That was the problem with Sam.

He was exactly the kind of man ~~she~~ . He was cocky, rough and crude. H~~e~~ ~~something~~ about the way he loo~~ked~~ ~~made a~~ mockery of all ~~the~~

"Are you going ~~to~~ ~~while?"~~ That question, as ~~sent a dart~~ of tension straight ~~to her~~

She could *not* take ~~off the coat.~~ Because she was wearing nothing more than a scrap of red lace underneath it. And now, it was all she could think of. About how little stood between Sam and her naked body.

About what might happen if she just went ahead and dropped the coat and revealed all of that to him.

"It's cold," she snapped.

The maddening man raised his eyebrows, shooting her a look that clearly said *suit yourself*, then set about looking for the fuse box.

She let out an exasperated sigh and followed his path, stopping when she saw him examining the little black switches inside the box.

"It's not a fuse. That means there's something else going on." He slammed the door shut. Then he turned back to look at her. "You should come to my cabin."

* * *

Hold Me, Cowboy
is part of the Copper Ridge series from

Ne~~w~~

New York Times bestselling author Maisey Yates

HOLD ME, COWBOY

BY
MAISEY YATES

First Published in Great Britain 2016
By Mills & Boon, an imprint of HarperCollins*Publishers*
1 London Bridge Street, London, SE1 9GF

© 2016 Maisey Yates

ISBN: 978-0-263-91883-0

51-1116

Our policy is to use papers that are natural, renewable and recyclable products and made from wood grown in sustainable forests. The logging and manufacturing processes conform to the legal environmental regulations of the country of origin.

Printed and bound in Spain
by CPI, Barcelona

Maisey Yates is a *USA TODAY* bestselling author of more than thirty romance novels. She has a coffee habit she has no interest in kicking, and a slight Pinterest addiction. She lives with her husband and children in the Pacific Northwest. When Maisey isn't writing she can be found singing in the grocery store, shopping for shoes online and probably not doing dishes. Check out her website, www.maiseyyates.com.

To KatieSauce, the sister I was always waiting for.
What a joy it is to have you in my life.

One

"Creative photography," Madison West muttered as she entered the security code on the box that contained the key to the cabin she would be staying in for the weekend.

She looked across the snowy landscape to see another home situated *far* too close to the place she would be inhabiting for the next couple of days. The photographs on the vacation-rental website hadn't mentioned that she would be sharing the property with anyone else.

And obviously, the example pictures had been taken from inventive angles.

It didn't matter. Nothing was going to change her plans. She just hoped the neighbors had earplugs. Because she was having sex this weekend. Nonstop sex.

Ten years celibate, and it was ending tonight. She had finally found *the one*. Not the one she was going to marry, obviously. *Please.* Love was for other people. People who hadn't been tricked, manipulated and humiliated when they were seventeen.

No, she had no interest in love and marriage. But she had abundant interest in orgasms. So much interest. And she had found the perfect man to deliver them.

All day, all night, for the next forty-eight hours.

She was armed with a suitcase full of lingerie and four bottles of wine. Neighbors be damned. She'd been hoping for a little more seclusion, but this was fine. It would be fine.

She unlocked the door and stepped inside, breathing a sigh of relief when she saw that the interior, at least, met with her expectations. But it was a little bit smaller than it had looked online, and she could only hope that wasn't some sort of dark portent for the rest of her evening.

She shook her head; she was not going to introduce that concern into the mix, thank you very much. There was enough to worry about when you were thinking about breaking ten years of celibacy without adding such concerns.

Christopher was going to arrive soon, so she figured she'd better get upstairs and start setting a scene. She made her way to the bedroom, then opened her suitcase and took out the preselected bit of lace she had chosen for their first time. It was red, which looked very good on her, if a bit obvious. But she was aiming for obvious.

Christopher wasn't her boyfriend. And he wasn't going to be. He was a very nice equine-vitamin-supplement salesman she'd met a few weeks ago when he'd come by the West estate. She had bought some products for her horses, and they'd struck up a conversation, which had transitioned into a flirtation.

Typically, when things began to transition into flirtation, Maddy put a stop to them. But she hadn't with him. Maybe because he was special. Maybe because ten years was just way too long. Either way, she had kept on flirting with him.

They'd gone out for drinks, and she'd allowed him to kiss her. Which had been a lot more than she'd allowed any other guy in recent years. It had reminded her how much she'd enjoyed that sort of thing once upon a time. And once she'd been reminded...well.

He'd asked for another date. She'd stopped him. Because wouldn't a no-strings physical encounter be way better?

He'd of course agreed. Because he was a man.

But she hadn't wanted to get involved with anyone in town. She didn't need anyone seeing her at a hotel or his house or with his car parked at her little home on her parents' property.

Thus, the cabin-weekend idea had been born.

She shimmied out of her clothes and wiggled into the skintight lace dress that barely covered her backside. Then she set to work fluffing her blond hair and applying some lipstick that matched the lingerie.

She was not answering the door in this outfit, however.

She put her long coat back on over the lingerie, then gave her reflection a critical look. It had been a long time since she had dressed to attract a man. Usually, she was more interested in keeping them at a distance.

"Not tonight," she said. "*Not* tonight."

She padded downstairs, peering out the window and seeing nothing beyond the truck parked at the small house across the way and a vast stretch of snow, falling harder and faster.

Typically, it didn't snow in Copper Ridge, Oregon. You had to drive up to the mountains—as she'd done today—to get any of the white stuff. So, for her, this was a treat, albeit a chilly one. But that was perfect, since she planned to get her blood all heated and stuff.

She hummed, keeping an eye on the scene outside, waiting for Christopher to pull in. She wondered if she should have brought a condom downstairs with her. Decided that she should have.

She went back upstairs, taking them two at a time, grateful that she was by herself, since there was nothing sexy about her ascent. Then she rifled through her bag, found some protection and curled her fingers around it before heading back down the stairs as quickly as possible.

As soon as she entered the living area, the lights flickered, then died. Suddenly, everything in the house seemed unnaturally quiet, and even though it was probably her imagination, she felt the temperature drop several degrees.

"Are you kidding me?" she asked, into the darkness.

There was no answer. Nothing but a subtle creak from the house. Maybe it was all that heavy snow on the roof. Maybe it was going to collapse. That would figure.

A punishment for her thinking she could be normal and have sex.

A shiver worked its way down her spine, and she jolted.

Suddenly, she had gone from hopeful and buoyant to feeling a bit flat and tragic. That was definitely not the best sign.

No. She wasn't doing this. She wasn't sinking into self-pity and tragedy. Been there, done that for ten years, thank you.

Madison didn't believe in signs. *So there.* She believed in fuses blowing in bad weather when overtaxed heaters had to work too hard in ancient houses. Yes, *that* she believed in. She also believed that she would have to wait for Christopher to arrive to fix the problem.

She sighed and then made her way over to the kitchen counter and grabbed hold of her purse as she deposited the two condoms on the counter. She pulled her phone out and grimaced when she saw that she had no signal.

Too late, she remembered that she had thought the lack of cell service might be an attraction to a place like this. That it would be nice if both she and Christopher could be cut off from the outside world while they indulged themselves.

That notion seemed really freaking stupid right now. Since she couldn't use the phone in the house thanks to the outage, and that left her cut off from the outside world all alone.

"Oh no," she said, "I'm the first five minutes of a crime show. I'm going to get ax-murdered. And I'm going to die a born-again virgin."

She scowled, looking back out at the resolutely blank landscape. Christopher still wasn't here. But it looked like the house across the way had power.

She pressed her lips together, not happy about the idea of interrupting her neighbor. Or of meeting her neighbor, since the whole point of going out of town was so they could remain anonymous and not see people.

She tightened the belt on her coat and made her way

slowly out the front door, bracing herself against the arctic wind.

She muttered darkly about the cold as she made her way across the space between the houses. She paused for a moment in front of the larger cabin, lit up and looking all warm and toasty. Clearly, this was the premium accommodation. While hers was likely beset by rodents that had chewed through relevant cords.

She huffed, clutching her coat tightly as she knocked on the door. She waited, bouncing in place to try to keep her blood flowing. She just needed to call Christopher and find out when he would be arriving and, if he was still a ways out, possibly beg her neighbor for help getting the power going. Or at least help getting a fire started.

The front door swung open and Madison's heart stopped. The man standing there was large, so tall that she only just came up to the middle of his chest. He was broad, his shoulders well muscled, his waist trim. He had the kind of body that came not from working out but from hard physical labor.

Then she looked up. Straight nose, square jaw, short brown hair and dark eyes that were even harder than his muscles. And far too familiar.

"What are *you* doing here?"

Sam McCormack gritted his teeth against the sharp tug of irritation that assaulted him when Madison West asked the question that had been on his own lips.

"I rented the place," he responded, not inviting her in. "Though I could ask you the same question."

She continued to do a little bounce in place, her arms folded tight against her body, her hands clasped beneath her chin. "And you'd get the same answer," she said. "I'm across the driveway."

"Then you're at the wrong door." He made a move to shut said door, and she reached out, stopping him.

"Sam. Do you always have to be this unpleasant?"

It was a question that had been asked of him more than once. And he gave his standard answer. "Yes."

"Sam," she said, sounding exasperated. "The power went out, and I'm freezing to death. Can I come in?"

He let out a long-suffering sigh and stepped to the side. He didn't like Madison West. He never had. Not from the moment he had been hired on as a farrier for the West estate eight years earlier. In all the years since he'd first met Madison, since he'd first started shoeing her horses, he'd never received one polite word from her.

But then, he'd never given one either.

She was sleek, blonde and freezing cold—and he didn't mean because she had just come in from the storm. The woman carried her own little snow cloud right above her head at all times, and he wasn't a fan of ice princesses. Still, something about her had always been like a burr beneath his skin that he couldn't get at.

"Thank you," she said crisply, stepping over the threshold.

"You're rich and pretty," he said, shutting the door tight behind her. "And I'm poor. And kind of an ass. It wouldn't do for me to let you die out there in a snowdrift. I would probably end up getting hung."

Madison sniffed, making a show of brushing snowflakes from the shoulders of her jacket. "I highly doubt you're poor," she said drily.

She wasn't wrong. A lot had changed since he'd gone

to work for the Wests eight years ago. Hell, a lot had changed in the past year.

The strangest thing was that his art had taken off, and along with it the metalwork and blacksmithing business he ran with his brother, Chase.

But now he was busier coming up with actual fine-art pieces than he was doing daily grunt work. One sale on a piece like that could set them up for the entire quarter. Strange, and not where he'd seen his life going, but true.

He still had trouble defining himself as an artist. In his mind, he was just a blacksmith cowboy. Most at home on the family ranch, most proficient at pounding metal into another shape. It just so happened that for some reason people wanted to spend a lot of money on that metal.

"Well," he said, "perception is everything."

She looked up at him, those blue eyes hitting him hard, like a punch in the gut. That was the other obnoxious thing about Madison West. She was pretty. She was more than pretty. She was the kind of pretty that kept a man up all night, hard and aching, with fantasies about her swirling in his head.

She was also the kind of woman who would probably leave icicles on a man's member after a blow job.

No, thank you.

"Sure," she said, waving her hand. "Now, I *perceive* that I need to use your phone."

"There's no cell service up here."

"Landline," she said. "I have no power. And no cell service. The source of all my problems."

"In that case, be my guest," he responded, turning away from her and walking toward the kitchen, where the lone phone was plugged in.

He picked up the receiver and held it out to her. She

eyed it for a moment as though it were a live snake, then snatched it out of his hand. "Are you just going to stand there?"

He shrugged, crossing his arms and leaning against the doorframe. "I thought I might."

She scoffed, then dialed the number, doing the same impatient hop she'd been doing outside while she waited for the person on the other end to answer. "Christopher?"

The physical response Sam felt to her uttering another man's name was not something he ever could have anticipated. His stomach tightened, dropped, and a lick of flame that felt a hell of a lot like jealousy sparked inside him.

"What do you mean you can't get up here?" She looked away from him, determinedly so, her eyes fixed on the kitchen floor. "The road is closed. Okay. So that means I can't get back down either?" There was a pause. "Right. Well, hopefully I don't freeze to death." Another pause. "No, you don't need to call anybody. I'm not going to freeze to death. I'm using the neighbor's phone. Just forget it. I don't have cell service. I'll call you if the power comes back on in my cabin."

She hung up then, her expression so sharp it could have cut him clean through.

"I take it you had plans."

She looked at him, her eyes as frosty as the weather outside. "Did you figure that out all by yourself?"

"Only just barely. You know blacksmiths aren't known for their deductive reasoning skills. Mostly we're famous for hitting heavy things with other heavy things."

"Kind of like cavemen and rocks."

He took a step toward her. "Kind of."

She shrank back, a hint of color bleeding into her

cheeks. "Well, now that we've established that there's basically no difference between you and a Neanderthal, I better get back to my dark, empty cabin. And hope that you aren't a secret serial killer."

Her sharp tongue left cuts behind, and he had to admit he kind of enjoyed it. There weren't very many people who sparred with him like this. Possibly because he didn't talk to very many people. "Is that a legitimate concern you have?"

"I don't know. The entire situation is just crazy enough that I might be trapped in a horror movie with a tortured artist blacksmith who is also secretly murdery."

"I guarantee you I'm not murdery. If you see me outside with an ax, it will only be because I'm cutting firewood."

She cocked her head to the side, a glint in her blue eyes that didn't look like ice making his stomach—and everything south of there—tighten. "Well, that's a relief. Anyway. I'm going. Dark cabin, no one waiting for me. It promises to be a seriously good time."

"You don't have any idea why the power is out, or how to fix it?" he asked.

"No," she said, sounding exasperated, and about thirty seconds away from stamping her foot.

Well, damn his conscience, but he wasn't letting her go back to an empty, dark, cold cabin. No matter that she had always treated him like a bit of muck she'd stepped in with her handmade riding boots.

"Let me have a look at your fuse box," he said.

"You sound like you'd rather die," she said.

"I pretty much would, but I'm not going to let *you* die either." He reached for his black jacket and the matching black cowboy hat hanging on a hook. He put both on and nodded.

"Thank you," she muttered, and he could tell the little bit of social nicety directed at him cost her dearly.

They headed toward the front door and he pushed it open, waiting for her to go out first. Since he had arrived earlier today, the temperature had dropped drastically. He had come up to the mountain to do some planning for his next few art projects. It pained him to admit, even to himself, that solitude was somewhat necessary for him to get a clear handle on what he was going to work on next.

"So," he said, making conversation not so much for the sake of it but more to needle her and see if he could earn one of her patented death glares, "Christopher, huh? Your boyfriend?" That hot spike drove its way through his gut again and he did his best to ignore it.

"No," she said tersely. "Just a friend."

"I see. So you decided to meet a man up here for a friendly game of Twister?"

She turned slightly, arching one pale brow. "Yahtzee, actually. I'm very good at it."

"And I'm sure your...*friend* was hoping to get a full house."

She rolled her eyes and looked forward again, taking quick steps over the icy ground, and somehow managing to keep sure footing. Then she opened the door to her cabin. "Welcome," she said, extending her arm. "Please excuse the shuddering cold and oppressive darkness."

"Ladies first," he said.

She shook her head, walking into the house, and he followed behind, closing the door against the elements. It was already cold in the dark little room. "You were just going to come back here and sit in the dark if I hadn't offered to fiddle with the circuit breaker?"

"Maybe I know how to break my own circuits, Sam. Did you ever think of that?"

"Oh, but you said you didn't, Madison."

"I prefer Maddy," she said.

"Sorry, Madison," he said, tipping his hat, just to be a jerk.

"I should have just frozen to death. Then there could have been a legend about my tragic and beautiful demise in the mountains." He didn't say anything. He just looked at her until she sighed and continued talking. "I don't know where the box thingy is. You're going to have to hunt for it."

"I think I can handle that." He walked deeper into the kitchen, then stopped when he saw two purple packets sitting on the kitchen counter. That heat returned with a vengeance when he realized exactly what they were, and what they meant. He looked up, his eyes meeting her extremely guilty gaze. "Yahtzee, huh?"

"That's what the kids call it," she said, pressing her palm over the telling packets.

"Only because they're too immature to call it fucking."

Color washed up her neck, into her cheeks. "Or not crass enough."

In that moment, he had no idea what devil possessed him, and he didn't particularly care. He turned to face her, planting his hands on the countertop, just an inch away from hers. "I don't know about that. I'm betting that you could use a little crassness in your life, Madison West."

"Are you trying to suggest that I need *you*?" she asked, her voice choked.

Lightning streaked through his blood, and in that moment, he was lost. It didn't matter that he thought she was insufferable, a prissy little princess who didn't appreciate any damn thing she had. It didn't matter that he'd come up here to work.

All that mattered was he hadn't touched a woman in a long time, and Madison West was so close all he would have to do was shift his weight slightly and he'd be able to take her into his arms.

He looked down pointedly at her hand, acting as though he could see straight through to the protection beneath. "Well," he said, "you have a couple of the essential ingredients to have yourself a pretty fun evening. All you seem to be missing is the man. But I imagine the guy you invited up here is *nice*. I'm not very nice, Madison," he said, leaning in, "but I could damn sure show you a good time."

Two

The absolute worst thing was the fact that Sam's words sent a shiver down her spine. Sam McCormack. Why did it have to be Sam McCormack? He was the deadly serpent to her Indiana Jones.

She should throw him out. Throw him out and get back to her very disappointing evening where all orgasms would be self-administered. So, basically a regular Friday night.

She wanted to throw herself on the ground and wail. It was not supposed to be a regular Friday night. She was supposed to be breaking her sex fast. Maybe this was why people had flings in the spring. Inclement weather made winter flings difficult. Also, mostly you just wanted to keep your socks on the whole time. And that wasn't sexy.

Maybe her libido should hibernate for a while. Pop up again when the pear trees were blooming or something.

She looked over at Sam, and her libido made a dash to the foreground. That was the problem with Sam. He irritated her. He was exactly the kind of man she didn't like. He was cocky. He was rough and crude.

Whenever she'd given him very helpful pointers about handling the horses when he came to do farrier work at the estate, he was always telling her to go away and in general showing no deference.

And okay, if he'd come and told her how to do her job, she would have told him where he could stick his hoof nippers. But still. Her animals. So she was entitled to her opinions.

Last time she'd walked into the barn when he was doing shoes, he hadn't even looked up from his work. He'd just pointed back toward the door and shouted, *out!*

Yeah, he was a jerk.

However, there was something about the way he looked in a tight T-shirt, his muscles bulging as he did all that hard labor, that made a mockery of that very certain hatred she felt burning in her breast.

"Are you going to take off your coat and stay awhile?" The question, asked in a faintly mocking tone, sent a dart of tension straight down between her thighs.

She could *not* take off her coat. Because she was wearing nothing more than a little scrap of red lace underneath it. And now that was all she could think of. About how little stood between Sam and her naked body.

About what might happen if she just went ahead and dropped the coat now and revealed all of that to him.

"It's cold," she snapped. "Maybe if you went to work getting the electricity back on rather than standing there making terrible double entendres, I would be able to take off my coat."

He lifted a brow. "And then do you think you'll take me up on my offer to show you a good time?"

"If you can get my electricity back on, I will consider a good time shown to me. Honestly, that's all I want. The ability to microwave popcorn and not turn into a Maddycicle."

The maddening man raised his eyebrows, shooting her a look that clearly said *Suit yourself*, then set about looking for the fuse box.

She stood by alone for a while, her arms wrapped around her midsection. Then she started to feel like an idiot just kind of hanging out there while he searched for the source of all power. She let out an exasperated sigh and followed his path, stopping when she saw him leaning up against a wall, a little metal door fixed between the logs open as he examined the small black switches inside.

"It's not a fuse. That means there's something else going on." He slammed the door shut. Then he turned back to look at her. "You should come over to my cabin."

"No!" The denial was a little bit too enthusiastic. A little bit too telling. "I mean, I can start a fire here—it's going to be fine. I'm not going to freeze."

"You're going to curl up by the fire with a blanket? Like a sad little pet?"

She made a scoffing sound. "No, I'm going to curl up by the fire like the Little Match Girl."

"That makes it even worse. The Little Match Girl froze to death."

"What?"

"How did you not know that?"

"I saw it when I was a kid. It was a *cartoon*. She really died?" Maddy blinked. "What kind of story is that to present to children?"

"An early lesson, maybe? Life is bleak, and then you freeze to death alone?"

"Charming," she said.

"Life rarely is." He kept looking at her. His dark gaze was worrisome.

"I'm fine," she said, because somebody had to say something.

"You are not. Get your suitcase—come over to the cabin. We can flip the lights on, and then if we notice from across the driveway that your power's on again, you can always come back."

It was stupid to refuse him. She knew him, if not personally, at least well enough to know that he wasn't any kind of danger to her.

The alternative was trying to sleep on the couch in the living room while the outside temperatures hovered below freezing, waking up every few hours to keep the fire stoked.

Definitely, going over to his cabin made more sense. But the idea filled her with a strange tension that she couldn't quite shake. Well, she knew exactly what kind of tension it was. *Sexual tension.*

She and Sam had so much of it that hung between them like a fog whenever they interacted. Although, maybe she read it wrong. Maybe on his end it was just irritation and it wasn't at all tinged with sensual shame.

"Why do you have to be so damned reasonable?" she asked, turning away from him and stalking toward the stairs.

"Where are you going?"

She stopped, turning to face him. "To change. Also, to get my suitcase. I have snacks in there."

"Are snacks a euphemism for something interesting?" he asked, arching a dark brow.

She sputtered, genuinely speechless. Which was unusual to downright unheard of. "No," she said, her tone sounding petulant. "I have *actual snacks*."

"Come over to my place. Bring the snacks."

"I will," she said, turning on her heel, heading toward the stairs.

"Maybe bring the Yahtzee too."

Those words hit her hard, with all the impact of a stomach punch. She could feel her face turning crimson, and she refused to look back at him. Refused to react to that bait at all. He didn't want *that*. He did not want to play euphemistic board games with her. And she didn't want to play them with him.

If she felt a little bit…on edge, it was just because she had been anticipating sex and she had experienced profound sex disappointment. That was all.

She continued up the stairs, making her way to the bedroom, then changed back into a pair of jeans and a sweatshirt as quickly as possible before stuffing the little red lace thing back in the bag and zipping everything up.

She lugged it back downstairs, her heart slamming against her breastbone when Sam was in her line of sight again. Tall, broad shouldered and far too sexy for his own good, he promised to be the antidote to sexual disappointment.

But an emotionless hookup with a guy she liked well enough but wouldn't get emotionally involved with was one thing. Replacing him at the last moment with a guy she didn't even like? No, that was out of the question.

Absolutely and completely out of the question.

"Okay," she said, "let's go."

By the time she got settled in the extra room in the cabin, she was feeling antsy. She could hide, but she was hungry. And Maddy didn't believe in being hungry when food was at hand. Yes, she had some various sugar-based items in her bag, but she needed protein.

In the past, she had braved any number of her father's awkward soirees to gain access to bacon-wrapped appetizers.

She could brave Sam McCormack well enough to root around for sustenance. She would allow no man to stand between herself and her dinner.

Cautiously, she made her way downstairs, hoping that maybe Sam had put himself away for the night. The thought made her smile. That he didn't go to bed like a normal person but closed himself inside…not a coffin. But maybe a scratchy, rock-hewn box that would provide no warmth or comfort. It seemed like something he would be into.

In fairness, she didn't really know Sam McCormack that well, but everything she did know about him led her to believe that he was a supremely unpleasant person. Well, except for the whole him-not-letting-her-die-of-frostbite-in-her-powerless-cabin thing. She supposed she had to go ahead and put that in the Maybe He's Not Such a Jackass column.

Her foot hit the ground after the last stair silently, and she cautiously padded into the kitchen.

"Looking for something?"

She startled, turning around and seeing Sam standing there, leaning in the doorway, his muscular arms crossed over his broad chest. She did her best to look cool. Composed. Not interested in his muscles. "Well—" she tucked her hair behind her ear "—I was hoping to find some food."

"You brought snacks," he said.

"Candy," she countered.

"So, that made it okay for you to come downstairs and steal my steak?"

Her stomach growled. "You have steak?"

"It's *my* steak."

She hadn't really thought of that. "Well, my...you know, *the guy*. He was supposed to bring food. And I'm sorry. I didn't exactly think about the fact that whatever food is in this fridge is food that you personally provided. I was protein blind." She did her best to look plaintive. Unsurprisingly, Sam did not seem moved by her plaintiveness.

"I mean, it seems cruel to eat steak in front of you, Madison. Especially if I'm not willing to share." He rubbed his chin, the sounds of his whiskers abrading his palm sending a little shiver down her back. God knew why.

"You *would* do that. You would... You would tease me with your steak." Suddenly, it was all starting to sound a little bit sexual. Which she had a feeling was due in part to the fact that everything felt sexual to her right about now.

Which was because of the other man she had been about to sleep with. Not Sam. Not really.

A slow smile crossed his face. "I would never tease you with my steak, Madison. If you want a taste, all you have to do is ask. Nicely."

She felt her face getting hotter. "May I please have your steak?"

"Are you going to cook it for me?"

"Did you want it to be edible?"

"That would be the goal, yes," he responded.

She lifted her hands up, palms out. "These hands don't cook."

His expression shifted. A glint of wickedness cutting through all that hardness. She'd known Sam was mean. She'd known he was rough. She had not realized he was wicked. "What do those hands do, I wonder?"

He let that innuendo linger between them and she practically hissed in response. "Do you have salad? I will fix salad. *You* cook steak. Then we can eat."

"Works for me, but I assume you're going to be sharing your candy with me?"

Seriously, everything sounded filthy. She had to get a handle on herself. "Maybe," she said, "but it depends on if your behavior merits candy." That didn't make it better.

"I see. And what, pray tell, does Madison West consider candy-deserving behavior?"

She shrugged, making her way to the fridge and opening it, bending down and opening the crisper drawer. "I don't know. Not being completely unbearable?"

"Your standards are low."

"Luckily for you."

She looked up at him and saw that that had actually elicited what looked to be a genuine grin. The man was a mystery. And she shouldn't care about that. She should not want to unlock, unravel or otherwise solve him.

The great thing about Christopher was that he was simple. He wasn't connected to her life in any way. They could come up and have an affair and it would never bleed over to her existence in Copper Ridge. It was the antithesis of everything she had experienced with David. David, who had blown up her entire life, shattered her career ambitions and damaged her good standing in the community.

This thing with Christopher was supposed to be sex. Sex that made nary a ripple in the rest of her life.

Sam would not be rippleless.

The McCormack family was too much a part of the fabric of Copper Ridge. More so in the past year. Sam and his brother, Chase, had done an amazing job of re-vitalizing their family ranch, and somewhere in all of that Sam had become an in-demand artist. Though he would be the last person to say it. He still showed up right on schedule to do the farrier work at her family ranch. As though he weren't raking in way more money with his ironwork.

Sam was… Well, he was kind of everywhere. His works of art appearing in restaurants and galleries around town. His person appearing on the family ranch to work on the horses. He was the exact wrong kind of man for her to be fantasizing about.

She should be more gun-shy than this. Actually, she had spent the past decade being more gun-shy than this. It was just that apparently now that she had allowed her-self to remember she had sexual feelings, it was difficult for her to turn them off. Especially when she was trapped in a snowstorm with a man for whom the term *rock-hard body* would be a mere description and not hyperbole.

She produced the salad, then set about to preparing it. Thankfully, it was washed and torn already. So her responsibility literally consisted of dumping it from bag to bowl. That was the kind of cooking she could get behind. Meanwhile, Sam busied himself with preparing two steaks on the stovetop. At some point, he took the pan from the stovetop and transferred it to the oven.

"I didn't know you had actual cooking technique," she said, not even pretending to herself that she wasn't watching the play of his muscles in his forearms as he worked.

Even at the West Ranch, where she always ended up sniping at him if they ever interacted, she tended to linger around him while he did his work with the horses because his arms put on quite a show. She was hardly going to turn away from him now that they were in an enclosed space, with said arms very, very close. And no one else around to witness her ogling.

She just didn't possess that kind of willpower.

"Well, Madison, I have a lot of eating technique. The two are compatible."

"Right," she said, "as you don't have a wife. Or a girlfriend…" She could have punched her own face for that. It sounded so leading and obvious. As if she cared if he had a woman in his life.

She didn't. Well, she kind of did. Because honestly, she didn't even like to ogle men who could be involved with another woman. Once bitten, twice shy. By which she meant once caught in a torrid extramarital affair with a man in good standing in the equestrian community, ten years emotionally scarred.

"No," he said, tilting his head, the cocky look in his eye doing strange things to her stomach, "I don't."

"I don't have a boyfriend. Not an actual boyfriend." Oh, good Lord. She was the desperate worst and she hated herself.

"So you keep saying," he returned. "You really want

to make sure I know Christopher isn't your boyfriend."
She couldn't ignore the implication in his tone.

"Because he isn't. Because we're not… Because
we've never. This was going to be our first time." Being
forthright and making people uncomfortable with said
forthrightness had been a very handy shield for the past
decade, but tonight it was really obnoxious.

"Oh really?" He suddenly looked extremely interested.

"Yes," she responded, keeping her tone crisp, refus-
ing to show him just how off-kilter she felt. "I'm just
making dinner conversation."

"This is the kind of dinner conversation you normally make?"

She arched her brow. "Actually, yes. Shocking people
is kind of my modus operandi."

"I don't find you that shocking, Madison. I do find
it a little bit amusing that you got cock-blocked by a
snowbank."

She nearly choked. "Wine. Do you have wine?" She
turned and started rummaging through the nearest cabinet. "Of course you do. You probably have a baguette
too. That seems like something an artist would do. Set
up here and drink wine and eat a baguette."

He laughed, a kind of short, dismissive sound. "Hate
to disappoint you. But my artistic genius is fueled by
Jack." He reached up, opening the cabinet nearest to
his head, and pulled down a bottle of whiskey. "But I'm
happy to share that too."

"You have diet soda?"

"Regular."

"My, this *is* a hedonistic experience. I'll have regular, then."

"Well, when a woman was expecting sex and doesn't get it, I suppose regular cola is poor consolation, but it is better than diet."

"Truer words were never spoken." She watched him while he set about to making a couple of mixed drinks for them. He handed one to her, and she lifted it in salute before taking a small sip. By then he was taking the steak out of the oven and setting it back on the stovetop.

"Perfect," he remarked when he cut one of the pieces of meat in half and gauged the color of the interior.

She frowned. "How did I never notice that you aren't horrible?"

He looked at her, his expression one of mock surprise. "Not horrible? You be careful throwing around compliments like that, missy. A man could get the wrong idea."

She rolled her eyes. "Right. I just mean, you're funny."

"How much of that whiskey have you had?"

"One sip. So it isn't even that." She eyeballed the food that he was now putting onto plates. "It might be the steak. I'm not going to lie to you."

"I'm comfortable with that."

He carried their plates to the table, and she took the lone bottle of ranch dressing out of the fridge and set it and her drink next to her plate. And then, somehow, she ended up sitting at a very nicely appointed dinner table with Sam McCormack, who was not the man she was supposed to be with tonight.

Maybe it was because of the liquored-up soda. Maybe it was neglected hormones losing their ever-loving minds in the presence of such a fine male specimen. Maybe it was just as simple as want. Maybe there was no justification for it at all. Except that Sam was actually beautiful. And she had always thought so, no matter how much he got under her skin.

That was the honest truth. It was why she found him so off-putting, why she had always found him so off-putting from the moment he had first walked onto the West Ranch property. Because he was the kind of man a woman could make a mistake with. And she had thought she was done making mistakes.

Now she was starting to wonder if a woman was entitled to one every decade.

Her safe mistake, the one who would lift out of her life, hadn't eventuated. And here in front of her was one that had the potential to be huge. But very, very good.

She wasn't so young anymore. She wasn't naive at all. When it came right down to it, she was hot for Sam. She had been for a long time.

She'd had so much caution for so long. So much hiding. So much *not doing*. Well, she was tired of that.

"I was very disappointed about Christopher not making it up here," she said, just as Sam was putting the last bite of steak into his mouth.

"Sure," he said.

"Very disappointed."

"Nobody likes blue balls, Maddy, even if they don't have testicles."

She forced a laugh through her constricted throat. "That's hilarious," she said.

He looked up at her slowly. "No," he said, "it wasn't."

She let out a long, slow breath. "Okay," she said, "it wasn't that funny. But here's the thing. The reason I was so looking forward to tonight is that I hadn't had sex with Christopher before. In fact, I haven't had sex with anyone in ten years. So. Maybe you could help me with that?"

Three

Sam was pretty sure he must be hallucinating. Because there was no way Madison West had just propositioned him. Especially not on the heels of admitting that it had been ten years since she'd had sex.

Hell, he was starting to think that *he* was the celibacy champion. But clearly, Maddy had him beat. Or she didn't, because there was no way in hell that she had actually said any of that.

"Are you drunk, Madison?" It was the first thing that came to mind, and it seemed like an important thing to figure out.

"After one Jack Daniel's and Coke? Absolutely not. I am a West, dammit. We can hold our liquor. I am…reckless, opportunistic and horny. A lot horny. I just…I need this. Sam, do you know what it's like to go *ten years* without doing something? It becomes a whole thing. Like, a whole big thing that starts to define you, even if it shouldn't. And you don't want anyone to know. Oh, my gosh, can you even imagine if my friends knew that it has been ten years since I have seen an actual…?" She took a deep breath, then forged on. "I'm rambling and I just *really* need this."

Sam felt like he had been hit over the head with a metric ton of iron. He had no idea how he was supposed to respond to this—the strangest of all propositions—from a woman who had professed to hate him only a few moments ago.

He had always thought Madison was a snob. A pain in his ass, even if she was a pretty pain in the ass. She was always looming around, looking down her nose at him while he did his work. As though only the aristocracy of Copper Ridge could possibly know how to do the lowly labor he was seeing to. Even if they hadn't the ability to do it themselves.

The kinds of people who professed to have strengths in "management." People who didn't know how to get their hands dirty.

He hated people like that. And he had never been a fan of Madison West.

He, Sam McCormack, should not be interested in taking her up on her offer. No, not in any way. However, Sam McCormack's dick was way more interested in it than he would've liked to admit.

Immediately, he was rock hard thinking about what it would be like to have her delicate, soft hands skimming over him. He had rough hands. Workman's hands. The kind of hands that a woman like Madison West had probably never felt against her rarefied flesh.

Hell, the fact that it had been ten years since she'd gotten any made that even more likely. And damn if that didn't turn him on. It was kind of twisted, a little bit sick, but then, it was nothing short of what he expected from himself.

He was a lot of things. Good wasn't one of them.

Ready to explode after years of repressing his desires, after years of pushing said desire all down and pretending it wasn't there? He was that.

"I'm not actually sure you want this," he said, wondering what the hell he was doing. Giving her an out when he wanted to throw her down and make her his.

Maddy stood up, not about to be cowed by him. He should have known that she would take that as a challenge. Maybe he had known that. Maybe it was why he'd said it.

That sounded like him. That sounded a lot more like him than trying to do the honorable thing.

"You don't know what I want, Sam," she said, crossing the space between them, swaying her hips just a little bit more than she usually did.

He would be a damn liar if he said that he had never thought about what it might be like to grab hold of those hips and pull Maddy West up against him. To grind his hardness against her soft flesh and make her feel exactly what her snobby-rich-girl mouth did to him.

But just because he'd fantasized about it before, didn't mean he had ever anticipated doing it. It didn't mean that he should take her up on it now.

Still, the closer she got to him, the less likely it seemed that he was going to say no.

"I think that after ten years of celibacy a man could make the argument that you don't know what you want, Madison West."

Her eyes narrowed, glittering blue diamonds that

looked like they could cut a man straight down to the bone. "I've always known what I wanted. I may not have always made the best decisions, but I was completely certain that I wanted them. At the time."

His lips tipped upward. "I'm just going to be another *at the time*, Maddy. Nothing else."

"That was the entire point of this weekend. For me to have something that didn't have consequences. For me to get a little bit of something for myself. Is that so wrong? Do I have to live a passionless existence because I made a mistake once? Am I going to question myself forever? I just need to… I need to rip the Band-Aid off."

"The Band-Aid?"

"The sex Band-Aid."

He nodded, pretending that he understood. "Okay."

"I want this," she said, her tone confident.

"Are you…suggesting…that I give you…sexual healing?"

She made a scoffing sound. "Don't make it sound cheesy. This is very serious. I would never joke about my sexual needs." She let out an exasperated sigh. "I'm doing this wrong. I'm just…"

Suddenly, she launched herself at him, wrapping her arms around his neck and pressing her lips against his. The moment she did it, it was like the strike of a hammer against hot iron. As rigid as he'd been before—in that moment, he bent. And easily.

Staying seated in the chair, he curved himself around Madison, wrapping his arms around her body, sliding his hands over her back, down to the sweet indent of her waist, farther still to the flare of those pretty hips. The hips he had thought about taking hold of so many times before.

There was no hesitation now. None at all. There was only this. Only her. Only the soft, intoxicating taste of her on his tongue. Sugar, Jack Daniel's and something that was entirely Maddy.

Too rich for his blood. Far too expensive for a man like him. It didn't matter what he became. Didn't matter how much money he had in his bank account, he would always be what he was. There was no escaping it. Nobody knew. Not really. Not the various women who had graced his bed over the years, not his brother, Chase.

Nobody knew Sam McCormack.

At least, nobody alive.

Neither, he thought, would Madison West. This wasn't about knowing anybody. This was just about satisfying a need. And he was simple enough to take her up on that.

He wedged his thigh up between her legs, pressing his palm down on her lower back, encouraging her to flex her hips in time with each stroke of his tongue. Encouraging her to satisfy that ache at the apex of her thighs.

Her head fell back, her skin flushed and satisfaction grabbed him by the throat, gripping him hard and strong. It would've surprised him if he hadn't suspected he was the sort of bastard who would get off on something like this.

Watching this beautiful, classy girl coming undone in his arms.

She was right. This weekend could be out of time. It could be a moment for them to indulge in things they would never normally allow themselves to have. The kinds of things that he had closed himself off from years ago.

Softness, warmth, touch.

He had denied himself all those things for years. Why

not do this now? No one would know. No one would ever have to know. Maddy would see to that. She would never, no chance in hell, admit that she had gotten down and dirty with a man who was essentially a glorified blacksmith.

No way in hell.

That made them both safe. It made this safe. Well, as safe as fire this hot could be.

She bit his lip and he growled, pushing his hands up underneath the hem of her shirt, kissing her deeper as he let his fingertips roam to the line of her elegant spine, then tracing it upward until he found her bra, releasing it with ease, then dragging it and her top up over her head, leaving her naked from the waist up.

"I…" Her face was a bright shade of red. "I…I have lingerie. I wasn't going to…"

"I don't give a damn about your lingerie. I just want this." He lowered his head, sliding his tongue around the perimeter of one of her tightened nipples. "I want your skin." He closed his lips over that tight bud, sucking it in deep.

"I had a seduction plan," she said, her voice trembling. He wasn't entirely sure it was a protest, or even a complaint.

"You don't plan passion, baby," he said.

At least, he didn't. Because if he were thinking clearly, he would be putting her top back on and telling her to go back to her ice-cold cabin, where she would be safe.

"I do," she said, her teeth chattering in spite of the fact that it was very warm in the kitchen. "I plan everything."

"Not this. You're a dirty girl now, Madison West," he said, sliding his thumb over her damp nipple, moving it in a slow circle until she arched her back and cried out.

"You were going to sleep with another man this weekend, and you replaced him so damn easily. With me. Doesn't even matter to you who you have. As long as you get a little bit. Is that how it is?"

She whimpered, biting her lip, rolling her hips against him.

"Good girl," he said, his gut tightening, his arousal so hard he was sure he was going to burst through the front of his jeans. "I like that. I like you being dirty for me."

He moved his hands then, curving his fingers around her midsection, his thumbs resting just beneath the swell of her breasts. She was so soft, so smooth, so petite and fragile. Everything he should never be allowed to put his hands on. But for some reason, instead of feeling a bolt of shame, he felt aroused. Hotter and harder than he could ever remember being. "You like that? My hands are rough. Maybe a little bit too rough for you."

"No," she said, and this time the protest was clear. "Not too rough for me at all."

He slid his hands down her back, taking a moment to really revel in how soft she was and how much different he must feel to her. She squirmed against him, and he took that as evidence that she really did like it.

That only made him hotter. Harder. More impatient.

"You didn't bring your damn candy and forget the condoms, did you?"

"No," she said, the denial coming quickly. "I brought the condoms."

"You always knew we would end up like this, didn't you?"

She looked away from him, and the way she refused to meet his eyes turned a throwaway game of a question into something deadly serious.

"Madison," he said, his voice hard. She still didn't look at him. He grabbed hold of her chin, redirecting her face so that she was forced to make eye contact with him. "You knew this would happen all along, didn't you?"

She still refused to answer him. Refused to speak.

"I think you did," he continued. "I think that's why you can never say a kind word to me. I think that's why you acted like a scalded cat every time I walked into the room. Because you knew it would end here. Because you wanted this. Because you wanted me."

Her expression turned even more mutinous.

"Madison," he said, a warning lacing through the word. "Don't play games with me. Or I'm not going to give you what you want. So you have to tell me. Tell me that you've always wanted me. You've always wanted my dirty hands on you. That's why you hate me so damn much, isn't it? Because you want me."

"I…"

"Madison," he said, his tone even more firm, "tell me—" he rubbed his hand over her nipple "—or I stop."

"I wanted you," she said, the admission rushed but clear all the same.

"More," he said, barely recognizing his own voice. "Tell me more."

It seemed essential suddenly, to know she'd wanted him. He didn't know why. He didn't care why.

"I've always wanted you. From the moment I first saw you. I knew that it would be like this. I knew that I would climb up into your lap and I would make a fool of myself rubbing all over you like a cat. I knew that from the beginning. So I argued with you instead."

He felt a satisfied smile that curved his lips upward. "Good girl." He lowered his hands, undoing the snap on her jeans and drawing the zipper down slowly. "You just made us both very happy." He moved his fingertips down beneath the waistband of her panties, his breath catching in his throat when he felt hot wetness beneath his touch. It had been way too long since he felt a silky-smooth desirable woman. Had been way too long in his self-imposed prison.

Too long since he'd wanted at all.

But Madison wasn't Elizabeth. And this wasn't the same.

He didn't need to think about her. He wasn't going to. Not for the rest of the night.

He pushed every thought out of his mind and instead exulted in the sound that Madison made when he moved his fingers over that place where she was wet and aching for him. When he delved deeper, pushing one finger inside her, feeling just how close she was to the edge, evidenced by the way her internal muscles clenched around him. He could thrust into her here. Take her hard and fast and she would still come. He knew that she would.

But she'd had ten years of celibacy, and he was pushing on five. They deserved more. They deserved better. At the very least they deserved a damn bed.

With that in mind, he wrapped his arms more tightly around her, moving his hands to cup her behind as he lifted her, wrapping her legs tightly around him as he carried them across the kitchen and toward the stairs.

Maddy let out an inelegant squeak as he began to ascend toward the bedrooms. "This is really happening," she said, sounding slightly dazed.

"I thought you said you weren't drunk."

"I'm not."

"Then try not to look so surprised. It's making me question things. And I don't want to question things. I just want you."

She shivered in his hold. "You're not like most men I know."

"Pretty boys with popped collars and pastel polo shirts? I must be a real disappointment."

"Obviously you aren't. Obviously I don't care about men in pastel polo shirts or I would've gotten laid any number of times in the past decade."

He pushed open the bedroom door, threw her down over the simply appointed bed that was far too small for the kind of acrobatics he wanted to get up to tonight. Then he stood back, admiring her, wearing nothing but those half-open jeans riding low on her hips, her stomach dipping in with each breath, her breasts thrust into greater prominence at the same time.

"Were you waiting for me?" He kept the words light, taunting, because he knew that she liked it.

She had always liked sparring with him. That was what they'd always done. Of course she would like it now. Of course he would like it now. Or maybe it had nothing to do with her. Maybe it had everything to do with the fact that he had years' worth of dirty in him that needed to be let out.

"Screw you," she said, pushing herself back farther up the mattress so that her head was resting on the pillow. Then she put her hands behind her head, her blue gaze sharp. "Come on, cowboy. Get naked for me."

"Oh no, Maddy, you're not running the show."

"Ten years," she said, her gaze level with his. "Ten years, Sam. That's how long it's been since I've seen a naked man. And let me tell you, I have never seen a naked man like you." She held up a finger. "One man. One insipid man. He wasn't even that good."

"You haven't had sex for ten years and your last lover wasn't even good? I was sort of hoping that it had been so good you were waiting for your knees to stop shaking before you bothered to go out and get some again."

"If only. My knees never once shook. In fact, they're shaking harder now and you haven't even gotten out of those pants yet."

"You give good dirty talk."

She lifted a shoulder. "I'm good at talking. That's about the thing I'm best at."

"Oh, I hope not, baby. I hope that mouth is good for a lot of other things too."

He saw her breasts hitch. Her eyes growing round. Then he smiled, grabbing hold of the hem of his shirt and stripping it off over his head. Her reaction was more satisfying than he could've possibly anticipated. It'd been a long time since he'd seen a woman looking at him that way.

Sure, women checked him out. That happened all the time. But this was different. This was raw, open hunger. She wasn't bothering to hide it. Why would she? They were both here to do this. No holds barred, no clothes, no nothing. Why bother to be coy? Why bother to pretend this was about anything other than satisfying lust. And if that was all it was, why should either of them bother to hide that lust.

"Keep looking at me like that, sweetheart, this is gonna end fast."

"Don't do that," she said, a wicked smile on her lips. "You're no good to me in that case."

"Don't worry, babe. I can get it up more than once."

At least, he could if he remembered correctly.

"Good thing I brought about three boxes of condoms."

"For two days? You did have high hopes for the weekend."

"Ten years," she reiterated.

"Point taken."

He moved his hands down, slowly working at his belt. The way that she licked her lips as her eyes followed his every movement ratcheting up his arousal another impossible notch.

Everything felt too sharp, too clear, every rasp of fabric over his skin, every downward flick of her eyes, every small, near-imperceptible gasp on her lips.

He hadn't been in a bedroom alone with a woman in a long damn time. And it was all catching up with him now.

Shutting down, being a mean bastard who didn't let anyone close? That was easy enough. It made it easy to forget. He shut the world out, stripped everything away. Reverted back to the way he had been just after his parents had died and it had been too difficult to feel anything more than his grief.

That was what he had done in the past five years. That was what he had done with his new, impossible loss that never should have happened. Wouldn't have if he'd had a shred of self-control and decency.

And now, tonight, he was proving that he probably still didn't have any at all. Oh well, just as well. Because he was going to do this.

He was going to do her.

He pushed his jeans down his lean hips, showing her the extent of his desire for her, reveling in the way her eyes widened when he revealed his body completely to her hungry gaze.

"I have never seen one that big before," she said.

He laughed. "Are you just saying that because it's what you think men need to hear?"

"No, I'm saying that because it's the biggest I've ever seen. And I want it."

"Baby," he said, "you can have it."

Maddy turned over onto her stomach and crawled across the bed on all fours in a move that damn near gave him a heart attack. Then she moved to the edge of the mattress, straightening up, raking her nails down over his torso before she leaned in, flicking her tongue over the head of his arousal.

He jerked beneath her touch, his length twitching as her tongue traced it from base to tip, just before she engulfed him completely in the warm heat of her mouth. She hummed, the vibration moving through his body, drawing his balls up tight. He really was going to lose it. Here and now like a green teenage boy if he didn't get a grip on himself. Or a grip on her.

He settled for the second option.

He reached back, grabbing hold of her hair and jerking her lips away from him. "You keep doing that and it really will end."

The color was high in her cheeks, her eyes glittering. "I've never, ever enjoyed it like that before."

She was so good for his ego. Way better than a man like him deserved. But damned if he wasn't going to take it.

"Well, you can enjoy more of that. Later. Right now? I need to be inside you."

"Technically," she said, her tone one of protest, "you were inside me."

"And as much as I like being in that pretty mouth of yours, that isn't what I want right now." He gritted his teeth, looking around the room. "The condoms."

She scrambled off the bed and shimmied out of her jeans and panties as she made her way across the room and toward her suitcase. She flipped it open, dug through it frantically and produced the two packets he had seen earlier.

All things considered, he felt a little bit triumphant to be the one getting these condoms. He didn't know Christopher, but that sad sack was sitting at home with a hard-on, and Sam was having his woman. He was going to go ahead and enjoy the hell out of that.

Madison turned to face him, the sight of that enticing, pale triangle at the apex of her thighs sending a shot straight down to his gut. She kept her eyes on his as she moved nearer, holding one of the condoms like it was a reward he was about to receive.

She tore it open and settled back onto the bed, then leaned forward and rolled it over his length. Then she took her position back up against the pillows, her thighs parting, her heavily lidded gaze averted from his now that she was in that vulnerable position.

"Okay," she said, "I'm ready."

She wasn't. Not by a long shot.

Ten years.

And he had been ready to thrust into her with absolutely no finesse. A woman who'd been celibate for ten years deserved more than that. She deserved more than one orgasm. Hell, she deserved more than two.

He had never been the biggest fan of Madison West,

but tonight they were allies. Allies in pleasure. And he was going to hold up his end of the bargain so well that if she was celibate after this, it really would be because she was waiting for her legs to work again.

"Not quite yet, Maddy," he said, kneeling down at the end of the bed, reaching forward and grabbing hold of her hips, dragging her down toward his face. He brought her up against his mouth, her legs thrown over his shoulders, that place where she was warm and wet for him right there, ready for him to taste her.

"Sam!" Maddy squeaked.

"There is no way you're a prude, Maddy," he said. "I've had too many conversations with you to believe that."

"I've never... No one has ever..."

"Then it's time somebody did."

He lowered his head, tasting her in long, slow passes, like she was an ice-cream cone that he just had to take the time to savor. Like she was a delicacy he couldn't get enough of.

Because she was.

She was all warmth and sweet female, better than he had ever remembered a woman being. Or maybe she was just better. It was hard to say. He didn't really care which. It didn't matter. All that mattered was this.

If he could lose himself in any moment, in any time, it would be this one.

It sure as hell wouldn't be pounding iron, trying to hammer the guilt out of his body. Certainly wouldn't be in his damn sculptures, trying to figure out what to make next, trying to figure out how to satisfy the customer. This deeply personal thing that had started being given to the rest of the world, when he wasn't sure he wanted the rest of the world to see what was inside him.

Hell, *he* didn't want to see what was inside him.

He made a hell of a lot of money, carving himself out, making it into a product people could buy. And he sure as hell liked the money, but that didn't make it a pleasant experience.

No, none of that mattered. Not now. Not when there was Maddy. And that sweet sugar-whiskey taste.

He tasted her until she screamed, and then he thrust his fingers inside her, fast and rough, until he felt her pulse around him, until her orgasm swept through them both.

Then he moved up, his lips almost touching hers. "Now," he said, his voice husky, "now you're ready."

Four

Maddy was shaking from head to toe, and she honestly didn't know if she could take any more. She had never—not in her entire life—had an orgasm like that. It was still echoing through her body, creating little waves of sensation that shivered through her with each and every breath she took.

And there was still more. They weren't done. She was glad about that. She didn't want to be done. But at the same time she wasn't sure if she could handle the rest. But there he was, above her, over her, so hot and hard and male that she didn't think she could deny him. She didn't want to deny him.

She looked at him, at the broad expanse of his shoulders and chest, the way it tapered down to his narrow waist, those flat washboard abs that she could probably actually wash her clothes on.

He was everything a man should be. If the perfect fantasy man had been pulled straight out of her deepest fantasies, he would look like this. It hit her then that Christopher had not even been close to being a fantasy man. And that was maybe why he had been so safe. It was why Sam had always been so threatening.

Because Christopher had the power to make a ripple. Sam McCormack possessed the power to engulf her in a tidal wave.

She had no desire to be swept out to sea by any man. But in this instance she had a life preserver. And that was her general dislike of him. The fact that their time together was going to be contained to only this weekend. So what did it matter if she allowed herself to get a little bit storm tossed. It didn't. She was free. Free to enjoy this as much as she wanted.

And she wanted. *Wanted* with an endless hunger that seemed to growl inside her like a feral beast.

He possessed the equipment to satisfy it. She let her eyes drift lower than just his abs, taking in the heart, the unequivocal evidence, of his maleness. She had not been lying when she said it was the biggest one she'd ever seen. It made her feel a little bit intimidated. Especially since she had been celibate for so very long. But she had a few days to acclimate.

The thought made her giddy.

"Now," she said, not entirely certain that she was totally prepared for him now but also unable to wait for him.

"You sure you're ready for me?" He leaned forward, bracing his hand on the headboard, poised over her like the very embodiment of carnal temptation. Just out of reach, close enough that she did easily inhale his masculine scent. Far enough away that he wasn't giving her what she needed. Not yet.

She felt hollow. Aching. And that, she realized, was how she knew she was going to take all of him whether or not it seemed possible. Because the only other option was remaining like this. Hollowed out and empty. And she couldn't stand that either. Not for one more second.

"Please," she said, not caring that she sounded plaintive. Not caring that she was begging. Begging Sam, the man she had spent the past several years harassing every time he came around her ranch.

No, she didn't care. She would make a fool out of herself if she had to, would lower herself as far down as she needed to go, if only she could get the kind of satisfaction that his body promised to deliver.

He moved his other hand up to the headboard, gripping it tight. Then he flexed his hips forward, the blunt head of his arousal teasing the slick entrance to her body. She reached up, bracing her palms flat against his chest, a shiver running through her as he teased her with near penetration.

She cursed. The sound quivering, weak in the near silence of the room. She had no idea where hard-ass Maddy had gone. That tough, flippant girl who knew how to keep everyone at a distance with her words. Who knew how to play off every situation as if it weren't a big deal.

This was a big deal. How could she pretend that it wasn't? She was breaking apart from the inside out; how could she act as though she weren't?

"Please," she repeated.

He let go of the headboard with one hand and pressed his hand down next to her face, then repeated the motion with the other as he rocked his hips forward more fully, entering her slowly, inch by tantalizing inch. She gasped when he filled her all the way, the intense stretching sensation a pleasure more than it was a pain.

She slid her hands up to his shoulders, down his back, holding on to him tightly there before locking her legs around his lean hips and urging him even deeper.

"Yes," she breathed, a wave of satisfaction rolling over her, chased on the heels by a sense that she was still incomplete. That this wasn't enough. That it would never be enough.

Then he began to move. Ratcheting up the tension between them. Taking her need, her arousal, to greater heights than she had ever imagined possible. He was measured at first, taking care to establish a rhythm that helped her move closer to completion. But she didn't need the help. She didn't want it. She just wanted to ride the storm.

She tilted her head to the side, scraping her teeth along the tendon in his neck that stood out as a testament to his hard-won self-control.

And that did it.

He growled low in his throat. Then his movements became hard, harsh. Following no particular rhythm but his own. She loved it. Gloried in it. He grabbed hold of her hips, tugging her up against him every time he thrust down, making it rougher, making it deeper. Making it hurt. She felt full with it, full with him. This was exactly what she needed, and she hadn't even realized it. To be utterly and completely overwhelmed. To have this man consume her every sensation, her every breath.

She fused her lips to his, kissing him frantically as he continued to move inside her and she held on to him tighter, her nails digging into his skin. But she knew he didn't mind the pain. She knew it just as she didn't mind it. Knew it because he began to move harder, faster, reaching the edge of his own control as he pushed her nearer to the edge of hers.

Suddenly, it gripped her fiercely, down low inside her, a force of pleasure that she couldn't deny or control. She froze, stiffening against him, the scream that lodged itself in her throat the very opposite of who she usually was. It wasn't calculated; it wasn't pretty; it wasn't designed to do anything. It simply was. An expression of what she felt. Beyond her reach, beyond her completely.

She was racked with her desire for him, with the intensity of the orgasm that swept through her. And then, just as she was beginning to find a way to breathe again, he found his own release, his hardness pulsing deep inside her as he gave himself up to it.

His release—the intensity of it—sent another shattering wave through her. And she clung to him even more tightly, needing him to anchor her to the bed, to the earth, or she would lose herself completely.

And then in the aftermath, she was left there, clinging to a stranger, having just shown the deepest, most hidden parts of herself to him. Having just lost her control with him in a way she never would have done with someone she knew better. Perhaps this was the only way she could have ever experienced this kind of freedom. The only way she could have ever let her guard down enough. What did she have to lose with Sam? His opinion of her was already low. So if he thought that she was a sex-hungry maniac after this, what did it matter?

He moved away from her and she threw her arm over

her face, letting her head fall back, the sound of her fractured breathing echoing in the room.

After she had gulped in a few gasps of air, she removed her arm, opened her eyes and realized that Sam wasn't in the room anymore. Probably off to the bathroom to deal with necessities. Good. She needed some space. She needed a moment. At least a few breaths.

He returned a little bit quicker than she had hoped he might, all long lean muscle and satisfied male. It was the expression on his face that began to ease the tension in her chest. He didn't look angry. He didn't look like he was judging her. And he didn't look like he was in love with her or was about to start making promises that she didn't want him to make.

No, he just looked satisfied. A bone-deep satisfaction that she felt too.

"Holy hell," he said, coming to lie on the bed next to her, drawing her naked body up against his. She felt a smile curve her lips. "I think you about blew my head off."

"You're so romantic," she said, smiling even wider. Because this was perfect. Absolutely perfect.

"You don't want me to be romantic," he returned.

"No," she said, feeling happy, buoyant even. "I sure as hell don't."

"You want me to be bad, and dirty, and to be your every fantasy of slumming it with a man who is so very beneath you."

That, she took affront to a little bit. "I don't think you're beneath me, Sam," she said. Then he grabbed hold of her hips and lifted her up off the mattress before bringing her down over his body. A wicked smile crossed his face.

"I am now."

"You're insatiable. And terrible."

"For a weekend fling, honey, that's all you really need."

"Oh, dammit," she said, "what if the roads open up, and Christopher tries to come up?"

"I'm not really into threesomes." He tightened his grip on her. "And I'm not into sharing."

"No worries. I don't have any desire to broaden my experience by testing him out."

"Have I ruined you for him?"

The cocky bastard. She wanted to tell him no, but she had a feeling that denting the masculine ego when a man was underneath you wasn't the best idea if you wanted to have sex with said man again.

"Ruined me completely," she responded. "In fact, I should leave a message for him."

Sam snagged the phone on the nightstand and thrust it at her. "You can leave him a message now."

"Okay," she said, grimacing slightly.

She picked up the phone and dialed Christopher's number quickly. Praying that she got his voice mail and not his actual voice.

Of course, if she did, that meant he'd gone out. Which meant that maybe he was trying to find sex to replace the sex that he'd lost. Which she had done; she couldn't really be annoyed about that. But she had baggage.

"Come on," she muttered as the phone rang endlessly. Then she breathed a sigh of relief when she got his voice mail. "Hi, Christopher, it's Madison. Don't worry about coming up here if the roads clear up. If that happens, I'm probably just going to go back to Copper Ridge. The weekend is kind of ruined. And…and maybe you should just wait for me to call you?" She looked up at Sam, who was nearly vibrating with forcibly contained laughter. She rolled her eyes. "Anyway, sorry that this didn't work out. Bye."

"That was terrible," he said. "But I think you made it pretty clear that you don't want to hear from him."

"I said I would call him," she said in protestation.

"Are you going to?"

"*Hell* no."

Sam chuckled, rolling her back underneath him, kissing her deep, hard. "Good thing I only want a weekend."

"Why is that?"

"God help the man that wants more from you."

"Oh, please, that's not fair." She wiggled, luxuriating in the hard feel of him between her thighs. He wanted her again already. "I pity the woman that falls for you, Sam McCormack."

A shadow passed over his face. "So do I."

Then, as quickly as they had appeared, those clouds cleared and he was smiling again, that wicked, intense smile that let her know he was about ready to take her to heaven again.

"It's a good thing both of us only want a weekend."

Five

"How did the art retreat go?"

Sam gritted his teeth against his younger brother's questioning as Chase walked into their workshop. "Fine," he returned.

"Fine?" Chase leaned against the doorframe, crossing his arms, looking a little too much like Sam for his own comfort. Because he was a bastard, and he didn't want to see his bastard face looking back at him. "I thought you were going to get inspiration. To come up with the ideas that will keep the McCormack Ranch flush for the next several years."

"I'm not a machine," Sam said, keeping his tone hard. "You can't force art."

He said things like that, in that tone, because he knew that no one would believe that cliché phrase, even if it was true. He didn't like that it was true.

But there wasn't much he was willing to do about it either.

"Sure. And I feel a slight amount of guilt over pressuring you, but since I do a lot of managing of your career, I consider it a part of my job."

"Stick to pounding iron, Chase—that's where your talents lie."

"I don't have talent," Chase said. "I have business sense. Which you don't have. So you should be thankful for me."

"You say that. You say it a lot. I think mostly because you know that I actually shouldn't be all that thankful for your meddling."

He was being irritable, and he knew it. But he didn't want Chase asking how the weekend was. He didn't want to explain the way he had spent his time. And he really didn't want to get into why the only thing he was inspired to do was start painting nudes.

Of one woman in particular.

Because the only kind of grand inspirational moments he'd had were when he was inside Maddy. Yeah, he wasn't going to explain that to his younger brother. He was never going to tell anybody. And he had to get his shit together.

"Seriously, though, everything is going okay? Anna is worried about you."

"Your wife is meddlesome. I liked her better when she was just your friend and all she did was come by for pizza a couple times a week. And she didn't worry too much about what I was doing or whether or not I was happy."

"Yeah, sadly for you she has decided she loves me. And by extension she has decided she loves you, which means her getting up in your business. I don't think she knows another way to be."

"Tell her to go pull apart a tractor and stop digging around in my life."

"No, thanks, I like my balls where they are. Which means I will not be telling Anna what to do. Ever."

"I liked it better when you were miserable and alone."

Chase laughed. "Why, because you're miserable and alone?"

"No, that would imply that I'm uncomfortable with the state of things. I myself am quite dedicated to my solitude and my misery."

"They say misery loves company," Chase said.

"Only true if you aren't a hermit."

"I suppose that's true." His brother looked at him, his gaze far too perceptive for Sam's liking. "You didn't used to be this terrible."

"I have been for a while." But worse with Maddy. She pushed at him. At things and needs and desires that were best left in the past.

He gritted his teeth. She pushed at him because he turned her on and that made her mad. He... Well, it was complicated.

"Yes," Chase said. "For a while."

"Don't psychoanalyze me. Maybe it's a crazy artist thing. Dad always said that it would make me a pussy."

"You aren't a pussy. You're a jerk."

"Six of one, half dozen of the other. Either way, I have issues."

Chase shook his head. "Well, deal with them on your own time. You have to be over at the West Ranch in less than an hour." Chase shook his head. "Pretty soon we'll be released from the contract. But you know until then we could always hire somebody else to go. You don't have to do horseshoes if you don't want. We're kind of beyond that now."

Sam gritted his teeth. For the first time he was actually tempted to take his brother up on the offer. To replace his position with someone else. Mostly because the idea of seeing Madison again filled him with the kind of reckless tension that he knew he wouldn't be able to do anything about once he saw her again.

Oh, not because of her. Not because of anything to do with her moral code or protestations. He could demolish those easily enough. It was because he couldn't afford to waste any more time thinking about her. Because he couldn't afford to get in any deeper. What had happened over the past weekend had been good. Damn good. But he had to leave it there.

Normally, he relished the idea of getting in there and doing grunt work. There was something about it that fulfilled him. Chase might not understand that.

But Sam wasn't a paperwork man. He wasn't a business mind. He needed physical exertion to keep himself going.

His lips twitched as he thought about the kind of physical exertion he had indulged in with Maddy. Yeah, it kind of all made sense. Why he had thrown himself into the blacksmithing thing during his celibacy. He needed to pound something, one way or another. And since he had been so intent on denying himself female companionship, he had picked up a hammer instead.

He was tempted to back out. To make sure he kept his distance from Maddy. He wouldn't, because he was also far too tempted to go. Too tempted to test his control and see if there was a weak link. If he might end up with her underneath him again.

It would be the better thing to send Chase. Or to call in and say they would have to reschedule, then hire somebody else to take over that kind of work. They could more than afford it. But as much as he wanted to avoid Maddy, he wanted to see her again.

Just because.

His body began to harden just thinking about it.

"It's fine. I'm going to head over. You know that I like physical labor."

"I just don't understand why," Chase said, looking genuinely mystified.

But hell, Chase had a life. A wife. Things that Sam was never going to have. Chase had worked through his stuff and made them both a hell of a lot of money, and Sam was happy for him. As happy as he ever got.

"You don't need to understand me. You just have to keep me organized so that I don't end up out on the street."

"You would never end up out on the streets of Copper Ridge. Mostly because if you stood out there with a cardboard sign, some well-meaning elderly woman would wrap you in a blanket and take you back to her house for casserole. And you would rather die. We both know that."

That made Sam smile reluctantly. "True enough."

"So, I guess you better keep working, then."

Sam thought about Maddy again, about her sweet, supple curves. About how seeing her again was going to test him in the best way possible. Perhaps that was why he should go. Just so he could test himself. Push up against his control. Yeah, maybe that was what he needed.

Yeah, that justification worked well. And it meant he would see her again.

It wasn't feelings. It was just sex. And he was starting to think just sex might be what he needed.

"I plan on it."

Maddy took a deep breath of clean salt air and arena dirt. There was something comforting about it. Familiar. Whenever things had gone wrong in her life, this was what she could count on. The familiar sights and sounds of the ranch, her horses. Herself.

She never felt stronger than when she was on the back of a horse, working in time with the animal to move from a trot to a walk, a walk to a halt. She never felt more understood.

A funny thing. Because, while she knew she was an excellent trainer and she had full confidence in her ability to keep control over the animal, she knew that she would never have absolute control. Animals were unpredictable. Always.

One day, they could simply decide they didn't want to deal with you and buck you off. It was the risk that every person who worked with large beasts took. And they took it on gladly.

She liked that juxtaposition. The control, the danger. The fact that though she achieved a certain level of mastery with each horse she worked with, they could still decide they weren't going to behave on a given day.

She had never felt much of that in the rest of her life. Often she felt like she was fighting against so much. Having something like this, something that made her feel both small and powerful had been essential to her well-being. Especially during all that crap that had happened ten years ago. She had been thinking more about it lately. Honestly, it had all started because of Christopher, because she had been considering breaking her celibacy. And it had only gotten worse after she actually had. After Sam.

Mostly because she couldn't stop thinking about him. Mostly because she felt like one weekend could never be enough. And she needed it to be. She badly needed it to be. She needed to be able to have sex with a guy without having lingering feelings for him. David had really done a number on her, and she did not want another number done on her.

It was for the best if she never saw Sam again. She knew that was unlikely, but it would be better. She let out a deep breath, walking into the barn, her riding boots making a strident sound on the hardpacked dirt as she walked in. Then she saw movement toward the end of the barn, someone coming out of one of the stalls.

She froze. It wasn't uncommon for there to be other people around. Her family employed a full staff to keep the ranch running smoothly, but for some reason this felt different. And a couple of seconds later, as the person came into view, she realized why.

Black cowboy hat, broad shoulders, muscular forearms. That lean waist and hips. That built, muscular physique that she was intimately acquainted with.

Dear Lord. Sam McCormack was here.

She had known that there would be some compromise on the never-seeing-him-again thing; she had just hoped that it wouldn't be seeing him now.

"Sam," she said, because she would be damned if she

appeared like she had been caught unawares. "I didn't expect you to be here."

"Your father wanted to make sure that all of the horses were in good shape before the holidays, since it was going to delay my next visit."

Maddy gritted her teeth. Christmas was in a couple of weeks, which meant her family would be having their annual party. The festivities had started to become a bit threadbare and brittle in recent years. Now that everybody knew Nathan West had been forced to sell off all of his properties downtown. Now that everyone knew he had a bastard son, Jack Monaghan, whose existence Nathan had tried to deny for more than thirty years. Yes, now that everybody had seen the cracks in the gleaming West family foundation, it all seemed farcical to Maddy.

But then, seeing as she had been one of the first major cracks in the foundation, she supposed that she wasn't really entitled to be too judgmental about it. However, she was starting to feel a bit exhausted.

"Right," she returned, knowing that her voice sounded dull.

"Have you seen Christopher?"

His question caught her off guard, as did his tone, which sounded a bit hard and possessive. It was funny, because this taciturn man in front of her was more what she had considered Sam to be before they had spent those days in the cabin together. Those days—where they had mostly been naked—had been a lot easier. Quieter. He had smiled more. But then, she supposed that any man receiving an endless supply of orgasms was prone to smiling more. They had barely gotten out of bed.

They had both been more than a little bit insatiable, and Maddy hadn't minded that at all. But this was a harsh slap back to reality. To a time that could almost have been before their little rendezvous but clearly wasn't, because his line of questioning was tinged with jealousy.

"No. As you guessed, I lied to him and didn't call him."

"And he call you?"

Maddy lifted her fingernail and began to chew on it, grimacing when she realized she had just ruined her manicure. "He did call," she said, her face heating slightly. "And I changed his name in my phone book to Don't Answer."

"Why did you do that?"

"Obviously you can't delete somebody from your phone book when you don't want to talk to them, Sam. You have to make sure that you know who's calling. But I like the reminder that I'm not speaking to him. Because then my phone rings and the screen says Don't Answer, and then I go, 'Okay.'"

"I really do pity the man who ends up wanting to chase after you."

"Good thing you don't. Except, oh wait, you're here."

She regretted that as soon as she said it. His gaze darkened, his eyes sweeping over her figure. Why did she want to push him?

Why did she always want to push him?

"You know why I'm here."

"Yes, because my daddy pays you to be here." She didn't know why she said that. To reinforce the difference between them? To remind him she was Lady of the Manor, and that regardless of his bank balance he was socially beneath her? To make herself look like a stupid rich girl he wouldn't want to mess around with anyway.

Honestly, these days it was difficult for her to guess at her own motives.

"Is this all part of your fantasy? You want to be… taken by the stable boy or something? I mean, it's a nice one, Maddy, and I didn't really mind acting it out with you last weekend, but we both know that I'm not exactly the stable boy and you're not exactly the breathless virgin."

Heat streaked through her face, rage pooling in her stomach. "Right. Because I'm not some pure, snow-white virgin, my fantasies are somehow wrong?" It was too close to that wound. The one she wished wasn't there. The one she couldn't ignore, no matter how much she tried.

"That wasn't the point I was making. And anyway, when your whole fantasy about a man centers around him being bad for you, I'm not exactly sure where you get off trying to take the moral-outrage route."

"I will be as morally outraged as I please," she snapped, turning to walk away from him.

He reached out, grabbing hold of her arm and turning her back to face him, taking hold of her other arm and pulling her forward. "Everything was supposed to stay back up at those cabins," he said, his voice rough.

"So why aren't you letting it?" she spat. Reckless. Shaky. She was a hypocrite. Because she wasn't letting it rest either.

"Because you walked in in those tight pants and it made it a lot harder for me to think."

"My breeches," she said, keeping the words sharp and crisp as a green apple, "are not typically the sort of garment that inspire men to fits of uncontrollable lust." Except *she* was drowning in a fit of uncontrollable lust.

His gaze was hot, his hands on her arms even hotter. She wanted to arch against him, to press her breasts against his chest as she had done more times than she could count when they had been together. She wanted… She wanted the impossible. She wanted more. More of him. More of everything they had shared together, even though they had agreed that would be a bad idea.

Even though she knew it was something she shouldn't even want.

"Your pretty little ass in anything would make a man lose his mind. Don't tell me those breeches put any man off, or I'm gonna have to call you a liar."

"It isn't my breeches that put them off. That's just my personality."

"If some man can't handle you being a little bit hard, then he's no kind of man. I can take you, baby. I can take all of you. And that's good, since we both know you can take all of me."

"Are you just going to be a tease, Sam?" she asked, echoing back a phrase that had been uttered to her by many men over the years. "Or is this leading somewhere?"

"You don't want it to lead anywhere, you said so yourself." He released his hold on her, taking a step back.

"You're contrary, Sam McCormack—do you know that?"

He laughed. "That's about the only thing anyone calls me. We both know what I am. The only thing that confuses me is exactly why you seem surprised by it now."

She was kind of stumped by that question. Because really, the only answer was sex. That she had imagined that the two of them being together, that the man he had been during that time, meant something.

Which proved that she really hadn't learned anything about sexual relationships, in spite of the fact that she had been so badly wounded by one in the past. She had always known that she had a hard head, but really, this was ridiculous.

But it wasn't just her head that was hard. She had hardened up a considerable amount in the years since her relationship with David. Because she'd had to. Because within the equestrian community, she had spent the years following that affair known as the skank who had seriously jeopardized the marriage of an upright member of the community. Never mind that she had been his student. Never mind that she had been seventeen years old, a virgin who had believed every word that had come out of the esteemed older man's mouth. Who had believed that his marriage really was over and that he wanted a life and a future with her.

It was laughable to her now. Any man nearing his forties who found himself able to relate to a seventeen-year-old on an emotional level was a little bit suspect. A married one, in a position of power, was even worse. She knew all of that. She knew it down to her bones. Believing it was another thing.

So sometimes her judgment was in doubt. Sometimes she felt like an idiot. But she was much more equipped to deal with difficult situations now. She was a lot pricklier. A lot more inured.

And that was what came to her defense now.

"Sam, if you still want me, all you have to do is say it. Don't you stand there growling because you're hard and sexually frustrated and we both agreed that it would only be that one weekend. Just be a man and admit it."

"Are you sure you should be talking to me like that

here? Anyone can catch us. If I backed you up against that wall and kissed your smart mouth, then people would know. Doesn't it make you feel dirty? Doesn't it make you feel ashamed?" His words lashed at her, made her feel all of those things but also aroused her. She had no idea what was wrong with her. Except that maybe part of it was that she simply didn't know how to feel desire without feeling ashamed. Another gift from her one and only love affair.

"You're the one that's saying all of this. Not me," she said, keeping her voice steely. She lifted a shoulder. "If I didn't know better, I would say you have issues. I don't want to help you work those out." A sudden rush of heat took over, a reckless thought that she had no business having, that she really should work to get a handle on. But she didn't.

She took a deep breath. "I don't have any desire to help you with your issues, but if you're horny, I can help you with that."

"What the hell?"

"You heard me," she said, crossing her arms and giving him her toughest air. "If you want me, then have me."

Sam could hardly believe what he was hearing. Yet again, Madison West was propositioning him. And this time, he was pissed off. Because he wasn't a dog that she could bring to heel whenever she wanted to. He wasn't the kind of man who could be manipulated.

Even worse, he wanted her. He wanted to say yes. And he wasn't sure he could spite his dick to soothe his pride.

"You can't just come in here and start playing games with me," he said. "I'm not a dog that you can call whenever you want me to come."

He let the double meaning of that statement sit between them. "That isn't what I'm doing," she said, her tone waspish.

"Then what are you doing, Madison? We agreed that it would be one weekend. And then you come in here sniping at me, and suddenly you're propositioning me. I gave in to all of this when you asked the first time, because I'm a man. And I'm not going to say no in a situation like the one we were in. But I'm also not the kind of man you can manipulate."

Color rose high in her cheeks. "I'm not trying to manipulate you. Why is it that men are always accusing me of that?"

"Because no man likes to be turned on and then left waiting," he returned.

The color in her cheeks darkened, and then she turned on one boot heel and walked quickly away from him.

He moved after her, reaching out and grabbing hold of her arm, stopping her. "What? Now you're going to go?"

"I can't do this. I can't do this if you're going to wrap all of it up in accusations and shame. I've been there. I've done it, Sam, and I'm not doing it again. Trust me. I've been accused of a lot of things. I've had my fill of it. So, great, you don't want to be manipulated. I don't want to be the one that has to leave this affair feeling guilty."

Sam frowned. "That's not what I meant."

She was the one who was being unreasonable, blowing hot and cold on him. How was it that he had been the one to be made to feel guilty? He didn't like that. He didn't like feeling anything but irritation and desire for her. He certainly didn't want to feel any guilt.

He didn't want to feel any damn thing.

"Well, what did you mean? Am I a tease, Sam? Is

that what I am? And men like you just can't help themselves?"

He took a step back. "No," he said. "But you do have
to make a decision. Either you want this, or you don't."

"Or?"

"Or nothing," he said, his tone hard. "If you don't
want it, you don't want it. I'm not going to coerce you
into anything. But I don't do the hot-and-cold thing."

Of course, he didn't really do any kind of thing anymore. But this, this back and forth, reminded him too
much of his interaction with Elizabeth. Actually, all of
it reminded him a little bit too much of Elizabeth. This
seemingly soft, sweet woman with a bit of an edge.
Someone who was high-class and a little bit luxurious.
Who felt like a break from his life on the ranch. His life
of rough work and solitude.

But after too much back and forth, it had ended. And
he didn't speak to her for months. Until he had gotten a
call that he needed to go to the hospital.

He gritted his teeth, looking at Madison. He couldn't
imagine anything with Madison ending quite that way,
not simply because he refused to ever lose his control
the way he had done with Elizabeth, but also because he
couldn't imagine Maddy slinking off in silence. She
might go hot and cold, but she would never do it quietly.

"Twelve days. There are twelve days until Christmas. That's what I want. Twelve days to get myself on
the naughty list. So to speak." She leveled her blue gaze
with his. "If you don't want to oblige me, I'm sure Christopher will. But I would much rather it be you."

"Why?" He might want this, but he would be damned
if he would make it easy for her. Mostly because he
wanted to make it a little harder on himself.

"Because I planned to go up to that cabin and have sex with Christopher. I had to, like, come up with a plan. A series of tactical maneuvers that would help me make the decision to get it over with after all that time. You," she said, gesturing at him, "you, I didn't plan to have anything happen with. Ever. But I couldn't stop myself. I think at the end of the day it's much better to carry on a sex-only affair with a man that you can't control yourself with. Like right now. I was not going to proposition you today, Sam. I promise. Not today, not ever again. In fact, I'm mad at you, so it should be really easy for me to walk away. But I don't want to. I want you. I want you even if it's a terrible idea."

He looked around, then took her arm again, dragging her into one of the empty stalls, where they would be out of sight if anyone walked into the barn. Then he pressed her against the wall, gripping her chin and taking her mouth in a deep, searing kiss. She whimpered, arching against him, grabbing hold of his shoulders and widening her stance so that he could press his hardened length against where she was soft and sensitive, ready for him already.

He slid his hand down her back, not caring that the hard wall bit into his knuckles as he grabbed hold of her rear, barely covered by those riding pants, which ought to have been illegal.

She whimpered, wiggling against him, obviously trying to get some satisfaction for the ache inside her. He knew that she felt it, because he felt the same way. He wrenched his mouth away from hers. "Dammit," he said, "I have to get back to work."

"Do you really?" She looked up at him, her expression so desperate it was nearly comical. Except he felt too desperate to laugh.

"Yes," he said.

"Well, since my family owns the property, I feel like I can give you permission to—"

He held up a hand. "I'm going to stop you right there. Nobody gives me permission to do anything. If I didn't want to finish the day's work, I wouldn't. I don't need the money. That's not why I do this. It's my reputation. My pride. I'm contracted to do it, and I will do what I promised I would. But when the contract is up? I won't."

"Oh," she said. "I didn't realize that."

"Everything is going well with the art business." At least, it would if he could think of something else to do. He supposed he could always do more animals and cowboys. People never got tired of that. They had been his most popular art installations so far.

"Great. That's great. Maybe you could…not press yourself up against me? Because I'm going to do something really stupid in a minute."

He did not comply with her request; instead, he kept her there, held up against the wall. "What's that?"

She frowned. "Something I shouldn't do in a public place."

"You're not exactly enticing me to let you go." His body was so hard he was pretty sure he was going to turn to stone.

"I'll bite you."

"Still not enticed."

"Are you telling me that you want to get bitten?"

He rolled his hips forward, let her feel exactly what she was doing to him. "Biting can be all part of the fun."

"I have some things to learn," she said, her blue eyes widening.

"I'm happy to teach them to you," he said, wavering on whether or not he would finish what they'd started here. "Where should I meet you tonight?"

"Here," she said, the word rushed.

"Are you sure? I live on the same property as Chase, but in different houses. We are close, but not that close."

"No, I have my own place here too. And there's always a lot of cars. It won't look weird. I just don't want anyone to see me…" She looked away from him. "I don't want to advertise."

"That's fine." It suited him to keep everyone in the dark too. He didn't want the kind of attention that would come with being associated with Madison West. Already, the attention that he got for the various art projects he did, for the different displays around town, was a little much for him.

It was an impossible situation for him, as always. He wanted things that seemed destined to require more of himself than he wanted to give. Things that seemed to need him to reach deep, when it was better if he never did. Yet he seemed to choose them. Women like Madison. A career like art.

Someday he would examine that. Not today.

"Okay," she said, "come over after it's dark."

"This is like a covert operation."

"Is that a problem?"

It really wasn't. It was hypocritical of him to pretend otherwise. Hell, his last relationship—the one with Elizabeth—had been conducted almost entirely in secrecy because he had been going out of town to see her. That had been her choice, because she knew her association with him would be an issue for her family.

And, as he already established, he didn't really want anyone to know about this thing with Maddy either. Still, sneaking around felt contrary to his nature too. In general, he didn't really care what people thought about him. Or about his decisions.

You're a liar.

He gritted his teeth. Everything with Elizabeth was its own exception. There was no point talking to anyone about it. No point getting into that terrible thing he had been a part of. The terrible thing he had caused.

"Not a problem," he said. "I'll see you in a few hours."

"I can cook," she said as he turned to walk out of the stall.

"You don't have to. I can grab something on my way."

"No, I would rather we had dinner."

He frowned. "Maddy," he began, "this isn't going to be a relationship. It can't be."

"I know," she said, looking up and away from him, swallowing hard. "But I need for it to be something a little more than just sex too. I just… Look, obviously you know that somebody that hasn't had a sexual partner in the past ten years has some baggage. I do. Shocking, I know, because I seem like a bastion of mental health. But I just don't like the feeling. I really don't."

His chest tightened. Part of him was tempted to ask her exactly what had happened. Why she had been celibate for so long. But then, if they began to trade stories about their pasts, she might want to know something about his. And he wasn't getting into that. Not now, not ever.

"Is there anything you don't like?"

"No," he said, "I'm easy. I thought you said you didn't cook?"

She shrugged a shoulder. "Okay, if I'm being completely honest, I have a set of frozen meals in my freezer that my parents' housekeeper makes for me. But I can heat up a double portion so we can eat together."

He shook his head. "Okay."

"I have pot roast, meat loaf and roast chicken."

"I'll tell you what. The only thing I want is to have your body for dessert. I'll let you go ahead and plan dinner."

"Pot roast it is," she said, her voice a borderline squeak.

He chuckled, turning and walking away from her, something shifting in his chest. He didn't know how she managed to do that. Make him feel heavier one moment, then lighter the next. It was dangerous. That's what it was. And if he had a brain in his head, he would walk away from her and never look back.

Sadly, his ability to think with his brain had long since ceased to function.

Even if it was a stupid idea, and he was fairly certain it was, he was going to come to Madison's house tonight, and he was going to have her in about every way he could think of.

He fixed his mouth into a grim line and set about finishing his work. But while he kept his face completely stoic, inside he felt anticipation for the first time in longer than he could remember.

Six

Maddy wondered if seductresses typically wore pearls. Probably pearls and nothing else. Maybe pearls and lace. Probably not high-waisted pencil skirts and cropped sweaters. But warming pot roast for Sam had put her in the mind-set of a 1950s housewife, and she had decided to go ahead and embrace the theme.

She caught a glimpse of her reflection in the mirror in the hall of her little house and she laughed at herself. She was wearing red lipstick, her blond hair pulled back into a bun. She rolled her eyes, then stuck out her tongue. Then continued on into the kitchen, her high heels clicking on the tile.

At least underneath the sweater, she had on a piece of pretty hot lingerie, if she said so herself. She knew Sam was big on the idea that seduction couldn't be planned, but Maddy did like to have a plan. It helped her feel more in control, and when it came to Sam, she had never felt more out of control.

She sighed, reaching up into the cupboard and taking out a bottle of wine that she had picked up at Grassroots Winery that afternoon. She might not be the best cook, or any kind of cook at all, but she knew how to pick a good wine. Everyone had their strengths.

The strange thing was she kind of enjoyed feeling out of control with Sam, but it also made her feel cautious. Protective. When she had met David, she had dived into the affair headlong. She hadn't thought at all. She had led entirely with her heart, and in the end, she had gotten her heart broken. More than that, the aftermath had shattered her entire world. She had lost friends; she had lost her standing within a community that had become dear to her… Everything.

"But you aren't seventeen. And Sam isn't a married douche bag." She spoke the words fiercely into the silence of the kitchen, buoyed by the reality of them.

She could lose a little bit of control with Sam. Even within that, there would be all of her years, her wisdom—such as it was—and her experience. She was never going to be the girl she had been. That was a good thing. She would never be able to be hurt like that, not again. She simply didn't possess the emotional capacity.

She had emerged Teflon coated. Everything slid off now.

There was a knock on her front door and she straightened, closing her eyes and taking a deep breath, trying to calm the fluttering in her stomach. That reminded her a bit too much of the past. Feeling all fluttery and breathless just because she was going to see the man she was fixated on. That felt a little too much like emotion.

No. It wasn't emotion. It was just anticipation. She was old enough now to tell the difference between the two things.

She went quickly to the door, suddenly feeling a little bit ridiculous as she pulled it open. When it was too late for her to do anything about it. Her feeling of ridiculousness only increased when she saw Sam standing there, wearing his typical black cowboy hat, tight T-shirt and well-fitted jeans. Of course, he didn't need to wear anything different to be hotter to her.

A cowboy hat would do it every time.

"Hi," she said, taking a step back and gesturing with her hand. "Come in."

He obliged, walking over the threshold and looking around the space. For some reason, she found herself looking at it through his eyes. Wondering what kinds of conclusions he would draw about the neat, spare environment.

She had lived out in the little guesthouse ever since she was nineteen. Needing a little bit of distance from her family but never exactly leaving. For the first time, that seemed a little bit weird to her. It had always just been her life. She worked on the ranch, so there didn't seem to be any point in leaving it.

Now she tried to imagine explaining it to someone else—to Sam—and she wondered if it was weird.

"My mother's interior decorator did the place," she said. "Except for the yellow and red." She had added little pops of color through throw pillows, vases and art on the wall. But otherwise the surroundings were predominantly white.

"Great," he said, clearly not interested at all.

It had felt weird, thinking about him judging her

based on the space, thinking about him judging her circumstances. But it was even weirder to see that he wasn't even curious.

She supposed that was de rigueur for physical affairs. And that was what this was.

"Dinner is almost ready," she said, reminding them both of the nonphysical part of the evening. Now she felt ridiculous for suggesting that too. But the idea of meeting him in secret had reminded her way too much of David. Somehow, adding pot roast had seemed to make the whole thing aboveboard.

Pot roast was an extremely nonsalacious food.

"Great," he said, looking very much like he didn't actually care that much.

"I just have to get it out of the microwave." She treated him to an exaggerated wink.

That earned her an uneasy laugh. "Great," he said.

"Come on," she said, gesturing for him to follow her. She moved into the kitchen, grabbed the pan that contained the meat and the vegetables out of the microwave and set it on the table, where the place settings were already laid out and the salad was already waiting.

"I promise I'm not trying to Stepford-wife you," she said as they both took their seats.

"I didn't think that," he said, but his blank expression betrayed the fact that he was lying.

"You did," she said. "You thought that I was trying to become your creepy robot wife."

"No, but I did wonder exactly why dinner was so important."

She looked down. It wasn't as if David were a secret. In fact, the affair was basically open information. "Do you really want to know?"

Judging by the expression on his face, he didn't. "There isn't really a good way to answer that question."

"True. Honesty is probably not the best policy. I'll think you're uninterested in me."

"On the contrary, I'm very interested in you."

"Being interested in my boobs is not the same thing."

He laughed, taking a portion of pot roast out of the dish in the center of the table. "I'm going to eat. If you want to tell me…well, go ahead. But I don't think you're trying to ensnare me."

"You don't?"

"Honestly, Maddy, nobody would want me for that long."

Those words were spoken with a bit of humor, but they made her sad. "I'm sure that's not true," she said, even though she wasn't sure of any such thing. He was grumpy. And he wasn't the most adept emotionally. Still, it didn't seem like a very kind thing for a person to think about themselves.

"It is," he said. "Chase is only with me because he's stuck with me. He feels some kind of loyalty to our parents."

"I thought your parents…"

"They're dead," he responded, his tone flat.

"I'm sorry," she said.

"Me too."

Silence fell between them after that, and she knew the only way to break it was to go ahead and get it out. "The first guy…the one ten years ago, we were having a physical-only affair. Except I didn't know it."

"Ouch," Sam said.

"Very. I mean, trust me, there were plenty of signs. And even though he was outright lying to me about his intentions, if I had been a little bit older or more experienced, I would have known. It's a terrible thing to find out you're a cliché. I imagine you wouldn't know what that's like."

"No, not exactly. Artist-cowboy-blacksmith is not really a well-worn template."

She laughed and took a sip of her wine. "No, I guess not." Then she took another sip. She needed something to fortify her. Anything.

"But other woman that actually believes he'll leave his wife for you, that is." She swallowed hard, waiting for his face to change, waiting for him to call her a name, to get disgusted and walk out.

It occurred to her just then that that was why she was telling him all of this. Because she needed him to know. She needed him to know, and she needed to see what he would think. If he would still want her. Or if he would think that she was guilty beyond forgiving.

There were a lot of people who did.

But he didn't say anything. And his face didn't change. So they just sat in silence for a moment.

"When we got involved, he told me that he was done with her. That their marriage was a mess and they were already starting divorce proceedings. He said that he just wore his wedding ring to avoid awkward questions from their friends. The dressage community around here is pretty small, and he said that he and his wife were waiting until they could tell people themselves, personally, so that there were no rumors flying around." She laughed, almost because she was unable to help it. It was so ridiculous. She wanted to go back and shake seventeen-year-old her. For being such an idiot. For caring so much.

"Anyway," she continued, "he said he wanted to

protect me. You know, because of how unkind people can be."

"He was married," Sam said.

She braced herself. "Yes," she returned, unflinching.

"How old were you?"

"Seventeen."

"How old was he?"

"Almost forty."

Sam cursed. "He should have been arrested."

"Maybe," she said, "except I did want him."

She had loved the attention he had given her. Had loved feeling special. It had been more than lust. It had been neediness. For all the approval she hadn't gotten in her life. Classic daddy issues, basically. But, as messed up as a man his age had to be for wanting to fool around with a teenager, the teenager had to be pretty screwed up too.

"How did you know him?"

"He was my... He was my trainer."

"Right, so some jackass in a position of power. Very surprising."

Warmth bloomed in her chest and spread outward, a strange, completely unfamiliar sensation. There were only a few people on earth who defended her when the subject came up. And mostly, they kept it from coming up. Sierra, her younger sister, knew about it only from the perspective of someone who had been younger at the time. Maddy had shared a little bit about it, about the breakup and how much it had messed with her, when Sierra was having difficulty in her own love life.

And then there were her brothers, Colton and Gage. Who would both have cheerfully killed David if they had ever been able to get their hands on him. But Sam was the first person she had ever told the whole story to. And he was the first person who wasn't one of her siblings who had jumped to her defense immediately.

There had been no interrogation about what kinds of clothes she'd worn to her lessons. About how she had behaved. Part of her wanted to revel in it. Another part of her wanted to push back at it.

"Well, I wore those breeches around him. I know they made you act a little bit crazy. Maybe it was my fault."

"Is this why you got mad about what I said earlier?"

She lifted a shoulder. "Well, that and it was mean."

"I didn't realize this had happened to you," he said, his voice not exactly tender but full of a whole lot more sympathy than she had ever imagined getting from him. "I'm sorry."

"The worst part was losing all my friends," she said, looking up at him. "Everybody really liked him. He was their favorite instructor. As far as dressage instructors go, he was young and cool, trust me."

"So you bore the brunt of it because he turned out to be human garbage and nobody wanted to face it?"

The way he phrased that, so matter-of-fact and real, made a bubble of humor well up inside her chest. "I guess so."

"That doesn't seem fair."

"It really doesn't."

"So that's why you had to feed me dinner, huh? So I didn't remind you of that guy?"

"Well, you're nothing like him. For starters, he was… much more diminutive."

Sam laughed. "You make it sound like you had an affair with a leprechaun."

"Jockeys aren't brawny, Sam."

He only laughed harder. "That's true. I suppose that causes trouble with wind resistance and things."

She rolled her eyes. "You are terrible. Obviously he had some appeal." Though, she had a feeling it wasn't entirely physical. Seeing as she had basically been seeking attention and approval and a thousand other things besides orgasms.

"Obviously. It was his breeches," Sam said.

"A good-looking man in breeches is a thing."

"I believe you."

"But a good-looking man in Wranglers is better." At least, that was her way of thinking right at the moment.

"Good to know."

"But you can see. Why I don't really want to advertise this. It has nothing to do with what you do or who you are or who I am. Well, I guess it is all to do with who I am. What people already think about me. I've been completely defined by a sex life I barely have. And that was… It was the smallest part of that betrayal. At least for me. I loved him. And he was just using me."

"I hope his life was hell after."

"No. His wife forgave him. He went on to compete in the Olympics. He won a silver medal."

"That's kind of a karmic letdown."

"You're telling me. Meanwhile, I've basically lived like a nun and continued giving riding lessons here on the family ranch. I didn't go on to do any of the competing that I wanted to, because I couldn't throw a rock without hitting a judge who was going to be angry with me for my involvement with David."

"In my opinion," Sam said, his expression turning dark, focused, "people are far too concerned with who women sleep with and not near enough as concerned as they should be about whether or not the man does it well. Was he good?"

She felt her face heat. "Not like you."

"I don't care who you had sex with, how many times or who he was. What I do care is that I am the best you've ever had. I'm going to aim to make sure that's the case."

He reached across the table, grabbing hold of her hand. "I'm ready for dessert," he said.

"Me too," she said, pushing her plate back and moving to her feet. "Upstairs?"

He nodded once, the slow burn in his dark eyes searing through her. "Upstairs."

Seven

"Well, it looks like everything is coming together for Dad's Christmas party," Sierra said brightly, looking down at the car seat next to her that contained a sleeping newborn. "Gage will be there, kind of a triumphant return, coming-out kind of thing."

Maddy's older brother shifted in his seat, his arms crossed over his broad chest. "You make me sound like a debutante having a coming-out ball."

"That would be a surprise," his girlfriend, Rebecca Bear, said, putting her hand over his.

"I didn't mean it that way," Sierra said, smiling, her slightly rounder post-childbirth cheeks making her look even younger than she usually did.

Maddy was having a difficult time concentrating. She had met her siblings early at The Grind, the most popular coffee shop in Copper Ridge, so that they could all get on the same page about the big West family soiree that would be thrown on Christmas Eve.

Maddy was ambivalent about it. Mostly she wanted to crawl back under the covers with Sam and burrow until winter passed. But they had agreed that it would go on only until Christmas. Which meant that not only was she dreading the party, it also marked the end of their blissful affair.

By the time Sam had left last night, it had been the next morning, just very early, the sun still inky black as he'd walked out of her house and to his truck.

She had wanted him to stay the entire night, and that was dangerous. She didn't need all that. Didn't need to be held by him, didn't need to wake up in his arms.

"Madison." The sound of her full name jerked her out of her fantasy. She looked up, to see that Colton had been addressing her.

"What?" she asked. "I zoned out for a minute. I haven't had all the caffeine I need yet." Mostly because she had barely slept. She had expected to go out like a light after Sam had left her, but that had not been the case. She had just sort of lay there feeling a little bit achy and lonely and wishing that she didn't.

"Just wondering how you were feeling about Jack coming. You know, now that the whole town knows that he's our half brother, it really is for the best if he comes. I've already talked to Dad about it, and he agrees."

"Great," she said, "and what about Mom?"

"I expect she'll go along with it. She always does. Anyway, Jack is a thirty-five-year-old sin. There's not much use holding it against him now."

"There never was," Maddy said, staring fixedly at her disposable coffee cup, allowing the warm liquid inside to heat her fingertips. She felt like a hypocrite saying that. Mostly because there was something about Jack that was difficult for her.

Well, she knew what it was. The fact that he was evidence of an affair her father had had. The fact that her father was the sort of man who cheated on his wife.

That her father was the sort of man more able to identify with the man who had broken Maddy's heart than he was able to identify with Maddy herself.

But Jack had nothing to do with that. Not really. She knew that logically. He was a good man, married to a great woman, with an adorable baby she really *did* want in her life. It was just that sometimes it needled at her. Got under her skin.

"True enough," Colton said. If he noticed her unease, he certainly didn't betray that he did.

The idea of trying to survive through another West family party just about made her jump up from the coffee shop, run down Main Street and scamper under a rock. She just didn't know if she could do it. Stand there in a pretty dress trying to pretend that she was something the entire town knew she wasn't. Trying to pretend that she was anything other than a disappointment. That her whole family was anything other than tarnished.

Sam didn't feel that way. Not about her. Suddenly, she thought about standing there with him. Sam in a tux, warm and solid next to her…

She blinked, cutting off that line of thinking. There was no reason to be having those fantasies. What she and Sam had was not that. Whatever it was, it wasn't that.

"Then it's settled," Maddy said, a little bit too brightly. "Jack and his family will come to the party."

That sentence made another strange, hollow sensation

echo through her. Jack would be there with his family. Sierra and Ace would be there together with their baby. Colton would be there with his wife, Lydia, and while they hadn't made it official yet, Gage and Rebecca were rarely anywhere without each other, and it was plain to anyone who had eyes that Rebecca had changed Gage in a profound way. That she was his support and he was hers.

It was just another way in which Maddy stood alone.

Wow, what a whiny, tragic thought. It wasn't like she wanted her siblings to have nothing. It wasn't like she wanted them to spend their lives alone. Of course she wanted them to have significant others. Maybe she would get around to having one too, eventually.

But it wouldn't be Sam. So she needed to stop having fantasies about him in that role. Naked fantasies. That was all she was allowed.

"Great," Sierra said, lifting up her coffee cup. "I'm going to go order a coffee for Ace and head back home. He's probably just now getting up. He worked closing at the bar last night and then got up to feed the baby. I owe him caffeine and my eternal devotion. But he will want me to lead with the caffeine." She waved and picked up the bucket seat, heading toward the counter.

"I have to go too," Colton said, leaning forward and kissing Maddy on the cheek. "See you later."

Gage nodded slowly, his dark gaze on Rebecca. She nodded, almost imperceptibly, and stood up. "I'm going to grab a refill," she said, making her way to the counter.

As soon as she was out of earshot, Gage turned his focus to her, and Maddy knew that the refill was only a decoy.

"Are you okay?"

This question, coming from the brother she knew the least, the brother who had been out of her life for seventeen years before coming back into town almost two months ago, was strange. And yet in some ways it wasn't. She had felt, from the moment he had returned, that there was something similar in the two of them.

Something broken and strong that maybe the rest of them couldn't understand.

Since then, she had learned more about the circumstances behind his leaving. The accident that he had been involved in that had left Rebecca Bear scarred as a child. Much to Maddy's surprise, they now seemed to be in love.

Which, while she was happy for him, was also a little annoying. Rebecca was the woman he had damaged—however accidentally—and she could love him, while Maddy seemed to be some kind of remote island no one wanted to connect with.

If she took the Gage approach, she could throw hot coffee on the nearest handsome guy, wait a decade and a half and see if his feelings changed for her over time. However, she imagined that was somewhat unrealistic.

"I'm fine," she said brightly. "Always fine."

"Right. Except I'm used to you sounding dry with notes of sarcasm and today you've been overly peppy and sparkly like a Christmas angel, and I think we both know that isn't real."

"Well, the alternative is me complaining about how this time of year gets me a little bit down, and given the general mood around the table, that didn't seem to be the best idea."

"Right. Why don't you like this time of year?"

"I don't know, Gage. Think back to all the years you

spent in solitude on the road. Then tell me how you felt about Christmas."

"At best, it didn't seem to matter much. At worst, it reminded me of when I was happy. When I was home with all of you. And when home felt like a happy place. That was the hardest part, Maddy. Being away and longing for a home I couldn't go back to. Because it didn't exist. Not really. After everything I found out about Dad, I knew it wouldn't ever feel the same."

Her throat tightened, emotion swamping her. She had always known that Gage was the one who would understand her. She had been right. Because no one had ever said quite so perfectly exactly what she felt inside, what she had felt ever since news of her dalliance with her dressage trainer had made its way back to Nathan West's ears.

"It's so strange that you put it that way," she said, "because that is exactly how it feels. I live at home. I never left. And I…I ache for something I can never have again. Even if it's just to see my parents in the way that I used to."

"You saw how it was with all of us sitting here," Gage said. "It's something that I never thought I would have. The fact that you've all been willing to forgive me, to let me back into your lives after I was gone for so long, changes the shape of things. We are the ones that can make it different. We can fix what happened with Jack— or move forward into fixing it. There's no reason you and I can't be fixed too, Maddy."

She nodded, her throat so tight she couldn't speak. She stood, holding her coffee cup against her chest. "I am looking forward to seeing you at the Christmas party." Then she forced a smile and walked out of The Grind.

She took a deep breath of the freezing air, hoping that it might wash some of the stale feelings of sadness and grief right out of her body. Then she looked down Main Street, at all of the Christmas lights gilding the edges of the brick buildings like glimmering precious metal.

Christmas wreaths hung from every surface that would take them, velvet bows a crimson beacon against the intense green.

Copper Ridge at Christmas was beautiful, but walking around, she still felt a bit like a stranger, separate and somehow not a part of it all. Everyone here was so good. People like her and Gage had to leave when they got too bad. Except she hadn't left. She just hovered around the edges like a ghost, making inappropriate and sarcastic comments on demand so that no one would ever look at her too closely and see just what a mess she was.

She lowered her head, the wind whipping through her hair, over her cheeks, as she made her way down the street—the opposite direction of her car. She wasn't really sure what she was doing, only that she couldn't face heading back to the ranch right now. Not when she felt nostalgic for something that didn't exist anymore. When she felt raw from the conversation with Gage.

She kept going down Main, pausing at the front door of the Mercantile when she saw a display of Christmas candy sitting in the window. It made her smile to see it there, a sugary reminder of some old memory that wasn't tainted by reality.

She closed her eyes tight, and she remembered what it was. Walking down the street with her father, who was always treated like he was a king then. She had been small, and it had been before Gage had left. Before she had ever disappointed anyone.

It was Christmastime, and carolers were milling around, and she had looked up and seen sugarplums and candy canes, little peppermint chocolates and other sweets in the window. He had taken her inside and allowed her to choose whatever she wanted.

A simple memory. A reminder of a time when things hadn't been quite so hard, or quite so real, between herself and Nathan West.

She found herself heading inside, in spite of the fact that the entire point of this walk had been to avoid memories. But then, she really wanted to avoid the memories that were at the ranch. This was different.

She opened the door, taking a deep breath of gingerbread and cloves upon entry. The narrow little store with exposed brick walls was packed with goodies. Cakes, cheeses and breads, imported and made locally.

Lane Jensen, the owner of the Mercantile, was standing toward the back of the store talking to somebody. Maddy didn't see another person right away, and then, when the broad figure came into view, her heart slammed against her breastbone.

When she realized it was Sam, she had to ask herself if she had been drawn down this way because of a sense of nostalgia or because something in her head sensed that he was around. That was silly. Of course she didn't *sense* his presence.

Though, given pheromones and all of that, maybe it wasn't too ridiculous. It certainly wasn't some kind of emotional crap. Not her heart recognizing where his was beating or some such nonsense.

For a split second she considered running the other direction. Before he saw her, before it got weird. But she hesitated, just for the space of a breath, and that was long enough for Sam to look past Lane, his eyes locking with hers.

She stood, frozen to the spot. "Hi," she said, knowing that she sounded awkward, knowing that she looked awkward.

She was unaccustomed to that. At least, these days. She had grown a tough outer shell, trained herself to never feel ashamed, to never feel embarrassed—not in a way that people would be able to see.

Because after her little scandal, she had always imagined that it was the only thing people thought about when they looked at her. Walking around, feeling like that, feeling like you had a scarlet *A* burned into your skin, it forced you to figure out a way to exist.

In her case it had meant cultivating a kind of brash persona. So, being caught like this, looking like a deer in the headlights—which was what she imagined she looked like right now, wide-eyed and trembling—it all felt a bit disorienting.

"Maddy," Sam said, "I wasn't expecting to see you here."

"That's because we didn't make any plans to meet here," she said. "I promise I didn't follow you." She looked over at Lane, who was studying them with great interest. "Not that I would. Because there's no reason for me to do that. Because you're the farrier for my horses. And that's it." She felt distinctly detached and lightheaded, as though she might drift away on a cloud of embarrassment at a moment's notice.

"Right," he said. "Thank you, Lane," he said, turning his attention back to the other woman. "I can bring the installation down tomorrow." He tipped his hat, then moved away from Lane, making his way toward her.

"Hi, Lane," she said. Sam grabbed hold of her elbow and began to propel her out of the store. "Bye, Lane."

As soon as they were back out on the street, she rounded on him. "What was that? I thought we were trying to be discreet."

"Lane Jensen isn't a gossip. Anyway, you standing there turning the color of a beet wasn't exactly subtle."

"I am not a beet," she protested, stamping.

"A tiny tomato."

"Stop comparing me to vegetables."

"A tomato isn't a vegetable."

She let out a growl and began to walk away from him, heading back up Main Street and toward her car. "Wait," he said, his voice possessing some kind of unknowable power to actually make her obey.

She stopped, rooted to the cement. "What?"

"We live in the same town. We're going to have to figure out how to interact with each other."

"Or," she said, "we continue on with this very special brand of awkwardness."

"Would it be the worst thing in the world if people knew?"

"You know my past, and you can ask me that?" She looked around the street, trying to see if anybody was watching their little play. "I'm not going to talk to you about this on the town stage."

He closed the distance between them. "Fine. We don't have to have the discussion. And it doesn't matter to me either way. But you really think you should spend the rest of your life punishing yourself for a mistake that happened when you were seventeen? He took advantage of you—it isn't your fault. And apart from any of that, you don't deserve to be labeled by a bunch of people that don't even know you."

That wasn't even it. And as she stood there, staring him down, she realized that fully. It had nothing to do with what the town thought. Nothing to do with whether or not the town thought she was a scarlet woman, or if people still thought about her indiscretion, or if people blamed her or David. None of that mattered.

She realized that in a flash of blinding brilliance that shone brighter than the Christmas lights all around her. And that realization made her knees buckle, because it made her remember the conversation that had happened in her father's office. The conversation that had occurred right after one of David's students had discovered the affair between the two of them and begun spreading rumors.

Rumors that were true, regrettably.

Rumors that had made their way all the way back to Nathan West's home office.

"I can't talk about this right now," she said, brushing past him and striding down the sidewalk.

"You don't have to talk about it with me, not ever. But what's going to happen when this is over? You're going to go another ten years between lovers? Just break down and hold your breath and do it again when you can't take the celibacy anymore?"

"Stop it," she said, walking faster.

"Like I said, it doesn't matter to me…"

She whirled around. "You keep saying it doesn't matter to you, and then you keep pushing the issue. So I would say that it does matter to you. Whatever complex you have about not being good enough, this is digging at that. But it isn't my problem. Because it isn't about you. Nobody would care if they knew that we were sleeping together. I mean, they would talk about it, but they wouldn't care. But it makes it something more. And I just…I can't have more. Not more than this."

He shifted uncomfortably. "Well, neither can I. That was hardly an invitation for something deeper."

"Good. Because I don't have anything deeper to give."

The very idea made her feel like she was going into a free fall. The idea of trusting somebody again…

The betrayals she had dealt with back when she was seventeen had made it so that trusting another human being was almost unfathomable. When she had told Sam that the sex was the least of it, she had been telling the truth.

It had very little to do with her body, and everything to do with the battering her soul had taken.

"Neither do I."

"Then why are you… Why are you pushing me like this?"

He looked stunned by the question, his face frozen. "I just…I don't want to leave you broken."

Something inside her softened, cracked a little bit. "I'm not sure that you have a choice. It kind of is what it is, you know?"

"Maybe it doesn't have to be."

"Did you think you were going to fix me, Sam?"

"No," he said, his voice rough.

But she knew he was lying. "Don't put that on yourself. Two broken people can't fix each other."

She was certain in that moment that he was broken too, even though she wasn't quite sure how.

"We only have twelve days. Any kind of fixing was a bit ambitious anyway," he said.

"Eleven days," she reminded him. "I'll see you tonight?"

"Yeah. See you then."

And then she turned and walked away from Sam McCormack for all the town to see, as if he were just a casual acquaintance and nothing more. And she tried to ignore the ache in the center of her chest that didn't seem to go away, even after she got in the car and drove home.

Eight

Seven days after beginning the affair with Maddy, she called and asked him if he could come down and check the shoes on one of the horses. It was the middle of the afternoon, so if it was her version of a booty call, he thought it was kind of an odd time. And since their entire relationship was a series of those, he didn't exactly see why she wouldn't be up front about it.

But when he showed up, she was waiting for him outside the stall.

"What are you up to?"

She lifted her shoulder. "I just wanted you to come and check on the horse."

"Something you couldn't check yourself?"

She looked slightly rueful. "Okay, maybe I could have checked it myself. But she really is walking a little bit funny, and I'm wondering if something is off."

She opened the stall door, clipped a lead rope to the

horse's harness and brought her out into the main part of the barn.

He looked at her, then pushed up the sleeves on his thermal shirt and knelt down in front of the large animal, drawing his hand slowly down her leg and lifting it gently. Then he did the same to the next before moving to her hindquarters and repeating the motion again.

He stole a glance up at Maddy, who was staring at him with rapt attention.

"What?"

"I like watching you work," she said. "I've always liked watching you work. That's why I used to come down here and give orders. Okay, honestly? I wanted to give myself permission to watch you and enjoy it." She swallowed hard. "You're right. I've been punishing myself. So, I thought I might indulge myself."

"I'm going to have to charge your dad for this visit," he said.

"He won't notice," she said. "Trust me."

"I don't believe that. Your father is a pretty well-known businessman." He straightened, petting the horse on its haunches. "Everything looks fine."

Maddy looked sheepish. "Great."

"Why don't you think your dad would notice?"

"A lot of stuff has come out over the past few months. You know he had a stroke three months ago or so, and while he's recovered pretty well since then, it changed things. I mean, it didn't change *him*. It's not like he miraculously became some soft, easy man. Though, I think he's maybe a little bit more in touch with his mortality. Not happily, mind you. I think he always saw himself as something of a god."

"Well," Sam said, "what man doesn't?" At least, until

he was set firmly back down to earth and reminded of just how badly he could mess things up. How badly things could hurt.

"Yet another difference between men and women," Maddy said drily. "But after he had his stroke, the control of the finances went to my brother Gage. That was why he came back to town initially. He discovered that there was a lot of debt. I mean, I know you've heard about how many properties we've had to sell downtown."

Sam stuffed his hands in his pockets, lifting his shoulders. "Not really. But then, I don't exactly keep up on that kind of stuff. That's Chase's arena. Businesses and the real estate market. That's not me. I just screw around with metal."

"You downplay what you do," she returned. "From the art to the physical labor. I've watched you do it. I don't know why you do it, only that you do. You're always acting like your brother is smarter than you, but he can't do what you do either."

"Art was never particularly useful as far as my father was concerned," Sam said. "I imagine he would be pretty damned upset to see that it's the art that keeps the ranch afloat so nicely. He would have wanted us to do it the way our ancestors did. Making leatherwork and pounding nails. Of course, it was always hard for him to understand that mass production was inevitably going to win out against more expensive handmade things. Unless we targeted our products and people who could afford what we did. Which is what we did. What we've been successful with far beyond what we even imagined."

"Dads," she said, her voice soft. "They do get in your head, don't they?"

"I mean, my father didn't have gambling debts and a

secret child, but he was kind of a difficult bastard. I still wish he wasn't dead." He laughed. "It would kind of be nice to have him wandering around the place shaking his head disapprovingly as I loaded up that art installation to take down to the Mercantile."

"I don't know, having your dad hanging around disapproving is kind of overrated." Suddenly, her face contorted with horror. "I'm sorry—I had no business saying something like that. It isn't fair. I shouldn't make light of your loss."

"It was a long time ago. And anyway, I do it all the time. I think it's the way the emotionally crippled deal with things." Anger. Laughter. It was all better than hurt.

"Yeah," she said, laughing uneasily. "That sounds about right."

"What exactly does your dad disapprove of, Madison?" he asked, reverting back to her full name. He kind of liked it, because nobody else called her that. And she had gone from looking like she wanted to claw his eyes out when he used it to responding. There was something that felt deep about that. Connected. He shouldn't care. If anything, it should entice him not to do it. But it didn't.

"Isn't it obvious?"

"No," he returned. "I've done a lot of work on this ranch over the years. You're always busy. You have students scheduled all day every day—except today, apparently—and it is a major part of both the reputation and the income of this facility. You've poured everything you have into reinforcing his legacy while letting your own take a backseat."

"Well, when you put it like that," she said, the smile on her lips obviously forced, "I am kind of amazing."

"What exactly does he disapprove of?"

"What do you think?"

"Does it all come back to that? Something you did when you were seventeen?" The hypocrisy of the outrage in his tone wasn't lost on him.

"I'm not sure," she said, the words biting. "I'm really not." She grabbed hold of the horse's lead rope, taking her back into the stall before clipping the rope and coming back out, shutting the door firmly.

"What do you mean by that?"

She growled, making her way out of the barn and walking down the paved path that led toward one of the covered arenas. "I don't know. Feel free to choose your own adventure with that one."

"Come on, Maddy," he said, closing the distance between them and lowering his voice. "I've tasted parts of you that most other people have never seen. A little bit of honesty isn't going to hurt you."

She whipped around, her eyes bright. "Maybe it isn't him. Maybe it's me. Maybe I'm the one that can't look at him the same way."

Maddy felt rage simmering over her skin like heat waves. She had not intended to have this conversation—not with Sam, not with anyone.

But now she had started, she didn't know if she could stop. "The night that he found out about my affair with David was the night I found out about Jack."

"So, it isn't a recent revelation to all of you?"

"No," she said. "Colton and Sierra didn't know. I'm sure of that. But I found out that Gage did. I didn't know who it was, I should clarify. I just found out that he had another child." She looked away from Sam, trying to ignore the burning sensation in her stomach. Like there was molten lava rolling around in there. She associated that feeling with being called into her father's home office.

It had always given her anxiety, even before everything had happened with David. Even before she had ever seriously disappointed him.

Nathan West was exacting, and Maddy had wanted nothing more than to please him. That desire took up much more of her life than she had ever wanted it to. But then, she knew that was true in some way or another for all of her siblings. It was why Sierra had gone to school for business. Why Colton had taken over the construction company. It was even what had driven Gage to leave.

It was the reason Maddy had poured all of her focus into dressage. Because she had anticipated becoming great. Going to the Olympics. And she knew her father had anticipated that. Then she had ruined all of it.

But not as badly as he had ruined the relationship between the two of them.

"Like I told you, one of David's other students caught us together. Down at the barn where he gave his lessons. We were just kissing, but it was definitely enough. That girl told her father, who in turn went to mine as a courtesy."

Sam laughed, a hard, bitter sound. "A courtesy to who?"

"Not to me," Maddy said. "Or maybe it was. I don't know. It was so awful. The whole situation. I wish there had been a less painful way for it to end. But it had to end, whether it ended that way or some other way, so… so I guess that worked as well as anything."

"Except you had to deal with your father. And then rumors were spread anyway."

She looked away from Sam. "Well, the rumors I kind of blame on David. Because once his wife knew, there was really no reason for the whole world not to know. And I think it suited him to paint me in an unflattering light. He took a gamble. A gamble that the man in the situation would come out of it all just fine. It was not a bad gamble, it turned out."

"I guess not."

"Full house. Douche bag takes the pot."

She was avoiding the point of this conversation. Avoiding the truth of it. She didn't even know why she should tell him. She didn't know why anything. Except that she had never confided any of this to anyone before. She was close to her sister, and Sierra had shared almost everything about her relationship with Ace with Maddy, and here Maddy was keeping more secrets from her.

She had kept David from her. She had kept Sam from her too. And she had kept this all to herself, as well.

She knew why. In a blinding flash she knew why. She couldn't stand being rejected, not again. She had been rejected by her first love; she had been rejected by an entire community. She had been rejected by her father with a few cold dismissive words in his beautifully appointed office in her childhood home.

But maybe, just maybe, that was why she should confide in Sam. Because at the end of their affair it wouldn't matter. Because then they would go back to sniping at each other or not talking to each other at all.

Because he hadn't rejected her yet.

"When he called me into his office, I knew I was in trouble," she said, rubbing her hand over her forehead. "He never did that for good things. Ever. If there was something good to discuss, we would talk about it around the dinner table. Only bad things were ever talked about in his office with the door firmly closed. He talked to Gage like that. Right before he left town. So, I always knew it had to be bad."

She cleared her throat, looking out across the arena, through the gap in the trees and at the distant view of the misty waves beyond. It was so very gray, the clouds hanging low in the sky, touching the top of the angry, steel-colored sea.

"Anyway, I *knew*. As soon as I walked in, I knew. He looked grim. Like I've never seen him before. And he asked me what was going on with myself and David Smithson. Well, I knew there was no point in denying it. So I told him. He didn't yell. I wish he had. He said... He said the worst thing you could ever do was get caught. That a man like David spent years building up his reputation, not to have it undone by the temptation of some young girl." She blinked furiously. "He said that if a woman was going to present more temptation than a man could handle, the least she could do was keep it discreet."

"How could he say that to you? To his daughter? Look, my dad was a difficult son of a bitch, but if he'd had a daughter and some man had hurt her, he'd have ridden out on his meanest stallion with a pair of pliers to dole out the world's least sterile castration."

Maddy choked out a laugh that was mixed with a sob. "That's what I thought. It really was. I thought... I thought he would be angry, but one of the things that scared me most, at least initially, was the idea that he would take it out on David. And I still loved David then. But no. He was angry at me."

"I don't understand how that's possible."

"That was when he told me," she choked out. "Told me that he had mistresses, that it was just something men did, but that the world didn't run if the mistress didn't know her place, and if I was intent on lowering myself to be that sort of woman when I could have easily been a wife, that was none of his business. He told me a woman had had his child and never betrayed him." Her throat tightened, almost painfully, a tear sliding down her cheek. "Even he saw me as the villain. If my own father couldn't stand up for me, if even he thought it was my fault somehow, how was I ever supposed to stand up for myself when other people accused me of being a whore?"

"Maddy…"

"That's why," she said, the words thin, barely making their way through her constricted throat. "That's why it hurts so much. And that's why I'm not over it. There were two men involved in that who said they loved me. There was David, the man I had given my heart to, the man I had given my body to, who had lied to me from the very beginning, who threw me under the bus the moment he got the opportunity. And then there was my own father. My own father, who should have been on my side simply because I was born his. I loved them both. And they both let me down." She blinked, a mist rolling over her insides, matching the setting all around them. "How do you ever trust anyone after that? If it had only been David, I think I would have been over it a long time ago."

Sam was looking at her, regarding her with dark, intense eyes. He looked like he was about to say something, his chest shifting as he took in a breath that seemed to contain purpose. But then he said nothing.

He simply closed the distance between them, tugging her into his arms, holding her against his chest, his large, warm hand moving between her shoulder blades in a soothing rhythm.

She hadn't rested on anyone in longer than she could remember. Hadn't been held like this in years. Her mother was too brittle to lean on. She would break beneath the weight of somebody else's sorrow. Her father had never offered a word of comfort to anyone. And she had gotten in the habit of pretending she was tough so that Colton and Sierra wouldn't worry about her. So that they wouldn't look too deeply at how damaged she was still from the events of the past.

So she put all her weight on him and total peace washed over her. She shouldn't indulge in this. She shouldn't allow herself this. It was dangerous. But she couldn't stop. And she didn't want to.

She squeezed her eyes shut, a few more tears falling down her cheeks, soaking into his shirt. If anybody knew that Madison West had wept all over a man in the broad light of day, they wouldn't believe it. But she didn't care. This wasn't about anyone else. It was just about her. About purging her soul of some of the poison that had taken up residence there ten years ago and never quite left.

About dealing with some of the heavy longing that existed inside her for a time and a place she could never return to. For a Christmas when she had walked down Main Street with her father and seen him as a hero.

But of course, when she was through crying, she felt exposed. Horribly. Hideously, and she knew this was why she didn't make a habit out of confiding in people. Because now Sam McCormack knew too much about her. Knew more about her than maybe anybody else on earth. At least, he knew about parts of her that no one else did.

The tenderness. The insecurity. The parts that were on the verge of cracking open, crumbling the foundation of her and leaving nothing more than a dusty pile of Maddy behind.

She took a deep breath, hoping that the pressure would squeeze some of those shattering pieces of herself back together with the sheer force of it. Too bad it just made her aware of more places down deep that were compromised.

Still, she wiggled out of his grasp, needing a moment to get ahold of herself. Needing very much to not get caught being held by a strange man down at the arena by any of the staff or anyone in her family.

"Thank you," she said, her voice shaking. "I just… I didn't know how much I needed that."

"I didn't do anything."

"You listened. You didn't try to give me advice or tell me I was wrong. That's actually doing a lot. A lot more than most people are willing to do."

"So, do you want me to come back here tonight?"

"Actually," she said, grabbing hold of her hands, twisting them, trying to deal with the nervous energy that was rioting through her, "I was thinking maybe I could come out a little bit early. And I could see where you work."

She didn't know why she was doing this. She didn't know where she imagined it could possibly end or how it would be helpful to her in any way. To add more pieces of him to her heart, to her mind.

That's what it felt like she was trying to do. Like collecting shells on the seashore. Picking up all the shimmering pieces of Sam she possibly could and sticking them in her little pail, hoarding them. Making a collection.

For what? Maybe for when it was over.

Maybe that wasn't so bad.

She had pieces of David, whether she wanted them or not. And she'd entertained the idea that maybe she could sleep with someone and not do that. Not carry them forward with her.

But the reality of it was that she wasn't going to walk away from this affair and never think of Sam again. He was never going to be the farrier again. He would always be Sam. Why not leave herself with beautiful memories instead of terrible ones? Maybe this was what she needed to do.

"You want to see the forge?" he asked.

"Sure. That would be interesting. But also your studio. I'm curious about your art, and I realize that I don't really know anything about it. Seeing you in the Mercantile the other day talking to Lane…" She didn't know how to phrase what she was thinking without sounding a little bit crazy. Without sounding overly attached. So she just let the sentence trail off.

But she was curious. She was curious about him. About who he was when he wasn't here. About who he was as a whole person, without the blinders around him that she had put there. She had very purposefully gone out of her way to know nothing about him. And so he had always been Sam McCormack, grumpy guy who worked at her family ranch on occasion and who she often bantered with in the sharpest of senses.

But there was more to him. So much more. This man

who had held her, this man who had listened, this man who seemed to know everyone in town and have decent relationships with them. Who created beautiful things that started in his mind and were then formed with his hands. She wanted to know him.

Yeah, she wouldn't be telling him any of that.

"Were you jealous? Because there is nothing between myself and Lane Jensen. First of all, anyone who wants anything to do with her has to go through Finn Donnelly, and I have no desire to step in the middle of *that* weird dynamic and his older-brother complex."

It struck her then that jealousy hadn't even been a component to what she had felt the other day. How strange. Considering everything she had been through with men, it seemed like maybe trust should be the issue here. But it wasn't. It never had been.

It had just been this moment of catching sight of him at a different angle. Like a different side to a prism that cast a different color on the wall and made her want to investigate further. To see how one person could contain so many different things.

A person who was so desperate to hide anything beyond that single dimension he seemed comfortable with.

Another thing she would definitely not say to him. She couldn't imagine the twenty shades of rainbow horror that would cross Sam's face if she compared him to a prism out loud.

"I was not," she said. "But it made me aware of the fact that you're kind of a big deal. And I haven't fully appreciated that."

"Of course you haven't," he said, his tone dry. "It interferes with your stable-boy fantasy."

She made a scoffing sound. "I do not have a stable-boy fantasy."

"Yes, you do. You like slumming it."

Those words called up heated memories out of the depths of her mind. Him whispering things in her ear. His rough hands skimming over her skin. She bit her lip. "I like nothing of the kind, Sam McCormack. Not with you, not with any man. Are you going to show me your pretty art or not?"

"Not if you call it pretty."

"You'll have to take your chances. I'm not putting a cap on my vocabulary for your comfort. Anyway, if you haven't noticed, unnerving people with what I may or may not say next is kind of my thing."

"I've noticed."

"You do it too," she said.

His lips tipped upward into a small smile. "Do I?"

She rolled her eyes. "Oh, don't pretend you don't know. You're way too smart for that. And you act like the word *smart* is possibly the world's most vile swear when it's applied to you. But you are. You can throw around accusations of slumming it all you want, but if we didn't connect mentally, and if I didn't respect you in some way, this wouldn't work."

"Our brains have nothing to do with this."

She lifted a finger. "A woman's largest sexual organ is her brain."

He chuckled, wrapping his arm around her waist and drawing her close. "Sure, Maddy. But we both know what the most important one is." He leaned in, whispering dirty things in her ear, and she laughed, pushing against his chest. "Okay," he said, finally. "I will let you come see my studio."

She fought against the trickle of warmth that ran through her, that rested deep in her stomach and spread out from there, making her feel a kind of languid satisfaction that she had no business feeling over something like this. "Then I guess I'll see you for the art show."

Nine

Sam had no idea what in hell had possessed him to let Maddy come out to his property tonight. Chase and Anna were not going to let this go ignored. In fact, Anna was already starting to make comments about the fact that he hadn't been around for dinner recently. Which was why he was there tonight, eating as quickly as possible so he could get back out to his place on the property before Maddy arrived. He had given her directions to go on the road that would allow her to bypass the main house, which Chase and Anna inhabited.

"Sam." His sister-in-law's voice cut into his thoughts. "I thought you were going to join us for dinner tonight?"

"I'm here," he said.

"Your body is. Your brain isn't. And Chase worked very hard on this meal," Anna said.

Anna was a tractor mechanic, and formerly Chase's

best friend in a platonic sense. All of that had come to an end a few months ago when they had realized there was a lot more between them than friendship.

Still, the marriage had not transformed Anna into a domestic goddess. Instead, it had forced Chase to figure out how to share a household with somebody. They were never going to have a traditional relationship, but it seemed to suit Chase just fine.

"It's very good, Chase," Sam said, keeping his tone dry.

"Thanks," Chase said, "I opened the jar of pasta sauce myself."

"Sadly, no one in this house is ever going to win a cooking competition," Anna said.

"You keep *me* from starving," Sam pointed out.

Though, in all honesty, he was a better cook than either of them. Still, it was an excuse to get together with his brother. And sometimes it felt like he needed excuses. So that he didn't have to think deeply about a feeling that was more driving than hunger pangs.

"Not recently," Chase remarked. "You haven't been around."

Sam let out a heavy sigh. "Yes, sometimes a man assumes that newlyweds want time alone without their crabby brother around."

"We always want you around," Anna said. Then she screwed up her face. "Okay, we don't *always* want you around. But for dinner, when we invite you, it's fine."

"Just no unexpected visits to the house," Chase said. "In the evening. Or anytime. And maybe also don't walk into Anna's shop without knocking after hours."

Sam grimaced. "I get the point. Anyway, I've just been busy. And I'm about to be busy again." He stood up, anticipation shooting through him. He had gone a long time without sex, and now sex with Maddy was about all he could think about. Five years of celibacy would do that to a man.

Made a man do stupid things, like invite the woman he was currently sleeping with to come to his place and to come see his art. Whatever the hell she thought that would entail. He was inclined to figure it out. Just so she would feel happy, so he could see her smile again.

So she would be in the mood to put out. And nothing more. Certainly no emotional reasoning behind that.

He couldn't do that. Not ever again.

"Okay," Anna said, "you're always cagey, Sam, I'll give you that. But you have to give me a hint about what's going on."

"No," Sam said, turning to go. "I really don't."

"Sculpture? A woman?"

Well, sadly, Anna was mostly on point with both. "Not your business."

"That's hilarious," Chase said, "coming from the man who meddled in our relationship."

"You jackasses needed meddling," Sam said. "You were going to let her go." Of the two of them, Chase was undoubtedly the better man. And Anna was one of the best, man or woman. When Sam had realized his brother was about to let Anna get away because of baggage from his past, Sam had had no choice but to play the older-brother card and give advice that he himself would never have taken.

But it was different for Chase. Sam wanted it to be different for Chase. He didn't want his younger brother living the same stripped-down existence he did.

"Well, maybe you need meddling too, jackass," Anna said.

Sam ignored his sister-in-law and continued on out of the house, taking the steps on the porch two at a time, the frosted ground crunching beneath his boots as he walked across the field, taking the short route between the two houses.

He shoved his hands in his pockets, looking up, watching his breath float up into the dense sky, joining the mist there. It was already getting dark, the twilight hanging low around him, a deep blue ink spill that bled down over everything.

It reminded him of grief. A darkness that descended without warning, covering everything around it, changing it. Taking things that were familiar and twisting them into foreign objects and strangers.

That thought nibbled at the back of his mind. He couldn't let it go. It just hovered there as he made his way back to his place, trying to push its way to the front of his mind and form the obvious conclusion.

He resisted it. The way that he always did. Anytime he got inspiration that seemed related to these kinds of feelings. And then he would go out to his shop and start working on another Texas longhorn sculpture. Because that didn't mean anything and people would want to buy it.

Just as he approached his house, so did Maddy's car. She parked right next to his truck, and a strange feeling of domesticity overtook him. Two cars in the driveway. His and hers.

He pushed that aside too.

He watched her open the car door, her blond hair even paler in the advancing moonlight. She was wearing a hat, the shimmering curls spilling out from underneath it. She also had on a scarf and gloves. And there was something about her, looking soft and bundled up, and very much not like prickly, brittle Maddy, that made him want to pull her back into his arms like he had done earlier that day and hold her up against his chest.

Hold her until she quit shaking. Or until she started shaking for a different reason entirely.

"You made it," he said.

"You say that like you had some doubt that I would."

"Well, at the very least I thought you might change your mind."

"No such luck for you. I'm curious. And once my curiosity is piqued, I will have it satisfied."

"You're like a particularly meddlesome cat," he said.

"You're going to have to make up your mind, Sam," Maddy said, smiling broadly.

"About what?"

"Am I vegetable or mammal? You have now compared me to both."

"A tomato is a fruit."

"Whatever," she said, waving a gloved hand.

"Do you want to come out and see the sculptures or do you want to stand here arguing about whether or not you're animal, vegetable or mineral?"

Her smile only broadened. "Sculptures, please."

"Well, follow me. And it's a good thing you bundled up."

"This is how much I had to bundle to get in the car and drive over here. My heater is *not* broken. I didn't know that I was going to be wandering around out in the dark, in the cold."

He snorted. "You run cold?"

"I do."

"I hadn't noticed."

She lifted a shoulder, taking two steps to his every one, doing her best to keep up with him as he led them both across the expanse of frozen field. "Well, I'm usually very hot when you're around. Anyway, the combination of you and blankets is very warming."

"What happens when I leave?"

"I get cold," she returned.

Something about those words felt like a knife in the center of his chest. Damned if he knew why. At least, damned if he wanted to know why.

What he wanted was to figure out how to make it go away.

They continued on the rest of the walk in silence, and he increased his pace when the shop came into view. "Over here is where Chase and I work," he said, gesturing to the first building. "Anna's is on a different section of the property, one closer to the road so that it's easier for her customers to get in there, since they usually have heavy equipment being towed by heavier equipment. And this one is mine." He pointed to another outbuilding, one that had once been a separate machine shed.

"We remodeled it this past year. Expanded and made room for the new equipment. I have a feeling my dad would piss himself if he knew what this was being used for now," he continued, not quite able to keep the thought in his mind.

Maddy came up beside him, looping her arm through his. "Maybe. But I want to see it. And I promise you I won't…do *that*."

"Appreciated," he said, allowing her to keep hold of him while they walked inside.

He realized then that nobody other than Chase and Anna had ever been in here. And he had never grandly showed it to either of them. They just popped in on occasion to let him know that lunch or dinner was ready or to ask if he was ever going to resurface.

He had never invited anyone here. Though, he supposed that Maddy had invited herself here. Either way, this was strange. It was exposing in a way he hadn't anticipated it being. Mostly because that required he admit that there was something of himself in his work. And he resisted that. Resisted it hard.

It had always been an uncomfortable fit for him. That he had this ability, this compulsion to create things, that could come only from inside him. Which was a little bit like opening up his chest and showing bits of it to the world. Which was the last thing on earth he ever wanted to do. He didn't like sharing himself with other people. Not at all.

Maddy turned a slow circle, her soft, pink mouth falling open. "Wow," she said. "Is this all of them?"

"No," he said, following her line of sight, looking at the various iron sculptures all around them. Most of them were to scale with whatever they were representing. Giant two-ton metal cows and horses, one with a cowboy upon its back, took up most of the space in the room.

Pieces that came from what he saw. From a place he loved. But not from inside him.

"What are these?"

"Works in progress, mostly. Almost all of them are close to being done. Which was why I was up at the cabin, remember? I'm trying to figure out what I'm going to do next. But I can always make more things like this. They sell. I can put them in places around town and tourists will always come in and buy them. People pay obscene amounts of money for stuff like this." He let out a long, slow breath. "I'm kind of mystified by it."

"You shouldn't be. It's amazing." She moved around the space, reaching out and brushing her fingertips over the back of one of the cows. "We have to get some for the ranch. They're perfect."

Something shifted in his chest, a question hovering on the tip of his tongue. But he held it back. He had been about to ask her if he should do something different. If he should follow that compulsion that had hit him on the walk back. Those ideas about grief. About loss.

Who the hell wanted to look at something like that? Anyway, he didn't want to show anyone that part of himself. And he sure as hell didn't deserve to profit off any of his losses.

He gritted his teeth. "Great."

"You sound like you think it's great," she said, her tone deeply insincere.

"I wasn't aware my enthusiasm was going to be graded."

She looked around, the shop light making her hair look even deeper gold than it normally did. She reached up, grabbing the knit hat on her head and flinging it onto the ground. He knew what she was doing. He wanted to stop her. Because this was his shop. His studio. It was personal in a way that nothing else was. She could sleep in his bed. She could go to his house, stay there all night, and it would never be the same as her getting naked here.

He was going to stop her.

But then she grabbed the zipper tab on her jacket and shrugged it off before taking hold of the hem of her top, yanking it over her head and sending it the same way as her outerwear.

Then Maddy was standing there, wearing nothing but a flimsy lace bra, the pale curve of her breasts rising and falling with every breath she took.

"Since it's clear how talented your hands are, particularly here..." she said, looking all wide-eyed and innocent. He loved that. The way she could look like this, then spew profanities with the best of them. The way she could make her eyes all dewy, then do something that would make even the most hardened cowboy blush. "I thought I might see if I could take advantage of the inspirational quality of the place."

Immediately, his blood ran hotter, faster, desire roaring in him like a beast. He wanted her. He wanted this. There was nowhere soft to take her, not here. Not in this place full of nails and iron, in this place that was hard and jagged just like his soul, that was more evidence of what he contained than anyone would ever know.

"The rest," he said, his voice as uncompromising as the sculpture all around them. "Take off the rest, Madison."

Her lashes fluttered as she looked down, undoing the snap on her jeans, then the zipper, maddeningly slowly. And of course, she did her best to look like she had no idea what she was doing to him.

She pushed her jeans down her hips, and all that was left covering her was those few pale scraps of lace. She was so soft. And everything around her was so hard.

It should make him want to protect her. Should make him want to get her out of here. Away from this place. Away from him. But it didn't. He was that much of a bastard.

He didn't take off any of his own clothes, because there was something about the contrast that turned him on even more. Instead, he moved toward her, slowly, not bothering to hide his open appreciation for her curves.

He closed the distance between them, wrapping his hand around the back of her head, sifting his fingers through her hair before tightening his hold on her, tugging gently. She gasped, following his lead, tilting her face upward.

He leaned in, and he could tell that she was expecting a kiss. By the way her lips softened, by the way her eyes fluttered closed. Instead, he angled his head, pressing his lips to that tender skin on her neck. She shivered, the contact clearly an unexpected surprise. But not an unwelcome one.

He kept his fingers buried firmly in her hair, holding her steady as he shifted again, brushing his mouth over the line of her collarbone, following it all the way toward the center of her chest and down to the plush curves of her breasts.

He traced that feathery line there where lace met skin with the tip of his tongue, daring to delve briefly beneath the fabric, relishing the hitch in her breathing when he came close to her sensitized nipples.

He slid his hands up her arms, grabbed hold of the delicate bra straps and tugged them down, moving slowly, ever so slowly, bringing the cups down just beneath her breasts, exposing those dusky nipples to him.

"Beautiful," he said. "Prettier than anything in here."

"I didn't think you wanted the word *pretty* uttered in here," she said, breathless.

"About my work. About you… That's an entirely different situation. You are pretty. These are pretty." He leaned in, brushing his lips lightly over one tightened bud, relishing the sweet sound of pleasure that she made.

"Now who's a tease?" she asked, her voice labored.

"I haven't even started to tease you yet."

He slid his hands around her back, pressing his palms hard between her shoulder blades, lowering his head so that he could draw the center of her breast deep into his mouth. He sucked hard until she whimpered, until she squirmed against him, clearly looking for some kind of relief for the intense arousal that he was building inside her.

He looked up, really looked at her face, a deep, primitive sense of pleasure washing through him. That he was touching such a soft, beautiful woman. That he was allowing himself such an indulgence. That he was doing this to her.

He had forgotten. He had forgotten what it was like to really relish the fact that he possessed the power to make a woman feel good. Because he had reduced his hands to something else entirely. Hands that had failed him, that had failed Elizabeth.

Hands that could form iron into impossible shapes but couldn't be allowed to handle something this fragile.

But here he was with Madison. She was soft, and he wasn't breaking her. She was beautiful, and she was his.

Not yours. Never yours.

He tightened his hold on her, battling the unwelcome thoughts that were trying to crowd in, trying to take over this experience, this moment. When Madison was gone, he would go back to the austere existence he'd been living for the past five years. But right now, he had her, and he wasn't going to let anything damage that. Not now.

Instead of thinking, which was never a good thing,

not for him, he continued his exploration of her body. Lowering himself down to his knees in front of her, kissing her just beneath her breasts, and down lower, tracing a line across her soft stomach.

She was everything a woman should be. He was confident of that. Because she was the only woman he could remember. Right now, she was everything.

He moved his hands down her thighs, then back up again, pushing his fingertips beneath the waistband of her panties as he gripped her hips and leaned in, kissing her just beneath her belly button. She shook beneath him, a sweet little trembling that betrayed just how much she wanted him.

She wouldn't, if she knew. If she knew, she wouldn't want him. But she didn't know. And she never had to. There were only five days left. They would never have to talk about it. Ever. They would only ever have this. That was important. Because if they ever tried to have more, there would be nothing. She would run so far the other direction he would never see her again.

Or maybe she wouldn't. Maybe she would stick around. But that was even worse. Because of what he would have to do.

He flexed his fingers, the blunt tips digging into that soft skin at her hips. He growled, moving them around to cup her ass beneath the thin lace fabric on her panties. He squeezed her there too and she moaned, her obvious enjoyment of his hands all over her body sending a surge of pleasure through him.

He shifted, delving between her thighs, sliding his fingers through her slick folds, moving his fingers over her clit before drawing them back, pushing one finger inside her.

She gasped, grabbing his shoulders, pitching forward. He could feel her thigh muscles shaking as he pleasured her slowly, drawing his finger in and out of her body before adding a second. Her nails dug into his skin, clinging to him harder and harder as he continued tormenting her.

He looked up at her and allowed himself to get lost in this. In the feeling of her slick arousal beneath his hands, in the completely overwhelmed, helpless expression on her beautiful face. Her eyes were shut tight, and she was biting her lip, probably to keep herself from screaming. He decided he had a new goal.

He lowered his head, pressing his lips right to the center of her body, her lace panties holding the warmth of his breath as he slowly lapped at her through the thin fabric.

She swore, a short, harsh sound that verged on being a scream. But it wasn't enough. He teased her that way, his fingers deep inside her, his mouth on her, for as long as he could stand it.

Then he took his other hand, swept the panties aside and pushed his fingers in deep while he lapped at her bare skin, dragging his tongue through her folds, over that sensitized bundle of nerves.

And then she screamed.

Her internal muscles pulsed around him, her pleasure ramping his up two impossible degrees.

"I hope like *hell* you brought a condom," he said, his voice ragged, rough.

"I think I did," she said, her tone wavering. "Yes, I did. It's in my purse. Hurry."

"You want me to dig through your purse."

"I can't breathe. I can't move. If I do anything, I'm

going to fall down. So I suggest you get the condom so that I don't permanently wound myself attempting to procure it."

"Your tongue seems fine," he said, moving away from her and going to grab the purse that she had discarded along with the rest of her clothes.

"So does yours," she muttered.

And he knew that what she was referring to had nothing to do with talking.

He found the condom easily enough, since it was obviously the last thing she had thrown into her bag. Then he stood, stripping his shirt off and his pants, adding to the pile of clothing that Maddy had already left on the studio floor.

Then he tore open the packet and took care of the protection. He looked around the room, searching for some surface that he could use. That they could use.

There was no way to lay her down, which he kind of regretted. Mostly because he always felt like she deserved a little bit more than the rough stuff that he doled out to her. Except she seemed to like it. So if it was what she wanted, she was about to get the full experience tonight.

He wrapped his arm around her waist, pulling her up against him, pressing their bodies together, her bare breasts pressing hard against his chest. He was so turned on, his arousal felt like a crowbar between them.

She didn't seem to mind.

He took hold of her chin, tilting her face up so she had to look at him. And then he leaned in, kissing her lightly, gently. It would be the last gentle thing he did all night.

He slid his hands along her body, moving them to grip her hips. Then he turned her so that she was facing away from him. She gasped but followed the momentum as he propelled her forward, toward one of the iron figures—a horse—and placed his hand between her shoulder blades.

"Hold on to the horse, cowgirl," he said, his voice so rough it sounded like a stranger's.

"What?"

He pushed more firmly against her back, bending her forward slightly, and she lifted her hands, placing them over the back of the statue. "Just like that," he said.

Her back arched slightly, and he drew his fingertips down the line of her spine, all the way down to her butt. He squeezed her there, then slipped his hand to her hip.

"Spread your legs," he instructed.

She did, widening her stance, allowing him a good view and all access. He moved his hand back there, just for a second, testing her readiness. Then he positioned his arousal at the entrance to her body. He pushed into her, hard and deep, and she let out a low, slow sound of approval.

He braced himself, putting one hand on her shoulder, his thumb pressed firmly against the back of her neck, the other holding her hip as he began to move inside her.

He lost himself. In her, in the moment. In this soft, beautiful woman, all curves and round shapes in the middle of this hard, angular garden of iron.

The horse was hard in front of her; he was hard behind her. Only Maddy was soft.

Her voice was soft—the little gasps of pleasure that escaped her lips like balm for his soul. Her body was soft, her curves giving against him every time he thrust home.

When she began to rock back against him, her desperation clearly increasing along with his, he moved his hand from her hip to between her thighs. He stroked her in time with his thrusts, bringing her along with him, higher and higher until he thought they would both shatter. Until he thought they might shatter everything in this room. All of these unbreakable, unbending things.

She lowered her head, her body going stiff as her release broke over her, her body spasming around his, that evidence of her own loss of control stealing every ounce of his own.

He gave himself up to this. Up to her. And when his climax hit him, it was with the realization that it was somehow hers. That she owned this. Owned this moment. Owned his body.

That realization only made it more intense. Only made it more arousing.

His muscles shook as he poured himself into her. As he gave himself up to it totally, completely, in a way he had given himself up to nothing and no one for more than five years. Maybe ever.

In this moment, surrounded by all of these creations that had come out of him, he was exposed, undone. As though he had ripped his chest open completely and exposed his every secret to her, as though she could see everything, not just these creations, but the ugly, secret things that he kept contained inside his soul.

It was enough to make his knees buckle, and he had to reach out, pressing his palm against the rough surface of the iron horse to keep himself from falling to the ground and dragging Maddy with him.

The only sound in the room was their broken breathing, fractured and unsteady. He gathered her up against his body, one hand against her stomach, the other still on the back of the horse, keeping them upright.

He angled his head, buried his face in her neck, kissed her.

"Well," Maddy said, her voice unsteady, "that was amazing."

He couldn't respond. Because he couldn't say anything. His tongue wasn't working; his brain wasn't working. His voice had dried up like a desert. Instead, he released his grip on the horse, turned her to face him and claimed her mouth in a deep, hard kiss.

Ten

Maybe it wasn't the best thing to make assumptions, but when they got back to Sam's house, that was exactly what Maddy did. She simply assumed that she would be invited inside because he wanted her to stay.

If her assumption was wrong, he didn't correct her.

She soaked in the details of his home, the simple, completely spare surroundings, and how it seemed to clash with his newfound wealth.

Except, in many ways it didn't, she supposed. Sam just didn't seem the type to go out and spend large. He was too…well, Sam.

The cabin was neat, well kept and small. Rustic and void of any kind of frills. Honestly, it was more rustic than the cabins they had stayed in up in the mountain.

It was just another piece that she could add to the Sam puzzle. He was such a strange man. So difficult to find the center of. To find the key to. He was one giant sheet of code and she was missing some essential bit that might help her make heads or tails of him.

He was rough; he was distant. He was caring and kinder in many ways than almost anyone else she had ever known. Certainly, he had listened to her in a way that no one else ever had before. Offering nothing and simply taking everything onto his shoulders, letting her feel whatever she did without telling her it was wrong.

That was valuable in a way that she hadn't realized it would be.

She wished that she could do the same for him. That she could figure out what the thing was that made Sam… Sam. That made him distant and difficult and a lot like a brick wall. But she knew there was more behind his aloofness. A potential for feeling, for emotion, that surpassed what he showed the world.

She didn't even bother to ask herself why she cared. She suspected she already knew.

Sam busied himself making a fire in the simple, old-fashioned fireplace in the living room. It was nothing like the massive, modern adorned piece that was in the West family living room. One with fake logs and a switch that turned it on. One with a mantel that boasted the various awards won by Nathan West's superior horses.

There was something about this that she liked. The lack of pretension. Though, she wondered if it reflected Sam any more honestly than her own home—decorated by her mother's interior designer—did her. She could see it, in a way. The fact that he was no-nonsense and a little bit spare.

And yet in other ways she couldn't.

His art pieces looked like they were ready to take a breath and come to life any moment. The fact that such beautiful things came out of him made her think there had to be beautiful things in him. An appreciation for aesthetics. And yet none of that was in evidence here. Of course, it would be an appreciation for a hard aesthetic, since there was nothing soft about what he did.

Still, he wasn't quite this cold and empty either.

Neither of them spoke while he stoked the fire, and pretty soon the small space began to warm. Her whole body was still buzzing with the aftereffects of what had happened in his studio. But still, she wanted more.

She hadn't intended to seduce him in his studio; it had just happened. But she didn't regret it. She had brought a condom, just in case, so she supposed she couldn't claim total innocence. But still.

It had been a little bit reckless. The kind of thing a person could get caught doing. It was definitely not as discreet as she should have been. The thought made her smile. Made her feel like Sam was washing away some of the wounds of her past. That he was healing her in a way she hadn't imagined she could be.

She walked over to where he was, still kneeling down in front of the fireplace, and she placed her hands on his shoulders. She felt his muscles tighten beneath her touch. All of the tension that he carried in his shoulders. Why? Because he wanted her again and that bothered him? It wasn't because he didn't want her, she was convinced of that. There was no faking what was between them.

She let her fingertips drift down lower. Then she leaned in, pressing a kiss to his neck, as he was so fond of doing to her. As she was so fond of him doing.

"What are you doing?" he asked, his voice rumbling inside him.

"Honestly, if you have to ask, I'm not doing a very good job of it."

"Aren't you exhausted?"

"The way I see it, I have five days left with you. I could go five days without sleep if I needed to."

He reached up, grabbing hold of her wrist and turning, then pulling her down onto the floor, onto his lap. "Is that a challenge? Because I'm more than up to meeting that."

"If you want to take it as one, I suppose that's up to you."

She put her hands on his face, sliding her thumbs alongside the grooves next to his mouth. He wasn't that old. In his early to midthirties, she guessed. But he wore some serious cares on that handsome face of his, etched into his skin. She wondered what they were. It was easy to assume it was the death of his parents, and perhaps that was part of it. But there was more.

She'd had the impression earlier today that she'd only ever glimpsed a small part of him. That there were deep pieces of himself that he kept concealed from the world. And she had a feeling this was one of them. That he was a man who presented himself as simple, who lived in these simple surroundings, hard and spare, while he contained multitudes of feeling and complexity.

She also had a feeling he would rather die than admit that.

"All right," he said, "if you insist."

He leaned in, kissing her. It was slower and more luxurious than any of the kisses they had shared back in the studio. A little bit less frantic. A little bit less desperate.

Less driven toward its ultimate conclusion, much more about the journey.

She found herself being disrobed again, for the second time that day, and she really couldn't complain. Especially not when Sam joined her in a state of undress.

She pressed her hand against his chest, tracing the strongly delineated muscles, her eyes following the movement.

"I'm going to miss this," she said, not quite sure what possessed her to speak the words out loud. Because they went so much deeper than just appreciation for his body. So much deeper than just missing his beautiful chest or his perfect abs.

She wished that they didn't, but they did. She wished she were a little more confused by the things she did and said with him, like she had been earlier today. But somehow, between her pouring her heart out to him at the ranch today and making love with him in the studio, a few things had become a lot clearer.

His lips twitched, like he was considering making light of the statement. Saying something to defuse the tension between them. Instead, he wrapped his fingers around her wrist, holding her tight, pressing her palms flat against him so that she could feel his heart beating. Then he kissed her. Long, powerful. A claiming, a complete and total invasion of her soul.

She didn't even care.

Or maybe, more accurately, she did care. She cared all the way down, and what she couldn't bother with anymore was all the pretending that she didn't. That she cared about nothing and no one, that she existed on the Isle of Maddy. Where she was wholly self-sufficient.

She was pretty sure, in this moment, that she might

need him. That she might need him in ways she hadn't needed another person in a very long time, if ever. When she had met David, she had been a teenager. She hadn't had any baggage; she hadn't run into any kind of resistance in the world. She was young, and she didn't know what giving her heart away might cost.

She knew now. She knew so much more. She had been hurt; she had been broken. And when she allowed herself to see that she needed someone, she could see too just how badly it could go.

When they parted, they were both breathing hard, and his dark eyes were watchful on hers. She felt like she could see further than she normally could. Past all of that strength that he wore with ease, down to the parts of him that were scarred, that had been wounded.

That were vulnerable.

Even Sam McCormack was vulnerable. What a revelation. Perhaps if he was, everyone was.

He lifted his hand, brushing up against her cheek, down to her chin, and then he pushed her hair back off her face, slowly letting his fingers sift through the strands. And he watched them slide through his fingers, just as she had watched her own hand as she'd touched his chest. She wondered what he was thinking. If he was thinking what she'd been. If he was attached to her in spite of himself.

Part of her hoped so. Part of her hoped not.

He leaned down, kissing her on the shoulder, the seemingly nonsexual contact affecting her intensely. Making her skin feel like it was on fire, making her heart feel like it might burst right out of her chest.

She found herself being propelled backward, but it

felt like slow motion, as he lowered her down onto the floor. Onto the carpet there in front of the fireplace.

She had the thought that this was definitely a perfect component for a winter affair. But then the thought made her sad. Because she wanted so much more than a winter affair with him. So much more than this desperate grab in front of the fire, knowing that they had only five days left with each other.

But then he was kissing her and she couldn't think anymore. She couldn't regret. She could only kiss him back.

His hands skimmed over her curves, her breasts, her waist, her hips, all the way down to her thighs, where he squeezed her tight, held on to her as though she were his lifeline. As though he were trying to memorize every curve, every dip and swell.

She closed her eyes, gave herself over to it, to the sensation of being known by Sam. The thought filled her, made her chest feel like it was expanding. He knew her. He really knew her. And he was still here. Still with her. He didn't judge her; he didn't find her disgusting.

He didn't treat her like she was breakable. He could still bend her over a horse statue in his studio, then be like this with her in front of the fire. Tender. Sweet.

Because she was a woman who wanted both things. And he seemed to know it.

He also seemed to be a man who might need both too.

Or maybe everybody did. But you didn't see it until you were with the person you wanted to be both of those things with.

"Hang on just a second," he said, suddenly, breaking into her sensual reverie. She had lost track of time.

Lost track of everything except the feel of his hands on her skin.

He moved away from her, the loss of his body leaving her cold. But he returned a moment later, settling himself in between her thighs. "Condom," he said by way of explanation.

At least one of them had been thinking. She certainly hadn't been.

He joined their bodies together, entering her slowly, the sensation of fullness, of being joined to him, suddenly so profound that she wanted to weep with it. It always felt good. From the first time with him it had felt good. But this was different.

It was like whatever veil had been between them, whatever stack of issues had existed, had been driving them, was suddenly dropped. And there was nothing between them. When he looked at her, poised over her, deep inside her, she felt like he could see all the way down.

When he moved, she moved with him, meeting him thrust for thrust, pushing them both to the brink. And when she came, he came along with her, his rough gasp of pleasure in her ears ramping up her own release.

In the aftermath, skin to skin, she couldn't deny anymore what all these feelings were. She couldn't pretend that she didn't know.

She'd signed herself up for a twelve-day fling with a man she didn't even like, and only one week in she had gone and fallen in love with Sam McCormack.

"Sam." Maddy's voice broke into his sensual haze. He was lying on his back in front of the fireplace, feeling drained and like he had just had some kind of out-of-body experience. Except he had been firmly in his body and feeling everything, everything and then some.

"What?" he asked, his voice rusty.

"Why do you make farm animals?"

"What the hell kind of question is that?" he asked.

"A valid one," she said, moving nearer to him, putting her hand on his chest, tracing shapes there. "I mean, not that they aren't good."

"The horse seemed good enough for you a couple hours ago."

"It's good," she said, her tone irritated, because she obviously thought he was misunderstanding her on purpose.

Which she wasn't wrong about.

"Okay, but you don't think I should be making farm animals."

"No, I think it's fine that you make farm animals. I just think it's not actually you."

He shifted underneath her, trying to decide whether or not he should say anything. Or if he should sidestep the question. If it were anyone else, he would laugh. Play it off. Pretend like there was no answer. That there was nothing deeper in him than simply re-creating what he literally saw out in the fields in front of him.

And a lot of people would have bought that. His own brother probably would have, or at the very least, he wouldn't have pushed. But this was Maddy. Maddy, who had come apart in his arms in more than one way over the past week. Maddy, who perhaps saw deeper inside him than anyone else ever had.

Why not tell her? Why not? Because he could sense her getting closer to him. Could sense it like an invisible cord winding itself around the two of them, no matter that he was going to have to cut it in the end. Maybe it would be best to do it now.

"If I don't make what I see, I'll have to make what I feel," he said. "Nobody wants that."

"Why not?"

"Because the art has to sell," he said, his voice flat. Although, that was somewhat disingenuous. It wasn't that he didn't think he could sell darker pieces. In fact, he was sure that he could. "I don't do it for myself. I do it for Chase. I was perfectly content to keep it some kind of weird hobby that I messed around with after hours. Chase was the one who thought that I needed to pursue it full-time. Chase was the one who thought it was the way to save our business. And it started out doing kind of custom artistry for big houses. Gates and the detail work on stairs and decks and things. But then I started making bigger pieces and we started selling them. I say *we* because without Chase they would just sit in the shop."

"So you're just making what sells. That's the beginning and end of the story." Her blue eyes were too sharp, too insightful and far too close to the firelight for him to try to play at any games.

"I make what I want to let people see."

"What happened, Sam? And don't tell me nothing. You're talking to somebody who clung to one event in the past for as long as humanly possible. Who let it dictate her entire life. You're talking to the queen of residual issues here. Don't try to pretend that you don't have any. I know what it looks like." She took a deep breath. "I know what it looks like when somebody uses anger, spite and a whole bunch of unfriendliness to keep the world at a safe distance. I know, because I've spent the past ten years doing it. Nobody gets too close to the girl who says unpredictable things. The one who might come out and tell you that your dress does make you look fat and then turn around and say something crude about male anatomy. It's how you give yourself power in social situations. Act like you don't care about the rules that everyone else is a slave to." She laughed. "And why not? I already broke the rules. That's me. It's been me for a long time. And it isn't because I didn't know better. It's because I absolutely knew better. You're smart, Sam. The way that you walk around, the way you present yourself, even here, it's calculated."

Sam didn't think anyone had ever accused him of being calculated before. But it was true. Truer than most things that had been leveled at him. That he was grumpy, that he was antisocial. He was those things. But for a very specific reason.

And of course Madison would know. Of course she would see.

"I've never been comfortable sharing my life," Sam said. "I suppose that comes from having a father who was less than thrilled to have a son who was interested in art. In fact, I think my father considered it a moral failing of his. To have a son who wanted to use materials to create frivolous things. Things that had no use. To have a son who was more interested in that than honest labor. I learned to keep things to myself a long time ago. Which all sounds a whole lot like a sad, cliché story. Except it's not. It worked. I would have made a relationship with my dad work. But he died. So then it didn't matter anymore. But still, I just never…I never wanted to keep people up on what was happening with my life. I was kind of trained that way."

Hell, a lot of guys were that way, anyway. A lot of

men didn't want to talk about what was happening in their day-to-day existence. Though most of them wouldn't have gone to the lengths that Sam did to keep everything separate.

"Most especially when Chase and I were neck-deep in trying to keep the business afloat, I didn't like him seeing that I was working on anything else. Anything at all." Sam took a deep breath. "That included any kind of relationships I might have. I didn't have a lot. But you know Chase never had a problem with people in town knowing that he was spreading it around. He never had a problem sleeping with the women here."

"No, he did not," Maddy said. "Never with me, to be clear."

"Considering I'm your first in a decade, I wasn't exactly that worried about it."

"Just making sure."

"I didn't like that. I didn't want my life to be part of this real-time small-town TV program. I preferred to find women out of town. When I was making deliveries, going to bigger ranches down the coast, that was when I would…"

"When you would find yourself a buckle bunny for the evening?"

"Yes," he said. "Except I met a woman I liked a lot. She was the daughter of one of the big ranchers down near Coos County. And I tried to keep things business oriented. We were actually doing business with her family. But I…I saw her out at a bar one night, and even though I knew she was too young, too nice of a girl for a guy like me…I slept with her. And a few times after. I was pretty obsessed with her, actually."

He was downplaying it. But what was the point of

doing anything else? Of admitting that for just a little while he'd thought he'd found something. Someone who wanted him. All of him. Someone who knew him.

The possibility of a future. Like the first hint of spring in the air after a long winter.

Maddy moved closer to him, looking up at him, and he decided to take a moment to enjoy that for a second. Because after this, she would probably never want to touch him again.

"Without warning, she cut me off. Completely. Didn't want to see me anymore. And since she was a few hours down the highway, that really meant not seeing her. I'd had to make an effort to work her into my life. Cutting her out of it was actually a lot easier."

"Sure," Maddy said, obviously not convinced.

"I got a phone call one night. Late. From the hospital. They told me to come down because Elizabeth was asking for me. They said it wasn't good."

"Oh, Sam," Maddy said, her tone tinged with sympathy.

He brush right past that. Continued on. "I whiteknuckled it down there. Went as fast as I could. I didn't tell anyone I was going. When I got there, they wouldn't let me in. Because I wasn't family."

"But she wanted them to call you."

"It didn't matter." It was difficult for him to talk about that day. In fact, he never had. He could see it all playing out in his mind as he spoke the words. Could see the image of her father walking out of the double doors, looking harried, older than Sam had ever seen him look during any of their business dealings.

"I never got to see her," Sam said. "She died a few minutes after I got there."

"Sam, I'm so sorry..."

"No, don't misunderstand me. This isn't a story about me being angry because I lost a woman that I loved. I *didn't* love her. That's the worst part." He swallowed hard, trying to diffuse the pressure in his throat crushing down, making it hard to breathe. "I mean, maybe I could have. But that's not the same. You know who loved her? Her family. Her family loved her. I have never seen a man look so destroyed as I did that day. Looking at her father, who clearly wondered why in hell I was sitting down there in the emergency room. Why I had been called to come down. He didn't have to wonder long. Not when they told him exactly how his daughter died." Sam took a deep breath. "Elizabeth died of internal bleeding. Complications from an ectopic pregnancy."

Maddy's face paled, her lips looking waxen. "Did you...? You didn't know she was pregnant."

"No. Neither did anyone in her family. But I know it was mine. I know it was mine, and she didn't want me to know. And that was probably why she didn't tell me, why she broke things off with me. Nobody knew because she was ashamed. Because it was my baby. Because it was a man that she knew she couldn't have a future with. Nobody knew, so when she felt tired and lay down for a nap because she was bleeding and feeling discomfort, no one was there."

Silence settled around them, the house creaking beneath the weight of it.

"Did you ever find out why...why she called you then?"

"I don't know. Maybe she wanted me there to blame me. Maybe she just needed me. I'll never know. She was gone before I ever got to see her."

"That must have been…" Maddy let that sentence trail off. "That's horrible."

"It's nothing but horrible. It's everything horrible. I know why she got pregnant, Maddy. It's because…I was so careless with her. I had sex with her once without a condom. And I thought that it would be fine. Hell, I figured if something did happen, I'd be willing to marry her. All of that happened because I didn't think. Because I lost control. I don't deserve…"

"You can't blame yourself for a death that was some kind of freak medical event."

"Tell me you wouldn't blame yourself, Maddy. Tell me you wouldn't." He sat up, and Maddy sat up too. Then he gripped her shoulders, holding her steady, forcing her to meet his gaze. "You, who blame yourself for the affair with your dressage teacher even though you were an underage girl. You could tell me you don't. You could tell me that you were just hurt by the way everybody treated you, but I know it's more than that. You blame yourself. So don't you dare look at me with those wide blue eyes and tell me that I have no business blaming myself."

She blinked. "I…I don't blame myself. I don't. I mean, I'm not proud of what I did, but I'm not going to take all of the blame. Not for something I couldn't control. He lied to me. I was dumb, yes. I was naive. But dammit, Sam, my father should have had my back. My friends should have had my back. And my teacher should never have taken advantage of me."

He moved away from her then, pushing himself into a standing position and forking his fingers through his hair. She wasn't blaming him. It was supposed to push her away. She certainly wasn't supposed to look at him with sympathy. She was supposed to be appalled. Appalled that he had taken the chances he had with Elizabeth's body. Appalled at his lack of control.

It was the object lesson. The one that proved that he wasn't good enough for a woman like her. That he wasn't good enough for anyone.

"You don't blame yourself at all?"

"I don't know," she said. "It's kind of a loaded question. I could have made another decision. And because of that, I guess I share blame. But I'm not going to sit around feeling endless guilt. I'm hurt. I'm wounded. But that's not the same thing. Like I told you, the sex was the least of it. If it was all guilt, I would have found somebody a long time ago. I would have dealt with it. But it's more than that. I think it's more than that with you. Because you're not an idiot. You know full well that it isn't like you're the first man to have unprotected sex with a woman. You know full well you weren't in control of where an embryo implanted inside a woman. You couldn't have taken her to the hospital, because you didn't know she was pregnant. You didn't know she needed you. She sent you away. She made some choices here, and I don't really think it's her fault either, because how could she have known? But still. It isn't your fault."

He drew back, anger roaring through him. "I'm the one…"

"You're very dedicated to this. But that doesn't make it true."

"Her father thought it was my fault," he said. "That matters. I had to look at a man who was going to have to bury his daughter because of me."

"Maybe he felt that way," Maddy said. "I can understand that. People want to blame. I know. Because I've been put in that position. Where I was the one that people wanted to blame. Because I wasn't as well liked. Because I wasn't as important. I know that David's wife certainly wanted to blame me, because she wanted to make her marriage work, and if she blamed David, how would she do that? And without blame, your anger is aimless."

Those words hit hard, settled somewhere down deep inside him. And he knew that no matter what, no matter that he didn't want to think about them, no matter that he didn't want to believe them, they were going to stay with him. Truth had a funny way of doing that.

"I'm not looking for absolution, Maddy." He shook his head. "I was never looking for it."

"What are you looking for, then?"

He shrugged. "Nothing. I'm not looking for anything. I'm not looking for you to forgive me. I'm not looking to forgive myself."

"No," she said, "you're just looking to keep punishing yourself. To hold everything inside and keep it buried down deep. I don't think it's the rest of the world you're hiding yourself from. I think you're hiding from yourself."

"You think that you are qualified to talk about my issues? You. The woman who didn't have a lover for ten years because she's so mired in the past?"

"Do you think that's going to hurt my feelings? I know I'm messed up. I'm well aware. In fact, I would argue that it takes somebody as profoundly screwed up as I am to look at another person and see it. Maybe other people would look at you and see a man who is strong. A man who has it all laid out. A man who has iron control. But I see you for what you are. You're completely and totally bound up inside. And you're ready to crack apart. You can't go on like this."

"Watch me," he said.

"How long has it been?" she asked, her tone soft.

"Five years," he ground out.

"Well, it's only half the time I've been punishing myself, but it's pretty good. Where do you see it ending, Sam?"

"Well, you were part of it for me too."

He gritted his teeth, regretting introducing that revelation into the conversation.

"What do you mean?"

"I haven't been with a woman in five years. So I guess you could say you are part of me dealing with some of my issues."

Maddy looked like she'd been slapped. She did not, in any way, look complimented. "What does that mean? What does that mean?" She repeated the phrase twice, sounding more horrified, more frantic each time.

"It had to end at some point. The celibacy, I mean. And when you offered yourself, I wasn't in a position to say no."

"After all of your righteous indignation—the accusation that I was using you for sexual healing—it turns out you were using me for the same thing?" she asked.

"Why does that upset you so much?"

"Because...because you're still so completely wrapped up in it. Because you obviously don't have any intention to really be healed."

Unease settled in his chest. "What's me being healed to you, Maddy? What does that mean? I changed something, didn't I? Same as you."

"But..." Her tone became frantic. "I just... You aren't planning on letting it change you."

"What change are you talking about?" he pressed.

"I don't know," she said, her throat sounding constricted.

"Like hell, Madison. Don't give me that. If you've changed the rules in your head, that's hardly my fault."

She whirled around, lowering her head, burying her face in her hands. "You're so infuriating." She turned back to him, her cheeks crimson. "I don't know what either of us was thinking. That we were going to go into this and come out the other side without changing anything? We are idiots. We are idiots who didn't let another human being touch us for years. And somehow we thought we could come together and nothing would change? I mean, it was one thing when it was just me. I assumed that you went around having sex with women you didn't like all the time."

"Why would you think that?"

"Because you don't like anyone. So, that stands to reason. That you would sleep with women you don't like. I certainly didn't figure you didn't sleep with women at all. That's ridiculous. You're... *Look* at you. Of course you have sex. Who would assume that you didn't? Not me. That's who."

He gritted his teeth, wanting desperately to redirect the conversation. Because it was going into territory that would end badly for both of them. He wanted to leave the core of the energy arcing between them unspoken. He wanted to make sure that neither of them acknowledged it. He wanted to pretend he had no idea what she was thinking. No idea what she was about to say.

The problem was, he knew her. Better than he knew anyone else, maybe. And it had all happened in a week. A week of talking, of being skin to skin. Of being real.

No wonder he had spent so many years avoiding exactly this. No wonder he had spent so long hiding everything that he was, everything that he wanted. Because the alternative was letting it hang out there, exposed and acting as some kind of all-access pass to anyone who bothered to take a look.

"Well, you assumed wrong. But it doesn't have to change anything. We have five more days, Maddy. Why does it have to be like this?"

"Honest?"

"Why do we have to fight with each other? We shouldn't. We don't have to. We don't have to continue this discussion. We are not going to come to any kind of understanding, whatever you might think. Whatever you think you're pushing for here…just don't."

"Are you going to walk away from this and just not change? Are you going to find another woman? Is that all this was? A chance for you to get your sexual mojo back? To prove that you could use a condom every time? Did you want me to sew you a little sexual merit badge for your new Boy Scout vest?" She let out a frustrated growl. "I don't want you to be a Boy Scout, Sam. I want you to be you."

Sam growled, advancing on her. She backed away from him until her shoulder blades hit the wall. Then he pressed his palms to the flat surface on either side of her face. "You don't want me to be me. Trust me. I don't know how to give the kinds of things you want."

"You don't want to," she said, the words soft, penetrating deeper than a shout ever could have.

"No, you don't want me to."

"Why is that so desperately important for you to make yourself believe?"

"Because it's true."

She let silence hang between them for a moment. "Why won't you let yourself feel this?"

"What?"

"*This* is why you do farm animals. That's what you said. And you said it was because nobody would want to see this. But that isn't true. Everybody feels grief, Sam. Everybody has lost. Plenty of people would want to see what you would make from this. Why is it that you can't do it?"

"You want me to go ahead and make a profit off my sins? Out of the way I hurt other people? You want me to make some kind of artistic homage to a father who never wanted me to do art in the first place? You want me to do a tribute to a woman whose death I contributed to."

"Yes. Because it's not about how anyone else feels. It's about how you feel."

He didn't know why this reached in and cut him so deeply. He didn't know why it bothered him so much. Mostly he didn't know why he was having this conversation with her at all. It didn't change anything. It didn't change him.

"No," she said, "that isn't what I think you should do. It's not about profiting off sins—real or perceived. It's about you dealing with all of these things. It's about you acknowledging that you have feelings."

He snorted. "I'm entitled to more grief than Elizabeth's parents? To any?"

"You lost somebody that you cared about. That matters. Of course it matters. You lost… I don't know. She was pregnant. It was your baby. Of course that matters. Of course you think about it."

"No," he said, the words as flat as everything inside

him. "I don't. I don't think about that. Ever. I don't talk about it. I don't do anything with it."

"Except make sure you never make a piece of art that means anything to you. Except not sleep with anyone. Except punish yourself. Which you had such a clear vision of when you felt like I was doing it to myself but you seem to be completely blind to when it comes to you."

"All right. Let's examine your mistake, then, Maddy. Since you're so determined to draw a comparison between the two of us. Who's dead? Come on. Who died as a result of your youthful mistakes? No one. Until you make a mistake like that, something that's that irreversible, don't pretend you have any idea what I've been through. Don't pretend you have any idea of what I should feel."

He despised himself for even saying that. For saying he had been through something. He didn't deserve to walk around claiming that baggage. It was why he didn't like talking about it. It was why he didn't like thinking about it. Because Elizabeth's family members were the ones who had been left with a giant hole in their lives. Not him. Because they were the ones who had to deal with her loss around the dinner table, with thinking about her on her birthday and all of the holidays they didn't have her.

He didn't even know when her birthday was.

"Well, I care about you," Maddy said, her voice small. "Doesn't that count for anything?"

"No," he said, his voice rough. "Five more days, Maddy. That's it. That's all it can ever be."

He should end it now. He knew that. Beyond anything else, he knew that he should end it now. But if Maddy West had taught him anything, it was that he wasn't nearly as controlled as he wanted to be. At least, not where she was concerned. He could stand around and shout about it, self-flagellate all he wanted, but when push came to shove, he was going to make the selfish decision.

"Either you come to bed with me and we spend the rest of the night not talking, or you go home and we can forget the rest of this."

Maddy nodded mutely. He expected her to turn and walk out the door. Maybe not even pausing to collect her clothes, in spite of the cold weather. Instead, she surprised him. Instead, she took his hand, even knowing the kind of devastation it had caused, and she turned and led him up the stairs.

Eleven

Maddy hadn't slept at all. It wasn't typical for her and Sam to share a bed the entire night. But they had last night. After all that shouting and screaming and love-making, it hadn't seemed right to leave. And he hadn't asked her to.

She knew more about him now than she had before. In fact, she had a suspicion that she knew everything about him. Even if it wasn't all put together into a complete picture. It was there. And now, with the pale morning light filtering through the window, she was staring at him as though she could make it all form a cohesive image.

As if she could will herself to somehow understand what all of those little pieces meant. As if she could make herself see the big picture.

Sam couldn't even see it, of that she was certain. So she had no idea how she could expect herself to see it.

Except that she wanted to. Except that she needed to. She didn't want to leave him alone with all of that. It was too much. It was too much for any one man. He felt responsible for the death of that woman. Or at least, he was letting himself think he did.

Protecting himself. Protecting himself with pain.

It made a strange kind of sense to her, only because she was a professional at protecting herself. At insulating herself from whatever else might come her way. Yes, it was a solitary existence. Yes, it was lonely. But there was control within that. She had a feeling that Sam operated in much the same way.

She shifted, brushing his hair out of his face. He had meant to frighten her off. He had given her an out. And she knew that somehow he had imagined she would take it. She knew that he believed he was some kind of monster. At least, part of him believed it.

Because she could also tell that he had been genuinely surprised that she hadn't turned tail and run.

But she hadn't. And she wouldn't. Mostly because she was just too stubborn. She had spent the past ten years being stubborn. Burying who she was underneath a whole bunch of bad attitude and sharp words. Not letting anyone get close, even though she had a bunch of people around her who cared. She had chosen to focus on the people who didn't. The people who didn't care enough. While simultaneously deciding that the people who did care enough, who cared more than enough, somehow weren't as important.

Well, she was done with that. There were people in her life who loved her. Who loved her no matter what. And she had a feeling that Sam had the ability to be one of those people. She didn't want to abandon him to this.

Not when he had—whether he would admit it or not—been instrumental in digging her out of her self-imposed emotional prison.

"Good morning," she whispered, pressing her lips to his cheek.

As soon as she did that, a strange sense of foreboding stole over her. As though she knew that the next few moments were going to go badly. But maybe that was just her natural pessimism. The little beast she had built up to be the strongest and best-developed piece of her. Another defense.

Sam's eyes opened, and the shock that she glimpsed there absolutely did not bode well for the next few moments. She knew that. "I stayed the night," she said, in response to the unasked question she could see lurking on his face.

"I guess I fell asleep," he said, his voice husky.

"Clearly." She took a deep breath. Oh well. If it was all going to hell, it might as well go in style. "I want you to come to the family Christmas party with me."

It took only a few moments for her to decide that she was going to say those words. And that she was going to follow them up with everything that was brimming inside her. Feelings that she didn't feel like keeping hidden. Not anymore. Maybe it was selfish. But she didn't really care. She knew his stuff. He knew hers. The only excuse she had for not telling him how she felt was self-protection.

She knew where self-protection got her. Absolutely nowhere. Treading water in a stagnant pool of her own failings, never advancing any further on in her life. In her existence. It left her lonely. It left her without any real, true friends. She didn't want that. Not anymore.

And if she had to allow herself to be wounded in the name of authenticity, in the name of trying again, then she would.

An easy decision to make before the injury occurred. But it was made nonetheless.

"Why?" Sam asked, rolling away from her, getting up out of bed.

She took that opportunity to drink in every detail of his perfect body. His powerful chest, his muscular thighs. Memorizing every little piece of him. More Sam for her collection. She had a feeling that eventually she would walk away from him with nothing but that collection. A little pail full of the shadows of what she used to have.

"Because I would like to have a date." She was stalling now.

"You want to make your dad mad? Is that what we're doing? A little bit of revenge for everything he put you through?"

"I would never use you that way, Sam. I hope you know me better than that."

"We don't know each other, Maddy. We don't. We've had a few conversations, and we've had some sex. But that doesn't mean knowing somebody. Not really."

"That just isn't true. Nobody else knows how I feel about what happened to me. Nobody. Nobody else knows about the conversation I had with my dad. And I would imagine that nobody knows about Elizabeth. Not the way that I do."

"We used each other as a confessional. That isn't the same."

"The funny thing is it did start that way. At least for me. Because what did it matter what you knew. We weren't going to have a relationship after. So I didn't have to worry about you judging me. I didn't have to worry about anything."

"And?"

"That was just what I told myself. It was what made it feel okay to do what I wanted to do. We lie to ourselves. We get really deep in it when we feel like we need protection. That was what I was doing. But the simple truth is I felt a connection with you from the beginning. It was why I was so terrible to you. Because it scared me."

"You should have kept on letting it scare you, baby girl."

Those words acted like a shot of rage that went straight to her stomach, then fired onto her head. "Why? Because it's the thing that allows you to maintain your cranky-loner mystique? That isn't you. I thought maybe you didn't feel anything. But now I think you feel everything. And it scares you. I'm the same way."

"I see where this is going, Maddy. Don't do it. Don't. I can tell you right now it isn't going to go the way you think it will."

"Oh, go ahead, Sam. Tell me what I think. Please. I'm dying to hear it."

"You think that because you've had some kind of transformation, some kind of deep realization, that I'm headed for the same. But it's bullshit. I'm sorry to be the one to tell you. Wishful thinking on a level I never wanted you to start thinking on. You knew the rules. You knew them from the beginning."

"Don't," she said, her throat tightening, her chest constricting. "Don't do this to us. Don't pretend it can stay the same thing it started out as. Because it isn't. And you know it."

"You're composing a really compelling story, Madison." The reversion back to her full name felt significant. "And we both know that's something you do. Make more out of sex than it was supposed to be."

She gritted her teeth, battling through. Because he wanted her to stop. He wanted this to intimidate, to hurt. He wanted it to stop her. But she wasn't going to let him win. Not at this. Not at his own self-destruction. "Jackass 101. Using somebody's deep pain against them. I thought you were above that, Sam."

"It turns out I'm not. You might want to pay attention to that."

"I'm paying attention. I want you to come with me to the Christmas party, Sam. Because I want it to be the beginning. I don't want it to be the end."

"Don't do this."

He bent down, beginning to collect his clothes, his focus on anything in the room but her. She took a deep breath, knowing that what happened next was going to shatter all of this.

"I need more. I need more than twelve days of Christmas. I want it every day. I want to wake up with you every morning and go to bed with you every night. I want to fight with you. I want to make love with you. I want to tell you my secrets. To show you every dark, hidden thing in me. The serious things and the silly things. Because I love you. It's that complicated and that simple. I love you and that means I'm willing to do this, no matter how it ends."

Sam tugged his pants on, did them up, then pulled his shirt over his head. "I told you not to do this, Maddy. But you're doing it anyway. And you know what that makes it? A suicide mission. You stand there, thinking you're being brave because you're telling the truth. But you know how it's going to end. You know that after you make this confession, you're not actually going to have to deal with the relationship with me, because I already told you it isn't happening. I wonder if you would have been so brave if you knew I might turn around and offer you forever."

His words hit her with the force of bullets. But for some reason, they didn't hurt. Not really. She could remember distinctly when David had broken things off with her. Saying that she had never been anything serious. That she had been only a little bit of tail on the side and he was of course going to have to stay with his wife. Because she was the center of his life. Of his career. Because she mattered, and Maddy didn't. That had hurt. It had hurt because it had been true.

Because David hadn't loved her. And it had been easy for him to break up with her because he had never intended on having more with her, and not a single part of him wanted more.

This was different. It was different because Sam was trying to hurt her out of desperation. Because Sam was lying. Or at the very least, was sidestepping. Because he didn't want to have the conversation.

Because he would have to lie to protect himself. Because he couldn't look her in the eye and tell her that he didn't love her, that she didn't matter.

But she wasn't certain he would let himself feel it. That was the gamble. She knew he felt it. She knew it. That deep down, Sam cared. She wasn't sure if he knew it. If he had allowed himself access to those feelings. Feelings that Sam seemed to think were a luxury, or a danger. Grief. Desire. Love.

"Go ahead and offer it. You won't. You won't, because you know I would actually say yes. You can try to make this about how damaged I am, but all of this is because of you."

"You have to be damaged to want somebody like me. You know what's in my past."

"Grief. Grief that you won't let yourself feel. Sadness you don't feel like you're allowed to have. That's what's in your past. Along with lost hope. Let's not pretend you blame yourself. You felt so comfortable calling me out, telling me that I was playing games. Well, guess what. That's what you're doing. You think if you don't want anything, if you don't need anything, you won't be hurt again. But you're just living in hurt and that isn't better."

"You have all this clarity about your own emotional situation, and you think that gives you a right to talk about mine?"

She threw the blankets off her and got out of bed. "Why not?" she asked, throwing her arms wide. She didn't care that she was naked. In fact, in many ways it seemed appropriate. That Sam had put clothes on, that he had felt the need to cover himself, and that she didn't even care anymore. She had no pride left. But this wasn't about pride.

"You think you have the right to talk about mine," she continued. "You think you're going to twist everything that I'm saying and eventually you'll find some little doubt inside me that will make me believe you're telling the truth. I've had enough of that. I've had enough of men telling me what I feel. Of them telling me what I should do. I'm not going to let you do it. You're better than that. At least, I thought you were."

"Maybe I'm not."

"Right now? I think you don't want to be. But I would love you through this too, Sam. You need to know that. You need to know that whatever you say right now, in this room, it's not going to change the way that I feel about you. You don't have that kind of power."

"That's pathetic. There's nothing I can say to make you not love me? Why don't you love yourself a little bit more than that, Madison," he said, his tone hard.

And regardless of what she had just said, that did hit something in her. Something vulnerable and scared. Something that was afraid she really hadn't learned how to be anything more than a pathetic creature, desperate for a man to show her affection.

"I love myself just enough to put myself out there and demand this," she said finally, her voice vibrating with conviction. "I love myself too much to slink off silently. I love myself too much not to fight for what I know we could have. If I didn't do this, if I didn't say this, it would only be for my pride. It would be so I could score points and feel like maybe I won. But in the end, if I walk away without having fought for you with everything I have in me, we will have both lost. I think you're worth that. I know you are. Why don't you think so?"

"Why do you?" he asked, his voice thin, brittle. "I don't think I've shown you any particular kindness or tenderness."

"Don't. Don't erase everything that's happened between us. Everything I told you. Everything you gave me."

"Keeping my mouth shut while I held a beautiful woman and let her talk? That's easy."

"I love you, Sam. That's all. I'm not going to stand here and have an argument. I'm not going to let you get in endless barbs while you try to make those words something less than true. I love you. I would really like it if you could tell me you loved me too."

"I don't." His words were flat in the room. And she knew they were all she would get from him. Right now, it was all he could say. And he believed it. He believed it down to his bones. That he didn't love her. That everything that had taken place between them over the past week meant nothing. Because he had to. Because behind that certainty, that flat, horrifying expression in his eyes, was fear.

Strong, beautiful Sam, who could bend iron to his will, couldn't overpower the fear that lived inside him. And she would never be able to do it for him.

"Okay," she said softly, beginning to gather her clothes. She didn't know how to do this. She didn't know what to do now. How to make a triumphant exit. So she decided she wouldn't. She decided to let the tears fall down her cheeks; she decided not to make a joke. She decided not to say anything flippant or amusing.

Because that was what the old Maddy would have done. She would have played it off. She would have tried to laugh. She wouldn't have let herself feel this, not all the way down. She wouldn't have let her heart feel bruised or tender. Wouldn't have let a wave of pain roll over her. Wouldn't have let herself feel it, not really.

And when she walked out of his house, sniffling, her shoulders shaking, and could no longer hold back the sob that was building in her chest by the time she reached her car, she didn't care. She didn't feel ashamed.

There was no shame in loving someone.

She opened the driver-side door and sat down. And then the dam burst. She had loved so many people who had never loved her in return. Not the way she loved them. She had made herself hard because of it. She had put the shame on her own shoulders.

That somehow a seventeen-year-old girl should have known that her teacher was lying to her. That somehow a daughter whose father had walked her down Main Street and bought her sweets in a little shop should have known that her father's affection had its limits.

That a woman who had met a man who had finally reached deep inside her and moved all those defenses she had erected around her heart should have known that in the end he would break it.

No. It wasn't her. It wasn't the love that was bad. It was the pride. The shame. The fear. Those were the things that needed to be gotten rid of.

She took a deep, shaking breath. She blinked hard, forcing the rest of her tears to fall, and then she started the car.

She would be okay. Because she had found herself again. Had learned how to love again. Had found a deep certainty and confidence in herself that had been missing for so long.

But as she drove away, she still felt torn in two. Because while she had been made whole, she knew that she was leaving Sam behind, still as broken as she had found him.

Twelve

Sam thought he might be dying. But then, that could easily be alcohol poisoning. He had been drinking and going from his house into his studio for the past two days. And that was it. He hadn't talked to anyone. He had nothing to say. He had sent Maddy away, and while he was firmly convinced it was the only thing he could have done, it hurt like a son of a bitch.

It shouldn't. It had been necessary. He couldn't love her the way that she wanted him to. He couldn't. There was no way in hell. Not a man like him.

Her words started to crowd in on him unbidden, the exact opposite thing that he wanted to remember right now. About how there was no point blaming himself. About how that wasn't the real issue. He growled, grabbing hold of the hammer he'd been using and flinging it across the room. It landed in a pile of scrap metal, the sound satisfying, the lack of damage unsatisfying.

He had a fire burning hot, and the room was stifling. He stripped his shirt off, feeling like he couldn't catch his breath. He felt like he was losing his mind. But then, he wasn't a stranger to it. He had felt this way after his parents had died. Again after Elizabeth. There was so much inside him, and there was nowhere for it to go.

And just like those other times, he didn't deserve this pain. Not at all. He was the one who had hurt her. He was the one who couldn't stand up to that declaration of love. He didn't deserve this pain.

But no matter how deep he tried to push it down, no matter how he tried to pound it out with a hammer, it still remained. And his brain was blank. He couldn't even figure out how the hell he might fashion some of this material into another cow.

It was like the thing inside him that told him how to create things had left along with Maddy.

He looked over at the bottle of Jack Daniel's that was sitting on his workbench. And cursed when he saw that it was empty. He was going to have to get more. But he wasn't sure he had more in the house. Which meant leaving the house. Maybe going to Chase's place and seeing if there was anything to take. Between that and sobriety it was a difficult choice.

He looked around, looked at the horse that he had bent Maddy over just three days ago. Everything seemed dead now. Cold. Dark. Usually he felt the life in the things that he made. Something he would never tell anyone, because it sounded stupid. Because it exposed him.

But it was like Maddy had come in here and changed things. Taken everything with her when she left.

He walked over to the horse, braced his hands on the

back of it and leaned forward, giving into the wave of pain that crashed over him suddenly, uncontrollably.

"I thought I might find you in here."

Sam lifted his head at the sound of his brother's voice. "I'm busy."

"Right. Which is why there is nothing new in here, but it smells flammable."

"I had a drink."

"Or twelve," Chase said, sounding surprisingly sympathetic. "If you get too close to that forge, you're going to burst into flame."

"That might not be so bad."

"What's going on? You're always a grumpy bastard, but this is different. You don't usually disappear for days at a time. Actually, I can pick up a couple of times that you've done that in the past. You usually reemerge worse and even more impossible than you were before. So if that is what's happening here, I would appreciate a heads-up."

"It's nothing. Artistic temper tantrum."

"I don't believe that." Chase crossed his arms and leaned against the back wall of the studio, making it very clear that he intended to stay until Sam told him something.

Fine. The bastard could hang out all day for all he cared. It didn't mean he had to talk.

"Believe whatever you want," Sam said. "But it's not going to make hanging out here any more interesting. I can't figure out what to make next. Are you happy? I have no idea. I have no inspiration." Suddenly, everything in him boiled over. "And I hate that. I hate that it matters. I should just be able to think of something to do. Or not care if I don't want to do it. But somehow,

I can't make it work if I don't care at least a little bit. I hate caring, Chase. I *hate* it."

He hated it for every damn thing. Every damn, fragile thing.

"I know," Chase said. "And I blame Dad for that. He didn't understand. That isn't your fault. And it's not your flaw that you care. Think about the way he was about ranching. It was ridiculous. Weather that didn't go his way would send him into some kind of emotional tailspin for weeks. And he felt the same way about iron that you do. It's just that he felt compelled to shape it into things that had a function. But he took pride in his work. And he was an artist with it—you know he was. If anything, I think he was shocked by what you could do. Maybe even a little bit jealous. And he didn't know what to do with it."

Sam resisted those words. And the truth in them. "It doesn't matter."

"It does. Because it's why you can't talk about what you do. It's why you don't take pride in it the way that you should. It's why you're sitting here downplaying the fact you're having some kind of art block when it's been pretty clear for a few months that you have been."

"It shouldn't be a thing."

Chase shrugged. "Maybe not. But the very thing that makes your work valuable is also what makes it difficult. You're not a machine."

Sam wished he was. More than anything, he wished that he was. So that he wouldn't care about a damn thing. So that he wouldn't care about Maddy.

Softness, curves, floated to the forefront of his mind. Darkness and grief. All the inspiration he could ever want. Except that he couldn't take it. It wasn't his. He didn't own it. None of it.

He was still trying to pull things out of his own soul, and all he got was dry, hard work that looked downright ugly to him.

"I should be," he said, stubborn.

"This isn't about Dad, though. I don't even think it's about the art, though I think it's related. There was a woman, wasn't there?"

Sam snorted. "When?"

"Recently. Like the past week. Mostly I think so because I recognize that all-consuming obsession. Because I recognize this. Because you came and kicked my ass when I was in a very similar position just a year ago. And you know what you told me? With great authority, you told me that iron had to get hot to get shaped into something. You told me that I was in my fire, and I had to let it shape me into the man Anna needed me to be."

"Yeah, I guess I did tell you that," Sam said.

"Obviously I'm not privy to all the details of your personal life, Sam, which is your prerogative. But you're in here actively attempting to drink yourself to death. You say that you can't find any inspiration for your art. I would say that you're in a pretty damn bad situation. And maybe you need to pull yourself out of it. If that means grabbing hold of her—whoever she is—then do it."

Sam felt like the frustration inside him was about to overflow. "I can't. There's too much… There's too much. If you knew, Chase. If you knew everything about me, you wouldn't think I deserved it."

"Who deserves it?" Chase asked. "Does anybody? Do you honestly think I deserve Anna? I don't. But I love her. And I work every day to deserve her. It's a work in progress, let me tell you. But that's love. You just kind of keep working for it."

"There are too many other things in the way," Sam said, because he didn't know how else to articulate it. Without having a confessional, here in his studio, he didn't know how else to have this conversation.

"What things? What are you afraid of, Sam? Having a feeling? Is that what all this is about? The fact you want to protect yourself? The fact that it matters more to you that you get to keep your stoic expression and your who-gives-a-damn attitude intact?"

"It isn't that. It's never been that. But how—" He started again. "How was I supposed to grieve for Dad when you lost your mentor? How was I supposed to grieve for Mom when you were so young? It wasn't fair." And how the hell was he supposed to grieve for Elizabeth, for the child he didn't even know she had been carrying, when her own family was left with nothing.

"Of course you could grieve for them. They were your parents."

"Somebody has to be strong, Chase."

"And you thought I was weak? You think somehow grieving for my parents was weak?"

"Of course not. But…I was never the man that Dad wanted me to be. Now when he was alive. I didn't do what he wanted me to do. I didn't want the things that he wanted."

"Neither did I. And we both just about killed ourselves working this place the way that he wanted us to while it slowly sank into the ground. Then we had to do things on our terms. Because actually, we did know what we were talking about. And who we are, the gifts that we have, those mattered. If it wasn't for the fact that I have a business mind, if it wasn't for the fact that you could do the artwork, the ranch wouldn't be here. McCormack Ironworks wouldn't exist. And if Dad had lived, he would be proud of us. Because in the end we saved this place."

"I just don't…I had a girlfriend who died." He didn't know why he had spoken the words. He hadn't intended to. "She wasn't my girlfriend when she died. But she bled to death. At the hospital. She had been pregnant. And it was mine."

Chase cursed and fell back against the wall, bracing himself. "Seriously?"

"Yes. And I want… I want to do something with that feeling. But her family is devastated, Chase. They lost so much more than I did. And I don't know how…I don't know what to do with all of this. I don't know what to do with all of these feelings. I don't feel like I deserve them. I don't feel like I deserve the pain. Not in the way that I deserve to walk away from it unscathed. But I feel like it isn't mine. Like I'm taking something from them, or making something about me that just shouldn't be. But it's there all the same. And it follows me around. And Maddy loves me. She said she loves me. And I don't know how to take that either."

"Bullshit," Chase said, his voice rough. "That's not it."

"Don't tell me how it is, Chase, not when you don't know."

"Of course I know, Sam. Loss is hell. And I didn't lose half of what you did."

"It was just the possibility of something. Elizabeth. It wasn't… It was just…"

"Sam. You lost your parents. And a woman you were

involved with who was carrying your baby. Of course you're screwed up. But walking around pretending you're just grumpy, pretending you don't want anything, that you don't care about anything, doesn't protect you from pain. It's just letting fear poison you from the inside."

Sam felt like he was staring down into an abyss that had no end. A yawning, bottomless cavern that was just full of need. All the need he had ever felt his entire life. The words ricocheted back at him, hit him like shrapnel, damaging, wounding. They were the truth. That it was what drove him, that it was what stopped him.

Fear.

That it was why he had spent so many years hiding.

And as blindingly clear as it was, it was also clear that Maddy was right about him. More right about him than he'd ever been about himself.

That confession made him think of Maddy too. Of the situation she was in with her father. Of those broken words she had spoken to him about how if her own father didn't think she was worth defending, who would? And he had sent her away, like he didn't think she was worth it either. Like he didn't think she was worth the pain or the risk.

Except he did. He thought she was worth defending. That she was worth loving. That she was worth everything.

Sam felt… Well, nothing on this earth had ever made him feel small before. But this did it. He felt scared. He felt weak. Mostly he felt a kind of overwhelming sadness for everything he'd lost. For all the words that were left unsaid. The years of grief that had built up.

It had never been about control. It had never been

based in reality. Or about whether or not he deserved something. Not really. He was afraid of feeling. Of loss. More loss after years and years of it.

But his father had died without knowing. Without knowing that even though things weren't always the best between them, Sam had loved him. Elizabeth had died without knowing Sam had cared.

Protecting himself meant hurting other people. And it damn well hurt him.

Maddy had been brave enough to show him. And he had rejected it. Utterly. Completely. She had been so brave, and he had remained shut down as he'd been for years.

She had removed any risk of rejection and still he had been afraid. He had been willing to lose her this time.

"Do you know why the art is hard?" he asked.

"Why?"

"Because. If I make what I really want to, then I actually have to feel it."

He hated saying it. Hated admitting it. But he knew, somehow, that this was essential to his soul. That if he was ever going to move on from this place, from this dry, drunken place that produced nothing but anguish, he had to start saying these things. He had to start committing to these things.

"I had a lot behind this idea that I wasn't good enough. That I didn't deserve to feel. Because…the alternative is feeling it. It's caring when it's easier to be mad at everything. Hoping for things when so much is already dead."

"What's the alternative?" Chase asked.

He looked around his studio. At all the lifeless things. Hard and sharp. Just like he was. The alternative was living without hope. The alternative was acting like he was dead too.

"This," he said finally. "And life without Maddy. I'd rather risk everything than live without her."

Thirteen

Madison looked around the beautifully appointed room. The grand party facility at the ranch was decorated in evergreen boughs and white Christmas lights, the trays of glittering champagne moving by somehow adding to the motif. Sparkling. Pristine.

Maddy herself was dressed in a gown that could be described in much the same manner. A pale yellow that caught the lights and glimmered like sun on new-fallen snow.

However, it was a prime example of how appearances can be deceiving. She felt horrible. Much more like snow that had been mixed up with gravel. Gritty. Gray.

Hopefully no one was any the wiser. She was good at putting on a brave face. Good at pretending everything was fine. Something she had perfected over the

years. Not just at these kinds of public events but at family events too.

Self-protection was her favorite accessory. It went with everything.

She looked outside, at the terrace, which was lit by a thatch of Christmas lights, heated by a few freestanding heaters. However, no one was out there. She took a deep breath, seeing her opportunity for escape. And she took it. She just needed a few minutes. A few minutes to feel a little bit less like her face would crack beneath the weight of her fake smile.

A few minutes to take a deep breath and not worry so much that it would turn into a sob.

She grabbed hold of a glass of champagne, then moved quickly to the door, slipping out into the chilly night air. She went over near one of the heaters, wrapping her arms around herself and simply standing for a moment, looking out into the inky blackness, looking at nothing. It felt good. It was a relief to her burning eyes. A relief to her scorched soul.

All of this feelings business was rough. She wasn't entirely certain she could recommend it.

"What's going on, Maddy?"

She turned around, trying to force a smile when she saw her brother Gage standing there.

"I just needed a little bit of quiet," she said, lifting her glass of champagne.

"Sure." He stuffed his hands in his pockets. "I'm not used to this kind of thing. I spent a lot of time on the road. In crappy hotels. Not a lot of time at these sorts of get-togethers."

"Regretting the whole return-of-the-prodigal-son

thing? Because it's too late to unkill that fatted calf, young man. You're stuck."

He laughed. "No. I'm glad that I'm back. Because of you. Because of Colton, Sierra. Even Jack."

"Rebecca?"

"Of course." He took a deep breath, closing the distance between them. "So what's going on with you?"

"Nothing," she said, smiling.

"I have a feeling that everybody else usually buys that. Which is why you do it. But I don't. Is it Jack? Is it having him here?"

She thought about that. Seriously thought about it. "No," she said, truthful. "I'm glad. I'm so glad that we're starting to fix some of this. I spent a long time holding on to my anger. My anger at Dad. At the past. All of my pain. And Jack got caught up in that. Because of the circumstances. We are all very different people. And getting to this point…I feel like we took five different paths. But here we are. And it isn't for Dad. It's for us. I think that's good. I spent a lot of time doing things in response to him. In response to the pain that he caused me. I don't want to do that anymore. I don't want to act from a place of pain and fear anymore."

"That's quite a different stance. I mean, since last we talked at The Grind."

She tried to smile again, wandering over to one of the wooden pillars. "I guess some things happened." She pressed her palm against the cold surface, then her forehead. She took a deep breath. In and out, slowly, evenly.

"Are you okay?"

She shook her head. "Not really. But I will be."

"I know I missed your first big heartbreak. And I feel like I would have done that bastard some bodily harm. I have quite a bit of internalized rage built up. If you need me to hurt anyone…I will. Gladly."

She laughed. "I appreciate that. Really, I do. It's just that…it's a good thing this is happening. It's making me realize a lot of things. It's making me change a lot of things. I just wish it didn't hurt."

"You know…when Rebecca told me that she loved me, it scared the hell out of me. And I said some things that I shouldn't have said. That no one should ever say to anyone. I regretted it. But I was running scared, and I wanted to make sure she didn't come after me. I'm so glad that she forgave me when I realized what an idiot I was."

She lifted her head, turning to face him. "That sounds a lot like brotherly advice."

"It is. And maybe it's not relevant to your situation. I don't know. But what I do know is that we both have a tendency to hold on to pain. On to anger. If you get a chance to fix this, I hope you forgive the bastard. As long as he's worthy."

"How will I know he's worthy?" she asked, a bit of humor lacing her voice.

"Well, I'll have to vet him. At some point."

"Assuming he ever speaks to me again, I would be happy to arrange that."

Gage nodded. "If he's half as miserable as you are, trust me, he'll be coming after you pretty quick."

"And you think I should forgive him?"

"I think that men are a bunch of hardheaded dumbasses. And some of us need more chances than others. And I thank God every day I got mine. With this family. With Rebecca. So it would be mean-spirited of me not to advocate for the same for another of my species."

"I'll keep that under advisement."

Gage turned to go. "Do that. But if he keeps being a dumbass, let me know. Because I'll get together a posse or something."

"Thank you," she said. "Hopefully the posse won't be necessary."

He shrugged, then walked back into the party. She felt fortified then. Because she knew she had people on her side. No matter what. She wasn't alone. And that felt good. Even when most everything felt bad.

She let out a long, slow breath and rested her forearms on the railing, leaning forward, staring out across the darkened field. If she closed her eyes, she could almost imagine that she could see straight out to the ocean in spite of the fact that it was dark.

She was starting to get cold, even with the artificial heat. But it was entirely possible the chill was coming from inside her. Side effects of heartbreak and all of that.

"Merry Christmas Eve."

She straightened, blinking, looking out into the darkness. Afraid to turn around. That voice was familiar. And it didn't belong to anyone in her family.

She turned slowly, her heart stalling when she saw Sam standing there. He was wearing a white shirt unbuttoned at the collar, a black jacket and a pair of black slacks. His hair was disheveled, and she was pretty sure she could see a bit of soot on his chest where the open shirt exposed his skin.

"What are you doing here?"

"I had to see you." He took a step closer to her. "Bad enough that I put this on."

"Where did you get it?"

"The secondhand store on Main."

"Wow." No matter what he had to say, the fact that Sam McCormack had shown up in a suit said a whole lot without him ever opening his mouth.

"It doesn't really fit. And I couldn't figure out how to tie the tie." And of course, he hadn't asked anyone for help. Sam never would. It just wasn't him.

"Well, then going without was definitely the right method."

"I have my moments of brilliance." He shook his head. "But the other day wasn't one of them."

Her heart felt as if it were in a free fall, her stomach clenching tight. "Really?"

"Yeah."

"I agree. I mean, unreservedly. But I am open to hearing about your version of why you didn't think you were brilliant. Just in case we have differing opinions on the event."

He cursed. "I'm not good at this." He took two steps toward her, then reached out, gripping her chin between his thumb and forefinger. "I hate this, in fact. I'm not good at talking about feelings. And I've spent a lot of years trying to bury them down deep. I would like to do it now. But I know there's no good ending to that. I know that I owe you more."

"Go on," she said, keeping her eyes on his, her voice trembling, betraying the depth of emotion she felt.

She had never seen Sam quite like this, on edge, like he might shatter completely at any moment. "I told you I thought I didn't deserve these feelings. And I believed it."

"I know you did," she said, the words broken. "I know that you never lied on purpose, Sam. I know."

"I don't deserve that. That certainty. I didn't do any-thing to earn it."

She shook her head. "Stop. We're not going to talk like that. About what we deserve. I don't know what I deserve. But I know what I want. I want you. And I don't care if I'm jumping the gun. I don't care if I didn't make you grovel enough. It's true. I do."

"Maddy…"

"This all comes because we tried to protect ourselves for too long. Because we buried everything down deep. I don't have any defenses anymore. I can't do it anymore. I couldn't even if I wanted to. Which you can see, because I'm basically throwing myself at you again."

"I've always been afraid there was something wrong with me." His dark eyes were intense, and she could tell that he was wishing he could turn to stone rather than finish what he was saying. But that he was deter-mined. That he had put his foot on the path and he wasn't going to deviate from it. "Something wrong with what I felt. And I pushed it all down. I always have. I've been through stuff that would make a lot of people crazy. But if you keep shoving it on down, it never gets any better." He shook his head. "I've been holding on to grief. Hold-ing on to anger. I didn't know what else to do with it. My feelings about my parents, my feelings about Elizabeth, the baby. It's complicated. It's a lot. And I think more than anything I just didn't want to deal with it. I had a lot of excuses, and they felt real. They even felt maybe a little bit noble?"

"I can see that. I can see it being preferable to grief."

"Just like you said, Maddy. You put all those defenses in front of it, and then nothing can hurt you, right?"

She nodded. "At least, that's been the way I've handled it for a long time."

"You run out. Of whatever it is you need to be a person. Whatever it is you need to contribute, to create. That's why I haven't been able to do anything new with my artwork." He rolled his eyes, shaking his head slightly. "It's hard for me to…"

"I know. You would rather die than talk about feelings. And talk about this. But I think you need to."

"I told myself it was wrong to make something for my dad. My mom. Because they didn't support my work. I told myself I didn't deserve to profit off Elizabeth's death in any way. But that was never the real issue. The real issue was not wanting to feel those things at all. I was walking across the field the other night, and I thought about grief. The way that it covers things, twists the world around you into something unrecognizable." He shook his head. "When you're in the thick of it, it's like walking in the dark. Even if you're in a place you've seen a thousand times by day, it all changes. And suddenly what seemed safe is now full of danger."

He took a sharp breath and continued. "You can't trust anymore. You can't trust everything will be okay, because you've seen that sometimes it isn't. That's what it's like to have lost people like I have. And I can think about a thousand pieces that I could create that would express that. But it would mean that I had to feel it. And it would mean I would have to show other people what I felt. I wanted… From the moment I laid my hands on you, Maddy, I wanted to turn you into something. A sculpture. A painting. But that would mean looking at how I felt about you too. And I didn't want to do that either."

Maddy lifted her hand, cupping Sam's cheek. "I understand why you work with iron, Sam. Because it's just like you. You're so strong. And you really don't want to bend. But if you would just bend...just a little bit, I think you could be something even more beautiful than you already are."

"I'll do more than bend. If I have to, to have you, I'll break first. But I've decided...I don't care about protecting myself. From loss, from pain...doesn't matter. I just care about you. And I know that I have to fix myself if I'm going to become the kind of man you deserve. I know I have to reach inside and figure all that emotional crap out. I can't just decide that I love you and never look at the rest of it. I have to do all of it. To love you the way that you deserve, I know I have to deal with all of it."

"Do you love me?"

He nodded slowly. "I do." He reached into his jacket pocket and took out a notebook. "I've been working on a new collection. Just sketches right now. Just plans." He handed her the notebook. "I want you to see it. I know you'll understand."

She took it from him, opening it with shaking hands, her heart thundering hard in her throat. She looked at the first page, at the dark twisted mass he had sketched there. Maybe it was a beast, or maybe it was just menacing angles—it was hard to tell. She imagined that was the point.

There was more. Broken figures, twisted metal. Until the very last page. Where the lines smoothed out into rounded curves, until the mood shifted dramatically and everything looked a whole lot more like hope.

"It's hard to get a sense of scale and everything in the drawings. This is just me kind of blocking it out."

"I understand," she whispered. "I understand perfectly." It started with grief, and it ended with love. Unimaginable pain that was transformed.

"I lost a lot of things, Maddy. I would hate for you to be one of them. Especially because you're the one thing I chose to lose. And I have regretted it every moment since. But this is me." He put his fingertip on the notebook. "That's me. I'm not the nicest guy. I'm not what anybody would call cheerful. Frankly, I'm a grumpy son of a bitch. It's hard for me to talk about what I'm feeling. Harder for me to show it, and I'm in the world's worst line of work for that. But if you'll let me, I'll be your grumpy son of a bitch. And I'll try. I'll try for you."

"Sam," she said, "I love you. I love you, and I don't need you to be anything more than you. I'm willing to accept the fact that getting to your feelings may always be a little bit of an excavation. But if you promise to work on it, I'll promise not to be too sensitive about it. And maybe we can meet somewhere in the middle. One person doesn't have to do all the changing. And I don't want you to anyway." She smiled, and this time it wasn't forced. "You had me at 'You're at the wrong door.'"

He chuckled. "I think you had me a lot sooner than that. I just didn't know it."

"So," she said, looking up at him, feeling like the sun was shining inside her, in spite of the chill outside, "you want to go play Yahtzee?"

"Only if you mean it euphemistically."

"Absolutely not. I expect you to take the time to woo me, Sam McCormack. And if that includes board games, that's just a burden you'll have to bear."

Sam smiled. A real smile. One that showed his heart, his soul, and held nothing back. "I would gladly spend the rest of my life bearing your burdens, Madison West."

"On second thought," she said, "board games not required."

"Oh yeah? What do you need, then?"

"Nothing much at all. Just hold me, cowboy. That's enough for me."

* * * * *

Meet all the cowboys in Copper Ridge!

SHOULDA BEEN A COWBOY (prequel novella)
PART TIME COWBOY
BROKEDOWN COWBOY
BAD NEWS COWBOY
A COPPER RIDGE CHRISTMAS (novella)
HOMETOWN HEARTBREAKER (novella)
TAKE ME, COWBOY
ONE NIGHT CHARMER
TOUGH LUCK HERO
LAST CHANCE REBEL
HOLD ME, COWBOY

Look for more COPPER RIDGE *books,*
coming soon!

If you can't get enough Maisey Yates,
try her bestselling books
from Mills & Boon Modern!

Don't miss
THE PRINCE'S PREGNANT MISTRESS
Second in her fabulous
HEIRS BEFORE VOWS *series.*
Available next month!

Kayla stopped the moment her eyes lit on him.

"Good to see you again, Van," she said in that husky, *come to bed* voice of hers.

No, she hadn't changed. Still with the flip attitude.

"I take it you're the one upsetting my receptionist?"

He saw the surprised hurt reflected in her clear blue gaze and wished he'd thought before speaking.

But that was how it always was with Kayla. She brought out the worst in him.

"I'm sorry," he said. "What can I do for you?"

A rapid pulse beat at the base of her throat, and he remembered just how silky soft her skin had been beneath his tongue, remembered just how she'd tasted. Desire heated his blood but he resisted, hard.

"Kayla, why are you here?"

She drew in a deep breath. "Like I said, I need your help."

"And a phone call wouldn't do?"

His secretary arrived in the doorway looking totally nonplussed, and no wonder, because she had a baby in her arms. A baby?

Van looked to Kayla. "Yours, I presume?"

And then the baby looked up and he was struck by the eyes that caught his.

"Yours, too, to be precise," Kayla said softly.

* * *
One Heir...or Two?
is part of Mills & Boon Desire's No.1 bestselling series,
Billionaires and Babies: Powerful men...
wrapped around their babies' little fingers.

ONE HEIR...
OR TWO?

BY
YVONNE LINDSAY

A typical Piscean, *USA TODAY* bestselling author **Yvonne Lindsay** has always preferred her imagination to the real world. Married to her blind-date hero and with two adult children, she spends her days crafting the stories of her heart, and in her spare time she can be found with her nose in a book reliving the power of love, or knitting socks and daydreaming. Contact her via her website, www.yvonnelindsay.com.

To my amazing fellow Writers in the Wild,
this book is dedicated to you with grateful thanks
for all your support and companionship on
our magical Tuesday mornings.

One

Van slipped the ring into his breast pocket and snapped the lid closed on the jeweler's box in his hand. The very large near-flawless white diamond was precisely what Dani would expect when he asked her to marry him at lunch today.

He knew that wasn't all she was expecting. He cast an eye over the merger documents on his desk. The amalgamation of Dani's family business, Matthews Electronics, and his DM Security would be a match made in corporate heaven. It only made sense to carry their relationship from the boardroom into the bedroom. They were kindred spirits—both focused on their business targets, both leading professional, uncluttered lives and neither of them wanting the burden of parenthood. Neither of them expected—or particularly wanted—passionate love and romance. But they'd share respect, attraction and compatible interests—and what more could he want than that? Yep, life was pretty much perfect for the boy who grew up never feeling like he belonged anywhere, and this ring would help seal the deal.

A subtle ping on his computer screen alerted him to a message from Reception. Using his Bluetooth earpiece, he connected to Anita—his dragon at the gate, as the rest of the staff called her.

"There's a woman here to see you, Mr. Murphy. She doesn't have an appointment but she is most insistent."

He could hear the disapproval in every syllable of Anita's perfect diction. Despite himself, Van felt a smile tug at his lips.

"Does the woman have a name?" he prompted. Clearly his receptionist was flustered, a reaction infrequent enough to amuse him. It was unlike her not to give him her usual shorthand summary of details that he needed to make a decision about any unexpected visitor.

"She says she's an old friend and doesn't need an appointment."

A prickle of foreboding made the hairs on the back of Van's neck stand up. That sensation had kept him alive more than once doing his tours of duty and since, in the private sector, and he wasn't about to ignore it now.

"Get her contact details and tell her to make an appointment to come back. Thank you, Anita."

A lot could be learned from a name and contact details, especially by a man with his resources. Just before he clicked off the call, he heard a slight commotion in the background.

"No," he heard Anita say very firmly. "I most definitely will not hold—"

Then all he heard was a scuffling sound. He frowned. What on earth was going on? He didn't have to wait long to find out. The commotion he'd heard in his earpiece was very definitely coming toward him down the corridor. Van gritted his teeth in frustration. His was a spe-

cialized international security company. How secure was
it really if someone could walk in off the street and cause
this much of a ruckus? He was up and moving from his
chair before he even completed the thought, but before
he could reach the door to his office, it swung open and a
woman swept in. In that split second, every notion, even
the breath in his lungs, stalled right where it was.

Kayla Porter.

Damn.

The last time he'd seen her, five years ago, she'd been
curled up asleep on the sofa bed of the substandard apartment she'd shared with her late sister. The bed they'd
shared for a few intense, incredibly hot hours before he'd
pulled himself away.

Kayla stopped in her tracks the moment her eyes lit
on him. Five years since he'd last seen her and she hadn't
changed a bit. Still dressed like an escapee hippie from
the sixties and still with the long flowing blond hair. He
could even remember the scent of the shampoo she'd used
back then. Something herbal and sweet and essentially
Kayla. The memory was visceral and hit him hard.

"Good to see you again, Van," she said in that husky
"come to bed" voice of hers as she took a few steps into
his office.

Her eyes flicked over him, from the top of his head and
his precisely mussed, expensive haircut to the tips of his
highly polished handmade shoes. She smiled.

"I see you can take the man out of the army but you
can't quite take the army out of the man, right?" she commented with a nod to his gleaming footwear.

No, she hadn't changed. Still with the flip attitude. Still
thinking she was welcome wherever she went and that
people would pretty much forgive her anything.

"I take it you're the one upsetting my receptionist? You
couldn't have made an appointment?"

The second the words were out of his mouth and he saw the surprised hurt reflected in her clear blue gaze, he wished he'd thought before speaking. But that was how it always was with Kayla. She brought out the worst in him. Always had, even when they were kids growing up next door to one another. Granted, she was four years younger than Van and her sister, Sienna, and her nuisance factor had correlated with the age difference. But it hadn't gotten any easier to deal with her once they'd grown up. Somehow, she always put him on edge, made him feel out of control. And that was why, after their one-night stand, he'd walked away and never looked back. Even though it made him ashamed of himself whenever he thought of it—or remembered how before Sienna had died, he'd promised her he'd always look out for Kayla.

The past always had a habit of biting you in the ass.

"I'm sorry—" he started again, moving toward her. "You're here now. What can I do for you?"

He tried not to look too closely at where a rapid pulse beat at the base of her throat, because if he did, he'd remember just how silky soft her skin had been beneath his tongue, remember just how she'd tasted. A flush of desire heated his blood but he pushed back, hard. He wasn't that man anymore. Not driven by emotional and physical need. No, he'd finally learned to control himself and his behavior. Learned not to act on impulse. Learned to weigh and consider and recognize when a situation was just risky or out-and-out dangerous. And for some reason his senses were screaming red alert right now.

Another sound from the corridor outside filtered into his office. A sound that made Kayla turn, a look of dismay on her face.

She moved toward him, her hands outstretched. "Van, I need to talk to you about something important. I really need your help. I—"

Anita arrived in the doorway looking totally non-plussed, and no wonder, because she had a baby in her arms. A baby? Van looked from his flustered receptionist to the strand of pearls clutched in a chubby fist and thrust in a gummy drooling mouth, and then to Kayla again.

"Yours, I presume?" he asked.

And then the baby looked up from her prize and he was struck instantly by the eyes that caught his. Eyes that were identical to the ones that reflected back at him every morning in the mirror.

"Yours, too, to be precise," Kayla said, softly, finding her voice again.

Kayla could see Van's mind casting back to that one night they'd shared after Sienna's funeral, gauging the age of the baby, doing the math and coming up with numbers that made no sense at all. The baby began to fret and she moved forward to take her from her very reluctant minder. If Kayla's sitter hadn't fallen through…well, if her sitter hadn't up and left her with no notice, her baby girl wouldn't be here at all.

"Come on, Sienna. We'll have none of that. Let the nice lady's necklace go."

"Sienna?"

Van's attention, locked for the past minute on the baby, now transferred to her.

"She's named for her mother. Appropriate, don't you think?"

Van gave her another hard look, leaving her in no doubt she was in for a grilling. He'd never actually said what he'd done in the Special Forces but she had no doubt that interrogation had probably been on an extensive list of lethal skills.

"Her mother? Sienna?"

Kayla turned to the receptionist, who still hovered in the doorway. "Thank you, I think we'll be fine now."

The woman looked from Kayla to Van and back again. Van seemed to come to attention.

"Yes, thank you, Anita. Could you please call Dani and tell her I'll be delayed for lunch today. Perhaps we can reschedule for dinner instead."

"Yes, sir, right away. Are you sure about...?" Anita gestured vaguely toward Kayla and the baby.

"I think I can handle them," he said firmly.

His eyes remained locked on Kayla's—silently demanding an explanation. At his words, Kayla couldn't help but feel a tingle run down her spine. Part anticipation, part fear, part sensual memory. But Van had made it perfectly clear when he'd left her without a note or a word since that he was very definitely not interested in her. She shored up her defenses and clutched Sienna to her a little more tightly, earning a surprised squawk from her little girl. Again, she wished she hadn't had to bring her precious child into this meeting. If she'd had any other choice, she'd have taken it.

As soon as the door closed, Van spoke.

"Kayla, why are you here?"

She drew in a deep breath. "Like I said, I need your help."

"And a phone call wouldn't do?"

It stung to hear him sound so dismissive, but it served to strengthen her resolve. "No, it wouldn't. Last time we saw each other—" Her mouth dried and she swallowed to moisten it. She began again, more resolutely this time. "After Sienna's funeral, you said to call you if I needed anything."

"And I meant it. But, Kayla, even you have to realize that you can't just waltz into my place of business and expect to see me straightaway."

"I'm sorry, but it's really important—otherwise I wouldn't have…"

Darn, she should just come right out with it. She looked up at him and saw a stranger. Gone was the boy next door—the one who'd received more beatings from his father than he'd ever earned, the one who'd allowed her sister to befriend him and bring him into their home, the one who as a teenager had gotten her out of more scrapes than she could remember. Gone was the soldier, gone was the passionate lover who had rocked her entire world. In his place stood a cold, controlled and distant individual. A man so unfamiliar to her now that she began to wonder if she'd ever really known him at all.

"Is it to do with her?" He gestured toward the baby.

"In a way, yes. Do you want to hold her?"

Without waiting for an answer, Kayla crossed the short distance between them and held Sienna out to her father. It should have been a beautiful moment but Van looked alternately horrified and annoyed as he instinctively put his hands out to receive his daughter.

"There, see? She's not that bad, is she?"

For a second Sienna seemed as though she'd cry and looked back at Kayla, her lip starting to wobble. Kayla forced herself to smile at her baby girl and make an encouraging sound. It seemed to work because Sienna turned her attention back to the man holding her—one dimpled little hand gripping the lapel of his suit jacket, the other reaching up for his mouth. Kayla stifled a giggle at the look on Van's face. You'd have thought she just handed him a live grenade.

There was a knock at the door to his office and an exquisitely groomed woman walked in without waiting for Van's response.

"Sorry to bother you, Donovan, but I was already in

the parking garage downstairs when Anita called, so I thought—"

She stopped dead in her tracks as she looked at first Kayla, then Van holding a baby.

"I see you're busy. I'm so sorry. I'll come back later."

"No, Dani, wait. Please."

Van thrust the baby back to Kayla, eliciting a howl of disapproval from Sienna. "Don't say anything," he growled quietly at Kayla before moving to the other woman's side.

Kayla rolled her eyes at him, then faced the new arrival and, juggling Sienna on one hip, put out her free hand. "Hello," she said. "I'm Kayla. My sister and I grew up with Van."

The woman moved to accept Kayla's proffered hand. "Dani Matthews," she said smoothly but not without directing a speaking look Van's way.

The look Van shot Kayla could have cut through steel.

"If you'll excuse us a moment," Van said to Dani, waiting for her nod of acceptance.

Polished and unflappable, she inclined her head in the most fluid of actions, the movement making the perfectly blunt-edged cut of her hair swoosh forward a moment before reassuming its almost regimental perfection with not a strand out of place. Kayla found herself fascinated by it. How was that even possible with the humidity of a regular San Francisco fog? Her own hair was a perpetual tousle of long blond waves no matter what she did with it.

"Thank you," he murmured. "I'll be back shortly."

"Take your time," she replied with a charming curve of her lips, but Kayla could see her eyes remained full of questions.

Without wasting another second, Van took Kayla by her upper arm and steered her out of his office and toward Reception. She made a sound of protest but he ignored it until he'd shown her into a small conference room and the door behind them was closed.

"No more beating around the bush, Kayla. I want answers from you and they had better be good."

"Van, I wasn't kidding around. I really need your help."

Sienna whimpered a little and Kayla smoothed her hand over the baby's head nervously. Suddenly this didn't seem like a good idea after all. But she'd thought and thought and she hadn't been able to come up with any other way she could raise the money she needed.

"What's wrong with her?" Van demanded, the roughness of his voice making Sienna's whimper grow louder.

"She's hungry, and in a strange place. This is messing with her routine. I'm sorry. The timing of this is all out of whack, isn't it? I should have thought this out a bit better."

Even now her breasts tingled with that full heavy warning that accompanied nursing.

"You think? But when has that ever stopped you?" he muttered.

She ignored his question. "Five years ago you offered to be there when I needed someone. Did you mean what you said?"

She had to hope that his offer still held. Without it, she had nothing and no one and her plans for the future, her promise to her sister, would all be shattered.

Van flashed a glance at his wristwatch. A Breitling with more whizzes and bangs on it than her food processor, she noted, unimpressed. But his action was a reminder for her, as well. Time was fleeting.

He flung her another look of irritation. "I don't say anything I don't mean. How about you explain it to me. You've got ten minutes, max."

"Thank you."

She moved forward and put her hand on his chest. Even through his suit she could feel the heat that poured from his body, feel the muscled perfection of his chest beneath the expertly tailored fabric. Against her will, her body began to react—her heart rate kicking up a beat, her senses that much more focused. He stared down at her hand and then back at her. She felt a rush of color stain her cheeks and let her hand drop.

Kayla's innate ability to push his buttons hadn't lessened with the time and distance between them. He reined in his impatience and directed her to sit down. The baby fussed again, tugging at Kayla's top. Mesmerized, he watched as Kayla lifted her blouse and did something with her bra, exposing one breast and guiding her nipple to the baby's mouth. It wasn't the first time he'd seen a woman breast-feeding and it probably wouldn't be the last, but he couldn't help the fascination that poured through him at the sight.

His child—the child he'd never believed would be born—being nurtured, here, right in front of him. Her birth shouldn't have happened, not with her biological mother dead these five years. But that was one puzzle he didn't need her to piece together for him. He remembered agreeing to be a donor for Sienna so that she could have embryos stored before starting cancer treatment. The logistics of how this little girl could be his baby and Sienna's were perfectly clear. What he didn't know was why—why had Kayla carried his child?

"Explain," he said curtly, trying to fight the sensation of awe that threatened to overwhelm him.

He hadn't wanted to be a father—he'd immediately signed his paternity rights away. And that had been before he'd found out the truth about his own birthright. Before he'd learned that the alcoholism that had plagued his birth parents' lives and seen him removed from their custody as a toddler could, in part at least, be hereditary.

Before he'd realized he had been heading down the same path and made a decision that he would never pass that potential legacy on, ever.

"I need money. A loan."

"That explains why you're here now but doesn't explain *her*." He pointed at the baby. "Sienna and I had an agreement. If she couldn't go through with embryo transfer, they'd be donated to research or—"

Destroyed. Even he couldn't bring himself to say the word out loud. At the time it hadn't meant all that much to him. But now, faced with living proof? It was another thing entirely.

Kayla filled the silence. "Before she died, she changed her mind. With her lawyer's help, she amended the paperwork and donated the embryos to me so that the children she'd always wanted would still have a chance. I promised her that her dream would still come true."

"And now you want money from me for maintenance, is that it? For a child I don't want?"

The words hung baldly in the air between them. He'd been deliberately provocative with his phrasing and could see Kayla fighting back her instinctive response to snap back—they'd frequently rubbed each other the wrong way in the past and today was a perfect example of that. When she'd composed herself, she spoke.

"Not for maintenance for Sienna, no. You may find it hard to believe, but I didn't enter into parenthood lightly. I saved hard, I have a job I love and she has had excellent care while I work. But things have changed and I wouldn't be asking you for help if it wasn't vitally important. We've…" She seemed to choose her next words very carefully. "We've suffered a bit of a setback and I just need a loan, until we're back on our feet."

"A loan?" He searched her face to see if she was lying. "How much?"

He reached in a pocket for his cell phone, flicked out the stylus, opened a blank memo and put the device on the table next to her. "Here, put your account details in there and I'll get my bank to transfer the money directly to your account."

When Kayla didn't move to pick up the stylus, he paused.

"What is it?" he asked.

"Just like that?"

"Like what?"

"Any sum I mention. You'll just give it to me?"

That sense of foreboding washed through him again. "What's this about, Kayla?"

She adjusted the baby in her arms, and when she looked back up at him, he could see her eyes shimmer with tears.

"I miss her. Don't you?" she whispered.

Van felt his gut twist in a knot. Yes, he missed her sister—she'd been his best friend growing up, after all, and it hurt to think of a world without her in it—but in many ways she was a reminder of his failures, of a past he was none too proud of. After she died, and particularly after that night with Kayla, he'd resolved to never look back, to only look forward.

"Yeah, I do," he acknowledged. "But we have to move on, right?"

She nodded. "That's what I'm doing. I'm moving on. I've made plans, very specific plans."

Van's spider senses were screaming. "Tell me," he intoned cautiously.

"I'm going to have the rest of your babies, Sienna's remaining two embryos. I was on track. I was going to space each of the pregnancies two years apart but—"

Whatever she said next was lost in the buzzing sound in his ears. *Babies?* Everything in him protested. Kayla's voice finally penetrated the fog.

"—and with the clinic closing down, I can't wait until I've built up my savings account to support two more individual pregnancies. Time is running out."

A shudder of horror rippled through him. This couldn't be happening. Not now that he knew about the awful heritage that had been passed down through generations on both sides of his family. And certainly not now that he was on the verge of expanding DM Security and merging not only with Dani Matthews's company but with the woman herself.

Suddenly the diamond solitaire ring he had in his breast pocket felt like it was burning through the lining of his suit. He and Dani were totally on the same page on this subject. They gave to the community through their philanthropy and their skills. They had no desire to add to the world by having children. In fact, it was something they both specifically planned to avoid. Bad enough that Kayla already had one baby with his DNA. One child with a genetic predisposition for alcoholism was more than enough. But more? Being raised by a mother as flighty and unreliable as Kayla? It was a recipe for disaster.

"No," he said emphatically.

A small frown pulled between Kayla's brows. "No, you're not going to loan me the money?"

"No, you're not going to have those babies."

Two

"I beg your pardon?"

"It's not going to happen. Not again."

Kayla began to protest. She couldn't believe her ears. "Five years ago, you said—"

He cut her off. "I will fight you on this with every last cent I have if necessary. I made a mistake agreeing to Sienna's request to serve as her donor in the first place. I'm not compounding that mistake by assisting you now."

"Well, that's where you're wrong. I'm the one who makes the decisions about what happens with the embryos, not you."

"Not once my legal team gets a hold of this. I can keep this tied up through the courts for as long as it takes, and I will."

Who was this man? She barely recognized him. But once upon a time he'd been different. He'd wanted to help. Maybe she could still reach that man somehow. She had to try. For her sister's sake.

"We both loved her, Van. Don't you remember why you wanted to help her in the first place? Because you supported her and wanted her to fulfill her dreams. That's exactly what I'm trying to do here. See her dreams come to fruition."

"Don't, Kayla!" He spoke sharply and baby Sienna, startled, popped off her breast.

Kayla quickly covered herself up again. "Don't what, Van?"

"Don't try to use Sienna to manipulate me. Everything is different now. Sienna's dead. Her dream of motherhood died with her," he said bluntly.

Kayla rose to her feet and rested Sienna against her shoulder, rubbing her little back more for her own comfort than for the child's.

"No, Van, they didn't. This beautiful little girl is proof of that. And I'm going to see to it that she doesn't grow up without a brother or a sister. You, more than anyone, should understand why I'm determined to do that."

"Be prepared for a long fight, then, because there is no way I'm sanctioning the birth of any more of my children. Not now. Not ever."

Kayla forced a smile to her lips. "It doesn't really matter whether you sanction them or not. You have no say. You signed your paternal rights away, remember?"

"Nothing is ever carved completely in stone, Kayla. And I have more than enough money to ensure that you won't be permitted to go ahead with this."

"We'll see about that," she answered with an equally determined tone. "You know, I feel sorry for you. You've become cold and unfeeling. Somewhere in the last five years you lost your heart."

Kayla could barely think straight on the drive home. Some of it she put down to hormones. After all, she'd already begun the preparation for the embryo transfer as soon as she got the letter from the clinic to say they were closing. But now she had to decide if she was going to go through with it. And she had to decide whether to go with the single transfer, like she'd done with Sienna, and hope for the best or take the option of a multiple transfer of both remaining embryos with its higher likelihood of a multiple pregnancy. If only she wasn't on such a short time frame. She'd budgeted so carefully to ensure she could have her sister's children without putting herself in dire financial straits. It wasn't cheap raising a kid, but with lots of overtime, diligent planning and a strict savings plan, she'd tucked away a tidy nest egg. But would it stretch to cover a multiple birth? No matter which way she looked at it, she'd be coming up short somewhere.

Well, she told herself optimistically, it wasn't as if she couldn't keep working and continuing to build her nest egg for now—even if the cost of day care for Sienna would now eat into her earnings. She wondered why her housemate, Zoe, had just up and left her like that. No notice, no anything. It was just weird. She and Kayla had enjoyed what Kayla thought was a fair arrangement—in exchange for an allowance, room and board, Zoe cared for Sienna while Kayla was at work. Zoe had never once mentioned she was unhappy with their situation.

Mind you, compared to living on the street, as Zoe had been when Kayla met her—down on her luck and down to her last five dollars—staying with Kayla must have been a massive relief. In fact, it was Zoe, an out-of-work child-care provider, who'd suggested she look after Sienna in the first place. So why had she just up and left?

By the time Kayla reached the two-bedroom apartment she rented on the outskirts of Lakeshore, she was no closer to finding an answer. She let herself inside and put Sienna, who'd fallen asleep in the car, into her crib.

Kayla paused and gazed lovingly at the little girl. The daughter of her heart, but very much Sienna and Van's child at the same time.

Why had Van been so distant, so determined that no more of his and Sienna's children be born? It didn't make sense. He'd willingly entered into the arrangement with her sister.

Well, whatever, she would still go ahead. She'd made a vow and she wasn't going to break it. It would take a lot of planning, a lot of organization—two things that had never been her strong suits. But she'd built those skills over time. She'd needed to, in order to prepare herself for becoming a single mother. The important thing, she knew, was to take things one step at a time. So for now, her first major headache would be getting the baby back into the day care where she'd been before Zoe had moved in.

Kayla reached for her phone and noticed she had a message waiting. She frowned slightly, wondering why she hadn't heard the phone ring before realizing the sound had been turned off. Strange, she didn't remember doing that. She started to listen to the message, hoping that maybe it was from Zoe, with an explanation about where the heck she'd taken off to today.

But no, it wasn't from Zoe—it was an automated message from her bank, notifying her that her account had gone into overdraft. That couldn't be right—in fact, it had to be downright impossible. Nausea rose in Kayla's gut as she pulled up her online banking app on her phone and checked her balance. But there it was on the screen, plain to see. The entire balance of her account had transferred out last night. But how...?

With shaking fingers, she keyed in the phone number for the bank and went through the menu options that would finally lead her to a human voice. Kayla felt her throat choke as she told the customer service rep just

how much money should be in her account. She ought
to know. After all, she checked it on her phone every
night. And last night... The sick dread that enveloped
her thickened and made her stomach flip uncomfortably.
Last night she'd been checking her balance when there'd
been a knock at the door to her apartment. She'd left her
phone on the coffee table when she'd gone to answer and
Zoe had been alone in the living room for about five minutes. Through the roaring sound in her ears, she could
just hear the customer service rep.

"You made a large withdrawal last night, Ms. Porter.
It's all there on the screen—a payment to one of your
regular payees, a Ms. Zoe Thompson."

"But I didn't do it. She must have done it herself."

Kayla swallowed back the tears that collected in her
throat. All her money. Gone. How the heck was she going
to cope?

"Did you give Ms. Thompson access to your account?
Under the terms and conditions—"

"I'm well aware of the terms and conditions, and no, I
didn't give her permission to access my account."

"Ms. Porter, even if the payment was made by mistake,
please be advised that we cannot reverse that payment
without the consent of the person who owns the account
the funds were paid into."

"But I didn't authorize the payment!"

Kayla's voice rose on a desperate note and in the bedroom she heard Sienna stir—the sound of her mother's
distress obviously having woken her.

"Ma'am, if we assist you to recover a payment made
from your authorized mobile device, we will have to
charge you an electronic credit recovery fee. You'll find
the fees set out in our guide."

"Whatever, do whatever you can, whatever your fees
are. I accept. I need my money back."

It was only later, when the bank called her back to say that Zoe had closed out her accounts and the funds could not be retrieved, that Kayla felt all hope die. After filing a claim with the bank and reporting the theft to the police, Kayla finally gave in to the tears that had burned at the back of her throat for what felt like hours.

Kayla looked around her. Her only remaining belongings were her furniture, her personal things and the small amount of cash in her purse. Zoe had left her with nothing else. No backup money, no nest egg. Zip. Zero. Nada. Rage, fear, confusion and a deep sense of violation all jangled within her. When she'd brought Zoe into her apartment, adamant in her belief that giving another person a fair chance to make a good life would help put something worthwhile back into the universe, she'd thought she was making a positive difference in the other woman's life. And she'd trusted her. So much so that she'd left Sienna with her on a day-to-day basis.

She knew Zoe had had a hard past, having to look out for herself after losing her job and being thrown out of her apartment by her boyfriend. Kayla knew Zoe didn't trust easily, but she'd believed they'd gotten past that and thought Zoe had learned to see the good things that life had to offer. And Zoe had at that, a scathing little voice inside Kayla said. She'd seen what Kayla had to offer and she'd taken it—all of it.

Kayla brushed tears from her cheeks. It was all her fault. She trusted people. Always. Now it had bitten her well and truly in the backside. The hard reality of what this meant pressed down on her like a ton of lead.

"Think, Kayla, think. And breathe. You can't lose it now," she said firmly to herself, desperately trying to calm the shudders that now began to ripple through her body.

She tried to center herself—to breathe in slow and

deep and find the inner calm that was usually never far from the surface of her mind—but all to no avail. The police hadn't been optimistic about her chances of getting her money back. Despite the information she'd given them about Zoe, she was just one opportunistic thief in a great big city full of them. She could even have gone out of state by now.

What the heck was she going to do? Her mind remained a blank. It was hopeless. She was hopeless. She needed money—those precious savings had been for her babies' future and to help her raise them, not to mention covering rent and utilities while she couldn't work—but who would loan her what she needed? The bank clearly wouldn't be any help, since they seemed to hold her responsible for losing the money in her account. She didn't have any family left. Most of her friends were in the same financial situation as she had been before she'd decided to have Sienna's kids—choosing to live in the present rather than plan for the future. So, if her friends were out, who did that leave?

One name whispered through her mind, making her nerves vibrate with tension and a swarm of butterflies skitter about in her stomach—Van Murphy. Even though he'd made his position painfully clear today, perhaps with time he'd soften his stance. Surely any man with a shred of decency left in him would want to help his children? It wasn't as if he was strapped for cash.

But no, she remembered the coldness on his face as he'd threatened to keep her from using Sienna's remaining embryos. He wouldn't help her. In fact, he'd do whatever he could to stop her.

There was no way she could afford a legal battle—especially against the kind of lawyers he could afford. She'd have to scrape together whatever resources remained and go through the procedure without any kind of nest egg.

The alternative was giving up on those babies and her promise to her sister completely—and that was something she would never do.

Van ended the call with his lawyer and calmly and deliberately slid his cell phone back into his pocket. He didn't dare move, or he might destroy something, although right now a bar brawl would come in handy to help him relieve the anger that infused every cell in his body.

She'd gone and done it.

Despite what he'd said, or maybe in spite of it, she'd carried on with the transfer of Sienna's remaining embryos before he could arrange an injunction to stop her. Two embryos, to be precise, if his lawyer's information was correct. Van slowly let go of the breath he'd been holding and focused on the picture on the wall of his office. Normally the vista, painted from the balcony of his home overlooking the sea on the Monterey Peninsula, calmed him. Reminded him of just how far he'd come. But nothing calmed him now.

This was his worst nightmare come to life.

For the first time in a long time, he was lost for what to do. Automatically he pulled out his car keys. He shrugged into his suit jacket and walked down the corridor and into his private elevator. Down in the parking garage, he slid onto the fine dove-gray leather seat of his late-model Audi and activated the GPS—inputting the address he'd committed to memory about two hours after Kayla had left his office just over a month ago.

He hadn't wanted to see her again—hadn't wanted to need to have this conversation—but with her decision to ignore his wishes, he had no other option. Anger rolled in waves beneath the surface, forcing him to utilize every last ounce of training he'd ever endured to keep it under control. One step at a time, he reminded himself. His primary objective right now was to see her, talk to her. What he wanted to say—well, he had no idea yet, nothing civil, anyway, but he knew something would come to him.

The roads were relatively quiet heading out of the city and he made the journey to Lakeshore in good time. Van's brows pulled into a frown when he saw the red-and-blue flashing lights as he drove up to Kayla's apartment building. He got out of his car and locked the doors.

He scanned the numbers on the rows of apartments and his frown deepened as he saw that Kayla's was very near where two police cars jutted out from the curb, along with an ambulance. Even from where he was, Van could hear the angry yelling of a woman the cops were guiding toward one of the cruisers.

"You owe me, Kayla! You owe me! You were supposed to help."

Van's blood ran cold. Had this crazy woman attacked Kayla? He quickened his step and drew closer to the crowd that had gathered on the sidewalk. Two police officers tried to restrain the wild-eyed woman, who spat and bucked and twisted and fought them with every step. Where the hell was Kayla in all this? Van looked up to a second-story balcony where a curtain billowed out through a broken glass slider. Without realizing he'd made a decision, he pushed his way through the crowd and started toward the building, only to be stopped by another officer on the sidewalk.

"Sir, you can't go up there."

Like hell he couldn't. "Kayla Porter, where is she?"

"And you are?" The officer gave him a hard stare.

"A friend. A *family* friend," he emphasized.

"She's over there in the ambulance, sir, with the baby."

Ambulance? A cold rush of fear washed through him.

Was she hurt? Was the baby hurt? Without another word to the officer, he strode toward the ambulance. As he neared the back of the vehicle, he spied Kayla inside, a stark white dressing on her forehead. His gut knotted until he saw the sleeping baby in her arms—not crying, not visibly injured, he noted almost immediately. He felt his taut muscles begin to ease. They were okay. A ridiculous sense of relief coursed through him, replacing the chill of alarm that had been there only seconds ago.

From the look on Kayla's pale face, she was shaken, but aside from that dressing, it looked like she and Sienna were all right. Kayla hadn't seen him yet. Her eyes were fixed on the woman being bundled into the back of the patrol car. Even from here he could see the way shock and strain had drawn Kayla's blanched features into a mask of horror and disbelief. She grew visibly paler at the vitriol being flung at her by the woman as one of the officers closed the back door of the cruiser and the vehicle pulled away. A paramedic moved inside the ambulance, blocking Van's view. As much as it frustrated him, he reminded himself it was okay for now. Kayla was getting the care she needed. The baby was fine. There was nothing else he could do right now but wait.

After another ten minutes he saw Kayla being helped down to the street. He resisted the urge to rush forward. A female officer led Kayla and Sienna back across the street and into the building. He followed them up the stairs.

The front door to what had to be Kayla's apartment was wide open. He stepped through the threshold, his gaze instantly assessing the chaos inside—the overturned side tables, the broken lamp, the cupboard doors hanging open—their shelves denuded of whatever had been inside.

"Sir, this is a crime scene. Please go back downstairs," the officer instructed when she caught sight of him.

"I'm a friend of Ms. Porter's," he repeated, then forced himself to say his next words. "And the father of the baby."

"Is that right, Kayla? Do you want him here?"

Kayla came through a doorway and closed it quietly behind her. The second her eyes lit on him, she seemed to jolt in surprise. Shock, rapidly followed by something else—guilt, probably, he surmised, since she likely knew good and well why he was here—shot across her face.

"Yes, that's okay," she said. She averted her gaze and studiously avoided looking at him again.

The officer turned to Van. "Fine," she said. "You can come in."

He gave the woman a curt nod and moved farther inside, picking his way through the debris to where Kayla stood near an overturned sofa. Shudders racked her body even though the evening air coming through the broken window was pretty mild for May. She was clearly feeling the effects of whatever had transpired here. Looking around, he knew it couldn't have been pleasant. Van shucked off his suit jacket and placed it over her shoulders. She flinched at his touch as his hands briefly rested on her upper arms, but she didn't refuse the warmth his jacket offered.

He waited patiently while she gave her statement, his hands curled into impotent fists as she described the invasion of her home by a woman she'd once trusted. But his interest sharpened at the officer's next words.

"And you say this is the woman who cleared out your bank account last month?"

"I...I can't talk about this right now," she said, glancing at Van, her voice jittering with nerves.

"Don't let me stop you making a full statement," Van responded smoothly. "Give the officer the information she needs."

At his prompting, Kayla carried on, although he sensed she was choosing her words carefully because of him. But no amount of care could disguise the facts, and by the end of her statement he was boiling under the surface. Not only had she brought some homeless person into her apartment, she'd left Sienna with her on a regular basis. Was she completely out of her mind? Van swallowed back the fierce wave of frustration that clogged his throat. He'd just have to bide his time until they were alone so he could have this out with Kayla.

He didn't have to wait much longer before the officer was leaving, with an admonition to Kayla to get her locks changed in the morning.

"I'll take care of it tonight," Van said firmly. "Thank you, officer."

The woman looked from him to Kayla and back again. Then, with a slight nod, she closed the door behind her. Van turned to face Kayla. Silence stretched out between them like a palpable being. He couldn't hold back a moment longer.

"What the hell were you thinking?"

"Tonight? How to stay alive, mostly."

Her attitude did nothing to assuage the burning anger that smoldered deep inside him.

"Nice try, Kayla. You know that's not what I'm talking about. You owe me an explanation and I'm not leaving until I get it."

Three

Kayla righted an armchair and sank into it. She was shattered. If having Zoe return to her apartment, tripping out on the drugs she'd spent all of Kayla's hard-earned savings on, hadn't been enough, now she had to deal with Van, as well?

She swallowed against the sudden dryness in her throat and looked at him. While she might not have been able to see the fury that emanated off him in waves, she could certainly feel it.

"Can't this wait until tomorrow? As you can see, I have a lot on my plate right now."

Her head ached where one of Zoe's missiles had caught her on the forehead and Kayla gingerly touched the dressing the paramedic had put over the cut and closed her eyes. She sensed rather than saw Van move to her side.

"Are you okay? Do you need further medical attention?"

She let her hand drop into her lap and opened her eyes

again. "No, I'm okay. It was a glancing blow. Nothing major. I'm just really tired right now. I'm not up for a big argument." She dredged up the last of her courage and fired her next words straight at him. "Perhaps you could call and make an appointment."

He looked startled for a second and then reluctantly amused. But frustration and fury soon took over again. "You're not getting rid of me that easily. You know exactly why I'm here. You owe me answers and I'm not leaving until I get them."

"They'll have to wait until I can get this all sorted out," she said with a weary wave of her hand at the mess that was once her sitting room and kitchen.

"Fine. We do that, then we talk."

"Van, no. It's late, I'm tired and I just want to go to bed."

"Without changing the lock? With that hole in your sliding door?"

She just shook her head, unable to find words. Tonight had been terrifying. When Zoe had shown up, letting herself in with her old key and demanding more money from Kayla, she'd thought she could talk the other woman down. How wrong had she been? Zoe went crazy and grabbed Sienna from her crib, making wild threats. Kayla didn't stop to think. Maternal instinct simply took over and she launched herself at Zoe. Both of them fell onto the bed and she tussled with her, determined to free her little girl from the madwoman's clutches. It was the last thing Zoe had anticipated and Kayla quickly wrested her baby free. After putting Sienna back in her crib, Kayla shoved Zoe out of the bedroom and barricaded them both inside. Sienna screamed her lungs out through the whole ordeal.

Zoe went completely over the edge at that stage and all Kayla could do was listen helplessly while the other woman destroyed the rest of the apartment. She couldn't even call the police, because her phone was in the living room. Thankfully, several of her neighbors had heard the commotion.

Another shudder racked her body. It had been only two days since the implantation procedure. She wasn't supposed to undertake any strenuous activity and things had gotten pretty strenuous when she and Zoe had struggled together—not to mention the strain of dragging her grandmother's old wooden dresser across the door to stop Zoe from breaking her way back into the bedroom. Already she could feel aches and pains in every part of her body. She wrapped her arms across her stomach, holding herself tight. She couldn't lose the babies, not now.

"Kayla?"

Van said her name impatiently, forcing her to drag her thoughts together.

"I'm insured. I'll call someone after I get a hold of the building manager to report the damage," she said weakly.

"And how long do you think it'll take before they can get contractors here? Leave it to me."

Without waiting for her response, Van pulled up a number on his cell phone and started talking. She dropped her head against the back of the chair and closed her eyes again, opening them only when he finished his call.

"A team will be here in about thirty minutes."

He could do that? Just how much pull did he have these days? She didn't want to think about the answer to that question. Van gave her a look, as if he could see exactly what she was thinking.

"You look awful," he said. "Can I get you anything?"

"Sure, a million dollars would be nice, since you're asking," she answered flippantly, then cringed, realizing that probably wasn't going to help her cause.

She hastened to head him off before he verbalized

some cutting comeback. "I'm sorry. It's just the shock talking. Maybe…" She turned toward the kitchen, staring at the empty cupboards, some doors hanging drunkenly on their hinges. "I'd have said a cup of tea would be good about now, but she's trashed the kitchen, hasn't she?"

"Leave it to me," Van said again, righting Sienna's high chair on his way through the mess. He picked up her battered electric kettle and held it aloft. "We have progress," he said, then proceeded to rinse it out before refilling it and plugging it back in to heat. While he waited, he started to put things back in the cupboards—what hadn't been smashed to pieces, at least.

"You don't have to do that," she protested.

"You said you'll talk when this is all cleaned up. I'm cleaning up."

The not-so-subtle reminder that he still expected to talk with her tonight did not go unnoticed. While Kayla sipped her tea, Van continued to work through the kitchen, setting it to rights as much as he could. Broken crockery went in a cardboard box. Undamaged food was stacked in the small pantry. Steadily, he restored order. By the time his crew arrived, he was almost done with the kitchen.

Kayla was surprised at the men who came through her front door. One had a prosthetic leg, another severe burn scars down one side of his face and neck, along with several missing fingers. After greeting Van with a camaraderie that obviously went back years, they got to work fast—replacing the shattered pane in her sliding door and putting in new locks. While they worked, Van made and received several calls. Kayla could do nothing but watch and tell them where she wanted the remaining unbroken pieces of furniture set. She thought they were finally all done, but when she saw them begin to install a wireless security system, she started to protest.

"Van, what's that? I don't need some fancy security system and I certainly can't afford it, either."

"Humor me," he said darkly. "Security is my business, and, correct me if I'm wrong, it is my daughter in that bedroom, and those are my children you're carrying, aren't they?"

If she was still carrying them. "Y-yes," she managed to say on the swell of emotion that threatened to overwhelm her.

It was the first time she'd heard him actually acknowledge the babies as his. The intimation that he'd take care of them, all of them, was loud and clear. Relief seeped through her whole body. He was going to help her. Hadn't he just said as much?

It was after midnight when his team finished. Van saw them to the door and locked it behind them. Double locked and chained, Kayla noted. She fought back a yawn as Van walked back toward her, pocketing one set of keys and handing the other set to her.

"You're keeping a set?" she asked, a little confused.

"Let's call it protecting my investment," he said cryptically.

"Investment?"

"Since you seem to be incapable of looking after yourself responsibly, obviously it's up to me to do so."

The warm buzz of hope that had filled her only a short while ago faded fast.

"What exactly do you mean by that?"

"It's too late for me to do anything about the embryo transfer. As much as I vehemently disagree with what you did, I can't undo it. But I can make sure that my children are brought up safe."

"That's what I want, too," Kayla agreed.

"Really? And yet you were the one who brought a stranger in off the street to live with you and Sienna. A woman whose background you hadn't investigated, some-one with no references. Honestly, Kayla—a drug addict? That's your idea of safe?"

"She wasn't on drugs when I invited her to stay here. And she showed me her qualifications. She is a trained child-care worker and she loved Sienna."

No matter how much she remonstrated, Kayla knew in her heart that Van was right. She trusted people too eas-ily and look where that had left her. Broke and broken.

"Did you know she was suspended from her last place of employment because she failed a drug test—not once but twice?"

Kayla felt sick to her stomach, and not just because she was pregnant. "No, I didn't know that."

"Obviously." Van pushed his fingers through his hair, messing it into a wild tousle that only made him look even more lethal, more attractive, than ever. "I want custody of the children."

"Shared custody, of course. I think it's important that the children get to know their father."

Van cast her a look, his green eyes as deep and unfath-omable as a forest lake. "No, Kayla, you misunderstand me. Not shared custody, full custody. It starts with Sienna and will continue with the new babies when they're born."

That sick feeling inside her surged. "You can't mean that. You can't take her away from the only parent she's ever known. It would be cruel. Besides, she's mine. No judge will award you full custody. You signed away your rights already."

"No judge? Really? And when shown your unstable background, your bad choices and your deadbeat friends, do you really think a judge isn't going to look more favor-ably upon me? Let's see, shall we?" He began to enumer-ate a few of the escapades she'd gotten caught up in as a teenager, some of which had involved the police.

"Look, everyone makes mistakes when they're young and foolish. Half the population of this country wouldn't have children if what you did as a kid was the only measure of how appropriate a parent you'd be."

"And now, Kayla? You're what, a masseuse?"

He said the word as if she was no more than a street-corner prostitute.

"I'm a fully trained massage therapist. There is a difference, you know. I'm respected and I'm good at my job."

"A job that takes you away from Sienna, right? A job that makes you leave her in the care of someone phenomenally unfit. And tell me, Kayla, does this job of yours pay so well that you can afford to stop work and care for three children under the age of two? Or were you planning to go to the local homeless shelter and find more day-care options there?"

"I'll manage—with your help, of course."

"With my help," he repeated grimly. "You're a piece of work, you know that? How much money do you have left in the bank?"

"That's none of your business."

She'd saved a few hundred dollars since Zoe had cleaned her out. Not much, but it was a start.

"I'm guessing that even if you're saving, it's nowhere near enough for you to even make the rent here when you have to stop working after the babies are born, is it?"

"I'll manage. I always have before and I will again. I'll sell Sienna's jewelry if I have to."

Kayla lifted a hand to finger the gold chain at her throat. Van's eyes tracked the movement and she felt the burn of his gaze as if it was a physical touch searing her skin.

"And you think that'll help? And what about when that's all gone—have you thought about that? Be honest with yourself, Kayla. No court is going to declare you a fit parent—especially not in comparison to me. I'm a decorated veteran, a stable and successful businessman, I'm engaged to be married and I have a debt-free home."

He was engaged?

For some reason that one piece of information sent a wave of desolation through her—as though she'd lost something very important without even realizing it. It was stupid, she told herself. It wasn't as if she and Van had ever been close growing up, and that one-night stand the evening after Sienna's funeral had been more of a re-lease of mutual grief than attraction. But even so, she still couldn't look at Van without remembering that night with him. That night she'd wondered if—no, hoped, she finally admitted to herself—they could move forward from that point and discover whether they could have more together.

But he'd run away, hadn't he? Just like he'd done when he'd turned eighteen and joined the army. Just like he'd done when Sienna's diagnosis had come through and he'd transferred to Special Forces. It seemed that when the chips were down, Van Murphy couldn't be relied upon. So how good a father would he be?

She stood up and squared her shoulders, ignoring the dull throb emanating from her forehead, and looked him in the eye.

"You might think that all it takes is money to be a par-ent, Van Murphy, but prepare yourself for a monumental fight. A man like you could never be a decent father and my children—yes, *mine*—deserve better than a man who cuts and runs whenever the going gets tough. They de-serve love and I'm betting that's something you're never going to be capable of giving to anyone."

Van listened to her words, felt each one like a hot round of lead attempting to pierce the shield he'd wrapped around his emotions a long time ago. She was probably right. The children certainly did deserve more love and affection than he knew how to offer, but the alternative was emphatically not her lackadaisical approach to life, either.

He forced himself to smile. "You haven't changed a bit, have you, Kayla? Still the dreamer, still thinking everything will all work out in the end if you just *believe* in it enough. But life, real life, is not like that."

"Isn't it? Tell me, then, the men you had working for you here tonight. You served with them?"

Where the hell was she going with this? He crossed his arms and nodded.

"And when they came home, they were broken, weren't they. Physically and probably mentally, too."

He grimaced. Those had been bad days.

"And you gave them something, didn't you? You gave them a purpose, gave them back their pride. Because you believed in them, you made them see that they still had skills and worth and something to offer. And they're happy now, aren't they? So don't tell me that things don't work out in the end."

He didn't like the way she made him feel or the way she made him think. He turned and went to the door.

"Yes, that's right, Van. You run away, and you keep on running!" she said forcefully at his retreating back.

From the bedroom, he heard Sienna's cry. "My daughter needs you," he said coldly. "Best you attend to her."

"Yes, that's right. I'm what's best for her and don't you forget it."

He wasn't likely to forget the fierce look on Kayla's pale face, nor the impassioned glare in her eyes. Her expression haunted him as he pounded down the stairs and along the sidewalk toward his car. She was right about his running, he thought as he drove back to the city. But what she didn't understand was that running meant survival. It meant staying safe both physically and emotionally. And if that was what he had to do, then that was what would happen.

He glanced at the time on the dashboard display. Almost 1:00 a.m. It wouldn't be worth the hour-and-a-half drive south to head to his home. Even if he filed a night flight and took the chopper, he'd no sooner be asleep before he'd need to be up and flying back to San Francisco. He might as well stay in his apartment.

After putting his car in the parking garage in the basement of the building, he took his private elevator up to the apartment. The moment the doors swished open, a tingle of awareness warned him that he wasn't alone.

A single light shone in the sitting room, bathing the woman who curled up in a corner of his sofa in a golden glow. Dani. He wondered how long she'd been waiting here. She must have sensed his arrival because she stretched like a cat and opened her eyes.

"Everything okay?" she asked, getting gracefully to her feet and walking toward him. "I called Imelda to see if you'd gone back to the house tonight but she said you weren't home, so I assumed you'd show up here eventually. Are you happy to see me?"

She lifted her face to his and kissed him. He met her kiss perfunctorily.

"I wasn't expecting you," he said.

She frowned, her mouth a moue of disappointment at his lukewarm reception. "I know, but we're here now, right? We can still make the most of what's left of the night."

Dani lifted her left hand and tucked her hair behind one ear. The movement caused her diamond to flash, reminding him of the decision he'd reached in the car on the way over here. She started to smile invitingly, but when she realized he still wasn't responding in kind, her expression grew serious.

"What is it, Donovan? Is everything okay?"

He sighed. No, everything most certainly was not.

"We need to talk," he said.

"That doesn't sound promising. Can it wait? Maybe things will look better in the morning and…" she arched one brow and gave him a look full of sensual promise "…perhaps I can distract you in the meantime."

Any other day, any other week, he'd have taken her up on the offer. Not after tonight, though, and not after the decision he'd made.

"I'm sorry, Dani—" he started.

"It's her, isn't it?"

"What?"

"The woman with the baby last month. Is it yours?"

Van wiped his face with one hand. This was going to be harder than he thought.

Dani continued. "Of course it is. She's a beautiful child and looks a lot like you. But it doesn't have to be a problem. Everyone can be bought for the right price, Van. Even past lovers. Pay her mother to leave you alone. If you take care of that little problem, we can carry on as we'd always intended."

"It's not as simple as that," Van said.

He explained, in the barest terms possible, about his arrangement with Sienna and about Kayla's decision to have her sister's children—*his* children.

"I don't see the issue. There's no need for you to be involved in their lives. She came to you for money—give it to her. Make the problem go away, Donovan."

There was a steely tone to her voice that showed a side of her he'd always known lingered beneath her smooth surface. Dani Matthews did not like to be thwarted. Normally, neither did he. But something had changed in the course of tonight. Instincts he hadn't known he possessed had pushed up through his barriers. Protective instincts, fatherly instincts.

His mother and father had abandoned him in the pursuit of their next alcoholic buzz. His adoptive parents had been of the "spare the rod and spoil the child" variety, never showing love, never admitting pride in any of his achievements and never, ever, giving encouragement. He wouldn't be like any of them. He had a chance to make things right for his children. To give them the stability and the opportunities his upbringing had never given him.

"No," he said firmly. "I'm sorry, Dani, but our engagement is off. I'm going to be a father."

Four

Kayla lay on the bed staring hard at the screen, willing the sonographer to find that second heartbeat.

"Please," she implored. "Look again."

"Kayla, one out of two is still a good thing. A lot of women don't even progress this far," the woman said encouragingly.

Even though she knew the odds, Kayla couldn't help but feel a sense of devastation that one of her babies hadn't made it.

"You're right, of course," she made herself say in response. "I'm very lucky."

And she kept telling herself that all the way back to work, but the instant she walked into the rooms she shared in a holistic wellness clinic, she felt her hard-fought-for composure begin to crumble. Susan, her boss and fellow therapist at the clinic, took one look at her face and raced forward to envelop Kayla in her arms.

"Oh, hon. Is the news that bad?" she said, sympathetically rubbing Kayla's back.

"I've lost one, Susan. The scan showed only one heartbeat."

"That's still good news, though, isn't it? You have one baby?" Susan loosened her embrace and held Kayla at arm's length. "Look at you. I thought all hope was gone."

Kayla gave her a watery smile. "I'm sorry. I'm just… It's just…"

She couldn't find the words to describe the aching sense of loss—and guilt—that had settled deep inside her. Every time she argued with herself that there was nothing she could have done differently to ensure the success of both the embryos, she was reminded of that night with Zoe. Of how physical it had gotten. Of how all of that was her fault. *She'd* brought Zoe into her home, into her and Sienna's world. *She'd* left her phone on the coffee table, open to her internet banking. *She'd* done nothing about changing her locks after Zoe had left.

No matter which way she looked at it, it was all her fault. She felt like she'd failed—both the lost embryo and her sister. The day had started bad enough when, before she left for the scan this morning, the papers had arrived from Van's lawyers; he was suing for custody of Sienna. It felt like an assault on her right to be Sienna's mother and the mother of the babies—no, baby, she corrected herself—she carried and she had nothing to fight it with. Tears filled her eyes and began to roll helplessly down her cheeks.

"There, there, hon. Don't take on so. Must be all those hormones heading into overdrive in your body, hmm? Why don't you take the rest of the day off? You only have three bookings. I'll cover for you, okay?"

Kayla reluctantly accepted Susan's offer. She couldn't

really afford to take extra time off, not when she was
so financially strapped, but right now the idea of working and investing what was left of her energy into other
people was just too much for her. Sienna was in day care
until five o'clock, so she decided to let her stay there and
headed to her apartment. She hadn't been sleeping all that
well. Maybe she could just take a nap and be in a better
headspace to figure out her next move.

She'd been dozing on her sofa for a couple of hours
when she heard a knock at the door. Still fuzzy, she got to
her feet and rubbed her face, surprised to find her fingers
came away wet. She'd been crying even in her sleep. The
reality of it all hit her again. There was another knock
at the door.

"Kayla? I know you're in there."

Van. Of course it had to be him. The man had the worst
timing in the world. She dragged herself to the door.

"I'm not really up for visitors right now. Can you come
another time?" she said at the solid block of wood with
its shiny new locks.

"This isn't a social call. Open up."

"Look, if you're wondering if your papers got here
today, they did. Okay? You can go now."

"I'm here because I'm worried about you," he interrupted. "Now open the door."

Kayla's shoulders drooped as emotion swelled through
her again. He was worried about her? Worried about his
progeny, more like. She had no doubt that she was nothing but a peripheral thought to him. She slipped the chain
off, twisted the two locks open and swung the door wide.

"Come in," she said listlessly.

She hadn't been kidding when she said she wasn't up
to visitors, but most especially, she wasn't up to him. She
turned her back on him to head back to the couch, but
not before she caught a whiff of his cologne. Funny how

it didn't make her stomach twist and revolt like so many other scents already did. The fragrance summed him up perfectly with its masculine woody blend and sharper citrus top note, and it reminded her anew of the difference between this man and the boy she'd known growing up—not to mention the man she'd sought oblivion with after Sienna's funeral.

Van came in, locked the door behind him and came to stand by the sofa, where she'd reassumed her position lying down under a soft blanket. His eyes raked her, almost as if he was trying to see inside her.

"I went to see you at work," he started.

Kayla felt her spirits dip even lower. Susan was a lovely woman but confidentiality was a foreign concept to her. She'd have told Van everything. His next words confirmed it.

"Your boss told me one of the embryos didn't take." He paused a moment, took in a deep breath. "Will you be all right? Is there anything I can do?"

"No, there's nothing anyone can do. It happens. I was half expecting it but I still…I still hoped, you know?"

Van moved around the room. Kayla surreptitiously watched him from her supine position on the sofa. He carried himself straight and tall, using every inch of his six-foot-two frame to fill the space he occupied. And all around him, like some cape imbued with superpowers, he wore an air of suppressed energy. As if he was coiled, ready to strike at a moment's notice. As if nothing and no one would ambush or surprise him. He'd always been like that, even as a kid—except, when it was just her and Sienna, he'd sometimes let his guard down. She guessed it was only natural that the army had enhanced this hyperawareness in him. But he wasn't in a war zone now—unless you counted the legal attack he'd launched on her this morning.

The reminder made her swing her legs to the floor and sit up straight.

"What do you want, Van? To see I'm okay? You've seen me. You can leave now."

"Tell me about the scan," he demanded, settling into the chair opposite and leaning toward her, his elbows resting on the tops of his thighs and his hands loosely clasped. "What's it like? What did you see?"

She briefly outlined the procedure and told him about the indistinct image on the screen.

"You really can't see a lot. It's still early days," she finished.

"But the sonographer heard a heartbeat?"

"I did, too."

He leaned back against the chair and thrust his hands through his hair. "Wow."

"Like I said, it's still early days."

Yes, there had been a heartbeat, but that could still change. There was a long time before the fetus would be considered viable. Right now it didn't even look like a baby—the scan had just been a collection of light and dark shapes to her—but the audio had confirmed the baby was there. She needed to hold on to that, take joy in that confirmation. It wasn't like her to be downcast, and she hated it, but she was mourning the missing heartbeat—and with it, mourning her sister all over again.

Van was unaccustomed, these days, at least, to feeling helpless. He was the kind of man who took action. He served, he protected, he saved. That he had virtually no control over any of this situation with Kayla was enough to drive a man to drink—except he didn't drink anymore. Ever. Not since he'd learned the truth about his parents. Actually, no, his decision had come earlier than that. It started in the cold gray dawn after that night with

Kayla, after her sister's funeral. A night when they'd had too much to drink and then— He shut down the thought before it could form fully in his mind. No, he did dumb things when he'd been drinking—made dumb choices. No more.

Of course, it looked like the dumbest decision he'd ever made was agreeing to be Sienna's donor. But then, he'd never expected things to turn out like this. Now he had a kid and another on the way.

It was his worst nightmare come true but he had to take control to make sure their childhoods wouldn't be the disaster zone his had been. They needed a strong role model, someone who could guide them into being good human beings who made the right choices in life. He had to be that person no matter how many times he'd told himself he couldn't, or wouldn't, raise kids of his own.

He had an ethical obligation to see that his children had the best of everything—morally and materially. That meant being the best damn father he could be. His kids would have a solid, safe, reliable upbringing. And no matter what impractical ideas Kayla had about parenting, he'd made himself a promise—he'd be the one making the hard decisions in their lives. He'd be the one keeping them safe, now and in the future. If that meant making sure their birth mother was cared for 24/7 until the new baby was born, then that was what he'd do.

Kayla needed his help right now, and she was going to get it—even though he knew she'd fight him on this. But what she probably hadn't counted on was that in the last several years he'd become quite used to succeeding—in everything. He wasn't about to stop now and he wasn't above using some heavy emotional leverage to achieve his objective, either.

He picked his next words very carefully. "You know, you don't need to make things so hard on yourself."

She made a noise that fell somewhere between a snort and a laugh. "Really? That's rather ironic, when you're the one making things hard on me."

Kayla leaned forward and gave the legal envelope sitting in front of her on the coffee table a dismissive shove toward him with her fingertips. He ignored it and the quick surge of frustration that threatened to cloud his thinking.

"I mean, you don't need to do this all on your own," he rephrased.

"Oh, you think I should just give in to your demands? Hand Sienna over to you without another thought? Forget I carried her in my body, birthed her, nurtured her and raised her on my own these past ten months? Forget that she's my sister's baby and that I promised to raise her?"

Her voice wobbled, betraying her vulnerability. Out of nowhere came the urge to wrap her in his arms, to tell her that everything was going to be okay. It was most inconvenient. He didn't want to feel that way toward her. He didn't want to feel that way toward anybody. He'd drilled that sap out of himself, taught himself not to feel anything more than he wanted to feel when he wanted to feel it. He compartmentalized and planned; he didn't wing it. He made decisions based on analysis and structure, not emotion. He did not offer hugs to tearful females, even if they were carrying his kids.

Again, the unwelcome impulse to comfort her fought to rise to the surface. Again, he shoved it straight back down. It was time to bring in the big guns—he might not want to feel emotion but he wasn't above manipulating it to get what he wanted.

"Sienna wouldn't have wanted you to do this on your own, Kayla. You know that. You said yourself that she would have wanted me to be a part of this, to help you, to support you."

"To support me, yes. Not to rip everything I hold dear away from me."

Her face grew taut, her throat worked—swallowing almost convulsively—and he saw the stricken echo of sorrow reflect from her blue eyes. He averted his gaze. Damn, he couldn't have felt any worse right now if he'd just kicked a puppy. What was it with these feelings? Was she leaking hormones in the air or something? He had to move, to get out of the line of fire. He shoved up and out of his chair and started to pace, talking all the time—enumerating all the reasons it would be a good idea for her to accept his offer of household help, financial security, comfortable living. You name it, he'd provide it. Help to infinity and beyond. After all, hadn't that been her objective all along when she'd come to see him last month? Wasn't he giving her, albeit belatedly, exactly what she'd asked for?

When he finally wound down, her expression was more normal again. Granted, she was still pale and her eyes still red rimmed, but there was a light of battle in them again. A light that reminded him of old Kayla. The one who got a harebrained idea in that head of hers and went off, damning the consequences without a second thought—just like she had with this pregnancy.

"So you're saying I should give up the lease on this apartment, give up a job I love, move south to your no doubt obscenely luxurious home on the hills outside Monterey, hand over Sienna to some faceless nanny and spend my time growing your next child like some uninvolved incubator until it's born, whereupon you plan to take it and my daughter and show me the door? I don't think so."

He knew it wouldn't be easy. "Look, sure, when you present it like that, it doesn't sound appealing, I agree. But ask yourself this—what's your other option? How are you going to cope, pregnant and working without any help?

Your friend Susan, she told me how sick you were with Sienna. What did she call it? Hyper-something-or-other."

"Hyperemesis gravidarum," Kayla supplied.

"Yeah, that. What if you get that again?"

"I'd already started by now with Sienna. Maybe I won't get sick this time. Maybe everything will go textbook perfect."

She was grasping at straws. "My research shows that if you've had it before, you have an 86 percent chance of developing it again in a subsequent pregnancy."

"Your research." She shook her head and huffed that snort-laugh again. "You did what? Googled it?" She gave him a slow clap. "Well done, Van. Well done."

He felt hot color rise in his cheeks. "Even if it only lasts through your first trimester, how do you expect to work during that? And Sienna, let's not forget her needs—not to mention bodily functions. Can you really see yourself coping with all that on your own?"

"Of course I can. I'll do whatever I have to."

"You don't get it, do you? You need help. *My* help."

"On your terms," she said bitterly.

"My kids, my terms."

"You forget—I have custody, legally and figuratively, of your supposed kids."

He bent down and pushed the legal envelope back toward her across the table.

"But for how much longer, Kayla?"

He stared at her, secretly surprised that she was fighting him this hard. She'd never wanted children before. Her life had always been one adventure after another. Backpacking in Kathmandu. Hiking in Papua New Guinea. Digging for opals in Australia. The antithesis of her sister, she'd never wanted to be tied down to anything or anyone. The only permanent tie in her life had been to Sienna—and he knew that was what was driving this stubbornness now. She'd made a promise to her sister. But surely she knew that Sienna would have wanted her children to have a safe and stable home. He could provide that. Kayla couldn't. He doubted she truly wanted to. She'd always been such a free spirit—surely she couldn't have changed that much. He tried another tack.

"Look, it doesn't have to be like this. You don't have to keep fighting me. I'll pay you for the surrogacy—for Sienna and for this child. Then you can go forth and do whatever it is that you do."

"No. *These are my children.* I'm not abandoning them and especially not to you. You've already discarded them once, when you tried to stop me from undergoing the procedure. You're just as likely to forsake them again when the going gets rough or when you start to feel too much. It's what you always do."

Her words hurt, but he pushed back the pain like he always did. "Things have changed. *I've* changed."

"And what about your fiancée? Does she welcome this opportunity to have a ready-made family? One where she doesn't have to be involved in any of the messy stuff like nausea, stretch marks or giving birth?"

"Dani and I are no longer engaged," he said bluntly.

Dani had fought hard that night to change his mind about their engagement but he'd been adamant. They continued to work together because neither of them were about to let a broken engagement get in the way of a perfectly good business merger, but he knew she thought he was crazy to want to take on his children.

"Why?" Kayla demanded. "Did she want too much from you, Van? Make you feel too much, perhaps?"

"We had our reasons," he answered. There was no way he was going into the details with Kayla.

"And I have mine now," she was quick to retort.

"So, we're at an impasse."

She crossed her arms and looked up at him. "We certainly are."

Van shoved his hand through his hair again and took a couple of steps away before wheeling around.

"We both know I'll win custody. What if I'm prepared to discuss some kind of visitation after the children are born?"

"Visitation?" She gave him a scornful look. "Please don't insult me like that. You know that's not enough. These are *my* children—in every way."

"In every way except biologically."

Their eyes locked in a silent duel, but he was a master at this and he'd stared down far more determined enemies before today. She was the first to look away.

"Okay, fine," she said bitterly. "I'll consider your offer."

"Seriously consider it?" he pressed.

"I said I would, didn't I?"

He studied her face, checked her hands to make sure she hadn't crossed her fingers, as she used to when she was a kid. She appeared to be telling the truth. He'd have to take it.

"I'll be back at the end of the week for your answer."

His words caused a fissure in her carefully composed facade.

"The end of the week? But that's only a couple of days!" she objected.

"It's all I'm prepared to concede. If I don't have your answer by then, I'll be instructing my lawyers to fast-track my petition for custody of Sienna."

He stalked to the door.

"You can't do that to me. It's not right," she protested.

"I can't? Just watch me."

Five

Kayla went about her treatment room, making sure everything was ready for her next appointment. She was exhausted, the tiredness of early pregnancy and caring for Sienna taking a toll she hadn't expected, and the severe nausea she'd experienced with Sienna's pregnancy had asserted itself over the weekend with a vengeance.

But she'd work things out. She just had to. One of her girlfriends had flippantly suggested crowdfunding to help her get through this—even if it was only to raise the funds to fight Van through family court. She had to admit, the idea had briefly held appeal, but wouldn't that just be grasping at straws? And how would it look to a judge? She had no doubt that Van would use such a thing as yet another example of why she wasn't a fit parent.

She put her hands at the base of her spine and leaned backward, stretching out her lower back before straightening her shoulders and heading to Reception to welcome her next client. She heard voices as she approached—a male murmur followed by an almost flirtatious giggle from Susan. Then the male voice again, this time sounding so familiar that a ripple of nausea lurched from the pit of her stomach, making her falter in her tracks.

She rested a hand on her diaphragm and swallowed, closing her eyes just a moment. Opening them again, she reoriented herself. No, she couldn't possibly have just heard Van's voice. Not here. The clinic was primarily frequented by convalescent patients needing massage therapy, and Van was most definitely not convalescent. Kayla drew in a steadying breath and completed the short distance down the corridor.

"Ah, here she is," Susan said brightly as Kayla entered the reception area.

Van gave Kayla an assessing look. "Here she is indeed," he said in a voice that told her he was here for answers.

She swallowed again, but it did nothing to ease the unsettled feeling that racked her. His deadline had come and gone, and to avoid speaking to him, she'd studiously ignored her phone and had gone so far as to go and visit with a friend up the coast over the weekend just in case he came to her apartment. She might have known he'd track her down at work when he didn't get the answer he sought.

"Mr. Murphy," she said, acknowledging his presence with a short nod. "Can I help you?"

"I hope so. I have this pain in my neck." He made no attempt to gesture to any strained muscles, just keeping his eyes trained on her like a rifle scope and leaving her in no doubt as to what the source of his apparent pain was.

"We specialize in convalescent therapy here. I can't help you."

Kayla heard Susan's sharply indrawn breath. She'd never been rude to a client before.

"Mr. Murphy, please excuse us a moment," Susan said smoothly.

She cast Van a smile and took Kayla by the arm into a small side office.

"What are you doing?" she demanded. "I know you've told me about your problems with him but if the man wants his neck massaged, then you massage his neck."

"That's not what he's here for," Kayla protested.

"This is your place of work," Susan reminded her emphatically. "Not your personal battlefield. Now, I suggest you take him through to your treatment room and get to work."

Without waiting for her response, Susan left the office and returned to Reception.

"Thanks for your support," Kayla muttered under her breath before following her. She forced herself to smile at Van. "Please, come with me."

He smiled back at her, satisfied that he'd won this round. In her room, she directed him to remove his tie and shirt and to lie facedown on the table. Once he was in position, she moved to the head of the bed and, with oil-slicked hands, began to stroke the muscles of his shoulders and neck. She tried to ignore how his body felt beneath her palms and any thoughts of the last time she'd touched his bare skin.

He was still strong but perhaps not as heavily muscled as he'd been back then, before he'd mustered out of the army. But stroking his skin now brought back memories she'd rather forget. Memories of how well they'd fit together, of the pleasure they'd wrought from one another's bodies. Of the glimmer of hope that maybe things had changed between them, that they could forge a new relationship together—one as adults who could be good for one another instead of the children and teenagers who'd so often butted heads. But then she reminded herself of the devastation she'd felt when she'd realized, come morning, that he'd gone without another word.

She applied more pressure—working her fingertips into the stiffness of his shoulders. Working out some of the frustration and helplessness she felt from right now as well as from back then. He needed it, anyway—while the appointment might have been a ruse to force her to talk to him, the knots in his muscles were crying out for attention.

Under normal circumstances she would have spent more time warming up the muscles of her clients, who were generally weaker and older. But Van got no such consideration. For this moment, she could kid herself she had the upper hand on this man. She hated being manipulated, and he knew it.

"Could you enjoy this a little less," he grunted from the table.

"You came here for a therapeutic massage, didn't you?" she reminded him, putting extra pressure on a particularly hard knot of muscle. "You carry a lot of tension here. You should try relaxing a bit more."

"I'll relax when you give me your answer. Why have you been avoiding me?"

She started to speak, to lie and say she needed more time, but she knew that would be a waste of breath. He'd made it clear when they'd last seen each other that she had only a couple of days to make up her mind, and while she hadn't wanted to admit it at the time, she had already made her decision before he even pulled away from the curb outside her apartment. She just didn't like that she'd had to make it, or that it favored him. The crowdfunding idea had been fun to bat around with her friend but she'd known all along that it wouldn't work. Without her savings she had only one option left.

"Kayla?" he prompted.

"Sienna and I went away for the weekend. It was a pre-existing arrangement."

"I see. So rather than tell me that, you thought you'd just make me wait? Make me wonder if you'd skipped town altogether? You realize that avoiding me like that would have endangered your case, don't you? Sienna is the subject of a custody dispute. A good lawyer could make a case that what you'd done could be construed as abduction." He paused before adding, "I have very good lawyers."

Kayla stiffened, ready to argue—but decided against rising to the bait. It would just be a delaying tactic. She couldn't push back this conversation any longer.

"I'm sorry," she said, shifting and focusing her attention on a different section of his back. He groaned as she found another knot and began to work it out. "But if it's any consolation, I have reached a decision."

She felt him stiffen beneath her hands, probably undoing all her hard work.

"And?" he asked.

"I have a few conditions."

"Of course you do." The sarcasm of his words hung in the air. "Come on, then. Spit them out."

"I will consider a fifty-fifty shared custody agreement. In return, you will cover all my pre-and postnatal costs of a medical and personal nature."

"Personal?"

She bit back a smile. She'd been scrimping and saving every penny for the last five years so that she could support the children she planned to have. If Van was willing to throw all that money at lawyers to drag her through family court, he shouldn't mind using some of his seemingly endless funds to let her pamper herself a bit for a change. It wasn't a deal breaker, of course, but it would be a nice benefit to repay her for being cooperative. "Well, I'll need a new wardrobe, for a start."

"Why do I feel like you're not taking this seriously?" he muttered.

"Oh, I'm definitely serious."

Van slowly counted to ten and forced himself to relax, not an easy thing to do when she seemed hell-bent on extracting as much discomfort from his muscles as she possibly could. Hell, and people regularly paid for this? But, he reminded himself, he was a step closer to getting exactly what he wanted. He needed to go softly.

"Anything else?" he asked, forcing his voice to remain civil.

"When you present my mandates to me in an acceptable document, I'll think about doing what you want."

"And you'll agree to give up work and move into my house?"

He could feel her tiring already. This work was intensely physical. Even he could see that she wouldn't be able to sustain the energy she needed to do this for long into her pregnancy.

"I'll need to work out notice, but, yes, if that's what it takes."

She was beaten and she knew it. He wanted to punch the air and shout "Hooah!" but he knew when to take his victories like a man.

"I'll see to the paperwork. Do you have a doctor already? Your records will need to be transferred to someone closer to home."

"I'll give you the information you need before you go today."

She leaned into the strokes she worked along his back now, putting her entire body weight into the massage. Now that she wasn't intent on punishing him, it felt great—a little too great. He reasserted control over his body, forcing every part of him to relax, to stop fighting her mentally and physically. He had what he wanted. Her motions grew lighter, gentler, and then, after the merest pressure at the base of his spine, she wiped his back with a warmed towel and then he heard her step away from the table.

"That's it—you're done. You can get up when you're ready."

He heard the clink of a glass and the sound of running water as he rolled over and got up. She handed him the water.

"Here—you'll need to drink. The last thing you need is a toxic headache."

He accepted the glass, noting that now that the massage was over, she assiduously avoided touching him. She turned and he watched as she consulted her phone and then transferred a name and details onto a piece of paper.

"There, my obstetrician's details."

He glanced at the small sheet before pocketing it. "When will you move in?"

"You haven't presented me with the agreement yet."

"Still hedging, Kayla?"

She sighed. "I guess. I don't like giving up my independence, and aside from that, I'm not convinced this is going to be the best thing for any of us."

How could it not be? "You say you have to work out notice here. What's that—a month? Two weeks?"

"A month," she confirmed. "And I need to give my landlord a month's notice, too."

"I'll see to it that the agreement is delivered to you tomorrow morning. You'll be here?"

She nodded. "I have a full day, so, yes, I'll be here."

He studied her a moment. In every line of her body, she looked defeated.

"It's not a prison sentence, Kayla. You won't regret this."

She returned his gaze just as steadily. "I already do but I don't really have a choice, do I?"

He could lie to her, but he wouldn't. "No, you don't."

"You know the way out," she said, turning her back to him.

He waited a few more seconds, feeling somehow at a disadvantage. He should have been filled with a sense of victory. He had exactly what he'd asked for, albeit with an amendment regarding custody. And that wasn't really so much of a hurdle—sooner or later Kayla was bound to show her true, irresponsible colors. When that happened, it would be easy enough for him to press for full custody. If her wanderlust kicked in again, she might even give it up without a fight. This was all working out perfectly.

So why did he feel like he'd lost something even bigger?

Six

It shouldn't have been this easy to just pack up one life and move to another, Kayla thought as her car rounded a curve in the road. Still, she'd spent most of her life reinventing herself and moving on to new pastures, hadn't she? She had to look at this as simply another adventure. As she pulled up outside the address, she turned back to check on Sienna, who'd been awake for most of the journey from their apartment to this aerie overlooking the Pacific Ocean.

Kayla wasn't generally impressed by what she'd always deemed excesses of grandeur but this place was really something. Through massive iron gates, she spied the house—a double-storied Mediterranean-inspired mansion. Her heart began to hammer in her chest. Van lived *here*?

The property looked huge—certainly far too big for a man living on his own. Maybe things wouldn't be so bad after all. In a house this size, it would be easy not to have to see him.

The building itself was imposing yet welcoming at the same time. Situated as it was at the top of the hill, it would command an impressive view of the ocean, and even though it looked isolated in its setting, it was still relatively close to both Monterey and Carmel. He had the best of everything, didn't he? And now he had her and Sienna, too.

In front of her, the gates began to open.

"Looks like this is us," Kayla commented, putting her old Toyota into gear and driving through.

She looked back in her rearview mirror and saw the gates slide closed behind them. The sensation of feeling trapped fluttered against the periphery of her mind. *Don't be stupid*, she told herself. *This is the best thing for Sienna and the baby. If it wasn't, you wouldn't be here.* Van had been right about the physical toll her pregnancy would put on her body and her ability to continue working. Once the hyperemesis gravidarum had hit, she'd been unable to handle being around so many different people with all the various scents they carried with them, not to mention the aromatic oils they used in the clinic. Susan had managed to find another therapist to take on her position and had released her from her notice with good wishes for her future. Even though she could have moved to Van's house earlier, she'd stubbornly stayed on at the apartment until the very last day of her lease.

Kayla rolled to a halt near the front entrance. A movement there alerted her to Van's presence. Even from here she could see the concern painted on his face. It struck her that she should probably have let him know that a diaper change for Sienna midjourney had led to a severe bout of nausea for her that had forced her to take a long driving break. It had taken almost an hour before she could keep down a few sips of water and they'd been able to head on their way again. One of the worst things about being this sick through her pregnancy was that she'd had to wean Sienna rather abruptly, too. She barely kept enough fluid down to stop herself from becoming dehydrated, let alone enough to be able to continue to nurse.

Before she could even turn off her ignition, he had her door open.

"Did you have trouble on the way? I tried to call you."

"I'm sorry. I forgot to charge my phone before we left and we had to stop on the way."

She neglected to include her reasons for stopping, not wanting Van to lord her frailty over her again. Although he was unaware of just how sick she'd been, he'd still been reluctant to let her drive herself, but she'd been adamant, holding on to every last second of independence—and it hadn't been fun at all. She felt his gaze rake over her, sensed he wasn't happy.

He cleared his throat and offered her his hand. "It isn't important now. You're here and that's what matters."

There was a possessive note in his voice that made her give him a second glance. The lines of worry had already begun to fade from Van's face as he helped her from the car. He was dressed more casually than she was used to seeing him and for a moment she was reminded of the old Van. But the old Van didn't exist anymore, she told herself as she moved to the rear passenger door to release Sienna from her car seat. And this version, in a pair of well-washed jeans that were faded in all the right places and a T-shirt that fit his muscled shoulders just a little too snugly, was an unknown quantity. One that was equally as unsettling as he was infuriating.

Van gently elbowed her aside. "Here, let me do that."

"It's okay. She's just woken and she's not used to you yet. She might cry."

"She'll have to get used to me sooner or later," he said,

pulling open the door on Sienna's side and reaching in to unsnap the child restraints.

Kayla stood back, the impact of his words sinking in. She'd been so focused on finishing up at work and packing and sorting her things for going into storage that she hadn't looked past moving day. This was to be her new reality—their new home, together—at least until the new baby was weaned. The somber finality of the thought brought back that trapped feeling she'd experienced just a few minutes ago. She pressed one hand to her lower belly and drew in a deep breath.

In the process of lifting a surprisingly amenable Sienna from her car seat, Van turned his head to look at Kayla. His brows drew into a frown.

"Are you okay? You're a bit pale."

"Always telling me how great I look, Van," she said with an attempt to lighten his intensity. "I'm just tired, that's all."

"You should have let me drive you, like I offered. Or at least allowed me to provide you with a driver."

"Self-sufficient to the core, that's me," she emphasized and gave a reassuring smile to Sienna, who was looking from Van to Kayla and back again. "Besides, I can't really see you driving that," she said, gesturing to her dented but generally reliable car.

"I don't want to see *you* driving that," he commented with a disparaging glance at the car.

The baby looked uncertain about the man holding her, but when Van held her close and smiled at her, she answered with a reciprocal, albeit slightly more gummy, grin. Kayla watched him with interest and saw the exact moment that he became captivated by his daughter. The two locked gazes. Suddenly the expression in Van's green eyes deepened, as if he'd just realized something incredibly important, and his smile took on a tenderness that hadn't been there before. Sienna reached up and patted his cheek, a little chortle of delight escaping as she felt the stubble on his cheeks against her tiny palms.

Instead of feeling relief that at least Sienna wasn't about to throw a screaming fit at being held by a stranger, a curious sense of loss filtered through Kayla. Was this what she'd really been fighting all along? The truth that she would be sharing Sienna's affections with Van? Surely, she wasn't that petty—was she? Maybe she was, she forced herself to admit. Maybe both she and Van needed to make some major adjustments. The idea was a difficult fit and certainly not one she embraced.

Van pressed a kiss to Sienna's head, then looked up. "Come on inside, I'll get Jacob to put your car in the garage later. Just leave the keys in the ignition."

Kayla raised her eyebrows. "You have staff?"

Van cracked a half smile in her direction. "Does that make me a capitalist pig? If so, I'm sorry, but, yes, I have staff. Jacob, who takes care of the cars and the grounds, Imelda, his wife, who looks after the house and meals, and now, Annabelle, who will be helping you with Sienna."

"A nanny?" She couldn't keep the shock and irritation from her voice. "I told you when I signed your agreement, I don't need a nanny."

"*Our* agreement," he corrected. "Just think of her as a precautionary measure."

"Is this another attempt to undermine my position as Sienna's mom? Or are you planning ahead, hoping she'll transfer her affections to another woman so that when I'm forced to share custody with you, she won't miss me so much?"

"Jeez, Kayla, relax. Annabelle is here to help you—to take care of the day-to-day things that will become harder for you as time progresses, especially if you don't start to feel better soon. She comes well recommended and worked for years as a pediatric nurse before becoming a nanny. Whatever your feelings about me, don't judge her until you meet her, okay?"

"I'm ten weeks now. I should start to feel better anytime soon. Besides, I'm responsible for Sienna's care and I don't see why that should change just because I'm pregnant." She sniffed indignantly. "If you want this Annabelle to have a highly paid holiday in your luxury home, go ahead. No skin off my nose. I only hope she doesn't get bored."

Van laughed. Honest-to-goodness laughed from deep in his belly. It made Sienna's eyes open wide, before she too chuckled along with him. Feeling like little more than an outsider with her own dysfunctional little family, Kayla wrapped her arms around herself.

"I don't see what is so funny," she said stiffly.

Van was still smiling when he spoke. "Most women I know with kids would love to have a nanny to help out. Tell me you're not just being possessive about the time Annabelle will be spending with Sienna."

The way he phrased it, it sounded like a foregone conclusion that this Annabelle would be taking over Sienna's care. It also made Kayla sound like a bit of a brat.

"I'm her mother. It's only natural that I would be uncomfortable about yet another *stranger*," she said with a sharp look at Van that hopefully left him in no doubt that she lumped him in that same category, "taking care of my daughter."

"And yet you were happy to leave her with a drug addict in your own home?" Van replied equally piercingly.

"I didn't know—"

"You can rest assured that very thorough checks were made into Annabelle's suitability as a caregiver for Sienna. Now, if you've quite finished grandstanding over things you can't change, let's go inside."

Van started toward the front door with Sienna in his arms. Torn between stamping her foot in frustration and following him, she chose the latter.

Kayla was so ruffled she almost didn't notice the opulent entrance of Van's home, but a slight wave of dizziness caused her to pause in her steps as she crossed the threshold in Van's wake. She'd heard the phrase *take your breath away* a time or two and had thought it hugely appropriate when faced with the majestic vistas that nature provided during her world travels, but she had to admit that the foyer to Van's house was certainly spectacular. The double front doors opened into a two-storied and spacious tiled entrance. From where she stood, she saw a massive staircase with an ornate balustrade swirling to the upper level, and directly ahead, she spied a formal sitting room with wide floor-to-ceiling windows that opened out onto a terrace on the other side.

She took a few steps forward. Light spilled in through the windows, making everything look fresh and spacious and gilded, while the pale gold tile floor gave it an inviting warmth. To one side she glimpsed a formal dining room, to the other what looked like a wood-paneled library.

"I can't believe you have all this house for just one person. Oh, and staff," she added, the last part heavily weighted with derision.

"It's home," Van answered plainly. "You know what I came from. I promised myself that when I could, I would have the best of everything. I have it now."

He hadn't said a lot but Kayla felt as though she'd been very firmly put in her place. It made her feel as if her snide remarks had been both nasty and unnecessary. She was so busy focusing on what she perceived to be his materialistic overindulgence she'd forgotten where he'd come from. What he'd endured. His simple summation of this house being home struck her hard. She was about to apologize when Van continued.

"You're probably imagining how many homeless people you could fit in here, right?"

"It crossed my mind," she admitted.

"You don't have to live on the streets to be homeless," Van gestured through to an archway. "Come through here and meet Imelda. She'll give you two something to eat before showing you the house. Don't worry about your things. Jacob will bring them in shortly."

"Van?"

He paused in the archway, father and daughter perfectly framed and driving home to her just how much her life and Sienna's would change from this day forward.

"I'm sorry for being such a bitch."

He shrugged and didn't say anything, but his eyes never left her face. She felt her cheeks heat under his perusal. He and Sienna looked perfect together, both dark haired and green eyed. No one seeing them could doubt their fundamental connection to one another. Again, she felt as though she was the outsider, peripheral to everyone's needs. The sensation lasted until Sienna thrust out her chubby little arms and said, "Mamma!"

It galvanized Kayla into action and she reached for her daughter. *Her* daughter, she reminded herself, no matter the little girl's biological ties to the man holding her. Sienna was the child of Kayla's heart, as was the baby steadily growing inside her. She didn't need a legal agreement to know that. She took Sienna in her arms and felt a sense of rightness, of spiritual balance, ease through her.

Van continued to watch her. "I realize this is upsetting for you, Kayla, but it's for the best. For everyone."

"Sometimes it's just a bit hard to see that," she admitted, nuzzling the top of Sienna's head and immediately regretting it as her nose filled with the scent of the baby's shampoo. She swallowed back the fresh wave of nausea that threatened.

It was ridiculous to suddenly feel bereft when Sienna transferred to Kayla's arms, Van told himself, and yet it gave him some insight as to how she was probably feeling about having someone else step in to be Sienna's parent when she was used to having her daughter to herself.

"Yeah, well, we both have a lot of adjusting to do," he commented.

For him, everything so far had been about the logistics of getting them here. The legal agreement, getting confirmation that Kayla had indeed relinquished the lease on her apartment and given notice at her work. None of those were things he could ultimately control, and despite what he'd said, he found that now that the shock of discovering he was a father had worn away, he had no desire to make Kayla's life truly difficult. He simply had to do what was best for his children.

In the kitchen, he introduced Kayla to Imelda, who cooed over the baby with glee. He could see Kayla begin to relax by increments.

"Isn't she just a love?" Imelda said with a doting smile. "And so like her daddy. Oh, that reminds me. Mr. Murphy, your Little Brother will be here tomorrow morning as arranged. He rang to confirm while you were outside."

"Little brother?" Kayla asked, looking at him in surprise.

"Well, not his real little brother," Imelda continued without missing a beat before Van could reply. "He's involved in the Big Brothers Big Sisters organization as a mentor. Young Alex has no dad and when he started to get into trouble at school, his mom knew he needed a strong male role model to help her guide him. Ben's gone from being a truant to an A-plus student since he's been matched with Mr. Murphy. You should see them together. You'd think they were both twelve year olds when they're in the pool. I swear my Jacob has to top it up every time Alex comes to visit."

"I can imagine," Kayla murmured absently.

"And Alex is just going to adore this young lady, here," Imelda continued, chucking Sienna under her chin.

Van felt his cell phone vibrate in his pocket, reminding him he still had work to attend to.

"Imelda, could you give these two ladies something to eat and then show them their rooms? I need to check in with the office but I'll be down for dinner."

Before he could leave the kitchen, however, Kayla bristled again.

"Rooms? Sienna has always slept in the same room as me. I don't want her to be more unsettled than necessary," Kayla remonstrated.

He sighed. Did everything have to be a battle with her?

"Your rest is vitally important. Annabelle is scheduled to take on night duties as required. Honestly, Kayla, have you seen yourself lately? You look like you could do with a decent night's sleep. How about you see if Sienna will settle in a room of her own first? If it distresses her, we'll move her in with you."

Kayla stared back at him and for a moment he thought she might argue, but then she seemed to weaken, her entire body drooping as if she'd had all the wind taken out of her sails.

"That sounds reasonable," she answered woodenly.

He reached out and put a hand on her shoulder. "Thank you, Kayla. I mean that."

He knew how much it must have cost her to give in to him on any point, especially on something that meant she'd have less time with Sienna. But he was adamant.

She really did look worn out and it made him feel guilty, even though he'd checked on her frequently by telephone. He should have been following up with her face-to-face this past month, but due to having to personally oversee a security installation overseas, he hadn't had an opportunity to visit her—and he hadn't made one, either, a little voice reminded him.

So what if he was trying to avoid conflict? She'd insisted everything was going fine, that she was fine, that the baby was fine—it had gotten to the stage where if he heard the word *fine* one more time, he thought he'd tear his hair out. But it was clear everything was not fine. She was pale and thinner than he remembered and exhaustion shadowed her eyes. If he'd had any qualms about coercing her into staying here with him, they flew out the window now.

"Can I offer you anything to eat, Ms. Porter? And what about Sienna? You'll need to let me know what foods she likes."

At the mention of food, Kayla went distinctly green around the gills. A stricken look passed over her face and her blue eyes sought him out, silently beseeching him for help. Sudden understanding dawned. He took Sienna from her arms and quickly handed her to the surprised housekeeper.

"Call Annabelle down to meet her charge," he said to Imelda quickly before taking Kayla's hand and leading her to a downstairs bathroom.

She barely had time to utter a brief thanks before she began to dry heave. Not knowing what else to do, and reluctant to leave her when she was obviously in such distress, Van rinsed a small hand towel under the cold tap and wrung it out before lifting her hair from her neck and gently placing the towel against her skin. He then continued to hold her hair to one side while she knelt on the tiled floor. After what felt like forever, she appeared to settle down.

"Thank you," she said shakily as he helped her to her feet. "I'm sorry you had to see that."

"It's hardly the first time I've seen you throw up," he said, remembering all too vividly Kayla's first highly illegal and disastrous encounter with alcohol when she was still a teenager. He and Sienna had taken turns looking after her that night so she wouldn't get in trouble with her parents. "Is this what happened to make you late on the way down, too?" he asked.

It was deeply concerning to realize she'd probably been driving while feeling so ill. It couldn't have been good for her concentration, let alone her and Sienna's safety.

"I didn't expect it to be so bad today. Honestly, it's been getting better, but…" Her voice trailed off.

"Kayla, really, you need to learn to accept help. It's clear you can't manage on your own. At least not until this has passed." If it passed, he reminded himself. The literature he'd read on the subject said some women struggled with hyperemesis gravidarum their entire pregnancy. Even beyond it.

"Well, you've seen to it that I don't have a choice in that now, haven't you," she snapped. She sighed again and shook her head. "I'm sorry, Van. I'm being evil today. This situation…it just makes me feel as if I've lost all say in my own life."

He studied her. This was the most honest she'd been with him since breezing into his office a couple of months ago and dropping her bombshell into his carefully ordered world.

"This affects me, too, Kayla," he said gently. "I appreciate it's caused the most upheaval for you, and I am sorry about that, but you can't do this alone."

"I managed okay last time."

"You weren't caring for an almost one-year-old at the same time, though. Cut yourself some slack. For Sienna's sake if not for your own. Look, I'll show you to your room—you can have a nap secure in the knowledge that Sienna is being well cared for. When you're up to it, come down and have something light to eat."

He could see she wanted to fight him on his suggestion but exhaustion obviously won out.

"Fine, take me to my dungeon," she said with a theatrical sigh.

He arched one brow at her. "Dungeon? Really? That's what you think of me? Like I'm your jailer?"

She remained silent.

"Never mind," he muttered. "Come this way. You have your own en suite bathroom, so you'll have privacy if you're feeling unwell again. If you need help, though, you can dial one on your house phone and it'll connect you to Imelda straightaway."

"And Sienna?"

"Will be competently cared for by my staff. I'll check on her again after I've been in touch with my office. Don't worry—she'll be fine."

Kayla wanted to disagree. Putting Sienna in day care had been one thing, but now that she wasn't working, *she* wanted to be the one seeing to Sienna's needs. Even so, she felt so wrung out right now that if she didn't lie down soon, she'd probably fall down. And Van had already seen her brought low enough. It really would just be simpler, while she still fought the insidious nausea that lingered no matter how many times she was sick, to give in for now.

She followed him through the house to the main stairs and noticed that he slowed his pace to match her more lethargic gait. He'd been like that as a boy, too. Whenever her shorter legs couldn't keep up with him and Sienna as they'd headed off for an adventure together, he'd always slow and allow her to catch up. Of course, he'd never missed an opportunity to tease her about it. Even so, the memory was bittersweet. Back then, neither of them would ever have imagined they'd be where they were right now.

Determined not to give in to the hormones that threatened to bring tears to her eyes at the memory, she blinked furiously and almost bumped into Van's back when he stopped at a doorway.

"This is your room. You should find everything you need here. The bathroom is through there." He gestured to one side.

"Some dungeon," Kayla commented with a wan smile as she walked over to the open French doors and private balcony.

Gauzy sheer curtains drifted in the ocean breeze, making the room look like something out of a movie set. A king-size bed was positioned so the first thing she'd see each morning was the view out over the sea. Everything was tasteful and elegant with clean and simple lines and yet it still managed to be welcoming at the same time.

Van remained just inside the door, a strange expression on his face. "You're not a prisoner here, Kayla. You can come and go as you please."

Yes, she thought as she bent her head in acknowledgment, and also no. She might not have been a prisoner, but he still most definitely controlled her life. Now and for the foreseeable future. And no matter how beautiful her cage, she didn't like it one bit.

Seven

Kayla woke to find a small bottle of club soda and a plate with a few crackers on it on the bedside table. She felt embarrassed that someone had obviously come in and found her sleeping. Not only sleeping, but sleeping so deeply she hadn't even heard the person enter.

Her mouth was dry, so she took a sip of the soda and sat back on her pillows, relieved when it stayed down. After a few minutes, she swung her feet to the floor and slowly rose and moved over to the open French doors. Below, she caught the glimmer of sunlight on the water of a pool. She wondered where Sienna was and who had her, but she didn't have to wonder for long. On the grassy area near the pool, she saw a tall, leggy brunette bent over Sienna, holding her hands and helping her to walk. *That* was Annabelle? The woman looked too young to have the kind of experience that Van had alluded to, or maybe her experience came in other areas, as well?

Kayla forced herself to change the direction of her

thoughts, putting them down to the fact that she just felt
so uprooted. She'd never been the jealous type and she
wasn't going to start now. And certainly not over Van.

It was weird. She'd spent the better part of her adult
life traveling and experiencing new things. Until she'd
lost her sister, it wouldn't have bothered her in the least
to have had to move to a luxury home for a visit. The
thing was, she'd grown used to the apartment she'd had
in Lakeshore. It had become home from the second she'd
brought Sienna back from the hospital. She'd worked hard
to afford it, to make the money to pay the rent and put
food on the table. It had been hers—she'd earned it. This
place, though? It felt as if she was living inside someone
else's dream.

That said, none of it was the nanny's fault, she reminded herself. It was childish to form a dislike for someone she'd never met based purely on a glimpse of them
in a garden while they were doing their job. The fact
that Van approved of her was also no reason to dislike
the other woman even if she did seem to be particularly
gifted when it came to grace and good looks. From the
grass, Sienna gurgled and laughed, the sound bringing a
faint smile to Kayla's face.

Her smile quickly died, though, when she saw Van
join them and reach for Sienna. The baby went happily
into her father's arms. The nanny touched Van's arm with
a lingering hand, the caress surprising Kayla and making her wonder just how long he'd known Annabelle before installing her in the house to assist in Sienna's care.
And hadn't he been on the verge of getting engaged to
some other woman? Dani something-or-other? It seemed
women came out of the woodwork to hang on his arm,
Kayla thought sourly. Sienna, of course, was oblivious to
the interplay of the two adults with her. Never one to be
overly shy of strangers, Sienna settled easily with Van and

didn't appear to be missing her mother at all. Watching the trio, Kayla felt again as though she was completely superfluous.

Van chose that exact moment to look up and he waved to Kayla and called out. "Are you feeling a little better? Come down and meet Annabelle."

Embarrassed at being caught spying on them, Kayla gave him a brief wave in response and rushed to her bathroom to freshen up. A few minutes later, showered, dressed in clothes that were less travel stained and with her hair brushed and pulled back in a ponytail, she made her way downstairs, wondering how to find her way to the lower terraced level where the pool was. Imelda bustled out from the kitchen and gave Kayla a smile and an approving nod when she saw Kayla carried the bottle of club soda.

"Mr. Murphy said for you to go down and meet them by the pool. I'll show you the way."

"Thank you," Kayla said with a smile in return. "And thank you for the snack and the soda water, too."

"Mr. Murphy asked me to leave it with you. He's very concerned for your health, and the baby's, too."

Imelda's words should have given Kayla some comfort but they made her feel more as if she was being managed—as if she was incapable of looking after herself. The housekeeper gave her a reassuring pat on the arm.

"Don't let him overwhelm you. He's just scared and isn't used to feeling that way—not to mention not being able to control what's happening. You and little Sienna are going to be good for him."

"Good for him? How?" Kayla blurted the question before stopping to think about it.

"He's locked himself up emotionally—I'm guessing that's something he taught himself to do a long time ago. It's why his engagement to Ms. Matthews worried both

Jacob and me. He didn't need someone like her. He's a man who needs warmth and care. Like a plant that requires gentle coaxing and nurturing."

Kayla frowned. Nurturing? Van?

"Oh, and listen to me. Bombarding you with conversation when you probably just want to check on your wee girl. Follow me."

Imelda turned and led the way to another staircase that stretched to a lower level of the house. Kayla noted the mostly open-plan layout of the downstairs section, with its gaming room complete with full-size pool table, what looked like a home theater and, from what she spied through an open door, a guest suite, as well. Kayla followed Imelda out onto a patio and saw Van and Sienna playing on the grass, Annabelle standing to one side and watching.

"Before I go, let me know what you'd like the little one to have for dinner and what time you'd like her to eat."

Kayla gave Imelda a list of foods that Sienna ate and what to avoid. Imelda took it all on board.

"I'll get onto it now, then. See you up in the kitchen later, perhaps? Or would you prefer to eat on the balcony outside, where you won't have to deal with too many different aromas?"

"The balcony, please. Just for today."

"Not a problem. Ah, it looks like Sienna has spied her mama," Imelda commented with an indulgent smile.

Sure enough, Sienna, who by the look of things had been rolling on the grass with her father, was now crawling at high speed across the manicured lawn. Kayla quickly moved forward and bent to swoop her baby girl up in her arms, relishing the feel of Sienna's little body pressed against hers and the sensation of rightness now that she held her again. Van followed close behind.

"The rest has done you good," he commented. "You look more like your old self."

"I feel much better now, too." She decided to take the lead when it came to Annabelle and stepped toward her, holding out her hand. "Hi, I'm Kayla Porter, Sienna's mom."

Annabelle smiled and shook her hand. "You have a beautiful daughter. I'm Annabelle Sorensen, but please call me Belle. Annabelle is such a mouthful."

The woman's smile was warm and friendly and Kayla felt something inside her ease. Apparently she'd been overreacting when she'd looked at them all before. Annabelle's manner was nothing but professional.

"Belle," Kayla repeated. "Good to meet you. I'm sorry I wasn't available earlier."

"No problem, Ms. Porter. My sister went through exactly the same thing with each of her pregnancies. I fully understand. You just tell me what you prefer for Sienna's routine and I'll do my best to ensure she's disrupted as little as possible during your time here."

And there it was. The reminder, unintentional or deliberate, that her time here was temporary. Kayla felt her smile stiffen but forced herself to relax. She had to be reading too much into Belle's statement. It seemed that being around Van was bringing out a defensive side of her that she didn't like. One that was as prickly as a desert cactus. She didn't like that person, she decided, and she was the only one who could change it.

Belle was looking at her, obviously awaiting a reply. Kayla summoned her best smile. Forget her antipathy toward Van; forget the obvious connection she'd witnessed between Van and Belle. She was going to play nice. Really nice.

"Thank you. I know it's just a job for you but I really appreciate it."

Okay, maybe not so nice, but she hadn't meant that to come out quite the way it did. Even Van shot her a startled look.

Belle was all grace and charm in response. "I know exactly what you mean. Seriously, though, I'm not here to undermine you—only to help when you need it."

There was a genuineness in the woman's voice that made Kayla feel about two feet high. Van's cell phone chimed in his pocket and he checked the screen.

"Sorry, ladies, something I have to deal with straightaway. I'll leave you to get better acquainted."

He gave them each a brief smile and put the phone to his ear. Kayla caught him saying Dani's name as he strode away toward the house. So, despite what he'd said, they were still an item? Where did that leave the beautiful Belle? More important, where did that leave her? She shifted uncomfortably, not at all happy with where her thoughts were going.

"Are you okay? Would you like me to take Sienna for you?" Belle offered.

"I'm fine, thanks."

"She has a lovely name. Van tells me it was your sister's name, is that right?"

Belle was trying hard to make conversation and Kayla forced herself to be polite.

"Yes, Sienna is her child, actually."

"Van told me. I think it's a truly wonderful thing you're doing, having your sister's children."

"Van told you? That's rather personal information to share." Kayla couldn't keep the surprise or censure from her voice. They sure must have some boss-nanny relationship if he was getting down to nitty-gritty details like biological parents.

"Oh, Van and I go way back."

Kayla just stared at the nanny, her brain working overtime. Belle looked taken aback by her expression for a moment, but then she laughed.

"Oh, no. Not like that." She shook her head and laughed again. "Really nothing like that at all. Van served with my brother. After Nicholas died, Van took it upon himself to keep an eye out for our whole family. When he heard I was taking a break from pediatric nursing, he asked me if I would be interested in taking this job on. I jumped at the chance. I mean, look at this place—who wouldn't want to live here? Even my partner is jealous. She told me not to get ideas above my station."

Kayla didn't miss the reference to Belle's partner being female. She felt herself loosen up incrementally. Not that it made any difference. She had no say in who Van shared romantic interests with anyway. So why did she feel so stupidly relieved?

Kayla woke the next morning to a gentle knock at her bedroom door, followed by the sound of a high-pitched squeal and much splashing outside at the pool. She looked at the clock and realized, with a shock, that she'd slept through the night and past Sienna's usual waking time.

"Who is it?" she called.

"It's Imelda, dear. I've brought you a light breakfast."

Imelda came in through the door, balancing a tray on one arm.

Kayla sat up in bed feeling embarrassed. "Oh, I don't expect you to wait on me."

"Mr. Murphy's orders. You're to be coddled and cared for."

"He said that?"

"Well, not in those words exactly," Imelda said with a wink. "But he's insistent that you have nothing to worry about and that you're to get your rest."

"I really need to see to Sienna," Kayla protested as the housekeeper gently steered her back to her bed.

"All taken care of. Belle brought her down for breakfast at six thirty and now she's got her out by the pool with Mr. Murphy and Alex."

Alex, Van's Little Brother. Kayla remembered he was visiting today. She was curious about how the two interacted. While Van seemed intrigued by Sienna, seeing his interaction with the older child might give her some ideas as to what kind of father he planned to be. The news that Sienna was already down there with her father and Belle triggered Kayla's maternal instinct.

"Sienna's sunscreen, it was in the side pocket of—"

"Her diaper bag. Don't worry—Belle is on it. Now, you sit back in bed and enjoy your breakfast and take your time coming down. Today is going to be a good day, yes?"

"Well, so far, so good," Kayla admitted.

She sat back on the bed and Imelda positioned the tray over her thighs before removing the cover. Neat sections of dry toast were arranged on a plate along with a small bowl of sliced fruit. Imelda poured from a small teapot into a delicate china cup.

"The tea is lemon and ginger. Please tell me if it's not to your taste and we'll find something that is."

Kayla lifted the cup to her face and cautiously inhaled. "That smells good."

Imelda smiled. "Excellent. I'll be sure to tell Mr. Murphy that his research paid off. Now, he said you're to have small meals every two hours and we're going to work to keep your fluids up, as well."

"Goodness. That makes me feel so indulged," Kayla said with a laugh that failed to conceal her irritation.

"I know it seems a bit over the top, but Mr. Murphy was deeply concerned for you when you arrived yesterday. He really only wants what's best for you and the baby."

And that was where his care began and ended, Kayla was certain—with the baby. She was just the carrier. She felt like little more than a commodity. She took a wary sip of the tea and waited for the familiar surge of nausea that usually accompanied anything by mouth at this time of day, but thankfully, her stomach decided to accept the new introduction.

"Everything okay?" Imelda asked, hovering at the edge of the bed.

"Thank you—that really is lovely."

Imelda gave her a satisfied smile. "Good. We'll see you downstairs in a bit, then?"

"Definitely."

Van knew the instant that Kayla arrived downstairs. That all-too-familiar awareness stroked the back of his neck even as Alex did his best to dunk him.

"Hold on a minute, Alex. We have a visitor."

He swam to the edge of the pool and pulled himself out of the water. Kayla approached from the house and made a beeline for Belle and Sienna, who were playing in a sheltered spot on the edge of the lawn. He searched her face for signs of the illness that had left her so run-down yesterday. He was relieved to see that Imelda's assessment of her health today had been correct. There was a faint blush of color in her cheeks and the shadows that had scored under her eyes yesterday were far less noticeable. Her skin still held a translucent quality, though—a fragility that he'd never associated with Kayla in the past. It spoke to him on a level that he was unaccustomed to these days, and the urge to protect her, and the child she carried, came stronger than he'd expected.

"Kayla," he said to acknowledge her approach. "I trust you slept well."

Her eyes flicked over his wet torso before settling back

on his face, as if she was uncomfortable with his near nakedness.

"Very well, thank you. Is this Alex?" she asked, looking beyond him to the boy who'd just come from the pool to join him.

"Yes, hi," the twelve-year-old said, offering his hand as Van had taught him. "I'm Van's Little Brother."

"Pleased to meet you," Kayla said, taking the boy's dripping-wet hand and shaking it. "I remember Van from when he was younger than you."

"Really? That's cool," the boy said exuberantly. "And you're still friends?"

Alex blushed as he realized the implication of what he'd just said.

"I'm sorry—" he started.

Kayla laughed and the sound was sweet and light and fresh. Everything he generally was not, Van thought. She always had been lightness to his dark. Sienna had fallen somewhere in between. The balancing rod that held them apart but kept them on an even keel at the same time.

"Nothing to be sorry about. I ask myself the same question," she said with a sharp look in Van's direction. "He was actually best friends with my sister, but, yeah, I guess we're still friends now."

"*Best* friends with a girl?" Alex gave Van a playful punch on the arm.

"A real guy can have girls for friends," Van retaliated.

"So where's your sister now?" Alex asked, giving Kayla his full attention again.

Van felt his gut clench and waited for Kayla's reply. She kept it brief.

"She died about five years back."

The boy looked uncomfortable, as if he'd just opened a can of worms he had no idea of how to deal with.

"Man, I'm sorry," he said with all the awkwardness of youth.

"Thank you," Kayla answered simply before smoothly changing the subject. "So, how long have you and Van been Brothers?"

Van watched as she captivated the boy—asking him questions, sharing a little of herself. She was natural with kids, he realized. She was already forming a friendship with Alex that had come a lot more quickly than his.

"And you're Sienna's mom?" Alex asked, his natural curiosity ignorant of the undercurrent that ran between Kayla and Van.

"Yes, that's right."

"How come she has a nanny, too?"

"Alex, remember we talked about this," Van interrupted. "Kayla hasn't been well and Belle is helping out."

"But Sienna is your baby, too, right? How does that work? Are you two together?"

Van thought about it carefully and settled on the clearest explanation he could come up with. "It's complicated."

"Why?"

He stifled a groan. He'd always encouraged Alex to ask questions—to delve deeper than the surface—in whatever he tackled. But this? How did you explain the situation to a twelve-year-old who was increasingly inquisitive about life? More important, how would he explain it in terms that wouldn't result in a call from Alex's mom tonight demanding to know what he was exposing her boy to? To his great relief, Kayla took over.

"Like Van said, it's complicated. Sienna always wanted kids, but she got sick and couldn't have them anymore. So I'm having them for her."

"Even though she's not alive anymore?"

"That's right."

Alex shrugged. "Sounds cool."

Van felt a surge of gratitude toward her for knowing exactly how much to say. No doubt he would have grossed Alex out with a far-too-detailed explanation.

The boy gave Van a cheeky grin and a light shove. "Last one in buys ice-cream sundaes in Carmel on the way home!" he yelled and took off back to the pool.

"Cheat!" Van answered with a laugh. "And no running beside the pool!" He turned to Kayla. "Thanks for that. He's a good kid, but he asks a lot of questions."

"No problem. You better go and join him. It's already going to cost you an ice-cream sundae. Who knows what else he'll add on if you take any longer?"

She gave him a smile that did strange things to his insides. He clamped down on the sensation. He didn't want to feel like that about Kayla. Not again. Attraction between them was a bad idea. They were polar opposites, for a start. Recognizing that he was beginning to try to rationalize his reactions, he decided it was a good time to go and join Alex. But as he started toward the pool again, he hesitated and turned toward her.

"You're welcome to come in, too. Bring Sienna in, if you like."

Oh, good one, Van, he silently growled. Like seeing her in an almost transparent muslin blouse and jeans wasn't doing stupid things to him already, he now wanted to see her in a bikini? He was certifiably nuts. She wouldn't accept. She'd made it pretty clear she wanted to be around him little more than he wanted to be in her vicinity.

Kayla appeared to consider his question. "It's still a little cold out, isn't it?"

"I can wait at the edge with a towel to wrap Sienna in the second she's ready to come out," Belle suggested from behind Kayla. "Really, the pool is lovely. Van keeps it temperature controlled all year round."

Kayla gave a brief nod. "Okay. She'd like that. She's

been a water baby right from the start. Just give me about ten minutes to get her ready, okay?"

"And you? Will you be coming in, too?" Van couldn't help asking. Maybe she'd refuse.

For a second he thought she was going to, but then she gave him another nod. "Sure."

"Okay. I'll wear some of the energy off this guy in the meantime," Van said.

He watched as she walked toward Belle, who was sitting in the shade with Sienna, and felt that uncomfortable pull in his chest again. Damn, why had he done that? He'd invited her here to his home so she could stay well while pregnant with his child. Just at the reminder that Kayla carried *his child*, the pull intensified and a rush of possessiveness swept through him.

"Damn," he muttered under his breath. No matter what he said, no matter what he did, he still wanted her. He deliberately turned his back and jogged toward the pool. Wanting her was one thing, he reminded himself. But having her was a complication he wasn't going near again—ever.

Eight

What on earth had she been thinking? Kayla asked herself as she carried Sienna upstairs to her nursery to change her into swim diapers and her little UV-protection sunsuit. She didn't want to spend any more time with Van than absolutely necessary and yet she had just agreed to do so—and swimming, no less.

For a moment she remembered how fine he'd looked coming out of the pool. His tanned skin glistening with water. Droplets caressing the contours of his body. Kayla felt her body react to the memory. Felt her heart rate increase and a flush of heat bloom deep inside. Well, at least it wasn't nausea, she told herself in an attempt to drag her attention away from just how very attractive he'd looked.

She should simply bring Sienna down ready for the water and forego a swim herself. But the lure of the pool with its temperature control was too strong. She loved the water. Loved the weightless feeling of floating. Besides, how much trouble could she get herself into when chaperoned by an eleven-month-old baby and a boy of twelve?

Even so, as she changed into her bikini, she began to reassess the wisdom of her decision. Her breasts were already fuller than normal and filled the cups of her halter-neck top and then some. This certainly wasn't appropriate wear in front of a couple of kids, she decided while checking her reflection in the mirror. She grabbed a thin T-shirt and pulled it on over the top. There, that was better. It also hid the slight bump that she was beginning to develop. She'd started to show so much earlier with this pregnancy, particularly with the weight loss she'd endured so far.

On the floor at her feet, Sienna looked a picture in her ruffled pink-and-white sunsuit.

"Aren't you just the cutest thing," she said, gathering her daughter up in her arms. "Your mommy would have loved you so much."

A wave of melancholy washed through her but she fought it back. Darn hormones were sending her emotions all over the place. But it felt good to remember Sienna, to think of how happy her sister would be to see her baby well cared for in such a beautiful place. She had to remember that she was living her dream of honoring her sister's wish—and not alone. Van was participating, too, albeit in a rather draconian way. She had to believe that things would work out the best for the children, and she had to hold on to that thought no matter what crazy ideas came into her head about Van.

Alex was out of the pool when she returned downstairs but Van remained in the water, now swimming strong laps back and forth. Some sixth sense must have warned him she'd returned because she had only just drawn close to the stairs when he stopped and swam toward her.

"Pass her to me," he said. "I'll play with her while you relax."

She was about to point out that she was perfectly capable of playing with her own daughter in the water but bit back the words that automatically sprang to her lips. She had felt a pang of envy when she'd seen Van swimming. It had been a while since she'd been able to do anything but paddle in the water with Sienna.

"Thanks," she said, handing a gleeful kicking baby to her father.

Sienna instantly splashed the water, making Van laugh. The sound was rich and deep and Kayla felt her lips pull into an answering smile. She watched the two of them as Van held Sienna carefully and began floating backward, kicking his legs like a lazy frog. They looked so perfect together, father and child. He'd missed so much of Sienna's development to date but he seemed resolved toward making the most of his time with her now. And there she went again with the waterworks springing to her eyes.

It had been her decision not to tell Van that she was having his children, even though she'd known her sister wouldn't have approved. His initial response to her a couple of months ago had made her glad she hadn't contacted him sooner, but seeing him with Sienna now was making her a little regretful on his behalf. Of course, back then, she hadn't known how he felt about having kids, but now that he had them…? Well, he certainly seemed to be adapting quickly.

If only she didn't still get this buzz of attraction simmering under her skin whenever she was around him. It made life difficult, to say the least. Did he feel the same thing, she wondered, that hint of physical memory of the passion they'd lost themselves in? Probably not. After all, if he had, he wouldn't have left without any further contact, would he? She had to remind herself of that. Had to hold on to the disappointment and anger she'd felt when she'd woken up alone after falling asleep in his arms. And hope like heck that he'd changed and that he wouldn't be a deserter when it came to his kids.

Kayla lowered herself into the pool, enjoying the texture of the water against her skin as she swam. The T-shirt she'd put on felt a little restrictive, though, as she did slow laps. She'd have to see if she could find a one-piece swimsuit. One that would see her through at least part of her pregnancy, with any luck. After a couple of minutes, she rolled onto her back and allowed herself to float.

"Enjoying it?" Van asked from nearby.

"Very much."

"Make use of the pool as much as you like. Day or night."

"Thank you."

She put her feet to the pool floor and looked at Sienna, who was happily still splashing and being floated around by Van. His hands were big and capable as they tucked under Sienna's armpits and his fingers closed around her little back. She looked safe with him, and incredibly happy. At the edge of the pool, Belle waited—her long legs dangling in the water and a thick fluffy white towel in her hands.

"Do you think she's had enough, Kayla?" Belle asked. "I'm taking Alex inside for a prelunch snack and I can take Sienna in, too, if you like."

"He's hungry again?" Van laughed. "That kid, he never stops eating."

"I'm a growing boy," Alex interjected from the deck chair where he'd been playing a game on his phone under the shade of the house's overhang.

Van turned to Kayla. "Kayla? You happy for Sienna to go with Belle?"

"I can take her," she protested.

"No, it's okay," Belle said. "You stay and enjoy your swim. We'll just be upstairs in the kitchen when you're finished."

If she refused now, she'd only appear churlish, Kayla forced herself to admit. "Okay, thanks. I won't be much longer."

"Take all the time you want," Belle answered with a smile and got to her feet so she could wrap Sienna in the towel.

Van made motorboat noises as he pushed the baby through the water, making her squeal with delight, and again, Kayla felt herself smiling in response. This really was good for her little girl. There was only so much the teachers at day care could do and this interaction with other people was opening up her tiny world beyond what she'd known to date. Kayla felt a sudden shame that she hadn't stopped to consider that aspect of what Van had to offer Sienna before today. She'd done her very best to make sure that Sienna had everything she needed, always. But she had the sense now that maybe it hadn't been enough.

Not liking the direction of her thoughts, Kayla returned to swimming laps. She kept her pace slow and steady, not wanting to wear herself out too much. Tiredness always exacerbated her nausea. She'd been at it for about ten more minutes before she felt a firm touch on her shoulder midstroke.

"You always were like a fish in water," Van said from right beside her. "But I think it's time you stopped for today."

She couldn't help it. Her temper flared. "Van, can we come to some kind of agreement that you will stop telling me what to do all the time? I'm an adult. I'm capable of looking after myself quite adequately."

"That's true," he answered, giving her a level look. "But in this case, with my baby inside you, adequate is not good enough."

She stared at him, seeing the unyielding determination in his gaze. His eyes seemed an even deeper green than usual as he stared back at her—his lashes black spikes from the pool and his dark hair matted close to his skull. He'd always been the only person who could match her in the water when they were kids and she realized that even back then, while he'd kept an emotional distance from her—trusting only her sister with his most personal secrets—he'd never physically been far away.

The thing was, when he'd been close before, she'd never felt the urge to place her hand on his bare chest the way she did now. Never wanted to trace the definition of his pectoral muscles or to run her fingers over the clearly defined six-pack of his abdomen. Or even to run the tip of her tongue along the cords of his neck and the line of his jaw.

She tried to focus on what he'd said. To draw her irritation to the surface, to use it to quench the slow-burning desire that had lit inside her, but it was useless. It seemed that, once lit, this fire couldn't be extinguished.

"Ms. Porter? It's time for your snack," Imelda called from the patio. The tension between them broke. Van took a step back and mustered up a false-looking half smile.

"See? Even Imelda thinks it's time you got out of the pool."

"Imelda is only doing what you tell her to do," Kayla muttered, annoyed with herself as much as she was with him.

But she didn't argue. Instead she swam to the edge of the pool and lifted herself out. Her T-shirt sucked onto her body like a second skin. Wet and now see-through as a result, it afforded her no protection from Van's gaze. She

stood and grabbed the hem of the garment, twisting and
wringing it to try to get rid of the excess moisture and to
pull it away from her body. Van watched her the whole
time, his eyes traveling over the prominent swell of her
breasts and lower to the tiny bump of her belly.

Color appeared along his cheekbones, and his jaw
firmed as though he clenched his teeth. Feeling uncomfortable under his stare, Kayla turned her back and walked
to where Imelda had set a small tray on a table under a
sun umbrella. Even so, she felt him continue to watch her.

Imelda picked up a robe off the back of the chair.
"Here—you should take that shirt off and wrap yourself
up in this before you get cold. It's not quite summer yet,"
she chided gently.

"Oh, that's not mine—" Kayla corrected.

"No, it's mine," Van said from behind her.

Kayla jumped. She hadn't heard him approach. He
stood behind her, swiping his body with a large towel,
which he then casually wrapped around his hips.

"But please, put it on," he continued.

Feeling awkward and already cold from the breeze
that came in off the sea, Kayla peeled the shirt off and
dropped it on the patio with a wet slap. Van had taken
the robe from Imelda and held it out for her. The second
the thick toweling wrapped around her, she felt warmer,
but no less uncomfortable as a faint trace of Van's scent
enveloped her.

"What about you? W-won't you get c-cold?" she stam-
mered.

"I'm okay for now. Will it bother you if I have coffee
with you here? I promise to stay downwind."

"Bother me? No, I don't think so." The aroma of coffee might not bother her right at this moment, but he most
certainly did. "But shouldn't you be with Alex?"

"He'll be okay for now, won't he, Imelda?"

"He's gone with Jacob for now, Mr. Murphy. They're stacking the flat rocks together for the water feature in the front garden. He's a very tactile child, isn't he?"

Van smiled, the brief flash of good humor sending a jolt of awareness through Kayla as if it was a lover's touch.

"That's one way of saying he wants to keep his fingers in as many pies as possible. Let Jacob know he's to send Alex to me if he's any bother."

Imelda smiled indulgently. "Oh, he's no bother. Jacob enjoys his company." She turned to Kayla. "Belle is putting Sienna down for a nap. She seemed a bit tired after her time in the pool. Belle said to tell you."

Kayla nodded. "That's good. She normally sleeps for an hour or so before lunch anyway."

Van raised a brow at her.

"What?" she demanded as Imelda returned upstairs.

"No dispute or argument at Belle's high-handedness?"

She took his teasing lightly. "No. She's merely following routine."

"And you have an hour or so to rest," he pointed out. "Is the food to your liking?"

Kayla looked at the plate of neatly cut raw vegetables and chose a slice of carrot to nibble on. "Tastes fine. Thank you, but I don't need to rest."

A frown of concern pulled between his brows.

"Don't bully me, Van," she interrupted before he could speak.

Van looked at her in surprise. "Bully you? Is that how you see it?"

"Tell me how else I should see it," she said. "You keep telling me what to do."

Her tone implied she was struggling to keep a grip on her temper. He'd never known her to be this fiery. She'd always had a sunny, easygoing nature. But then, he guessed a lot had changed since he'd known her truly well. And he'd never known her pregnant.

He looked at her. Dressed in his robe, she looked tiny, swamped, even. But when she'd gotten out of the pool just now, he hadn't missed the fullness of her breasts or the intriguing shape of her lower belly. If he hadn't already known how taut her body normally was, he probably wouldn't have thought much of it, but he couldn't help feeling that twinge of pride and possession when he'd considered that his child was nestled there.

It was strange and terrifying at the same time. He couldn't help wondering—had he unwittingly passed on the genetic predisposition of his family to his children? He wasn't certain he'd avoided it himself. He'd cut alcohol completely from his life—but was that enough? Even if he never took a drink again, the craving for it was still written in his DNA. It could still be inherited by his children.

He looked at Kayla's face and realized she was still waiting for his response. He scrambled to remember exactly what it was she'd said. Something about bullying.

"Perhaps, Kayla, it's more about caring. Have you ever considered that?"

He reached for the thermos coffee carafe Imelda had left on the table for him and poured the dark brew into his mug.

"Don't lie to me, Van. We both know you don't care about me. And I'm fine with that. Let's just agree to be honest with each other."

She shifted in her chair and the front of his robe opened, exposing the curves of her breasts and the shadowy valley between. Hell, he'd seen more of her when she was dressed in that clinging wet shirt than he did now and yet somehow this glimpse of her in his robe sent a punch of lust through his body that made his hand shake as he set the carafe back on the table.

"I'm all for being honest," he said, staring straight into her blue eyes. "Tell me, why does staying here chafe you so much?"

"I'm not used to being so—" she paused, her brow furrowing as she searched for the right word "—coddled."

"What, like an egg?" he teased, making himself keep his tone light.

"For want of a better analogy, yes. Except I'm the one coddling an egg, aren't I?"

He laughed. "Kind of. You know you can come and go as you please. Like I said yesterday, you're not a prisoner here."

"And Sienna? I can take her with me as I come and go as I please?"

He hesitated and it was enough to ignite the fuse on her anger.

"See? That's exactly what I'm talking about. I'm her mother, for goodness' sake! I carried her, I birthed her, I've been her primary carer from the day she arrived in this world. Me. Not some overpaid nanny. Not some man who suddenly wants to control every aspect about the children he stopped caring about before they were even born!"

"I care," he said softly, lethally. "Don't ever underestimate that, Kayla."

"No, controlling everything around you is not caring. It's smothering. Really, Van, you need a reality check."

"And I guess you think you're the person to give it to me?" he snapped back.

"I wouldn't even bother," she sniffed.

The gentle breeze swirled around them and he noticed that Kayla had suddenly blanched.

"Are you okay?" he asked, setting his mug down on the table.

"Oh, please. Enough with the concern. I just got a

whiff of your coffee. Neither it nor your company agrees with me. If you'll excuse me, I'm going inside."

She pushed her seat back sharply and rose from the table. The neckline of the robe gaped again, and damned if he didn't get that powerful burst of arousal once more. Despite the fighting, despite their obvious frustration with one another, his body and his brain were completely out of sync. He rose, too, putting a hand out to stop her. She stared at his fingers curled over the white toweling that encased her arm, then up at his face.

"If you don't want me to throw up on your feet, I'd advise you to let me go," she said in a voice that hinted that she was barely holding on to her control.

He let his hand drop and watched as she made her way back inside. What the hell was wrong with him? And why did she bring out the worst in him even now that he was a man grown and fully in charge of his senses? Well, fully in charge when he wasn't around her, at least.

"Van, Van! Come and see what we made!" Alex came dashing around the side of the house, dancing with excitement.

"I'm on my way," Van answered, grateful for the distraction.

And that was something Kayla Porter had always been. A distraction through and through. Maybe it hadn't been such a great idea bringing her here, but if he wanted a place in his children's lives, he had to accept she was part of the deal. For now, at least.

It didn't mean he didn't want to throttle her every now and then, though. Throttle her or something else? A tiny voice at the back of his mind poked at him, reminding him of his reaction to her just now. No, he wasn't going there, he thought. Not again. Because he knew that if he did, he'd never be able to walk away like he had the last time.

Nine

After her altercation with Van, Kayla worked hard to steer clear of him over the next few days. It wasn't too difficult. Early each morning, he drove to the Monterey Airport and piloted his helicopter to work in San Francisco. And he put in long hours. Whether that was all work and no play was none of her business, she reminded herself firmly as she looked at the clock in the main entrance on her way upstairs. So what if it was nine thirty and he was still nowhere to be seen? However, for a man who'd said he wanted to have more to do with his children, he was doing a mighty poor job of spending time with his daughter.

And there she was again. Annoyed at him. Angry. Neither of which were her natural state. She'd always been sunny natured. Cheerful. Able to look on the bright side of pretty much everything all the time. But living under the same, albeit expansive, roof as Van Murphy was totally doing her head in. The last few nights, she'd resumed doing a little yoga before bed. It helped her to center herself and she certainly needed centering right now.

Since she was already dressed in a loose-fitting pair of stretch pants and one of her favorite tie-dyed shirts, she walked across to the large square of carpet in the living room and slipped off her shoes. The fibers of the carpet were thick and spongy beneath her bare feet and she wriggled her toes in them, enjoying the sensation against her skin. When was the last time she'd taken a minute just to be in the moment? Sure, she'd been doing her exercises but more as a matter of rote, not so much as a state of mind.

She lowered into a deep squat, lifted her arms and pressed her palms together in front of her as though in prayer, then closed her eyes and consciously made an effort to relax. Slowly, she breathed in and out, clearing her mind of thoughts.

It lasted all of about two minutes before her mind was racing ahead thinking about Van again. She was annoyed with him for spending so long away from home. Sienna might not know any better now, but it wouldn't be long before she got old enough to notice. Was this really the kind of father he intended to be—an absentee one?

But then she remembered watching him with Alex last Saturday. It had been quite an eye-opener. He was different with the boy than he was with her. Not as dictatorial, for a start, she noted with a huff of irritation.

Stop it, she told herself. *Stop thinking about him. Relax. Empty your mind. Breathe in. Breathe out.* She worked through her sun-salutation warm-up routine but the Big Brother version of Van continued to intrude.

She'd been intrigued by the man she'd seen. To encourage Alex to continue to strive hard, he'd even promised the kid a ride in his helicopter if he kept his grades up until the end of the school year. He was firm with the boy but kind about it. *Almost*, dare she say it, *nurturing*. It was interesting to reflect on, she thought as she moved into her first pose with an ease and familiarity from years of experience. Maybe he was offering Alex what he'd missed out on all those years as a child himself.

Heaven knew his parents were stricter than most. His family situation had been so very different from hers growing up. Her parents had always made a fuss over a good report, having a special meal at home or buying a small trinket of one kind or another. Every achievement was celebrated, while any failures were looked upon as an opportunity to learn and receive encouragement. Van's parents, not so much. If he failed a class, or even got a bad grade on a test or a paper, he'd get a beating. But he'd always brush the bruises and scrapes off as a result of being clumsy, never admitting what had really happened.

He'd spent a lot of time at her house. She could still see him sitting at the table of her parents' dining room, watching silently as her dad made a little speech when she'd won a creativity award in elementary school. He'd kept himself aloof, yet he was clearly yearning to be a part of the warmth that had made their family's house a home. Was that what he'd meant when he'd told her this was home for him? That he wanted to re-create the sense of belonging that her family had always taken for granted? It was a question to tuck away and ponder later, she decided.

Kayla began her standing asanas, finally feeling as though she was in the moment. She was balanced on one leg, her hand holding the tip of her left foot as she extended it out beside her.

"Is that safe?"

As if her thoughts had summoned him, there he was. Standing right behind her with yet another disapproving frown creasing between his brows. Kayla lowered her leg and planted both feet firmly on the ground.

"If it wasn't, do you think I'd be doing it?" she countered in as reasonable a tone as she could manage.

While part of her was strangely relieved to see him, another was frustrated that just as she'd managed to focus on her meditation, he'd come along and yanked her back out of it.

He looked tired. His tie had been pulled loose and the top two buttons of his pristine white shirt were undone, exposing the hollow at the base of his tanned throat. She'd kissed him there, she remembered before snapping her mind back out of the past.

"Is everything okay?" she asked.

"Yeah, just busy. We're ironing out glitches in a new system and it's the usual—whatever can go wrong will go wrong."

"Sounds like you could use a bit of yoga yourself." She smiled. "Or a stiff whiskey."

His face froze. "I don't drink."

"Oh, I didn't realize you'd given it up. Any particular reason?" she probed without thinking. "Oh, heck, that was probably a bit personal. I'm sorry. You don't have to answer that if you don't want to."

He gave her a cursory smile and ignored her question altogether. "Have you made plans for tomorrow?"

"Plans? No, not really. Sienna's cutting a tooth at the moment but if she's not too grouchy, I thought I could take her to the aquarium in Monterey. I considered the zoo, but, you know, too many smells."

She gave a self-deprecating laugh. The nausea was more manageable now that she was getting so much more rest, but she didn't think she was up to facing the various aromas to be encountered on a late spring morning at the zoo.

"Sounds like a good idea. Do you mind if I join you?"

Kayla couldn't hide her surprise. "Isn't tomorrow a business day for you?"

"One of the perks of being the boss. I can take time off when I want. But I don't have to, if you'd rather take her on your own."

Kayla was reminded of the aloof boy of her childhood. Always on the fringe. Never inserting himself where he feared he wasn't wanted. She made a decision.

"No. I mean, she'd love it if you came, too."

Van's eyes met hers, a flicker of something in their emerald depths. "And you?"

Her breath caught in her throat. It was hard to put a label on how she felt about deliberately spending time with him. "I'd appreciate the extra pair of hands with Sienna, of course."

The flicker of light she thought she'd seen reflected in his eyes dimmed a little. "Have you been feeling better this week?" he asked, moving into the sitting room and relaxing onto one of the deep chairs.

"Each day seems to get a little better."

He nodded in apparent approval. "That's good. And you haven't been overdoing things?"

Kayla sighed. "No, your troops have made sure I barely lifted a finger all week."

His mouth quirked into that sweet half smile that seemed like a kindness compared to his usually somber visage. "They had their orders. You're looking a lot better for the rest. What time were you thinking of heading out tomorrow?"

"They don't open until ten, and Imelda tells me it only takes about fifteen minutes or so from here."

"So, leave at oh-nine-forty-five?"

She fought the urge to salute him. "Sure, that sounds fine. But like I said, it'll depend on how grumpy Sienna is."

"With both of us to distract her, I'm sure we'll man-age." He stifled a yawn. "If you'll excuse me, I'll head up to bed."

A vision of him, naked against crisp white sheets, flooded her mind. Kayla felt a warm blush spread across her face. "Sleep well," she said, her voice suddenly more husky than normal.

Van looked back at her and for the briefest moment she thought she saw that flare in his eyes again—something primal and heated. Something that reminded her of the man she'd taken to bed five years ago. Kayla's mouth grew dry, every cell in her body attuned to his next move. But all too quickly that look was gone, leaving her wondering if she hadn't imagined it after all.

She stood there transfixed by her imagination as he left the room and headed up the main staircase. A tremor rippled through her. He was an attractive man; of course she'd have some kind of physical reaction to him, espe-cially knowing what they'd been capable of together, but this felt like something more. Something she really didn't want to examine any further. Something that could be-come very messy emotionally if she allowed herself to think about it too much.

Hormones, she told herself. *You're just in crazy mode, where everything either drives you mad, makes you cry or...or turns you on*, whispered a little voice in the back of her mind. Kayla shook her head, as if the physical ac-tion could rid her of the reality she didn't want to admit. The truth that despite his deserting her after their one night together, despite the way he'd more recently run roughshod over her and taken control of her life, she still wanted him.

Wanted, yes. But having was another thing entirely and it so wasn't going to happen, she resolved sternly. Not only because she didn't want it to, but because he so clearly didn't, either. She wasn't about to set herself up for complete rejection again. It had been hard enough the last time. Now she was so much more vulnerable.

Kayla tried to resume her yoga routine but her mind simply wouldn't let go for long enough for anything to flow. Giving it up altogether, she switched off the lights and made her way to her room. Hours later she still couldn't get to sleep. Her mind kept offering alternative scenarios of where things could have gone with Van after he'd said good-night. Scenarios that left her feeling as though she had an itch somewhere that, no matter what, she simply couldn't relieve.

Van was up early the next morning and was surprised to find Kayla already downstairs with Sienna.

"Belle not up?" he said after wishing them a good morning.

He studiously tried to ignore the fact that Kayla was obviously still in her pajamas. The tank top clung to her full breasts and the bottoms hung low on her hips, exposing the slight roundness of her belly.

Kayla gave him a long-suffering look. "You can't expect the woman to have night duties with Sienna and then be up at the crack of dawn, as well. Besides, it's her day off today. You know, that time when normal people do normal things like, oh, I don't know—not work, maybe?"

He looked at her in surprise. "Did you get out on the wrong side of the bed this morning?"

"No, I did not and my morning has been perfectly lovely."

Until now. Even he could hear the unsaid words hanging in the air.

"Dadadadadad!"

Both adults turned to the baby in the high chair. Van felt a rush of elation thrill through him.

"What did she say?"

"You heard her. She's been saying it since she woke up this morning."

Ah, maybe that explained the bad mood, Van thought. He flashed a smile at Sienna, who reached out her arms toward him.

"You'll want to wipe her hands first," Kayla commented.

She rose from the kitchen table and moved toward the counter, where she rinsed a small muslin cloth under the tap before handing it to him. Van looked at her a moment before understanding. She expected him to wipe the baby's hands? That should be interesting, he thought. Aside from occasionally holding Sienna and playing with her in the pool the other day, he'd actually had very little to do with her. Right now a full-combat mission would have been less daunting.

"You'll get best results if you hold her lower forearm with one hand and then use your other with the cloth to clean her hand. And make sure you get between her fingers, too," Kayla advised.

She leaned against the counter and eyed him with a look that, if he hadn't known better, he'd have said was almost gleeful.

"What exactly is that muck she's got on her hands?"

"Mashed banana mostly."

"Mostly?"

"And some cereal. Sets pretty hard if you don't wash it out of your clothes or hair straightaway. Stains, too."

"Dadadadadad!" Sienna exclaimed cheerfully, suddenly putting her hands on her head and transferring a lot of the mess into her hair.

"Oh, hell, now what?" Van asked, instantly feeling utterly helpless.

Kayla chuckled. At first the sound was slight, as if it

had slipped out despite her best attempts not to laugh, but then it grew and took shape until she was in paroxysms of laughter.

"Your face," she wheezed between bouts of uncontrolled laughing. "I wish you could see your face."

Van shifted uncomfortably. He'd survived the regular beatings his adoptive dad had given him. He'd spent the better part of ten years in the army seeing active service. He'd built a multimillion-dollar company from the ground up. He would not let this defeat him.

"C'mon, Sienna. Be a good girl for your daddy," he coaxed.

He moved forward carefully, holding the cloth as if it was some magic talisman or enchanted weapon.

"She's a baby, not a wild animal," Kayla observed. Another chuckle escaped her.

The baby laughed, too, and the sound of her full-bellied little laugh coaxed a similar response from Van.

"Maybe I should just take her outside and hose her," he said.

"Yeah, I know it's tempting but I don't think that's completely necessary. Go on, she won't bite. Or are you scared?"

Her last words hardened his resolve. He surged forward, took one little arm and wiped the hand as quickly as he could, then did the same with the other. Sienna, of course, immediately put her hands back in the slop in her bowl and applied them straight to her hair again. Behind him, Kayla exploded into laughter once more, generating even more baby giggles from Sienna.

"You know, you really shouldn't encourage her. These are not nice table manners," he said grimly.

He took the bowl from the high-chair tray and set it in the kitchen sink before rinsing off the cloth and approaching Sienna again—this time with a determination that he would not fail. She tugged her tiny hands as he cleaned them but he was firm as he gently wiped them. Then he did the best he could with her hair before unbuckling her harness and lifting her from the chair.

"How's that?" he said as he faced Kayla again, feeling ridiculously triumphant.

She nodded slowly and pursed her lips. "Not bad. Needs work, but not bad at all."

She took the cloth off him and rinsed it out before teasing Sienna with it while managing to remove the last of the goop from her hair. He watched in surprise at how adept she was.

"You're really good at that," he commented.

"I've had a few more months of practice."

It struck him how much she'd dealt with on her own for so long—and how well she'd coped. He'd never have thought it of her. She'd always been the one that got into trouble at school with her teachers—mostly for daydreaming and not turning in her homework or assignments on time. She'd eschewed attending college, instead choosing to take a year to indulge her wanderlust. A year that turned into several years as she traveled around the world. But she'd been there for her sister when crunch time came and Sienna really started to go downhill, he remembered. Which was a damn sight more than he'd been.

"I know I've never acknowledged this before, but you've done a really good job with Sienna," he said in all seriousness. "She's a beautiful baby. Thank you."

"Well, I didn't have her for your sake," Kayla responded tartly, but he could see the gleam of pleasure that glowed in her eyes at his words.

"I know that, but I'm grateful."

"Grateful that I didn't tell you that you were going to be a father?"

He absently pressed his lips to the top of his daughter's

head and inhaled the lingering scents of banana, cereal and baby that mingled together.

"Yeah, I guess I am. I would have stopped you some-how and then…" He let his voice trail off.

"And then we wouldn't be here now," Kayla finished for him.

She turned away to rinse out Sienna's bowl and stack it in the dishwasher and he watched her, unmistakably drawn to the way the fabric of her pajama bottoms tightened around the curve of her bottom as she bent to insert the bowl. His body awakened in response and he tamped the sensation back. This was Kayla. The mother of the baby in his arms and now carrying another child he'd never expected to want or to love. He shouldn't feel this way about her. She straightened up and looked at him.

"What?" she demanded. "Have I ripped my pants or something?"

"No, no. Nothing like that."

"Are you okay with Sienna while I go and grab my shower? There's a stack of books in the box in the corner there," she said, gesturing to the more casual sitting room to the other side of the kitchen. "She likes to be read to."

"You're going to leave her alone…with me?"

"You're her father, aren't you? Being a dad is a bit more than cleaning her up once and taking her to the aquarium. You've been pretty scarce since we've been here. I thought you wanted to get to know your daughter," Kayla challenged him.

"I wanted to know she was safe and well cared for and that you were, too," he defended.

"But you didn't want to be hands-on?"

He hesitated. To be totally honest, he had no idea of how to be a good father. His birth parents had been deemed incapable of caring for him and at the age of three he'd been adopted by a couple who'd wanted to be parents but who'd had no idea of what it took to nurture a child. The only example of fatherhood he'd had was Kayla's own dad. He wondered if the man had ever felt as confused and cast adrift with his daughters as Van did right now.

"I don't know what I expected. But I do want to be a good father. I want to keep her safe, always."

Kayla's expression softened. "Van, you're not your father. You won't lift a hand to Sienna in anger. I know you're stronger than that. Is that what's bothering you? That you think you might turn into him?"

"He wasn't my father," Van shocked himself by answering. "I was adopted."

"You…you what? Adopted? Really? When did you find that out?"

"Not long after your sister died. I shouldn't have been surprised, really."

Kayla moved across the kitchen and put a hand on his arm. Her blue eyes reflected her concern for him. "It can't have been an easy discovery."

"It wasn't. It made me reassess things, though. And now I'm reassessing again."

He looked at the baby in his arms. A child that was a blend of both him and her biological mother. Could he do this? Could he be a good dad? Had he inadvertently passed on a potential death sentence to this beautiful sweet child?

Kayla moved a step back. He felt the loss of her touch instantly. "Every day is a new day, Van. You can start over as often as you like."

And that summed her up perfectly. Always starting over, always looking for the next adventure. He'd long considered her to be lacking in commitment, but the background search he'd ordered into her life showed that since her sister had passed away, she'd knuckled down, just like she'd said, and lived a stable lifestyle. With the exception of her providing a roof over the head of a series of home-less people, of course. But even then, she'd been trying to do something good. He understood that aside from the last incident, the people she'd helped had mostly gone on to better things and happier lives once they'd gotten onto their feet again. Maybe he needed to take a leaf out of her book for a change instead of trying to pigeonhole her where he thought she should fit.

The realization was sobering. Where exactly did he think she fitted? Right now he wanted her here to en-sure that she didn't endanger the baby she was carrying or herself—let alone the child he now held in his arms. But what about after the new baby came along? Where did he want Kayla to fit then?

Ten

It was quiet when Kayla came back downstairs after her shower. She knew Imelda wouldn't be far away when she left the kitchen, so she wasn't too worried about leaving Van with Sienna, but she was surprised that neither of them were in the room where she'd left them twenty minutes ago. She found Imelda bustling around with her customary efficiency.

"Good morning, Ms. Porter," the housekeeper said cheerfully. "Looks like when the cloud burns off, it's going to be a beautiful day."

"Yes, it does." No matter how many times Kayla asked Imelda to use her first name, the woman insisted on the more formal address. "Have you seen Van and Sienna? I left them here when I went for my shower a little while ago."

Imelda beamed. "Oh, yes. They've gone into the garage. Jacob arrived with a new delivery for Mr. Murphy. He said for you to go through when you were down."

The garage? Kayla frowned. "Do you know what that's about?"

The housekeeper continued grinning. "Yes, I do, but don't ask me what it is, because it's meant to be a surprise. You go on through and find out."

There was nothing left to do but obey so Kayla followed the corridor that led toward the three-car garage and pushed open the connecting door. She stopped in her tracks when she saw what was there. Or, more to the point, what wasn't.

"Where's my car?" she asked, looking through the open garage door to the driveway to see if it had been moved.

"Right here," Van said, straightening from the backseat, where he'd been securing Sienna in a car seat, and gesturing to the gleaming Audi SUV parked where her car should have been.

"That's not my car, Van. This isn't funny. You said I wasn't a prisoner here but now you've taken my car away from me?"

"Kayla, relax. This *is* your car now." He took a set of keys from his pocket and handed them to her. "Here— these are yours, too. Do you want to take it for a ride? Sienna's already in her seat and ready to go."

"I...I don't understand." She glanced from him to the vehicle in utter confusion. Had he just bought her a vehicle that was worth several times her usual salary? And gotten rid of her own car without even asking? "No, I can't accept it. I want my car back."

"Kayla, you and I both know that heap of rust and bolts wasn't going to last for much longer. I didn't like you driving it, especially not with Sienna on board. I've donated it to a trade school where the kids are going to use it as a project car for restoration."

Anger boiled so hot and so fast she thought steam might be coming out of her ears.

"You had no right. I owned that car fair and square. It was mine, not yours to do what you wanted with."

All the joy leeched from Van's face, and inside the car, Sienna began to whimper.

"I wanted you to be safer. All of you," he said firmly. "I did what any responsible adult would have done, and if you were more responsible yourself, you'd see that. Can't you just say thank you, take the keys and move on?"

She understood what he was saying, but that didn't make her any happier. She took a deep breath and forced herself to respond calmly.

"Van, a responsible adult would have sat me down for a conversation about how my car was unsafe for children. Then we could have discussed options for getting it repaired or replaced with something safe but affordable that I'd be comfortable in. Giving away my property without my permission and replacing it with something we both know I would have never chosen for myself isn't responsible—it's dictatorial. I'm not your employee, or one of your troops. You don't have the right to make all the decisions with the expectation that I'll just fall in line."

He looked stricken, which made her soften just a bit. Yes, he'd overstepped—but just how long had it been since there was someone in his life who *wasn't* a subordinate, just waiting to fulfill his orders? He ran a major business and had a lot of people counting on him to make the right decisions. He was used to taking the lead, and that was usually a good thing. Just not now—not here. Not with her.

"I understand that this is an adjustment for you," she continued. "You got thrown in the deep end with parenthood, and you're still trying to figure out how to make this work. And," she admitted, knowing it was only fair for her to admit her flaws, too, "I know that my past hasn't given you a lot of confidence in my ability to make smart decisions for myself. Plus, I've been fighting back on most of your actions since I got here. But I need to know that you're not going to make any more decisions like this—decisions that affect my life and my property—without consulting me. We're in this together, Van. Equal partners. And that means you can't go behind my back like this again. Is that understood?"

"Yes, I…I understand," he said. Then to her shock, he added, "And you're right. I'm sorry. I should have talked to you first. It can't be undone now but it won't happen again."

There was a pause as Kayla, baffled, tried to recall if she'd ever seen Van back down before. Finally she managed to push out a "Thank you."

"Are you up for giving the Audi a try?" he asked.

"I'll try not to hate it," she said teasingly, accepting the keys.

His lips quirked in his signature half smile, making her stomach do a little loop. "Thank you," he said gently.

Kayla got into the driver's seat while Van went around to the passenger side. He showed her how to adjust her seat and mirrors and set them as the driver default setting and instructed her on the features of the car. They were many and varied and Kayla began to wonder if she'd ever remember half the things he told her.

"Guys," she muttered under her breath.

"What's that?"

"Guys," she repeated. "Always about the features. Just tell me how to start the thing, okay?"

Van laughed, and after a quick demonstration of what to do, she put the SUV in gear and backed out of the garage.

The car moved smoothly up the driveway and out the gates. Kayla followed Van's instructions for a short ride around the neighborhood, then back to the house again. Kayla drove into the garage and turned off the engine.

"So, what do you think?" Van asked.

"What do you think I think?" she said, exasperated. "Of course I love it. I'd be mad not to. It drives like a dream, visibility is fantastic and it feels so darn good beneath my hands."

She caressed the leather-covered steering wheel and then the seat on either side of her thighs.

"You don't have to say that—we can trade it in for something else if you'd prefer."

Kayla sighed. "No, it was a good choice. I'll keep it. Thank you, Van. I'll probably spend the next twenty years terrified someone will scratch or steal it, but thank you."

"It has a remote-link antitheft device, so at least you won't have to worry about that."

She rolled her eyes. "Enough with the features. It's very nice and I'm very grateful."

Van nodded in satisfaction. "Good. Then we'll use this to go to the aquarium later?"

"Of course," she said. "There's no reason why not."

"So we're okay now?"

She looked at him, saw the seriousness behind his question reflected in his gaze. "Yes, we're okay."

His shoulders relaxed and his smile was a full one this time. "Good. Then let's go and get ready for the aquarium. I asked Imelda to pack us a picnic so we don't need to rush back."

"You've thought of everything," she said with a sprinkle of acerbity.

"It's what I do," he said simply. "I don't think I'll ever really change—but I can and will work on hearing you out when the situation involves you or the kids. I'll probably fight back pretty hard if we disagree on a situation involving your safety, though."

He was so focused on protecting the people around him. His words made her wonder when anyone, aside from her sister, had ever looked out for him, and she said so.

Van paused in the middle of unclipping Sienna's child restraint. "Why, I do, of course."

"Of course," Kayla repeated and reached out for her daughter. "Come on, Little Miss Muffet. Let's go get you all ready for the fishies, shall we?"

Sienna crowed with glee at the excitement in Kayla's voice, then shouted, "Dadadadad!" at the top of her voice.

"Yes, and your daddy is coming, too."

Van felt a keen sense of belonging that he hadn't experienced before. He wasn't sure how to take it. Or where it fit in his carefully constructed new world. He knew, of course, that once he'd decided to pursue this parenting thing, he would do whatever he could to ensure his children were properly cared for, but he hadn't looked terribly far past that. Suddenly here he was—part of what would appear to be a family outing.

His instincts told him to run for the hills—or at least the office—before it was too late, but a part of him really wanted to actively take part. To soak up Sienna's pleasure in the day. To actually be a dad. No one had ever mentioned how terrifying the prospect truly was. What if something happened? Not that anything had gone wrong so far. Kayla had said the baby was grumpy with her tooth coming through, but he'd seen little enough evidence of it today. In fact, while he'd had that quiet reading time with the child, he'd actually found himself relaxing and enjoying it.

Sienna had been captivated by the selection of pop-up books that were in the basket next to the chair. She selected one after the other herself, then demanded to be lifted into his lap, where she leaned with her warm little back against his stomach and listened as he read the words, then copied him in opening the book flaps. He wasn't sure if she was exceptionally bright for her age or if this was a normal developmental stage for a child, but he experienced an enormous sense of pride in her actions.

Pride, yes, and something else. There was an incredible closeness in having her sit with him—trusting him. He felt as if he would move mountains for her in that moment. Seeing her little fingers reach for the page flaps, listening to her baby babble as she mimicked him reading out loud. Every moment had been incredibly special and it made him realize just how much he'd missed out on already.

Suddenly the idea of shared custody with Kayla held a lot less appeal than it had before. He didn't want to be a part-time father. But maybe he needed to prove that to himself first. This past week he'd been so busy at work he'd stayed back each night as late as he could to get things done. A thought occurred to him. Had it been absolutely necessary that he be the one dotting the *i*'s and crossing the *t*'s? Wasn't that why he'd employed the best of the best in every department of his business, so he could leave when he wanted to?

But he hadn't really wanted to leave work, had he? He'd been staying at the office to avoid seeing Kayla. There, he'd admitted it to himself. What he wasn't prepared to admit just yet was why.

He heard Kayla and Sienna coming back downstairs and went into the foyer to meet them.

"Wow, you don't travel light, do you?" he teased as he relieved Kayla of a large bag she'd slung over one shoulder.

"Not me, her," she replied.

She'd changed into jeans and a colorful long-sleeved cotton top that had tiny mirrors embroidered onto the bodice. It was so her and yet chic at the same time. She was nothing like Dani and he certainly couldn't imagine his sleek business partner toting a baby and a bag with the same air of joy that Kayla seemed to carry inside her. The thought crept into his mind and took him by surprise. Even though he and Dani had planned to take their relationship toward something permanent, they hadn't wanted children, so of course he wouldn't ever have seen her like this. But it was still odd to compare the two women and find his business partner wanting. Dani had been everything he thought he wanted in a life partner. At least, that was what he'd been telling himself for the past year or more.

But she could never be the kind of woman who could simultaneously wipe drool from her child's chin and juggle a hefty tote while walking down stairs. Speaking of heavy totes… Van reached for the bag.

"Jeez, what have you got in here?"

"Just the usual. It's not like you can just sling your wallet in your back pocket and head out the door with a baby on your hip, you know."

"So I'm learning," he admitted ruefully.

"We need to stop in the kitchen for her bottle, too."

"Already on it. Imelda is putting it in its special container already for us and Jacob has probably already loaded it in the car."

"And her stroller?"

"That's in the car, too. Jacob transferred all your personal effects to the Audi last night. I don't know how you fit all that in your old car. You'll find you have a lot more room in the new one."

Kayla gave him a baleful look. "Van, you've already

convinced me to accept the new car, okay? You don't have to keep selling it to me."

He laughed, feeling genuinely lighthearted at their banter. "Good to know you haven't changed your mind in the last twenty minutes."

"I may be female but I'm not that fickle," she said with an exaggerated sniff. "Shall we get this show on the road? The aquarium will be opening soon and I'd rather go through before the crowds build."

In the end, they spent little time at the aquarium. Sienna enjoyed seeing the habitats but the sight of a giant Pacific octopus was enough to start her screaming. Fielding a mixture of concerned and sympathetic looks from the handful of other aquarium patrons, they hurried Sienna back outside. Van tried to soothe her, but ultimately, only Kayla could bring her sobbing to an end. He'd never felt so incredibly helpless in his life. If this was parenthood, he didn't want it.

The instant he thought it, he felt as if he'd betrayed something that ran deep to his moral core. It forced him to rethink, to reassess—and to realize that it wasn't that he didn't want parenthood; it was that he wanted to be the one who could soothe his daughter.

"It was easier when I still nursed her. Sometimes suckling helps her to settle. Can you get her bottle from the bag for me?"

Van reached into the tote and found the insulated container with Sienna's bottle. "Here it is," he said after removing the protective cap.

Kayla looked up gratefully. "Would you like to feed her?"

"Sure," he answered before he could overthink his reply.

"We can go get a seat over there in the shade."

Kayla started walking and Van pushed the stroller in

her wake. Once she found a bench seat, she gestured for him to sit down and put Sienna in his lap. For a moment it looked as though Sienna would start up howling again but then Van offered her the bottle and, distracted, the baby grabbed it and began to suck furiously.

"There, that's better, isn't it?" he found himself saying to Sienna.

The baby looked straight up into his eyes and inside him he felt an elemental shift. How could he have considered, even for a moment, not being a part of this—of handing over all care for this wonder of nature, this mini female version of himself, to others to look after?

"She's quite something, isn't she?" Kayla said softly. She sat down beside him and reached out to brush her fingers over Sienna's hair. "Every day I look at her and I marvel at how she was made and who she's growing up to be."

"She's a little miracle, all right," Van replied, his voice thickening with emotion.

He swallowed it back. He didn't do that kind of thing. He never showed weakness. He remained on the outer fringes, where it was safe, but as Sienna's eyes began to slide shut and she became heavier in his arms, he realized that he had fallen head over heels in love with this precious child. And he hated how vulnerable that made him.

"Should we put her back in the stroller now that she's asleep?" he asked.

"Sure, if you don't want to hold her any longer."

"It's not that—I just thought she might be more comfortable in there."

Kayla looked at him as though she could see right through him to the epiphany that had just occurred and to the terror that closed a cold fist around his heart. He held her gaze, not saying a word. She gave a little sigh

and turned to the stroller, adjusting something at the back
that lowered the seat into a reclining position.

"There you go. Just pop her in there. We can keep walking around, can't we? You're not in a rush to get back?"

"Sure. I took the day so we could spend it with Sienna.
It would be a shame to cut it short."

Through the next hour, they walked from one exhibit to
the next. Sienna woke just as they approached the otters,
and he was relieved to see she'd slept off her tantrum from
before. Then he noticed twin rosy spots had appeared
in her cheeks as she slept and he felt a pang of concern.

"Is she all right?" he said, pointing them out to Kayla.

"They're just another symptom of the teething," she
said.

Another thing he had no idea about, he reminded himself. The sense of being out of his depth just grew bigger
and bigger. How did anyone cope with it? None of the
books or articles he'd read had prepared him for the enor-
mity of all of this. It made him wonder why Kayla, who'd
always been the quintessential free spirit, had taken on
something so big—so *committed*.

"Why did you decide to have Sienna's babies rather
than donate the embryos?" he asked.

He realized that it was a question he should have asked
her right from the start months ago.

"I thought about it for a long time. It was a scary prospect. You saw how we were living when Sienna died."

He thought back to the crummy apartment Kayla had
taken him back to that night after the funeral and nodded.

Kayla continued. "All I could think of was that her
children deserved to be born to people who could tell
them about just how wonderful their mother was, and
my sister deserved to have her one life dream come true,
even if it was after she'd gone. I guess it's as simple as
that, really."

But it wasn't simple. Kayla's decision had opened up a whole new can of worms. Worms that invaded his every waking thought and a good many of his sleeping ones, as well.

"But the responsibilities attached," he started. "Didn't you stop to consider them? Don't they scare you?"

"The financial side of things, you mean?" She cocked her head to one side. "I didn't enter it at all lightly. I trained, I worked several jobs, I went without any form of luxury and I saved every penny before the transfer that gave me Sienna. I'd made a long-term plan that would let me have the babies—three, ideally—two years apart. It was only because the storage facility was closing and planning to destroy any embryos that weren't claimed that I was forced to take other action."

"Like approaching me?"

"Like approaching you," she agreed. "I didn't know what to expect when I came to see you, to be honest. I'd hoped that you'd be more open to things."

He mulled over what she'd said. "Would you have told me about the children at all if you hadn't needed my financial aid?"

A look of regret crept into her expression. "No. Probably not."

"Well," he said on a huff of air. "Thank you for being honest about that, at least."

Silence fell between them for a while and then he heard Kayla clear her throat.

"Do you wish I hadn't had Sienna? Or this baby?" she asked, smoothing her top down over her small baby bump. "Do you wish I'd just done nothing and let the embryos be destroyed when the clinic closed down?"

His heart hammered in his chest. A couple of months ago, he'd have said yes and thought nothing of it. But he couldn't even tolerate the thought now that he'd held

Sienna, read to her, cleaned her up, fed her…loved her. Loved her? Another shock wave of emotion flooded him. He didn't love. He didn't want to love. He didn't want to ever be that vulnerable to anyone—to be that hurt by anyone—ever again. But he couldn't admit any of that to Kayla, who stood there next to him holding *his* child— one who lived and breathed and grew and learned every second of the day—and be able to keep the emotional distance he knew he needed.

"It's all irrelevant now, isn't it," he heard himself say. "Sienna's here and in a few more months another baby. I'm just glad there weren't more."

He turned away from them both, ignoring Kayla's sharply indrawn breath, and focused on the otters playing in the water in front of them. He was glad there weren't more babies, he kept telling himself, because it was already next to impossible to realize that he loved Sienna. And what if it happened with the next baby, too? Loving this hard, this deeply, made him feel weak, defenseless. He knew better than most how dangerous it was to expose yourself in any way to anyone—be it an unloving adoptive parent or an unseen enemy in an unfriendly land. Could a man's heart honestly grow and expand that big and survive? Could his?

Eleven

For the rest of the outing, Van's vehement words kept playing over and over in her mind. It was her own fault for opening up the conversation in the first place but she certainly hadn't expected such a painfully blunt response. He'd begun to enjoy Sienna, she was sure of it, and his fatherly instincts to provide and protect, though they'd been slow to show, were more than evident now. And yet he'd made it absolutely clear that he didn't want more children. Why? Because of her as their mother?

Her enjoyment of the day was shattered and she found it hard to watch Van and Sienna together without wondering how much he must resent her for having brought the child into his life. When the now-infrequent nausea swept her with unusual ferocity just after they stopped for lunch, she was only too pleased to head home again. At least there she could lock herself away with her hurt and her worries. And maybe dissect where she'd gone so totally and utterly wrong with him.

Should she have told him about the children at all? Well, like he'd said, it was irrelevant now. She couldn't turn back time; she couldn't undo what she'd done even if she wanted to.

Later that night she couldn't sleep at all. No wonder, of course, when she'd ended up napping most of the afternoon away once they'd gotten back to the house. She stepped out onto the balcony outside her room and stared out into the distance. How had her life become so complicated? She'd always kept things so simple—no home, no ties, no responsibilities—all the way up until she realized that her sister's dream of being a mother was going to die along with her.

She'd told herself that she'd done this for her sister, but had she really? Maybe it was all too convenient for her to have her sister's babies. She could build a family without having to build a loving, mature relationship first.

Of course, she'd had relationships, but she'd always prided herself on not settling down in one place with one person for too long. Settling down created expectations that she'd never been prepared to fulfill. Looking back on her life, she could now see how superficial it had been. Oh, sure, she'd worn clothing made from renewable sources; she'd paid extra money to replant a forest wherever she'd traveled to offset her carbon footprint. She'd prided herself on her spontaneity, her ability to live in the moment without structure or planning. But what had that all been for if not to hide from the reality of being a grown-up?

Having Sienna had opened her eyes to a lot of things. Not least of which the idea that making her decisions based on her emotions was not always necessarily the right choice. It certainly hadn't been with Van, had it? How could she have thought it was a good idea to approach him for financial help when she hadn't even done him the most basic courtesy of informing him he was a father?

"It was dumb, dumb, *dumb*," she muttered out loud.

And she was paying the cost now. Not only her, though, but Sienna and Van, too—and possibly even the baby-to-be. The reality of what she'd done to Van and to his life and his plans for his future settled on her shoulders like a ton of lead. There had to be a silver lining in this somewhere, she told herself. Wasn't she the queen of being upbeat and seeing the bright side of everything?

She knew her impulsive nature could sometimes unintentionally cause hurt to people and that her inclination to meddle had led to some tricky situations—case in point, the situation that had blown up with Zoe—but her heart was always in the right place. At least, that was what she'd always told herself. But maybe she'd been wrong all this time. Kidding herself that she was doing things for other people when she was, in reality, doing them for herself and to heck with the consequences.

Her hands gripped the iron railing in front of her and hot tears began to slide down her cheeks. Had she destroyed everything for Van? Ruined any chance he had at future happiness with his children because of her actions? She could have sworn he was falling in love with Sienna, and believing that had made her heart begin to soar for her little girl's future and for that of the baby she carried. But his response to her questions today had made her doubt. Maybe it was too late for him to feel the bond he should have with his children. And if so, it was all her fault.

Had this all been a terrible mistake? No, she couldn't think that. Couldn't assign that awful word to two children she loved more than life itself. And they deserved more. They deserved two loving parents. Preferably ones who were on the same page about their children's futures.

Maybe it would have been simpler if she'd let Van take full custody of the children. But as soon as the thought entered her mind, she felt an overwhelming rejection of it surge through her. No. These were her children, too. She'd cleaned up her act, created stability in her life where before there'd been none, and she had become someone worthy of raising kids—and all for them. She had to believe she'd done the right thing.

Van would come around to that, surely. Wouldn't he?

She stumbled back into her room and closed the French doors to the damp night air before climbing back into her bed. Things had to improve again. They'd already done it once, gone from two people at an impasse to two people who could make compromises. It hadn't been easy and she'd given up a lot of her independence—heck, who was she kidding, pretty much all of her independence, to be honest. Gone was her work, her home, even her car. But she'd gotten plenty in exchange—and best of all were the opportunities for the children. Van could give them things they never could have experienced on just her resources. And he'd made sacrifices, too. Hadn't he broken off his engagement because he had learned he was a father?

Kayla had never stopped to think about what the other woman thought of the sudden change to her future. Right now she felt deeply ashamed. Dani what's-her-name must hate her. She'd had plans for her future with Van. Plans that had been smashed because Kayla didn't stop to think.

She'd created this situation. She had to find a way to make it work. If she didn't, then life would be very dark indeed, and she owed it to her children to make sure the darkness never touched their lives. And she owed it to Van, too.

Kayla noticed that Van made a concerted effort to spend time with Sienna every day, either in the morning or just before her bedtime at seven. But if he was home in the evening, he disappeared into his home office after putting Sienna down and remained there until long after Kayla was tucked up in her bed. At least the time he spent each day with Sienna was an improvement on how things had been before the aquarium day, she consoled herself, even if things between him and Kayla had become more stilted than ever.

So she was surprised to find Van waiting for her when she went downstairs to the kitchen for breakfast one morning two weeks later. He was seated at the kitchen table reading some bound report that he held in one hand while holding a coffee cup in the other. Not for the first time, Kayla found herself briefly mesmerized by his hands. He had beautiful hands for a man. Broad but with long, tapered fingers and with an interesting array of scars she knew he hadn't incurred before he entered the army. They were a reminder that there was so much about him that she didn't know. One day she'd get up the courage to ask him about them, she told herself and forced her gaze away before she could remember other, forbidden, things about those hands and what they were capable of.

"Good morning," she said as brightly as she could. "Late into work?"

"I'm taking you to your doctor's visit today," he said without looking up from his report.

Kayla stopped in her tracks. "Oh, you have time for that?"

The second the words were out of her mouth, she wished them back. Would she ever learn to think first and speak second? She wouldn't blame Van for a minute if he took what she'd said the wrong way.

"I'm sorry," she hastened to add before he could do more than glare at her over the rim of his mug. "I didn't mean it to come out that way. You've been really busy lately, obviously. I didn't expect you'd be able to make it."

"Is that why you didn't tell me about the appointment?"

Kayla felt her cheeks color in shame. To be honest, she hadn't told him about the appointment because she was terrified he'd show no interest in it, or her, and she hadn't wanted to face his rejection. Yes, it was the coward's way out, she fully admitted it, but she absolutely didn't see the point in inviting any more conflict into her life than she'd already created. Seemed she was destined to fail in that department.

He made a gesture with his hand. "Forget I said that. Imelda told me you were scheduled for a scan today. Your notes and everything transferred to an obstetrician in Monterey okay?"

"Yes, I certainly couldn't face the idea of a two-hour drive each way to see the doctor who cared for me through Sienna's gestation. Belle recommended someone."

"Good," he replied, getting up from the table. "It makes sense. Do you know how long the appointment will take?"

She shrugged. "I'm really not sure. I'm due for some tests, and since this is my first time with this doctor, I don't know how long they'll take."

"Tests?" He frowned. "What kind of tests? I thought today was just a routine scan."

"Well, it is. They'll be checking the baby's size and development, especially considering the hyperemesis gravidarum, but they're also doing blood tests and what they call a nuchal translucency test—it's made up of a blood test and the scan where they look to make certain there are no chromosomal abnormalities or other kinds of defects."

Van paled. "And if there are?"

"We'll cross that bridge when we get there," she said with a blitheness she was far from feeling.

"You'd go through with the pregnancy?" he pressed.

She shrugged, but she knew that if faced with that question, she would do what she thought her sister would have done. Bear and love the child no matter what his or her life might look like or how short-lived it might be.

"Like I said—" she tried to smile reassuringly "—we'll deal with it when we know for certain. No point in borrowing trouble."

"You forget, trouble is my business." He got up from the table and put his mug in the dishwasher. "Let me know when you're ready to leave. I'll be in my office."

And like that, he was gone again. Kayla didn't quite know how to feel. A part of her was glad she didn't have to drive herself to the appointment. At least that way, if there was any obvious bad news, she wouldn't be alone. But being with Van lately was akin to cuddling a porcupine, with the exception being that he certainly didn't get that physically close.

Van watched intently as the image came up on the screen and the sonographer made an indistinct sound.

"Is everything okay?" Van asked, leaning forward.

It was hard to make anything out, but the woman turned to him and smiled. "Just give me a moment or two, Mr. Murphy. I need to complete some measurements and send the information through to Ms. Porter's obstetrician. They'll be able to tell you the outcome."

He shifted in his seat, starting in surprise as Kayla's hand slipped into his.

"It'll be okay, Van. Just relax. There's no reason for anything to be wrong."

But bad things happened all the time. He knew that better than anyone. His fingers tightened around hers and she gave him a reassuring smile before turning her attention to the screen. He was surprised to hear her sniff and looked at her in time to see her surreptitiously wiping away a tear with her other hand.

"What's wrong?" he asked, feeling more terrified than he had been a moment ago.

"Nothing," she said through more tears. "It's just such a crazy miracle, isn't it? Look, you can see it there on the screen."

"And here's the heartbeat," the sonographer said.

The room was filled with a rapid drumming sound.

"Is that okay? It seems very fast," Van asked, staring hard at the screen.

"All perfectly normal," came the steady reply. She adjusted a setting on the equipment and the resolution of the image on the screen sharpened. "I see you've requested to know the baby's sex, if possible, so let's have a look here. And there he is."

"It's a boy?" Kayla asked, squeezing Van's hand so tight it actually hurt.

"He's being very accommodating and showing off, so, yes, it's definitely a boy. Congratulations. Was that what you were hoping for?"

"I didn't care. I just wanted another healthy baby. Don't you feel the same, Van?"

But he was beyond answering. First a daughter and now a son? This for a man who'd decided never to have children, who never expected to be a father? Emotion threatened to drown him and he focused on the pain of Kayla's fingernails digging into the palm of his hand. Allowed the discomfort to distract him from the crazy swirl of joy and fear and exhilaration that made his eyes burn and his chest ache.

Through the buzzing in his ears, he heard Kayla speaking to the sonographer.

"He's a bit overwhelmed. He missed out on the scans with our daughter, so this is all new to him."

"I understand," the woman said with a smile in his direction.

She turned her attention back to her equipment and continued with the various measurements she had to make. Van was fascinated—the tiny skull with the tiny brain developing inside it, the curve of the spinal cord, the limbs. This was a little human. A child. *His* son.

"Is he sucking his thumb?" Van asked.

"He certainly is."

"Wow."

Kayla had called it a crazy miracle and she wasn't wrong. It was almost beyond his comprehension seeing the image on the screen and correlating it to the fact the baby was nestled in her womb. And he'd wanted to miss out on all of this? But there was still the issue of his parents' DNA to contend with. What if his son, or Sienna, carried that same disposition to self-destruct by using substances? He had such a responsibility to see to it that they weren't tempted to go down that road and potentially destroy their lives. Lives that Kayla had fought so hard to ensure they had without realizing what kind of time bomb they could be carrying. These babies, his children, deserved his best. Could he give it to them? Would he be enough?

Those questions played on his mind for the balance of the day. He locked himself in his office in an attempt to avoid them, but it was useless. After a long video call with Dani regarding an ongoing and escalating issue with one of their clients in the Middle East, Van shut down his computer and pushed away from his desk. It was dark outside and far later than he'd realized. That was why he and Dani had always been so well suited, he thought. Both prepared to keep going to get the job done, no matter the hour. Would he still be able to continue to give his work everything with two children in the house? It was unlikely.

Life, as he'd made it, had begun to change irrevocably and he hated to admit it, but he was scared. He could count on one hand the number of times he'd felt this way before. The first time his adoptive father had lifted a hand to him, the first time he'd been deployed and the first time he'd seen active duty. But this was a whole new kettle of fish.

Van stretched and heard the kinks in his back crack. A swim would be a good idea about now, he decided. Maybe a few lazy laps of the pool would help ease some of the jittering sensation that danced along his nerves so insistently. Yeah, some mindless exercise was just what he needed.

It was a beautiful night. The air was cool but the pool felt like warm silk on her skin as she went down the steps and was submerged in its softness. Kayla flipped onto her back and floated for a while, staring up into the cloudless night sky. Even with the subtle pool lighting she could still see more stars than she could count. It made her feel as if she was in another world altogether. In so many ways, that was true.

She sensed rather than heard a movement by the side of the pool and turned her head to look. Van stood at the edge. Moonlight limning his powerful physique made him look almost ethereal. Something deep inside her clenched before releasing slowly on a wave of hunger that had nothing to do with food and everything to do with the man standing there, silent as a statue.

"Did you want the pool to yourself?" she asked, treading water now at the deeper end of the pool. "I can go in now."

"No, don't leave on my account."

His voice was gruff and he stayed there—standing still. She couldn't tear her eyes off him. She tracked the shadowed lines of muscle along his shoulders and her mouth went dry, forcing her to swallow convulsively. She tried to avert her gaze, but it was useless. She might be pregnant but she was first and foremost a woman and most certainly a woman with an eye of appreciation for a stark male beauty such as his.

Any male's? a voice inside her asked. *Or just his?*

She couldn't lie to herself. Her attraction specifically to him went deep. Physically, Van was perfection. And emotionally? She wasn't sure yet. So much had changed between them and yet still remained the same. When they were growing up, he'd always been the one looking out for her. Making decisions regarding her safety and bailing her out of difficulties when she slipped through his protective net. They'd always had a relationship, of sorts, she admitted. But it had been lopsided—at least to her way of thinking. He'd never respected her or viewed her as an equal. She'd thought she had a chance to balance it after Sienna died and look how that had worked out, she reminded herself. But now, well, this was another place in time. Maybe this time things could be different.

She felt a flush of heat build from her chest and work its way up to her cheeks. Kayla was glad for the darkness. She still hadn't gotten around to buying a new swimsuit, and believing she'd be alone tonight, she hadn't covered herself in a T-shirt before entering the water. Right now, unable to resist the magnetic attraction she felt toward Van, she felt as if her body was bursting from her bikini— and the slide of the water against her made her feel naked. Naked and Van were probably not a good combination in her head at the moment, but as hard as she tried to stop them, nerve endings all through her body sprang to life in the most persistent fashion. The pool, which had only seconds ago been a sanctuary of peace and tranquility, now transformed into a simmering melting pot of need.

She continued to watch him as he dove neatly into the pool and began to swim freestyle. One lap, then another, until she lost count. She felt a prick of chagrin that he could so easily ignore her and was on her way to the stairs at the shallow end when he surfaced beside her.

"Not swimming anymore?" he asked.

"I've pretty much been just floating. It's relaxing, but I should probably leave you to it," she said, doing her best not to stare at him.

His hair was plastered to his head and water ran in rivulets down his face, his neck and then his chest. Desire pulled with such a hard wrench from her core that she gasped with its intensity. If she could only reach out, touch him. Let her fingers trace the lines of his body. No! They'd already gone down that road once and look where that had ended, she told herself. Distraction. She needed distraction and latched on to the one thing she knew would drive any thought of sex from her mind.

"I think you're going to be a great dad, Van," she blurted. "I just wanted to say that."

He looked startled, as if that was the last thing he'd expected her to say. He inclined his head in acknowledgment but didn't say a word. Instead he kept looking into her eyes, perhaps trying to delve beyond her clumsy attempt at deflection and get straight to the burning-hot center of her. It made her feel an urge to fill the silence.

"Did you enjoy today?" she asked. "Seeing the new baby?"

A tiny frown pulled at his brows. "*Enjoy* is probably not the right word for it," he said. "But it was fascinating." His eyes dropped from her face to her belly—to where his son was nestled. "And terrifying at the same time."

"I know what you mean. The first time I saw Sienna, I

freaked. I mean, I never planned to have kids, and when I decided to have her, I didn't stop to think about every aspect of it. I just knew I had to fulfill my promise and planned to do that without considering all the aspects of it."

Van snorted a laugh. "That's so like you."

She allowed herself a smile. "I've done a lot of stupid things in my life. I just wanted to do something right for a change. Something where I put someone else's needs and hopes first. But I still kind of leaped in with both feet. I guess I haven't changed much, have I? But then, neither have you."

"You don't think I've changed? I thought I had. A lot." He sounded mildly disappointed.

She looked at him. Of course he was different now than he'd been as a boy. He'd achieved wealth and authority beyond what anyone could have expected. But essentially he hadn't changed at all. He was still the protector, still distant from everyone around him even while making sure they were all okay. She'd seen that reserved demeanor of his completely crack just the once. The night they'd made love after her sister's funeral. He'd been more open with her then than he'd ever been. With their bodies, they'd said all the things that their minds couldn't formulate words for, and in a mutual need for comfort, they'd clung to one another and soared to exquisite heights of pleasure in their bid to obliterate their grief.

"Changed?" she repeated, musing on the word. "You're maybe more driven than you were. You've obviously come a long way since leaving the army, that's for sure. It's not every man who creates an empire in the time you have."

"I'm lucky that my skill set translates to a very high-value commodity. People need security, and in the countries where we work, those people are prepared to pay an extremely high price for it. Besides, I didn't do it all on my own. I was fortunate to be able to recruit a pool of people with skills that complement mine."

"People like Dani? What skills did she bring to the table?" Kayla asked, then hated herself for perversely bringing the other woman into their conversation.

"Her company provides the electronics that make our job a whole lot easier. If I'd had to invest separately in development for that side of things, I certainly wouldn't be where I am now."

"I'm sorry you two didn't work out."

Kayla knew the words were a lie the moment she spoke them. She wasn't sorry at all. There'd been something so unfeeling about the other woman when they'd met, something so clinical and detached. Sure, she was stunning, but in the same way a cool marble sculpture could be stunning and yet cold, empty.

"We still work well together despite that," Van replied.

Somehow that seemed to be a shame. There should have been some fire between them, surely. If Kayla had been so close to a person that she'd considered marrying him just to have it fall apart, she knew she wouldn't have been able to calmly keep working with him. It seemed especially wrong that it had happened with Van. She knew how deep his passion lay. The kind of man he was with Dani Matthews felt false. As if he was fitting himself into a mold where he thought he ought to be, instead of going where he truly belonged. But hadn't he always been like that? As a boy, as a soldier? He'd delivered on expectations every time but when had he had an opportunity to truly be himself?

The thought brought her back to their one night, to the raw honesty they'd expressed in actions when words were no longer enough. Usually she tamped down her thoughts of that time, but right now they flared, hot and bright, to the forefront of her mind. Her body, already simmering, fired to life.

"I know I couldn't," she commented.

"Why not?"

"I guess because I feel too much. I'm not the kind of person who can compartmentalize my emotions and my needs so easily. If the man I wanted to marry broke off our engagement for the same reasons you did…" Her voice trailed away and she shook her head. No, she didn't want to go down that road.

"You'd what?" he prompted.

"Well, if he really meant anything to me and I thought we stood a chance together, I'd fight tooth and nail for him. I'd learn to compromise, to blend his wishes with my own—especially if his children were involved."

"And you think Dani didn't fight for me?"

Ah, now, there was a thought. Maybe she'd been too dismissive of the beautiful Ms. Matthews.

"Did she?" Kayla countered, suddenly curious.

"Not beyond our initial discussion, no."

"But you guys were in love, right?"

He dunked his head under the surface and rose back up again, pushing the water from his eyes with his hands. "Love didn't enter into it. It didn't have to."

"Then I'm sorry for you, and for her."

"Don't be. We're adults. It hasn't hurt our working arrangements."

"But don't you see? That's what's wrong. It should hurt—your heart, your mind. Everything!" Kayla argued.

"And that's your philosophy on life?"

"It's my philosophy on love."

"Then it's just as well you're not in love, isn't it. It sounds very painful to me."

His words couldn't have struck her any harder than if he'd slapped her.

"Are you saying you don't feel?"

"Not if I don't choose to."

"You still keep a wall between you and the rest of the world, don't you? I've only seen you take that wall down once."

"What are you talking about?"

"Our night together," she said passionately. "I know you felt that night. Be honest. You were hurting. I know I was. And, just for a while, we both made the hurt go away. We *felt* something together. Something that was bigger than the hurt, something that was special. Don't you ever think about it? Don't you want to feel like that again?"

"No, I absolutely do not. That night was nothing but a mistake."

He launched toward the edge of the pool and hauled himself out, distancing himself from the conversation both mentally and physically. The way he always did from anything that approached emotion, she reminded herself. She shouldn't feel as though she'd lost something precious, but she did. By the time Kayla got out of the pool and wrapped herself in the toweling robe she'd brought down with her, he was gone.

She'd never learn, she thought as she made her way up to her room. Always blurting stuff out. Well, at least it made life interesting, she consoled herself, as opposed to the frozen wasteland that was Van's chosen emotional spectrum. She closed her bedroom door behind her and leaned back against it, feeling loss and sorrow seep through her. A knock on the wooden surface behind her made her start. She turned to open the door.

Van stood there, a towel wrapped at his waist and a smoldering green fire burning in his eyes.

"Van?"

"I do think about that night. I think about how your

hair smelled, how your skin felt beneath my hands, the taste of you on my tongue, about the heat of your body when I was inside you, and all of it drives me crazy. I can't stop thinking about that night. Or you."

And then he reached for her.

Twelve

His hands grasped her shoulders and he tugged her toward him. Stunned, she offered no resistance. His lips were hot and dry as they descended on hers. A bolt of desire, searing and desperate, shuddered through her as their lips met, as his tongue swept across the seam of her mouth. She parted her lips on a cry of need and he wasted no time deepening the kiss.

Kayla's hands flew to his head, her fingers driving through his short dark hair, her nails gently scraping his scalp. He groaned into her mouth and the sound felt as though it vibrated throughout her entire body. She could already feel the press of his hips against her. Feel the hardness that spoke of his need for her. Inside, she turned molten.

A maelstrom of sensation poured through her as he wrenched free the knot in her robe's belt and pushed aside the lapel to expose her to his starving gaze. His hand shook as he reached for the neck tie of her bikini. One

quick tug and the too-small triangles of damp fabric fell
to her waist. With one finger he traced a faint blue vein
on her swollen breast, then followed it with the tip of his
tongue.

She tried to speak, to tell him how he made her feel,
but the second his mouth closed around her nipple, words
failed her. Her knees threatened to buckle and send them
both crashing to the floor. As if he sensed her weakness,
he scooped her into his arms and carried her next to the
bed and put her gently down on her feet again. Three
more flicks of his fingers and her bikini top was off and
her bottoms had fallen in a heap on the carpet. Her robe
followed. Then his towel.

Kayla traced her hands over his chest, down his rib
cage and lower to the waistband of his swimming shorts.
Her fingers closed over the bulge at the front and he
dropped his head to the crook of her neck. One of his
hands closed over hers, halting her when she would have
squeezed him.

His voice shook. "I want you, Kayla, but if you don't
want this, too, say it now while I can still, maybe, leave
this room."

"Want you? I need you, Van. Here. *Now*," she whimpered.

He felt like he'd waited a millennium to hear those
words and he didn't waste the invitation she offered. He
bent his head to kiss her again and pulled her hard to his
body. She felt just as perfect against him as she had the
last time. His world had been tilted off its axis for so long.
But here, now, things finally felt so very right.

His hands skimmed over her body, different now
than before. A voice inside him told him he should be
ashamed that he was so turned on by the lushness of her
new curves, by the fact that she was carrying his child,

but then he realized the voice wasn't his. It was merely
an echo of disapproval from far in his past. An echo that
deserved to be erased forever because nothing—absolutely nothing—had ever felt as right as holding Kayla
in his arms did now.

She was spectacular, her skin smooth and warm. He
coaxed her down onto the mattress so he could see all of
her, touch all of her, taste all of her. She was no passive
partner in this. Her hands reached for him, squeezing,
tracing, stroking until his skin was burning and his entire body shook with need. But he'd waited what felt like
forever for this. He didn't want to rush it now.

He settled over her, bearing his weight on his arms.

"Are you okay with this?" he rasped as he bent his head
to tease the tip of one pale pink nipple with his tongue.

"I'd be a lot more okay if you'd hurry up," she said,
squirming against him. "And if you'd remove those wet
shorts of yours."

"They're the only thing keeping me under control," he
admitted as he smiled against her skin, loving the fact that
she was so impatient for him. "And I meant with having
me on top of you."

"I'm more than okay. You're just perfect, right where
you are."

She thrust her hips against his groin again and groaned
deep in the back of her throat. He could see the hot flush
of desire on her skin and the glitter in her eyes as she
looked at him.

"Don't take forever about this, soldier," she said teasingly.

"I'll take...just...as...long...as...I...take," he answered, punctuating each word with a nip or a lick of
her breasts.

Her nipples had hardened and distended and he could
have spent forever paying homage to her physical perfec-

tion. A lifetime wouldn't be long enough to spend following the tracery of veins that glowed palest blue beneath her skin. To spend holding her breasts, gently squeezing those pink peaks and laving them with his tongue. Kayla's nails dug into his shoulders, spurring him to take as much time as he could to make this good for her.

But there was more of her to explore, to pleasure, and he was nothing if not dedicated. Beneath his hands, her rib cage felt so small and her skin pebbled with goose bumps as he traced his tongue over each rib, then followed the center line between them before finishing at her belly button. The thickening of her waist and the slight rise of her tummy were more noticeable lying down. An incredible sense of strength and pride fought through the haze of desire that wreathed him. His child. His woman.

"Van?" Her voice sounded unsure and he realized he'd been motionless for a minute or more. "Are you okay? Is everything all right?"

"Everything is perfect," he said through a throat that had suddenly clogged with emotion. "You are perfect."

Then he bent his head again, lower this time, to the neat thatch of blond curls at the apex of her thighs, then lower still to where her musky wetness called to him. Kayla's thighs were trembling as they fell wider apart, allowing him to nestle between them, to feel their silky softness against the breadth of his shoulders.

He blew a cool stream of air against her glistening flesh and smiled as he heard the hitch in her labored breathing.

"Van Murphy, if you think you're going to tease me now…" she threatened, closing her fingers in his short-cropped hair.

But he was far too much of a gentleman to keep her waiting. He nuzzled her tender spot and felt her thighs tighten around him.

"Yes, please. Right there."

Her voice shook and he drew pleasure from the fact that he could make her feel so much. This woman, who was the light to his darkness, who was his polar opposite in so many things but who was his perfect match in bed. Van swirled his tongue around her clitoris, increasing the pressure with each moment and then easing it off. Kayla was begging him incoherently to give her the release he knew boiled just beneath the surface and it took every ounce of his considerable self-control to keep her teetering on that edge before he closed his mouth around her and sucked hard, flicking his tongue against the swollen bud.

Beneath him, Kayla's hips rose involuntarily from the bed and her whole body tensed as the first wave hit her. He almost came in his shorts, her orgasm was so intense. Watching her, knowing he'd given her this pleasure, this moment of mindlessness beyond measure, made him feel stronger than anything he'd ever done before in his life. His shorts were an unwelcome constriction and he finally shucked them off. His erection, thick and heavy and aching so hard that he wondered if he'd be able to hold on as long as necessary, sprang free.

Van shifted, moving higher up Kayla's body, positioning himself at her entrance. The sensation of her core's heat against the sensitive head of his penis almost sent him hurtling over the brink. He paused, pulling on every ounce of reserve he had left.

"I don't want to hurt you," he stated.

"For goodness' sake, just make love to me, Van," Kayla demanded, her voice sounding drunk on bliss and need.

Her hands were at his hips, the heels of her feet pressing on his buttocks as he slid inside her. A massive shudder shook his body as he sank full length inside. This was home, he realized. Not a house, not a place. But this woman, this moment, together.

He began to move, his hips thrusting with more vigor on each stroke. Kayla's inner muscles tightened around him, increasing the intensity of his pleasure until with a cry she came undone again, her orgasm seeming to take control of them both as it pulled him over the edge and into a searing pleasure so powerful he felt as though his climax could go on into eternity.

The ripples of satisfaction were still running through him as he collapsed on the bed to her side and rolled her over him, still joined.

"If that's the last thing I ever feel for the rest of my days, I'll die a happy woman," Kayla said against his chest before kissing him there. "I love you, Van."

Her voice was thick, heavy, and within seconds she was asleep. Van lay there listening to her breathing, cradling her in his arms and waiting for his heart rate to return to some semblance of normal. But in the wake of her declaration, he knew that would be impossible. This should have been the moment when he felt at peace, but for some irrational reason, he'd never felt less peaceful in his life. The urge to get up and leave her was strong. He didn't do this kind of thing, this depth of emotion, this level of connection to anyone. She loved him. He couldn't—wouldn't—love her. It was too much and too terrifying to contemplate. It left a person too open, too raw, too exposed.

His brain tried to argue with him. This moment with her, her declaration, it was too much to lose—*she* was too much, meant too much. Maybe he'd always known that deep down, always sensed that Kayla was the one who could make him this vulnerable inside. Make him want things he'd told himself it was safer to live without. She made him begin to believe that he deserved these things—

a family, a rich life, love. But he knew he didn't. All it would take was one slip. He'd screw it up eventually—people with his background always did.

She shifted a little in his arms and the warm puffs of her breath against his chest were painfully endearing. It would be all too easy to stay here, to wake with her later and to explore their sensual journey together over and over.

He had the sense that the walls were closing in on him. That he was being buried in a mire of emotion he had no idea how to handle. He knew he couldn't do it. It had been a mistake the first time he'd made love with her and it had been a mistake this time, too. He couldn't give her what she wanted, what she deserved. He would always let her down in the long run. It might as well be sooner rather than later, he decided as he gently extricated himself from her arms and slid from the bed, pausing a moment to pull the covers over her.

He picked up his towel and damp shorts from the floor and headed for the door. It wouldn't have lasted between them anyway, even if he had been willing to try—he knew that. Nothing good ever did. Van flicked off the light switch and closed the door behind him.

Kayla woke the next morning and stretched languorously, reaching one arm over to stroke Van's back. But her hand met nothing but cool sheets. It didn't bother her at first. She knew he was an early riser and she'd become a late one recently with either Belle or Imelda getting Sienna up in the mornings. That would have to stop, she decided. It wasn't fair to Belle to make her handle mornings when she was on call all night. And Kayla was feeling so much better now that she could take over her duties as Sienna's mom properly again. Actually, today in particular she was feeling exceptionally well. She smiled and stretched again before swinging her legs over the side of the bed and getting up.

There was an energy surging in her body right now that made her want to step out onto her balcony, throw her arms out to the world and give thanks for the exceptional lovemaking she'd had with Van. That she was stark naked and that she could spy Jacob working the garden on the perimeter of the property were two very good reasons not to, she thought with a private smile.

She went to her bathroom and quickly showered and dressed for the day—eager to see Van and maybe suggest another family outing. Now that she'd admitted to herself and to him that she loved him, she wanted to explore those feelings further and, if possible, to coax his feelings out of him. The fact he'd come to her last night was a revelation. For once he'd put aside the distant businessman and become purely the man. And what a man. She still tingled and throbbed in the parts of her body that hadn't experienced such rich sensual pleasure in a very long time.

Kayla skipped downstairs and went to the kitchen. As she approached, she heard Imelda coaxing Sienna to eat her cereal.

"Good morning!" Kayla said.

She went straight to her daughter's high chair and plonked a kiss on the top of Sienna's head.

"Good morning to you, too, Ms. Porter. You're obviously feeling on top of the world today." Imelda smiled back.

"I am. And I'm starving. I might even manage two slices of toast today," she answered with a wink. Kayla then looked around. "Is Van around? I thought he might like to go out with Sienna and me today."

"No, Ms. Porter. He left while it was still dark."

A cold, sick sensation rippled through her. A sensa-

tion that was rapidly chased by a series of questions. He
left? Where to? When? Why had he gone without saying goodbye?

"He didn't mention anything about that to me. Did you
know he was going away?" She was proud of the fact that
none of her shock filtered through her voice.

"Not in advance, no. Some emergency overseas, apparently."

"Doesn't he have staff to deal with things like that?"

"You know Mr. Murphy. Always with the personal
attention to detail. He takes a lot of pride in his work."

"So where did he go?"

Imelda mentioned a well-known trouble spot and Kayla
felt a fist of fear clutch her heart. "So you see," Imelda
concluded, "he wouldn't have sent a staff member into
an area like that. It's such a volatile region and he's always said he'd never send anyone anywhere he wasn't
prepared to go himself."

Wouldn't he? Kayla asked herself. Or had he, in the
face of her declaration, just grabbed hold of an opportunity to run away—like he always did? With no goodbye,
no message of when he'd be back. Tears burned in the
back of her eyes and her throat choked on emotion. She
thought he'd changed, that he was prepared to live up to
his responsibilities here—to her, to his children. But she'd
been so very wrong.

"He'll miss Sienna's first birthday," she said bitterly.

Imelda nodded. "I know."

How could he do this? Leave now after everything
they'd shared? Kayla automatically went through the motions of putting her breakfast together but found she had
no appetite at all when it came to eating it. She felt as if all
the sunshine had suddenly fled her world. It was the past
repeating all over again. Why, though? she asked over and

over. Even if he wasn't ready to pursue something with her, why would a man deliberately put himself in danger when he didn't have to and when he had a responsibility to children here at home? It didn't make sense to her at all. His children needed him in their lives. Not just as some transient male role model who turned up from time to time, but as a father who would guide them and love them and teach them about life and living it.

None of it made sense at all. He was the one who'd threatened to take both kids from her. He was the one who'd ensconced them here in this house and took over her life. He was the one who'd come to her last night and who'd made love to her like a man who felt love, not fear of where love would lead.

On the heels of her sorrow at discovering he'd gone came a sudden rise of burning anger. How dare he? He'd changed the parameters of their relationship with his actions last night—he had no right to renege on that by morning. And his duty to Sienna—how could he expect to swan in and out of her little world and *choose* to go somewhere from where he might not return?

Kayla had no trouble feeding the flames of her fury. In fact, they buoyed her through her day and the days that followed until Van's return. The sweet, passionate, loving night they'd spent together was nothing but a distant memory two weeks later when he finally returned home, and she wasted no time cornering him in his office.

He was pale with exhaustion and still dressed in dusty fatigues, his T-shirt stretched across the broadness of his shoulders and his chest like a second skin.

"So," she started without even a greeting. "You decided to stop hiding."

Her words and tone were as sharp as shattered glass. It was no more than he deserved.

"Hello to you, too," he replied, looking up from a stack of papers that had been couriered from his office in San Francisco earlier that day.

"Why, Van?"

He continued to look at her, drinking in her beauty. Even as angry as she clearly was, she pulled at him like a powerful magnet. A magnet he'd tried to ignore when he'd chosen to leave the way he had. The similarities between that night and their first together hadn't escaped him. He'd slipped away like a thief in the night, telling himself it was for the best even while his heart argued that he should stay. But then, he'd long since gotten accustomed to ignoring his heart.

"What?" she prompted, folding her arms across her midsection. The look she gave him should have withered him on the spot. "Got nothing to say? Well, that's just dandy because I have plenty."

He stood there and took it as she unleashed her wrath with guns blazing. He'd earned it, every word, every accusation, and he hated every second of it—especially when she brought up Sienna's birthday, which had been last week. He honestly hadn't known—hadn't bothered to find out. But it hurt to realize he'd missed it. Not that he'd ever show it.

It was one thing to come to a moment of truth by yourself; it was quite another to have it hurled at you. And everything inside him urged him to fight back. To tell her the truth. But he couldn't find the words to say that he wasn't enough for someone like her and he never would be.

"Are you quite finished?" he said when she finally wound down.

There were tear tracks on her face and he battled himself to ignore the deep regret that shafted him, together with the knowledge that he was the one solely responsible for putting them there.

"I'll be finished when you can admit that you choose to deliberately put your life in danger rather than face up to your issues!" she raged once more. "I'm guessing you ran away because I told you I love you. Well, guess what—that's not the worst thing that could happen to you. You won't die because someone loves you—or because *I* love you. You don't have to always be the hard man, the defender of the weak. You are allowed to show weaknesses yourself and to be vulnerable to another person, someone you can trust—like me."

"You don't know what you're talking about. I didn't run away. I had work to do," he said dismissively, even though he knew he was lying.

She hadn't said anything that he hadn't already thought of himself these past two weeks. But he wasn't ready to admit that to anyone—not now, not ever. That would mean opening up a part of himself that had been locked down and secured far too long for him to even consider changing. Not for her, not for anyone.

He continued, deliberately choosing the words that would push her away. "I wasn't running away from issues. I was running away from you."

She whitened and appeared to sway a little under the cruelty of his words. Van fought back every instinct to claw the words back, to apologize, to put out a hand to steady her when she was so obviously shaken. Instead he remained very firmly where he was.

"I see," she said quietly. "Well, thank you for being honest about that, at least."

She turned and walked away. Van's fists clenched tight at his sides, every muscle in his body locked as he held back the need to follow after her. It was better this way, he kept telling himself. She couldn't love him; he wouldn't let her. As vicious as he'd been, it was the right thing to do. It had to be because if it wasn't, then he'd just sent away the best thing that had ever happened to him his whole miserable life.

Thirteen

Loving a man who didn't love you and never would was a great deal more painful than Kayla could ever have imagined. Oh, sure, she'd had crushes on boys growing up, boys who hadn't returned the favor, but this was another thing entirely. It left her heart sore and miserable to the extent that it was an effort to be upbeat for Sienna each day. Even Imelda had noticed, and between her and Belle, they seemed to be hell-bent on trying to cheer her up. But this wasn't just a funk; this felt like the end of everything she'd never known she'd really wanted. And she wanted out.

She'd admitted to herself that despite everything, she truly wanted a real, permanent relationship with Van. But now she knew it to be an impossible dream. And living here, sitting across the table from him on the nights he was home for dinner or watching him spend time with Sienna, coaxing her to walk on her chubby little legs, was killing her inside. He'd never love her—she accepted that now—and she wasn't about to be a moth to his flame until she drove herself senseless with it. But she had to be here to fulfill the terms of their contract, even though staying in his house was a living hell—when he was here anyway, she reminded herself glumly.

Van was gone again on business—safely stateside this time, to her untold relief—when Imelda called her to the phone.

"Who is it?" Kayla asked as she reached for the handset Imelda held toward her.

"Ms. Matthews," the housekeeper answered with a sour twist to her mouth.

There weren't many people that Imelda disapproved of but there was no mistaking the antipathy reflected on her normally jovial face right now.

"Did she say what she wanted?"

"She didn't deign to tell me," Imelda sniffed.

Kayla took the call off hold and said hello.

"Kayla, I trust you're well?" The other woman's faultlessly modulated tones came down the line.

Kayla stifled the urge to rub her ear. "I'm fine, thank you. Van's not here right now. Did you want to leave a message for him with me?"

"No, it's you I wanted to speak to." Dani paused a moment before continuing. "I wondered if you and I could meet and have a chat. Perhaps tomorrow morning at Fisherman's Wharf in Monterey, say eleven thirty?"

Kayla couldn't hold back her surprise. "Why?"

"Let's discuss that then. Can I take it that you're amenable to that time and place? I trust you'll be able to find a babysitter."

Who the heck used words like *amenable* in conversation, Kayla thought before answering. Imelda, who could hear the conversation, rolled her eyes before nodding her assent.

"Yes, that's not a problem. Eleven thirty it is, then."

Dani mentioned the name of a restaurant and then ended the call.

"Mark my words," Imelda said taking the phone back from Kayla. "She's up to no good."

"I have to admit I'm surprised she wants to see me. What on earth do we have in common?"

"Mr. Murphy," Imelda replied with a fiery look in her eye.

"Oh, no, but we're not... He's not... It's not like that between us."

Imelda merely raised her brows.

"It's not," Kayla repeated adamantly. "Well, I guess I'll find out soon enough what she wants. Are you sure you'll be okay with Sienna tomorrow? I know Belle is on a rostered day off but I'm sure she wouldn't mind having her for a couple of hours. She told me she had no plans for tomorrow but lazing around the pool and reading a book."

"Shush now—you know I love to have Sienna to myself. But just you be careful around that woman. I don't trust her. It's not natural for a woman to be so—" She broke off and searched for the right word. "So soulless."

"Soulless?" Kayla asked with a frown. "I only met her the once and she struck me as very..." she tried to think of a nice word for *cold* and settled on "...self-possessed, but she can't be all that bad. She and Van were going to get married, weren't they?"

"Believe me, that woman never does or says anything that isn't in her personal interests. She has a calculator where her heart should be. It was a good thing when Mr. Murphy broke their engagement and confined their relationship to business only."

"You didn't think they suited one another?" Kayla knew she shouldn't be prompting Imelda to gossip, but she couldn't resist.

"On the surface, maybe, but she could never give him what he needs. Not like you can."

Kayla shook her head. "Oh, no. He doesn't want anything from me."

"Like a lot of men, he doesn't know what he needs. He's too busy looking out for everyone else to ever think about looking out for himself. You say he doesn't want anything from you—what's more to the point is that he doesn't want to want anything from anybody. And wanting is one thing, but needing is entirely another. He needs *you*. You should think on that," Imelda said.

Kayla found herself watching Imelda's back as she left the room and turned over the other woman's words in her mind. Imelda couldn't have been serious. Kayla had nothing to offer Van. Nothing he would admit to needing, anyway. As much as she hoped it could be possible for them to forge a new beginning together, he'd made it blatantly clear that it would never happen. Which left her wondering what the heck Dani wanted to talk to her about.

The next day, Dani was already waiting at the table when Kayla arrived at the restaurant. She stood and shook Kayla's hand when she approached. The nerves that had skittered and danced in the pit of her stomach tightened into an uncomfortable knot. She'd been feeling queasy again all morning. There was no doubt that a lot of her discomfort came from nerves right now. She'd considered canceling but believed if she put Dani off, she'd only have to reschedule, because she had a feeling that Dani was persistent once she wanted something.

"Please, sit," Dani directed. "What would you like to drink?"

"Just filtered iced water for me, please."

"Of course." Dani smiled in return and gestured for one of the waiters to take their drinks order.

Once he was gone, Dani turned her full attention on Kayla. Kayla studied her. She hadn't changed at all from the first time Kayla had seen her—still impeccably groomed and with her hair a perfect glossy swing about the china-doll perfection of her face. It made Kayla want to reach for her more tousled locks and try to tame them into some semblance of order but she forced herself to keep her hands still.

"I imagine that you're wondering why I called you."

Kayla could only nod.

"I want Donovan back, and you're going to help me get him," she said in a tone that, while perfectly pleasant, held undertones that made Kayla uncomfortable.

"I don't see how I have any influence in the matter. Van very much does as he pleases," Kayla replied as evenly as she could.

Dani smiled at her condescendingly, much as one would to a particularly dense person. "I thought you'd say as much. Let's be honest here. You and I both know that Donovan is miserable with the current state of affairs."

"I wouldn't say miserable, exactly," Kayla defended, but she knew he wasn't happy. There'd been a cloud hanging over him since their night together that made him more distant than ever.

"There's no point in lying to yourself," Dani continued. She waved her slender ringless hands extravagantly. "He made a commitment based on an emotional reaction to a situation that took him completely by surprise and he's too honorable to step away from it, even though he knows it's a huge mistake. It's up to you and me to make it right."

Dani reached into an impossibly elegant narrow leather briefcase and pulled out a thin sheaf of papers, which she then slid across the table to Kayla.

"I'd like you to look over this. I think you'll find the terms quite agreeable."

Kayla picked up the papers and read through the document. It was pretty clear, despite the legal jargon contained inside. Dani was offering her money, a great deal of money, to move out of Van's home and away to another city. In return, all she had to do was promise not to contact Van again. On paper, it all looked quite simple and straightforward but everything in Kayla revolted at the idea. Even though she knew she had no future with Van, what about the children? What about his relationship with them?

An all-too-familiar sick feeling bloomed in her stomach. She reached for her iced water and took a sip to try to settle her nerves but it was no use.

"Excuse me," she blurted and rose to her feet.

Kayla let the papers fall to the table and rushed toward where she'd seen the restrooms. Once there, her stomach convulsed, forcing her to lose the light breakfast she'd eaten a couple of hours ago and leaving her feeling weak and wrung out. With shaking hands, she flushed the toilet and went to the basin and washed her hands, running cold water over her wrists for some time before grabbing a paper towel, moistening it, and wiping her face and the back of her neck before the nausea could swell again.

Her eyes swam with the words printed on the agreement Dani had presented to her. It was painfully clear-cut. Dani wanted her to leave Van, and she was prepared to pay richly for what she wanted. Kayla would have unfettered access to a trust fund established for her and the children and the security of a fully serviced apartment to help her so she could afford to raise the children on her own. All she had to do was cut Van from her life, and the lives of the children, completely. Dani had even offered new identities for them all so she wouldn't have to worry about Van coming after them to claim custody. That was how far she was prepared to go.

Kayla had thought things like that were to be found solely in soap operas and the movies, not in everyday people's lives. It seemed too impossible to contemplate. Besides, she'd already signed a contract with Van. She was still bound by that, wasn't she? She balled up the paper towel and cast it in the trash bin. Could she do that to him? Disappear without a trace? Wouldn't that be the utmost cruelty?

But what about the way he'd just excised himself from their lives when he'd taken that job overseas? she asked herself. Was that really the kind of father she wanted for her children? A man who would come and go at will without any consideration for them?

Kayla looked at her reflection in the mirror. She was pale but relatively composed. Dani would be waiting at the table and she needed to go back and face up to the other woman's offer. Even as she left the restroom and walked back to their table, she had no idea what to say. However, once she was settled back in her chair, Dani didn't waste any time on working to convince her to see things her way.

"All under control again now, are we?" she said with a saccharine smile.

"Yes, thank you."

"I couldn't go through what you're suffering, not to mention what else it's doing to your body." She gave an elegant shudder. "Far too messy and so undignified."

Kayla didn't say anything; she simply couldn't, because she knew if she opened her mouth, she'd say something she'd probably regret. She was beginning to see what Imelda had warned her of. Dani obviously had no maternal urge at all—no idea of the love a mother bore for her child, no matter what carrying that child did to her. Dignity didn't even begin to enter into the equation. But it also made her wonder what Dani felt she offered

Van. Surely no woman that focused on composure could truly feel passion for anyone. She didn't love him—she seemed to want to acquire him instead.

"So, what do you think of my offer?" Dani continued. "It's more than generous, and with the additional college funds established for the children, you should have no concerns for their future, either. Like I said, I want Donovan back. We're good together, and since you've been back on the scene with your growing brood, he's been different. Unhappy. Unfocused. He needs me more than he knows, and with you and the children out of the way, he won't have the distractions that have derailed our plans for our business and for a future together."

Unhappy? Maybe he'd been unhappy recently, but certainly not all the time. Kayla thought for a moment of the laughter she'd heard when he'd been playing with Sienna out on the lawn the other day. He certainly hadn't sounded unhappy then. But then she remembered the expression on his face when he caught her watching them and what an outsider it had made her feel like. "He said he wants the children. It was his choice to be a part of their lives."

"Is that what he told you?" Dani shook her head sorrowfully. "Oh, you poor deluded girl. Of course Donovan would want you to believe that, because that would be the right thing to do. But trust me, deep down, he doesn't want children cluttering up his life. He would do whatever he had to to ensure they were taken care of, of course. But he never, ever, wanted to be involved in raising children himself.

"With all the pressure this situation has put on him, he's been distracted at work and I'm sure you will agree that such a thing in his line of business can be dangerous. It's my desire to rid him of said distractions so he can put his mind where it's most valuable."

"On business, or on you?" Kayla asked bitterly.

"Both, of course. We are one and the same, after all. Donovan and I are meant to be together, Kayla. Surely you can see that. We're similar in so many ways—we have the same dreams, the same purpose. We're perfect for one another and we always will be. I understand he has needs. He is, after all, such a lusty creature, as I'm sure you know." Dani trilled a little laugh that scraped along Kayla's nerve endings and made her bristle with anger.

"Why would I know that?" She kept her voice cool, desperate not to betray the emotions that burned just beneath the surface.

"Oh, you know what I'm talking about." Dani gave her a conspiratorial look. "Donovan and I don't keep secrets from one another."

He'd told her about sleeping with Kayla? How could he? More important, why would he? Unless it had meant absolutely nothing to him at all. Unless he'd merely done it to try to work an itch out of his system.

Kayla stared at the pen. Gold, of course, with some fancy name engraved on it. It probably cost more than her last car did. Could she do this? Could she sign the offer that Dani had presented her and simply vanish from Van's life with his children? She wondered about the legal ramifications of that, about whether or not he'd pursue her.

"Questions, Kayla?" Dani pushed into her thoughts.

"Van threatened me with legal action if he didn't have access to the children the last time. Who's to say he won't do that again if I agree to your terms?"

"Should such a thing happen, and I assure you it won't, I will take care of everything for you, I promise. Here, I'll even write that in." She took the contract back and wrote in an addendum on the last page, marking her initials beside it. Skimming over it, Kayla noticed that it transferred legal liability for any conflicts to Dani. "He'll listen to me," Dani assured her.

"And you're certain he doesn't want the children anymore? He fought me hard to have shared custody of them. You're absolutely sure he's changed his mind about that now?"

"Well, obviously." Dani looked quite pointedly at the new contract. "As I said, his sense of honor demanded he do something about his children even though he didn't want them."

"And his sense of honor has disappeared now? Why didn't he talk to me about this? Why leave it to you?"

"Let's just say that the reality of being a father has turned into something he didn't expect. And, let's be honest, it's all getting so untidy, isn't it? Far better I deal with it and present him with a lovely clean slate to move forward with."

Dani's words had a ring of truth to them, but could Kayla trust them—or even trust the woman herself? She looked at the contract and thought hard about it. She'd admitted to herself only yesterday that she wanted out of the situation she'd found herself in. And there was no way she'd leave Sienna behind if she did find a way to leave. Dani was offering her a way out for both of them. A very lucrative way. As much as she hated to admit it, the woman's offer was tempting.

Kayla's biggest concern all along had been that Van would bail on his new family when things became too much for him on an emotional level. And hadn't he already proved that to be true after the night they'd slept together? He'd shut down completely since, ensuring she understood she had no future with him, nothing at all. And here she had a gold-plated opportunity to get out and stay out. A chance to start her life over.

"He wouldn't need to know where I've gone, would he?" she asked.

Dani, obviously sensing she was getting closer to her

goal, gave Kayla the most genuine smile Kayla had seen from her so far. "Not at all. I'll make sure that Donovan is completely unaware of the finer details of our agreement and I've promised to ensure you're protected from him legally. He won't bother you again, trust me—we'll be too busy building our future."

Everything in Kayla screamed at her not to do it. She *wanted* Van to bother her—she wanted him in her life and in the lives of their children. But did he want the same thing?

No, he did not.

She made her decision, all the while feeling as though she was watching from the outside of some kind of glass prison. Her fingers clasped around the ornate gold pen. She had to do this, didn't she? It was what was best for Sienna and for Kayla's unborn son—and, ultimately, no matter how much it hurt, it was what was best for her. Their little family of three would want for nothing under the terms of the agreement. They'd have their own place, not be in forced living conditions under the roof of a man who now barely tolerated her presence.

"This is costing you a lot of money," she hedged. "Are *you* certain you want to do this?"

Dani made a shooing motion with her hand. "It's nothing to me financially. Donovan, however, is everything to me and as I said earlier, I'll do whatever it takes to have him back and make him happy again."

The last four words she uttered echoed in Kayla's mind. Yes, she was doing this not just for herself and for the children; she was doing this for Van, too. He deserved to be happy, didn't he?

She picked up the pen and scored her signature on the page.

Fourteen

He'd irrationally looked forward to coming home for days now. Normally he had no difficulty staying away, doing his job, losing himself in the work, but this trip had felt different. He'd had plenty of time at night, when he couldn't sleep, to search his soul for why and it had come as a painful revelation to admit to himself that he missed Kayla and Sienna with an ache that went soul deep.

Initially he'd dismissed it—putting it down to the fact that he was on the East Coast, a long way from the life he'd carved out for himself, and the fact that he was averaging sixteen-to eighteen-hour days and less than four hours' sleep each night. It was hard on a body and sleep deprivation could do awful things to a man's mind. He knew that intimately from his time in the army.

It only made sense that he'd crave an alternate existence, he'd reasoned, especially when that alternative lived so enticingly under his very roof. But, he'd reminded himself often, even that wouldn't last. As soon as his son was born and weaned, Kayla would be gone again and they'd share custody of the two children. Live sensible, detached parallel lives just the way he'd dictated all along. The way he wanted it, he reminded himself.

Somehow, though, he didn't want to live like that anymore. Somewhere along the line he'd felt a shift in his thinking—sensible and detached wasn't nearly enough now. And he couldn't use the argument that Kayla was unreliable—she was not the flighty dreamer she'd been in her younger years. Yes, she still had an impulsive and giving heart and always wanted to help those in worse circumstances than her own—to her detriment, as he'd seen—but that in itself didn't make her a bad person. She was a really good, loving and consistent mom, and considering the toll her pregnancies had taken on her physically, he had to admire that she hadn't let her physical complications deter her from her vow to her sister. That took guts no matter which way you looked at it.

"You need to man up," he said out loud, thumping the steering wheel beneath his hands. "Be honest with yourself."

And maybe, like Kayla had said, stop running scared from his emotions. But could he learn to trust like she wanted him to? Could he open himself up to his fears of inadequacy, rejection and failure? First it had been the parents who'd brought him up who'd scarred his heart. Then it had been the truth about his birth family that had put the seal on it. And he was damaged goods, let's face it. With a predisposition to alcoholism and a past in which he'd done unspeakable things to unspeakable people in the line of duty, he was no prize. And yet she said she loved him.

Would she love him as much if she knew all of it? Was it too late to make amends? Could he mend the rift he'd created when he'd shoved her love away as if it didn't matter—as if *she* didn't matter?

But she mattered, as did Sienna and his as-yet-unborn son. They mattered far more than he'd ever believed possible. He had to make things right—there really was no other option. His life would be incomplete if he couldn't fix things and create the true home he'd always wished for. Van slowed down for the turn into his driveway and waited for the electronic gates to slide open. Now that he was here, he was filled with an equal mix of foreboding and anticipation. It wouldn't be easy asking for Kayla's forgiveness, but he was prepared to humble his pride, go on his knees and beg if it meant she'd give him another chance. And this time, please, God, he wouldn't mess it up.

Van could sense something was wrong the minute he pulled into the garage. He looked around. Kayla's car was there, baby seat secured in the back, just like it always was—and yet he still felt as though something was terribly out of kilter.

He couldn't dismiss the feeling. His instincts had saved him from bad situations more times than he could count— both as a kid and as an adult. He hefted his laptop case from his car and went inside. There, his unease grew and it wasn't until he bumped into Imelda, who was coming down the hall toward him, that he realized something had to be very wrong. There was a sadness about her, an emptiness in her eyes that struck fear deep into his chest.

"Imelda? What is it? What's wrong?" he demanded.

"You don't know?"

"Know what? Tell me." Van fought the urge to shake it from her. "Is Kayla all right? The babies?"

"As far as I know, they're all very well. Perhaps I should let Ms. Matthews tell you. She's waiting for you out on the balcony."

"As far as you… Dani?"

But Imelda pushed past him with a sniff that sounded suspiciously like she was holding back tears. Without wasting another moment, Van strode through the house and headed outside. Dani lounged on one of the outdoor chairs, looking as exquisitely beautiful as always but so cold and emotionless that as he watched her unfold from her seat and rise to greet him, he wondered how he could ever have thought he'd be happy with someone like her.

"Donovan, darling," Dani greeted him, presenting a cheek to be kissed. "I've missed you."

Van couldn't bring himself to touch her. Not now.

"I'm surprised to see you here," he said through gritted teeth, forcing himself to be civil when all he wanted to do was demand she tell him where Kayla was and why she wasn't here. "I wasn't expecting to see you until tomorrow at the office."

"I know—isn't it delicious? I love my little surprises." She turned to the table and lifted a bottle of champagne from the sweating ice bucket in the center of the table. "Now you're back, this calls for a celebration."

"Dani, what the hell is going on?" he growled.

"Oh, no need to go all caveman on me, Donovan. You know that doesn't appeal to me. Besides, you're going to be so pleased when you know what I've done."

She passed him a crystal champagne flute, which he promptly put back on the table. "You know I don't drink," he bit out.

"But this is a very special occasion. Surely you can make an exception, just this once? Just a sip?"

"I don't make exceptions. Not on this, ever. Why are you here?"

"I thought you might be pleased to know I've managed to sort out your little situation and get rid of it permanently so we can go back to how we were before. You've been so wretched since you've had that woman and her brat under your roof. Someone had to do something."

"That's my child you're referring to," he said, pressing down the fury that threatened to boil over. His anger would have to wait until he got all the information he needed, and if he knew Dani at all, that was probably going to take a lot longer than he wanted.

"One you didn't want, remember. And now she's gone. And her mother, too."

"What did you do to them?"

"Do? Why, nothing. I merely offered them an alternative and now the situation is resolved to everyone's satisfaction. We can go back to our plans to marry without any unwanted babies cluttering up our future."

Was he going to have to drag everything out of her word by painful word? "Where are they?"

"They're quite happy where they are. At Kayla's request, you're not to know the exact location. We both felt it would be better that way. Otherwise, given your unfortunate knight-in-shining-armor tendencies, you'd be inclined to haring after her, wouldn't you?"

"You had no right to interfere. We're over as a couple, Dani. Our relationship remains a business one only."

She fluttered an elegant hand and he noted the solitaire diamond ring he'd given her glittered once more on her ring finger. "But we both know we want more than that. We were happy before she came along."

Happy? He might have thought he'd been happy but he hadn't realized quite how empty his life had been.

"Dani, I made a mistake when I asked you to marry me. It wasn't fair to either of us."

For the first time, her confidence wavered a bit. Apparently this was not what she'd expected him to say. "What are you saying, Donovan? Please, think very hard before you answer me. We have so much riding on this. Our business, our future, everything."

Was she insinuating that their business would always come first? Hell, what was he thinking? Of course it did. It was what had brought them together, after all. He'd been an idiot to think that would ever have been enough to build a marriage on.

"You deserve better than me, Dani," he said firmly. "You deserve a man who will love you through and through—everyone does. We might have been happy together, initially, at least, but long-term I think we both know we would have been left wanting more."

"But I want you, Donovan."

She said the words flatly, as if wanting was all that was important.

"I'm not the man you think I am anymore. Maybe I never was. I'm sorry, but it really is over between us."

A look of regret flashed through her eyes. "And the business? Do you still expect me to work beside you knowing you've rejected me like this?" She hadn't objected before…but she must have thought the situation between them could still be resolved. Kayla had been wrong about Dani—she'd fought for him after all. But not out of love, simply out of pride. Dani hadn't wanted to lose out on the relationship she'd decided would suit her best. And now that he'd injured that pride by clearly rejecting her, she evidently wanted nothing more to do with him.

He sighed. It would probably take every penny he had, and maybe the house, as well, but he could buy her out. He'd miss her business acumen, but he realized that a man needed more than that by his side and in his bed.

It was probably a testament to how little her heart was invested in their relationship that they managed to hammer out a verbal agreement there and then regarding the transfer of her company shares. Their lawyers would get rich taking care of the rest.

"I'm sorry it had to come to this," Dani said as she rose from the table.

"So am I," he said, taking her hand and clasping it warmly. For a long time he'd thought she'd be the woman he'd spend the rest of his life with. She had his respect at the very least. But there was one question still burning in the back of his mind. "You know where Kayla is, don't you?"

"I do, but Donovan, I won't tell you where to find her. Trust me on this. You may think you know what you want but I think in this instance I know you better. She's no good for you. She's moved away of her own choice. Yes, I helped her, of course I did. She had no one else, did she? Let's face it—you have never really been there since she moved in with you, have you? Your work has always been the most important thing to you and that's why we were so good together." Tears gleamed in Dani's eyes. "But remember this—she could have told me no. She could have stayed, and she didn't."

"I have a responsibility to see to it that my children are going to be okay." That was only a fraction of the reason, but he thought it was the one most likely to get a positive response from Dani. She wouldn't like hearing that Kayla had won his heart when Dani hadn't even made a dent in it.

"Already seen to," Dani said with a slight wobble in her voice. "Think of it as my parting gift to you. I set up generous funds for them and an excellent housing situation. They're fine, and Kayla, well, she'd be happier if she never saw you again, too."

Would she? He'd find that out for himself, he decided as he showed Dani to the door and called for Jacob to organize someone to take her to the airport and for a pilot to fly her back to San Francisco. The moment she left the house, he was on the phone to his immediate team with instructions.

"Find her and soon," he directed. "This takes priority over everything else right now."

The apartment just outside Sacramento held everything she needed, Kayla thought, and was far nicer than the one she'd been living in before she'd moved to Van's. Sienna had adjusted easily to the move and aside from the occasional tantrum when she would utter "Dadadadad!" in imperious tones as only a thirteen-month-old could do, she didn't seem to miss Van, either. But Kayla did. With an ache that went deep into her very being and that kept her awake nights and tearful at the least opportune times. Just hormones, she told herself. Life would settle into a new pattern soon and she'd adjust, like she always did.

The baby's movements had become more frequent and stronger of late. As if Van's little boy was trying to make a statement of his own. Maybe he was simply expressing his approval of the move. She wondered what Van had felt when he'd arrived home and found she and Sienna were gone. Relief, probably. While he definitely had a strong urge to control and protect, there was an emptiness in him where his heart should have been. She felt sorry for him, truly sorry, but at the same time she felt sorry for herself, too.

Sienna was curled up in bed after a busy day. They'd joined a local playgroup and Kayla was tentatively making new friendships. The fact that the babies' father wasn't on the scene hadn't been easy to gloss over and the sympathy reflected in a couple of the other moms' eyes had almost been her undoing but she'd held it together. The gentle offers of help and support from her new friends had been welcome and made her feel just a little less alone than she had when she arrived.

She was just settling down with a cup of lemon ginger tea, and trying not to think about Van, when there was a buzz from downstairs. She checked the security screen to see who was at her door. Van? A visceral shudder ran through her body—even the grainy black-and-white image on the screen did nothing to reduce the impact seeing him again had on her. No, a thousand times, no! How had he found her? Dani had told her that her location here would be a complete secret.

But then again, Kayla hadn't factored in what Van did for a living. Part of providing security was gathering intelligence. She should have thought about that further. Clearly changing her name hadn't been enough. She should have moved across the country, as well. Either way, it was too late now.

The buzzing became insistent.

"Go away," she said through the intercom.

"I need to see you, Kayla. Let me into the building."

"Look, I made my decision and I'm sticking with it. Please, Van, respect me on this if nothing else," she begged.

"I'm not leaving until we've talked. Now, I can spend all night leaning on this buzzer, and the buzzers for all your neighbors, or you can let me in and we can talk."

"I'll call the police," she threatened, knowing in her heart of hearts she would do no such thing.

"And explain to them that you have abducted my daughter? Please, by all means, go ahead. I'll be more than happy to show them the court-issued document I have in my pocket awarding me full custody of Sienna."

"You've come to take her away? You can't do that!"

Through the crackle of the speaker, she heard him sigh.

"No, Kayla, that's not what I'm here for, but I'm not above using this document to get to you if that's what it takes."

There was a determination in his tone that left her in no doubt that he'd do exactly as he'd said.

"All you want to do is talk?"

She couldn't hide the tremor in her voice as she spoke and gripped her hands into fists of frustration beside her. How would she ever maintain the upper hand in a discussion with him if she couldn't even talk to him through a speaker without getting overemotional?

"For now," he replied. She could hear his impatience.

"And then you'll be on your way?"

"For now," he repeated.

She hit the button that unlocked the downstairs door and said, "Apartment 303."

"I know."

He probably knew everything by now. In some ways the thought was a relief, but in others? Well, she'd cross those bridges when she got to them, just like she always did. She opened her front door and waited for the chime of the elevator down the hall. She didn't have to wait long.

If she'd thought her gut response to Van's image on the screen had been strong, it was nothing compared to how she felt as he strode out of the elevator and down the corridor toward her. As dark and saturnine as ever and dressed in a black fitted T-shirt and black jeans, he looked as if he was on a stealth mission. A frisson of fear rippled across the back of her neck and she stepped away the moment he drew near.

Van's eyes scanned her thoroughly and she felt their intensity as if it was a physical touch. Her body responded in kind, her nipples beading into tight points, a flare of desire burning at her core.

"Come in. Make yourself at home," she said pithily as he stepped inside. "Just close the door behind you."

He did exactly that and she stood in the middle of the room, watching him as he made himself quite comfortable on her sofa and stretched his legs out before him. He looked as if he was here for no more than a social visit, but she knew the truth.

"How did you find me? Did Dani—?"

"She didn't tell me a word and she was better at hiding you than I thought she'd be. Did you know she set up a corporation to rent this place for you and to administer the money for your upkeep?"

Kayla nodded. She, too, had been surprised at the lengths Dani had been prepared to go to hide her trail, but she'd been so glad for an out that she hadn't stopped to think about the how—she'd just wanted to be gone.

"Why, Kayla? Why leave me? I thought that was my specialty," he said ruefully.

His attempt at humor fell dreadfully flat, at least as far as she was concerned.

"I had to do what was best for the children," she said vehemently. At least, that was what she'd constantly told herself as she lay in bed at night, reliving their lovemaking and wishing she could convince herself it was better to be away and trying to be happy than to be with him and miserable instead.

"How is Sienna doing?"

Kayla nodded. "She's fine. Adjusting happily and making friends at playgroup."

"They make friends at this age?"

"Well, they play alongside one another," she conceded.

"Good. I'm glad she's okay. And the baby? Have you been to the doctor? I'm assuming you transferred to a new doctor up here?"

She nodded. "Everything is textbook perfect. Look, Van, stop beating around the bush. Sienna's fine, the baby's fine and I'm fine. What do you want?"

"I want you back."

"That's not going to happen. We tried it—it didn't work. In my newfound maturity I'm trying to learn from my mistakes. Besides, Dani told me that the two of you were together again, that you wanted me gone."

Finally a slow-burning anger began to take over the anxiety. She fed on it, allowed it to grow and take shape, knowing she'd need it to buoy her through the next few minutes.

"Look, Van, we're happy here without you. We don't need you. We never did, to be honest." She crossed her fingers behind her back. "My children deserve stability and constancy in their lives. And we both know you're incapable of that. I know you can shower them with everything that money can buy and send them to the best schools, but I also know that you won't be there for them when they really need you, because you won't let yourself love them—or anyone else."

Van looked at her, pain reflected in his eyes. She felt a pang of remorse for being so blunt but someone had to say it. The time for tiptoeing around the truth was long past.

"That might have been true of me before, but it's not true now. And as to Dani—she's in my past, where she belongs. She might have hoped we'd get back together, but that's never going to happen. We no longer even work together. She should never have interfered. I mean it when I say I want you back home, Kayla. You and Sienna."

Kayla sighed and shook her head as she sat in one of the armchairs opposite the sofa. "Van, you say you want us there now, but how can you be sure? You can't just turn love on and off like a tap—there when it's convenient for you and gone when it's not."

"You're right, but I can learn if you'll let me."

"And if you decide it's not for you after all? What then? You just make yourself emotionally and physically unavailable to your son and daughter and carry on with your life with a clear conscience, telling yourself you *tried*? That's not good enough. They deserve better than that. *I* deserve better than that."

And there it was. The crux of her pain, the center of everything. As much as she loved him, he just couldn't be the man she needed, and she'd rather have no one than suffer a life with a man who had a yawning cavern where his heart should be.

"I won't. I want to make a commitment to them, to you all, that I'll always be there for you. Being with you, well..." he shook his head "...it opened my eyes, made me see things I didn't want to see. Reminded me of things I always wanted but convinced myself I could do without—things I didn't deserve to have. For the first time since I was a kid and you and your sister lived next door, I started to feel like I belonged somewhere, to someone."

"None of that guarantees me anything," she retorted. "I don't want to live with the fear that one day I'll wake up again and reach for you and you'll be gone. And what if, next time, you don't come back? How on earth am I supposed to deal with that? More important, how are the children?"

"It won't happen," he insisted.

"But how do I know that?"

"Because I'm stepping back from operations, for good. The company is undergoing some restructuring and the operations division is going to be under the control of a team I trust implicitly. A team on which I am only to be an adviser rather than an on-site operator. I've always prided myself on the fact that I wouldn't send my people into the field unless I was prepared to go there myself—it's who I've always been. But I learned that I've changed. I have a responsibility to the ones I love, to be there for them. I don't want to put myself in a position where I might die and leave you behind, Kayla."

Kayla looked at him in disbelief. "You really expect me to believe that?"

"I wish you would. The same as I wish you would give me a last chance to show you I can be the man you need, the father the children need. I've learned a lot these past few weeks, not least of which is that emotion is not always a weakness. It can be a strength, too. I've always been too afraid to feel, because when I did, it only hurt or led to being a weapon that allowed others to hurt me. It was easier to simply stop caring."

Her eyes filled with tears and they began to spill down her cheeks unhindered. "Van, I'm so sorry."

"Don't be sorry for me, Kayla. Just tell me that you love me. Just tell me…" His voice broke and he dragged in a breath before continuing. "Just tell me, please, that you'll let me love you, too."

"I want to, Van, I really do, but I don't know if I can trust you. And it's not just me I'm talking about, but Sienna and this little guy here, too." She rubbed her small round belly protectively. "I can't let you into our lives again if you're only going to walk out when the going gets tough."

"I don't want to be that man anymore. I want to feel. I want to experience love and enjoy my life and I know I won't be able to do that without you by my side. I don't know why I never saw it before, why I kept pushing it away. I want to go to sleep at night and know that the first ray of sunshine in my life each morning will be seeing you there by my side. I know I've treated you badly but I can't let you go. I never understood why, Kayla, but it's because I love you—even when I didn't want to, I loved you. I just didn't know how to deal with it."

She wiped her face dry. He was saying all the right

things but did he believe them himself? Could she? "What makes you think you can deal with it now?"

"That's a good question. I think I've finally realized what's important in life. I've spent all my years trying to find myself worthy in one way or another. When I didn't find that at home, with my adoptive parents, I looked for it in the army. And I was a damn good soldier. I fit there. I could hone my instincts and my skills and be great at something and be proud that what I was doing was serving the greater good. But I still never found that elusive sense of home that I was searching for. When I quit the army, I knew I had the skills to make a lot of money, so I did. I carved a new niche for myself, created a place where I thought I'd made a home. But it wasn't a home until you lived there, too. Having you and Sienna under my roof reminded me of what it felt like being at your parents' house. Feeling the love your family shared for one another. Even when your parents were angry at you, you could still feel that they loved you. It was something that was constant and I wanted that constancy but I didn't feel like I'd ever earned it. And when you offered it, I didn't know how to handle it."

Kayla stared at him. She'd never seen him look this shattered or broken inside. Not even when Sienna died, or on that awful morning years ago when she and her sister had found him curled up asleep on their front porch with bruises from head to foot courtesy of his dad.

"Van, you don't *earn* love. It's not a reward for good behavior. It's something freely given," she said softly.

"I'm learning that now," he said with an ironic quirk of his lips. "Your family was the only thing that kept me from running away as a kid. Did you know that?"

Kayla nodded. Her sister had told her one night after they'd heard yelling from Van's house that she wished Van would just run away because then he might get put into foster care and surely that would be better than what he endured in his own home. But he stayed, until he was eighteen.

"What made you join the army?" she asked. "You could have gone away to college, gone anywhere. But you enlisted."

"I had a lot of anger in me. I needed to channel it somewhere with a purpose or I knew I'd go off the rails. I'd started drinking already, using a fake ID or stealing my dad's beers from the fridge. It was a problem before I even knew it. And that's something else you need to know, Kayla. I'm an alcoholic. There, I've said it. That's the first time I've admitted it to myself—did you know that? I'm an alcoholic and I come from a long line of alcoholics. The reason I was put up for adoption was because my birth parents had fallen so deep into substance abuse that they could no longer care for me. And the scary thing is, their DNA is in me, and in our children."

He dropped his head and stared at the floor, Kayla battled the desire to go to him and comfort him. She was beginning to understand a whole lot more about Van Murphy and the way he'd behaved. Both his self-destructive behaviors and the ones that were the exact opposite, when he found it necessary to control and protect everything around him.

"DNA is one thing, but you still make your own choices, Van."

He coughed a humorless laugh. "Yeah, I read somewhere that DNA loads the gun and environment pulls the trigger. Well, I kept pushing myself into environments that made me very dangerous. It got to the point where I chased death. You know, when I agreed to be a donor for your sister, I never believed I'd live long enough to see her bear her children. It was only after she died that I realized that I didn't want to stay on that fast road to a short future." He sat up and looked Kayla straight in the eye. "The first time we made love was the first time I felt truly alive, but it terrified me so much more than anything I'd ever done before. That's why I left you. I didn't know how to deal with how you made me feel or how much I wanted to stay with you. I felt like I had to punish myself for wanting to be with you. Like I'd failed you somehow, or disrespected you. I had to punish myself for that, so I had to leave. In the end, I decided to blame the whole episode on the drink, y'know? And I stopped drinking from that night on to make sure I wouldn't make the same mistake again.

"Not long after that, I discovered the truth about my birth parents and everything slotted into place about who and what I was. I was glad I'd left you then. I wasn't worthy of love or family. I was glad that my parents' problem ended with me. That was my choice, my decision. And with your sister gone, God rest her beautiful soul, I wouldn't have kids, ever."

The last pieces fell into place and painful understanding dawned. "Until I turned up in your office with one and wanting to have more of them. I'm so sorry, Van. I had no idea."

"I've tried to be strong. I've worked hard to make the right choices. But deep down, I'm still a weak man. I have no idea how to be a good father, Kayla. With my background of violence and alcohol and the very fact it's ingrained into me, how could I be?"

Her heart fractured on his words. Despite what she'd kept telling herself, she could see he had a heart. One that was broken and bruised and buried deep beneath so many years of abuse that it was a fragile thing. One that needed constancy and tenderness to thrive. She could do that— she could help his love thrive and grow. And together they could give their children the love, devotion and stability they needed to teach them what was right and wrong and guide them through their lives. They would give their all to them and hope that it would be enough.

"All it takes is love, Van. Just love. Together we can do this, I promise."

"Together?"

The look in his eyes, the yearning and hope she saw there, shrank all her fears into a tiny knot in the recesses of her heart. Maybe someday the knot would go away, and maybe it wouldn't, but she knew if it didn't, she'd learn to manage it because Van deserved for her to try. When had he ever known unconditional love? When had he ever been told he deserved it just as much as anyone else? Someone had to show him and that started with her.

"Yes, together," she said firmly. She got up from her chair and dropped to her knees in front of him. "I love you, Van Murphy. You don't need to be alone anymore, ever, but promise me you won't push me away when you most need me. Promise me you'll let me love you the way you deserve to be loved."

"I do promise. I know I'm not worthy of you," he said. "But I want you so much I don't feel like a whole person unless you're with me. Does that make me weak, Kayla?"

His honesty drove right through her. "No," she assured him. "Admitting it is what makes you strong. Fear is what makes us brave in the long run. Doing what's right, even when we're scared. That's what makes the difference. And, Van, loving you is what's right for me. We'll make it through this."

Van reached for her and pulled her to him. "You know, I believe you. I love you so much, Kayla. Please, don't ever leave me again."

She smiled up at him. "Only if you promise the same."

"I do," he said fervently. "I really do. Will you come

home with me tomorrow? You and Sienna? Will you be my family?"

"We already are," she answered.

Kayla lifted her face to his and as his lips claimed hers in a seal of their declaration to one another, she knew they'd weather the storms that would undoubtedly come their way.

Together.
Always.

* * * * *

If you liked this story of a billionaire tamed by the love of the right woman—and her baby— pick up these other novels from
USA TODAY *bestselling author*
Yvonne Lindsay
A FATHER'S SECRET
THE CHILD THEY DIDN'T EXPECT
WANTING WHAT SHE CAN'T HAVE
FOR THE SAKE OF THE SECRET CHILD

Available now from Mills & Boon Desire!

And don't miss the next
BILLIONAIRES AND BABIES *story,*
THE BABY PROPOSAL
by Andrea Laurence
Available December 2016!

MILLS & BOON®

Desire™

PASSIONATE AND DRAMATIC LOVE STORIES

A sneak peek at next month's titles...

In stores from 17th November 2016:

- **The Baby Proposal** – Andrea Laurence *and*
  The Pregnancy Project – Kat Cantrell

- **The Texan's One-Night Standoff** – Charlene Sands *and*
  Maid Under the Mistletoe – Maureen Child

- **Rich Rancher for Christmas** – Sarah M. Anderson *and*
  Married to the Maverick Millionaire – Joss Wood

Just can't wait?
Buy our books online a month before they hit the shops!
www.millsandboon.co.uk

Also available as eBooks.

Give a 12 month subscription to a friend today!

Call Customer Services
0844 844 1358[*]

or visit
millsandboon.co.uk/subscription